WHISH'T DADDY

James McCormack

authorHOUSE®

AuthorHouse™
1663 Liberty Drive
Bloomington, IN 47403
www.authorhouse.com
Phone: 1 (800) 839-8640

Cover art by Diane Stimson

Published by AuthorHouse 02/08/2016

ISBN: 978-1-5049-7454-7 (sc)
ISBN: 978-1-5049-7452-3 (hc)
ISBN: 978-1-5049-7453-0 (e)

Library of Congress Control Number: 2016901121

Print information available on the last page.

For my Grandchildren – Gennaro, Charlotte, Milania and those to come – go be Champions one and all!

When the Irish tell someone to hush they say whish't. If they were to tell their father to hush they would say whish't daddy!

“The wind of heaven is that which blows between a horse’s ears!” Arabian Proverb

Prologue

Saratoga, New York – 2009

My Grandfather's belongings all smelled of hay and barn and horses. This was not surprising as he had lived most of his life in a small building close by the grounds of Saratoga Racetrack in upstate New York. He'd lived in that tiny cottage for over eighty-seven years since coming to America as a young lad of fifteen nearly a century ago. He was born and raised in County Kildare, the second child and only son in a family with three sisters. He rarely spoke of the days back in Ireland and if myself or one of his other grandchildren tried to drag a story or two out of him, he'd only tell us he'd lived a happy and nondescript childhood and left Ireland to find opportunity and a good livelihood in this grand country. For most of my life I had accepted this version of Michael Francis Walsh's upbringing and reason for emigration. But as I'd spent the good part of the past day sorting through his things I was beginning to wonder. My Grandfather died a week ago at the ripe old age of one hundred and two and the task of cleaning out his small home and sifting through his possessions had fallen to me. Most of what I had found would be what one might expect – tattered pairs of jeans and overalls, most stained and some crudely patched, heavy cotton shirts and nylon zip up jackets and countless pairs of working gloves, a dozen or so hats (my grandfather had a fondness for caps of a wide variety,) one good suit of gray wool and two ties to match the two dress shirts I found hanging in the closet or "the press" as he would say. Several pairs of work boots, all well worn with cracked leather and a few missing eyelets, one pair of suede moccasins and a good pair of black dress shoes, highly polished and with brand new laces, rounded out his wardrobe. He had several shelves of books, mostly fiction, a considerable number of Philip Marlowe mysteries, a few weighty volumes about horses, a small collection of stamps, two sets of cufflinks, and at least a dozen photographs of my Grandfather with his wife Nellie and with their two sons, my father and my Uncle Tom. There was one photo of a young man sitting aboard a beautiful and immense horse and I could see my Grandfather's deep set eyes in that picture despite the many decades that had passed. He was rubbing the horse's head and smiling broadly, pride and satisfaction beaming from his youthful countenance. All these things were to be expected, raising little suspicion regarding his past. But in the bottom of a small desk occupying a tight space at the back of the small house, beside the kitchen in a hallway leading to the back door, I found several items that fanned my curiosity. The first was a small metal box, the size many people use to store important documents like passports, birth certificates and social security cards. Judging by its appearance, very old, dented in several places, with rusty hinges and clasp and more scratches than I could count, the box was ancient. At first I thought the clasp was locked but with a little work I managed to snap it open and to my surprise the box held a number of shiny medals of different sorts – what looked to be gold and silver to my untrained eye. The medals were attached to an array of colorful ribbons and almost all the ribbons had some inscription written across them – *First Place – Sainte Leger – 1920, Champion Carlow Plate – 1920, Punchestown Stakes – Second Place – 1920.* Others had inscriptions I could not read – they were legible but the language was nothing I had ever seen before – *Geallta Bhaile Atha Cliath – 1920.* I was mystified. I laid the medals and ribbons across the small kitchen table and counted them up – eight in all, six with the word "First" or "Champion" scrolled across the ribbon. Two were written in the mysterious language and most of the medals were emblazoned with images of a horse in full stride or a horse's head or a castle, abbey or town. The more I handled the medals the more certain I was that they were made of real gold or silver, the weight of the awards considerable and impressive. I began placing them back into the safety box but noticed the bottom of it was lined by a thin folder. It stuck to the box stubbornly and then came out with a distinctive pop. The folder, made of old cardboard, was as fragile as a flower petal. It flaked and peeled from my touch so I gently placed it on the desk. Turning over the cover I found a small number of newspaper clippings and what looked like several letters, mostly yellowed around the edges, more fragile than the cardboard cover. Half the newspaper articles were in English and half in the language I assumed was the same as on the ribbons. It was not a very great leap of faith or intelligence to guess the language was Gaelic, the ancient Celtic language of the Irish people. All of the letters were in the native Irish tongue. Gingerly, I flipped through the newspaper clippings, separating them into two piles by language. Five were written in English and four of those were articles about horse races, all written between 1920 and 1921 and every one of the four featured a horse named *Whish't Daddy*. One article contained a picture of an immense and beautiful beast mounted by a young man with a jubilant smile and I had only to glance back to the box of photographs taken down from the wall to confirm the horse and rider were the same – my Grandfather and a horse I now knew as *Whish't Daddy. T*he articles written in Gaelic looked to span a wider spectrum of topics. Three were clearly about the horse and racing and one showed a picture of the young boy with the blond hair and a man with a strong family resemblance hugging him closely. I could make out the name of Francis Walsh in the caption and knew that to be my Great-grandfather, a man I'd never met and to my knowledge someone who never left the Emerald Isle. Even in the grainy black and white newsprint picture, the family resemblance was strong, especially around the eyes and the square, hard edged jaw and in the smile the two men shared. I felt a twinge of pride in knowing the bond of familial love and affection stretched back across the century and across a great, wide ocean. It was harder to make out what the other articles referenced. One had a picture of a small cottage burning on a hill and others were most likely political as they showed pictures and names I knew to be vaguely familiar – Michael Collins, Eamon de Valera, Sinn Fein. One article had a headline that read *Dubh agus Tan* and showed pictures of four very rough looking men under the banner and the men wore uniforms with the insignia of the British government. I could only assume this newspaper was notifying the local Irish citizenry of the presence of these enemies and someone had circled in rough red pencil one of the men in the picture, a large and dangerous looking man. I skimmed through the clippings again but could draw no further conclusions. Placing them all back carefully into the cardboard folder, I made a mental note to make copies for further inspection and to put the originals into individual plastic covers for protection. I went back to piling the clothing, books, pictures, and other belongings into various boxes and I was almost done when I decided to check the desk one more time to make sure I left nothing behind. Starting from the bottom, I opened every drawer finding only dust and scratches for my effort. But directly below the writing surface there was a small draw I had not noticed earlier. It looked to be ornamental but on closer inspection I found two holes where the draw handle once had been. Obviously it had come unscrewed over the years and disappeared to God knows where. I took a pen from my pocket and tried jamming it into one of the holes hoping to pry the small drawer open. I only managed to snap the pen in half. I worked on it for a good twenty minutes and needed to get underneath the desk and find a small lock which I pried apart with a screwdriver and finally the desk draw slid open. It was jammed full with pens and pencils and crayons and old notepads and coins of various denominations and a few receipts and pictures - a junk drawer like so many others in every house in America, if not the world. Rummaging through the junk and discarding almost all of it, I was almost done when I reached into the back of the drawer and my fingers bumped into a book. It was wedged in the corner, almost too thick to have fit inside the small desk and I had to yank it very hard to get it out. It was a leather bound book, about five by seven, with several rubber bands wrapped around the covers, some papers sticking out at the top and bottom, the whole thing looking old and ominous and anxious to be opened. My hands trembling, I undid the rubber bands, two of them snapping in my hands like brittle, old chicken bones. I opened the cover and it was immediately clear that this was not just a book, it was a diary. Inside the cover there was a small black and white picture. The horse was standing in a field, rolling hills in the distance, a cottage close by on a hill. He was huge and majestic and beautiful. I knew for certain it was Whish't Daddy – the white line down the center of the horse's great head looked almost to be an exclamation point – one that cried out with joy and conviction – "*Have you ever seen such a horse*?" He looked directly into the camera, his eyes bright and intelligent and knowing. He seemed to be smiling, acknowledging the relationship between the photographer and his subject. I slid the picture out and at first I thought the writing in the small journal might again be in Gaelic, it was hard to decipher, the script blurred and uneven, most likely the writing of a young boy full of excitement and purpose. I squinted carefully and moved a little closer to the light. Slowly the words began to take shape; slowly the story began to be told.

Yesterday my horse was born. This is going to be his diary. I am going to write down something about my horse every day so the whole world knows what a great horse he is and what a great racing horse he is going to be. He is going to be the best racing champion ever and his name is Whish't Daddy!

And so the story begins.

Chapter One

Barreen, County Kildare, Ireland - April 1918

The anticipation of watching the broodmare foal paled in Mickey's memory only to the day nearly a year before when his father bought him down to the barn to watch the incredible scene of the massive stallion, Bellweather, mating with the broodmare on a cool evening in early March. Bellweather, a four year old who'd performed well for the stable over the past two years, was a mix of Irish Draft horse and Thoroughbred, with the size of the former and the athleticism of the latter. Normally a well behaved horse, Mickey could hear him neighing and whinnying and stomping around in the stable at the far end of the barn and wondered what would make the horse so anxious. The mare, imperially named Queen of the Isle, also a four year old thoroughbred, stood in the first stable, her feet chained together and a very nervous look in her dark brown eyes. She stomped around pulling at the lead to which she was tethered, jerking Da's arm again and again. Frank Walsh gently caressed the mare's face, whispered kindly in her ear, settling her down a wee bit. He called his thirteen year old son over, handing him the rope.

"Okay, Mick, I need you to hold her firm now boy, understand? When I bring Bellweather in he's going to be ornery as all hell and she may get skittish, she's got a hankering about what she's about to get so make sure you hold on tight." Mickey wasn't quite sure exactly what Queen of the Isle was about to get but he took the rope from his father and began gently stroking the mare's head, whispering to her as he had seen his father do. Frank went out to get the stallion and Mickey felt a tinge of excitement as he had a feeling whatever was about to happen would not be soon forgotten. And he was right. Da led Bellweather into the stable and the massive horse arrived in nearly violent fashion, his head rearing up and down, snorting like a steam engine, and whinnying to wake the dead. Despite her chains, the mare began pulling away, jerking Mickey half way across the stable before he could settle her down. She stood nervously looking back towards the stallion, shifting around and searching for a place to bolt.

"Steady, girl," Mick whispered over and over. He held the rope tightly with both hands. What happened next amazed him. With Da's careful attention, Bellweather approached the mare from behind sticking his nose directly between her haunches and seeming to be breathing deeply from inside the horse's arse. He did this for a few minutes and as he did so Mickey watched in awe as the stallion's penis, normally the size of nice chunk of turf, began to grow to two or three times its size, swelling with a slick wet sheen and eventually achieving the size of Mickey's arm if not bigger. Mick knew that sometimes his own penis grew larger when he had those bad thoughts about some of the girls in his class and that made him blush a little but mostly he was just shocked by the massive size of the horse's tool. Now the mare shifted again but this time it seemed more to position herself for what happened next. Bellweather suddenly reared up on his hind legs and tried wrapping his front hooves around the mare's middle but he slipped off jerking about while Da held him tightly. He reared again but still did not gain the hold he needed but on his third try he mounted the mare and Mickey's eyes almost burst from their sockets as he watched in amazement as the horse's huge cock entered the rear of the mare, disappearing completely as the stallion pushed in closer. Then Bellweather rocked back and forth a number of times and with a sudden grunt pushed into the mare very deeply. Gaining some kind of relief from his efforts, he dropped his head onto the back of the broodmare, lessening his hold on her midsection. Then he slipped off completely and Mick saw the huge penis dripping with a whitish liquid, glistening in the last light of the day and now beginning to shrink back to its normal size. Bellweather appeared to lose interest in Queen of the Isle and Da led him away quickly, back down the barn to the stall at the very end. Mickey stroked the mare, looking into her mournful eyes.

"Did that hurt?" he asked her gently, "I hope not, girl, I hope you're feeling alright." She nodded her head as if to assure him she was fine and Mick went to fetch a feedbag to reward her for her efforts.

Later that evening, he worked up the courage to ask his Da about what he'd seen. They were sitting by the turf fire. His mother and his sisters, Maureen and Deidre, were working away in the kitchen. His father had a book in his hand but he did not appear to be reading it. He was staring into the fire mulling over something very important Mickey was sure.

"Da, can I ask you something?" he said softly. His father moved his eyes slowly from the flames and smiled kindly at his son. He nodded for the boy to continue. "It's about the horses and what Bellweather was doing to the mare," Mick said sheepishly. His father nodded again and Mick thought he saw the smile on his face lengthen. He searched carefully for the right words to say. "What was he doing to her? I mean why would we let him get on top of the mare like that? I was thinking that maybe he would hurt her, he seemed angry to me and his, his, well his cock got so huge and he was poking so hard and it all looked very scary to me." Mickey looked away in embarrassment as his father's smile broadened again. He reached across the fire and gently patted his son on the head. He slipped his rough, calloused hand under the boy's chin and made him look directly into his father's face.

"They was mating, Mick," Da said softly. "Do you know what mating means, boy?" He waited for his son to shake his head from side to side and then he pulled him closer, speaking in a quiet and dignified tone. "We mate the horses so they can foal, you know, have a wee colt or a little filly." Mickey's eyes brightened slowly as what his father said began to take hold in his head. "Bellweather mounted the mare so he could make her pregnant, understand?" The look on his son's face told Frank Walsh that the boy had an inkling of understanding but much clarification was required. "Do you want to know exactly how it works?" he asked the boy. Mickey nodded slowly, unsure if he really did want to know. And then with something of a clinical detachment, Da explained very slowly the entire process from when the mare would be ready to get pregnant which seemed some magical time of the year to Mickey, to the stallion's desire to mount the mare and the way his penis would swell with anticipation to the actual act of mating and how the male would shoot some powerful liquid into the mare's rear and that would cause her egg to develop into a baby horse growing in the broodmare's belly. Mick recalled the site of Bellweather's huge tool glistening with wetness after the act had been concluded and how the horse appeared to relax after he had finished with the mare.

"Do you understand, son?" the father asked softly. Mickey nodded. "Do you have any questions about it?" Mick thought carefully for a few minutes. He looked into the kitchen and saw his mother working at the sink, her belly swollen to many times its normal size. The father followed the boy's gaze and let out a gentle laugh. "Yes, my son," he said with an embarrassing smile, "it works pretty much the same way with us humans too!" Mickey had trouble going to sleep that night. He could barely contain his excitement at the prospect of a new horse being born on the farm. And this would not be just any new horse. It was going to be his horse, that was one thing he was certain and he could not wait for the day to arrive.

And a year later, it was here. Da told him to keep an eye on Queen of the Isle and let him know when she lay in the straw and her belly began heaving. He'd come down in the afternoon, after school and noticed the mare seemed a little agitated. She moved around a great deal, lying down momentarily and then getting up to turn in circles. She was sweating a lot and her belly hung down and Mick thought he saw it swelling in and out. He gave her some water and rubbed her gently and she nestled her nose closely into his shoulder in thanks and he could feel her shuddering as she did so. Within the hour she lay down into the pile of straw they'd set aside for her and Mickey watched in wonder as her belly bucked and rolled like a skiff on a stormy lake. He pulled himself away from the amazing sight, racing up to the house to fetch his father.

As they moved back towards the barn, Da gave him instructions to fetch a blanket and a good number of burlap tarps, a clean supply of water and a sharp knife. Mick raced through the barn, knowing intimately where to find each item although he was uncertain of their intended use. But he never questioned his father's orders in any respect and certainly not when it had anything to do with horses. Frank Walsh knew more about horses, breeding them, raising them, training them, racing them and retiring them than any man in Kildare if not in all of Ireland and surely his young son would do nothing but obey. Still, he was curious. He placed all the items in the stable where the broodmare lie convulsing and breathing heavily. Mickey wondered if it had been so difficult on his Ma when the wee baby arrived six months earlier. He slipped beside the nervous horse, gently smoothing her withers and rubbing her haunches, whispering encouragement all along. The mare's brown eyes swept dolefully towards him but she looked anything but soothed by his touch.

Da put on his elbow length rubber gloves and stuck his hand in the rear of Queen of the Isle and felt around carefully. "It won't be long now, Mick, this evening at the latest," Da said confidently,

"How will we know?" the boy asked innocently, moving to a spot along the wall where he could sit and keep watch.

"Oh, we'll know," his father replied with a smile. "Just you wait and see."

About two hours later, after an interminable amount of shuddering and whinnying and heaving and trying to stand only to lie back into the bed of straw, the broodmare gave a final shudder and suddenly a burst of fluid coursed slowly from her rear washing indiscreetly across the straw bed and the dirt below. It was a mixture of fluids, some clear and watery, some red and bloody, some laced with mucus and other greenish and white matter. Mickey inhaled quickly, unsure if maybe the horse had just died, given birth or shat itself in some pathetic way.

Frank Walsh went right to work. Putting his gloves on again, he spread the blanket out a few feet away from where the mare laid thrashing about and piled the burlap sacks alongside the blanket. He gently approached the animal and felt around the midsection and inspected her rear. Nodding his head slowly, he pointed to a small mass beginning to protrude from the mare's rear section. It was slightly pointed and again covered with some kind of odd film.

"It's coming, Mickey, the babe is coming." For the next few minutes the boy looked on in wonder as the mass slid slowly out of the mare's body inch by inch. "Pay attention now, son," Frank instructed. He reached into the slimy mass with his burly hands and another small sack seemed to give way with more fluids spilling about the ground. Then he grabbed onto two small objects and it took a few moments for Mickey to realize they were the foal's legs. Da began pulling the foal out of the mare, no small task the boy observed. Frank grunted and tugged and twisted around for a number of minutes and then with a fearsome yank the young horse slid completely out of his mother and Mick looked on in complete astonishment as the shape and form of a young colt was revealed before him. It was covered in slime and blood and mucus but the new born horse raised his head, twisting from side to side. The boy saw the beautiful brown eyes, the pointed ears, the flaring nostrils and a dark mane of hair along his neck, almost black, against the chestnut coloring of his body. And down the center of his head, running between his glassy eyes and above the wet and shining nose was a white strip with a small white circle below it, a very distinctive marking to Mick's young eyes. His Da cleared the foal's nostrils of any mucus so he could breathe and then began the task of wiping the foal down with the burlap sacks, taking wet and sticky swabs of gunk and mucus from the animal's shiny fur. He told Mick to put down some clean straw and sliding the colt onto the blanket gently, he positioned it in such away that when the feeding would begin, the exhausted mare would not need to move very much. He dipped his hand in the bucket of water and gently cleared the slimy fluid from the colt's eyes and looked him over carefully, examining the head and ears and gums to make sure all was as it should be. He tossed one of the burlap sacks to his son and the boy was overjoyed to join in the wiping down of the new born and he smiled widely while rubbing vigorously, feeling the warmth and softness of the young horse beneath his hands. Mickey could only imagine the months and years ahead. As he cleaned the colt with loving care, he dreamed of working with his Da training the beautiful horse, grooming him, feeding him, learning to ride the animal and to teach him how to run and jump, watching him grow into the champion he was meant to be. Mick did not know at what point his father had left him alone with the horse or when it had grown so dark. But he watched for a long while as the colt fed hungrily from his mother's tit while Queen of the Isle cleaned her colt with gentle licks and by rubbing her big head against him. Later, Mick curled up within arm's reach of the animal, borrowing a corner of the blanket, and fell into a deep slumber full of wonderful dreams.

The next morning the chatter around the breakfast table was mostly about the new horse. Naming the colt was a very important and honored family tradition. Mammy was at the stove working up a massive breakfast of eggs, bacon, blood pudding, brown bread and potatoes. The small cottage smelled delightful. Mickey's eldest sister, Maureen, was pouring steaming hot tea for everyone while Deidre minded the wee child named Patricia. Da was looking over the morning racing form, not interested in the wagering but curious where two horses he had trained and were running that afternoon in Dublin would be stacked.

"They got River Run going off at twelve to one," he said with a chuckle. "That should be a money maker right there. Not saying the horse will win but I am as sure as my name is Frankie Walsh that he'll be in the money. Why he should be…"

"Whish't Daddy," Maureen said as she filled his cup with steaming brew. "We are a lot more interested in the new colt in the barn than we are with old River Run."

Da began to protest but this time Deidre cut him short. "Whish't, Daddy, Maureen is right. River Run was nothing more than a disappointment and we all are hoping that the new boy is going to be a fair amount better coming down the stretch."

But Da was not one to give up easily. "River Run is a damn fine horse, young lady," he protested. "He's just been on a run of bad luck of late. Why just the other day he was making the turn and …."

"Whish't, Daddy," Maureen admonished him again. She was seventeen years of age and as lovely as a spring morning. It was generally felt throughout the family that she was Daddy's favorite. She giggled at her father's astonished face and her laugh sounded like a bird's song. "Bellweather's little boy is going to be a champion racer!" she exclaimed with pride. She looked fondly towards her younger brother sitting at the kitchen table. "That's what Mickey said, didn't you Mick?" Mickey was shaking his head vigorously and trying to get a word in edgewise but Da could not resist a spirited reply.

"Oh, my lovely lass, you are quite right. All the horses trained by Frank Walsh are champions in one way or another and I am certain this fellow will be no different. If you go back as far as when I was your brother's age you'll find champions all along the way. Take the first one …" but before he could offer up the ancient horse's name it was Mammy that cut him short.

"Now whish't, Daddy," she said with a smile. "Breakfast is ready and we will all think better on a full belly. And the wee ones need to get off to school so if you can kindly hush and let me feed this brood I would greatly appreciate it." She filled Da's plate first and then spread the feast around the table. As she did so Frank ate with relish until suddenly he stopped. Pushing his plate back a little he began laughing great big, deep belly laughs. The whole family looked at him as if he'd gone mad but he just went on laughing to beat the band. He laughed so hard he almost choked on his food.

"Now whish't, Daddy," Mother said again, trying to restore order but it only made her husband laugh harder and begin shaking his head up and down. Finally he gained control of himself and holding up his hand, waited for absolute quiet in the small kitchen.

"Yes," he said with a grin, "that is what it will be!" When the children and his wife all looked at him quizzically he nodded again. "The name, it will be what you all have said to me so often this morning and now that I think about it, what you've all said to me for most of my life!' He waited another moment letting the suspense build. "The colt's name will be Whish't Daddy! For all the times I heard it and all the times I still will, at least when I hear his name being called on the track it will make me smile." He looked at their faces all full of surprise and slight astonishment. "Is it okay with you Mickey? Is that name for the horse going to be okay?" The young boy looked around the room and saw all eyes staring at him, waiting on his reply. Normally nothing he had to say had much importance in family decisions and he was surprised his father had asked for his approval. He gave it a few moments thought and then shook his head up and down enthusiastically.

"Surely, Da! That will be a great name for a great champion. Whish't Daddy, champion racer of the season! I like it. I surely like it a lot." The whole family joined in with laughter and shouts of approval and somewhere out in the barn the young colt began struggling to his feet. The name would befit a champion and a champion he would be. And Whish't Daddy would be his name.

Chapter Two

Barreen, County Kildare, Ireland – April 1918

Later that morning Frank entered the stable and found the new born colt sleeping a short distance from his mother. She eyed Frank carefully as he opened the gate to the stall. Da smiled at the mare and then laughed to himself when he saw his son nestled in tightly against the young horse. He glanced at the colt's mother, pleased and surprised to see Queen of the Isle having no problem with the boy tucking himself neatly beside her young one. Sometimes the mares were over protective and once in a while down right ornery with anyone getting too close to their newborn. But Mickey had one hand draped across the animal's belly and his other tucked behind his head as a pillow. Frank figured the boy had spent half the night out in the barn so he was not surprised to find him napping after breakfast. He would miss school but this did not overly concern the father. He gently pushed the toe of his boot into his son's ribs and the boy startled, jumping to his feet.

"Sorry, Da," the boy mumbled, rubbing sleep from his bright blue eyes. "I just come down to check on Whish't Daddy and I must have fallen asleep." Mickey looked sheepishly at his father wondering how much trouble he would be in for missing school. His father eyed him momentarily but then the young horse awoke and struggled to his feet. He ambled clumsily over to the mare and suckled hungrily at his mother's teat. Frank watched the amazement once again crawl across his son's handsome face and he figured Mick would learn more today at home than he'd ever learn in school. He tousled the boy's unruly hair, shaking some hay from the nest, gently kissing him on the head.

"I declare today your first day of higher education," Frank said to his son. The boy looked at him questioningly. "Today you'll work with me and the horses and tomorrow you go back to school. How does that sound, Mick?" The young boy looked at his father with great surprise. He'd mucked the stables many of times before for his father and he'd been charged with cleaning the water and blankets and some other supplies but he'd never really had the chance to work directly with the horses. He smiled at his father with unbridled love and affection, throwing his arms around Frank's waist and giving his Da a good strong hug.

"Really, Da? Oh, that is a grand thing, just a grand thing. I'll work as hard as I can, I promise, its all I really ever wanted to do." He looked up and smiled a bright and beautiful smile that nearly broke his father's heart.

"Okay, then, let's get going. First thing is to walk the colt out to the yard. I'll be taking the mare and two of the others. Your job is that new boy, right over there." He pointed his chin towards Whish't Daddy and Mick nodded enthusiastically. "Now watch what I do son, and try to do the same thing with the colt."

And that is how it started. Mick watched his Da carefully fit a bridle and lead over the mare's big head and he followed his father's instructions to only lightly loop a thin leather strap over the new born horse's head. Imitating his father, he gently stroked the horse's face and withers and shoulders and underbelly. He massaged the soft, warm hair on the colt's ears and laughed coyly as the young foal licked his face lovingly in return. Leading his horse, he followed his father out of the stall and down the barn and through the small paddocks and out into the grassy pasture where the horses spent much of their morning. It was a soft day in early spring, quite cool, the dampness of daybreak from the fog and mist still lingering in the meadow despite the valiant attempts of the sun to burst through the white-gray clouds. Da told him to remove the leather strap from the young horse and to let him mingle with the other horses as they were released into the field. The brood mare ambled over to her offspring and gently nudged the colt deeper into the pasture where the grasses were thick and tall and the mare began to feed. Whish't Daddy slid his head under the mare's belly and found a teat and drank hungrily from his mother.

Da brought several of the stallions from the barn, including Bellweather, but the big horses barely paid the new colt any mind. They walked and galloped in a small pack about the pasture, their long, muscular bodies bursting with energy, their dark manes and long tails flying in the breeze. Most were chestnut or browns, and the lone gray, a sleepy eyed five year old named Chipper, was dappled with white markings along his legs. Mickey loved to watch the stallions run and he thought to himself as he watched the new foal feeding from the mare, "One day you'll run faster than all of them, Whishy. One day you will be the fastest stallion in all of Ireland. You're going to be a champion, boy. You just wait and see."

His dad called him back to the barn and put him to familiar work mucking out the stables, changing out fresh hay, filling the feed bags and fetching clean water. Mickey spent most of the morning on these tasks and although some of the labor was arduous requiring much lifting and carrying, he performed admirably with a smile on his face and never once did his thoughts wander to school work or any of his friends. He felt so perfectly comfortable in the barn and working in the stables or walking the pasture along with the horses. After lunch, they returned the horses to the barn, each to their own stall. His chores for the afternoon included grooming the adult horses and changing out the grooming kits to ensure each of the horses had a separate supply of brushes, sponges, combs, clothes, pads and other sundry items. Da explained to him the importance of each horse having its own kit as it would prevent the spread of any illness or disease and that the horses sometimes reacted poorly to the scent of another horse on a brush or sponge. His father showed him how to securely cross tie the mighty stallions so they could be properly groomed. A horse not correctly anchored could twist or turn and bite at his groomer and Da assured him that would not happen with any of Athy House's horses. He spent hours brushing the mighty beasts, first working down one side of their massive bodies and legs and then the other. He was careful in brushing out their faces, avoiding their eyes and nose, fearing they might spook should he poke or touch them in an unexpected way. Da delicately addressed these areas with a special soft cloth, wiping out the mucus from the eyes and nose and cleaning out the dock. Then came the brushing of the thick manes and long bushy tails and some of the horses had hair matted and tangled and knotted together which required combing out with metal combs and lots of patience. The last operation on each horse was performed by his father but Da instructed him on what he was doing every step of the way. He told Mickey that a horse's legs and their hooves are complicated and potentially delicate marvels of creation requiring constant care and attention. Every horse needed to have his legs and hooves checked at least twice a day and the race horses even more often to see how their muscles and tendons reacted to their work outs and to be certain no irritants or abrasions or odd growths might take hold in their feet. Da carefully lifted the heavy legs of each horse feeling carefully along their knees, shins, canon bones and ankles, searching for any swelling or abrasions, watching the horse carefully for any signs of discomfort or pain. Then, using a small pick, he held each hoof between his own legs and gently removed any dirt, small pebbles, grass or muck from the foot or the shoe. He inspected the shoes for fit and shape and size, explaining to his son that the farrier, Old Man O'Malley, would be coming by later in the week to change the shoes on a few of the racers and to inspect the whole lot of them for safety. Da carefully cut away some of the hoof wall and then rubbed an oily mixture into the sole of the foot, telling his son they needed to keep the sole lubricated to prevent cracking and chafing. He showed the various parts of the hoof to Mickey giving special attention to a "V" like structure in the soul of the foot he called the frog. And indeed it did look to the boy like the spread legs of the frogs he often caught down by the lake.

"That's where a champion gets his traction, my boy," Da told him enthusiastically. He reinforced the importance of caring for this part of the horse with great dedication, ensuring Mick that no horse with bad feet ever ran a mile worth a damn. When they were done inspecting the five stallions and the two mares, Mickey asked his father about the new colt.

"When does Whish't Daddy get his shoes, Da?"

Father walked him over to the stall where the new colt stood alongside his mother. "We'll let him grow for the good part of a year. It depends on the size of his hooves and O'Malley is the best judge of when he should be shod. But let's have a look at the wee one's feet." Da moved towards the colt reaching down to pick up one of his spindly legs. But the young horse side-stepped, whinnying in thin complaint. He looked at Frank suspiciously. Da tried again but the horse skittered away a second time. Mick looked at his father and held up his hand cautiously, telling him to wait. The boy moved slowly towards the young colt, first petting him gently along the nose and whispering softly in his ear. The young horse nestled his nose into Mick's shoulder calming down completely. Da looked on with surprise as the boy held out his hand and the colt slowly offered the hoof of his front right leg. Mick did as he had watched his father do and tucked the hoof safely between his legs, beginning a thorough inspection, picking out any debris and checking for the formative frog, pointing it out to his Da with a smile.

"He's got good feet," Da said as he watched his child deftly handle the horse's hoof and leg. He stood aside and let Mick check all four of the colt's hooves and smiled approvingly at the ease and confidence with which the boy handled the new horse. When they were done they fed the horses again and made sure the water was fresh in every stall. As they walked back up towards the cottage together, Da put his hand across the boy's shoulder and gave him a gentle squeeze. "Well done, Mick, you seem to have a gift for it," he said with more than a little pride. Father and son hugged each other tightly and then made their way back up to their home where dinner awaited and the hearth burned warm in the cool April evening.

Chaapter Three

Barreen, County Kildare, Ireland – May 1920

Frank Walsh watched with pleasure as his fifteen year old son worked Whish't Daddy in the open paddock with the ease and skill of a man twice his years. He had the big two year old horse on a short lead and was putting him through his paces, loading him into and out of the covered trolley they used to transport the horses, making sure the animal was comfortable with the procedure and calm during the process. The boy also had him walking wide figure eights, cantering side to side, moving front and back and standing as still as a cobra on command. It occurred to Frank it was not so much a walk the boy and horse were doing, it was much more of a dance, an elegant, well-choreographed waltz, the horse responding perfectly to Mickey's gentle touch, his calming voice, his every nuance and whisper. The colt had grown into a huge, muscular chestnut beauty but with Mickey, barely as tall as the horse's shoulder, Whish't Daddy was as gentle as the May breeze. For Frank, the boy's skill and natural gift with the horse was a source of great pride and pleasure. He himself had been training horses for as long as he could remember and his father before him and his grandfather even earlier forming a long lineage of horsemen with hundreds of years of experience and intimacy with the equestrian kingdom. From generation to generation the deep, thorough, primal understanding of these tremendous animals was solemnly passed with time honored methods and well proven techniques, tools, training aids, equipment, medical procedures, conditioning secrets, and breeding traditions. Each and every aspect of raising, caring, training and racing the most sacred of God's creatures was honed and improved by the next generation and looked upon as sacred lore by those following in line receiving this special gift and great responsibility. As Frank watched his son work magically with this massive colt, he thought that perhaps in this young man, all the teachings and learning and skills and all the respect, passion and profound love of all the generations for the animal knows as a horse, might be perfected and made holy quite simply by this boy being alive. Frank smiled at this rather luminous adulation he was lavishing on a youngster that had yet to raise a horse to breeding age but he did know for certain Mick had something special about him, something the horses knew as well. Most of the horses seemed to feel it and in the big beautiful chestnut colt dancing with him, it was a defined certainty. And after all it should be. The boy seemed to be one of them, he had their complete faith and trust and he moved amongst these huge animals like one of their own. Two years ago, Frank decided that Whish't Daddy would be the boy's horse to raise and train. Frank had been there every step of the way providing instruction, advice, critique and praise and he would continue in this role. Thinking back to the early days of Whish't Daddy's training, he'd demonstrated for the boy many of the technical aspects of fitting a bridle, securing a bit, how to saddle and fit the stirrups and how to load and unload for transport. He'd instructed the boy on schedules and equipment and when to work the horse and when to rest him, how to inspect the colt's physical condition and how to deal with a wide range of ailments from colic and diarrhea to cuts and abrasions, fractures and laminitis. But the actual care and feeding and training and health of the animal fell to Mick completely. Frank had explained this to Mickey in the first few weeks of Whish't Daddy's life and the boy accepted this charge with great enthusiasm and excitement, performing in the most dedicated manner, wholly justifying Da's great confidence and faith in his son. Over the two years, Frank carefully observed Mick's growing skills and his mystic manner with the horse and he could not help the immense pride bursting within him for his boy and he felt a great sense of satisfaction in knowing that the line of great trainers stretching back generations would live on in Mickey and perhaps reach some new level of perfection.

Frank left his son and the horse alone in the paddock and wandered back towards the barn. As he strolled across the open field he felt the warm breeze of May on his weathered face and it filled him with a familiar feeling of gratitude for the many blessings in his life. The rolling green fields stretched wide around him, nearly fifteen acres in all, a small but solid cottage made of sturdy timber and good thatch sat perched on the highest parcel of land, a large barn held eight stalls, each stall bordered by a small grassy paddock and encircling the barn and paddocks a small make-shift race course served for training the horses. Beyond the course a wide expanse of rolling fields where the horses were put out for grazing and galloping stretched into the distance. Next to the cottage was a small fenced in garden where his wife Fiona scratched out a meager harvest of potatoes, carrots and parsnips. Being the oldest male in his family, Frank had inherited a small parcel of land from his Da, Bernard, who had purchased it from the Land Commission in 1885 shortly after the passing of the Ashbourne Act. Bernard's family had for many generations worked this same land when it was known as Castle Longpond, some in the fields providing the back-breaking labor for sowing and picking potatoes, barley and sugar beets but a select few worked in the stalls and barns taking care of Lord Longpond's many horses. The Lord's stable had an excellent reputation in horse racing circles throughout the adjoining counties and it was expected that the men working in the stables would continue producing elegant racers and jumpers with an occasional champion for the Castle. With the passage of the Ashbourne Act and the return of the Longpond family to England, the barns and stables grew into disrepair and were eventually sold off in small lots to the peasantry. But Frank had learned plenty from his father and other relatives over the many years and his position as *"Maistir Capaill"* or Master of Horses left him in great demand across all of Ireland. He was held on special retainer to several of the wealthy Lords still owning vast acreage and stables across the country. This work allowed him many advantages over the majority of his neighbors and fellow land owners, most of who owned very small plots with small farms barely providing enough of a harvest to feed their families let alone improve the state of their holdings. It was a common problem resulting from the Land Commission's decision to slice up the more sizeable estates purchased from wealthy nobles into tiny parcels to be sold off to the great number of peasants who had been working the land for decades and in some cases centuries. The small farms were prohibited from banding together and so each family struggled to coax a sufficient harvest from the hard and often rocky soil, fighting the often bitter Irish winters with the memory of the devastating Great Famine never far from the farmer's mind. Many of Frank's neighbors complained bitterly of the restrictions and limitations of the tiny farms but Frank often reminded them of the days not too long ago when the absentee landowners and their cruel agents inflicted a far more brutal existence. Frank knew it was easy for him to point out the advantages of the current system, the ability to at least own a little land and educate their children, because the horse training provided him with economic benefits unavailable to the wide majority of Irish families. So he made sure to share any surplus of food and wool and tooling he enjoyed with neighbors and community members in need of assistance. The smiling face of Harry the Horse crossed Frank's mind as it did whenever he thought of his great and unexpected fortune in acquiring the comparatively vast parcel of land surrounding him, the land known as Athy House upon which the cottage, farm and stables stood. Harry and his benefactor's business acumen and legal creativity allowed Frank to circumvent Irish laws limiting land and business ownership by Irish citizens. Leveraging their assistance and his knowledge of horses allowed Frank to realize a lifelong dream, to build his own stable of racers, horses he personally, if somewhat secretly, owned and to begin racing them under the mysterious banner of Athy House. He'd begun building his stable nearly fifteen years earlier using the unexpected investment from America to purchase a young colt born blind in one eye from an Earl in County Clare who felt the horse was somehow cursed. But Frank Walsh new the bloodlines and liked the horse's look, especially the powerful shoulders, forearms and thighs. He also liked the horse's pluck and the way he turned his head to look you directly in the face with his one good eye. It took a good number of months training him, at first with both eyes covered and gradually with only the blind eye in blinkers, but with enough repetition and practice the horse, renamed Look Once, grew into a competitive, spirited racer, finishing in the money three times as a two year old and winning two regional championships, at the age of three. Using his winnings from those races along with additional off shore investment and some money saved from his work as a trainer in great demand, Frank purchased a beautiful broodmare and another young colt that showed promise and his stable's humble roots were established! He was careful to maintain the veil of secrecy regarding his ownership of the stable. Although the laws were slowly changing he felt it best not to leave anything to chance when it came to the British Government. He also saw no purpose in notifying potential employers that he was now one of their competitors. Frank knew in his heart he would still go about his business of training their horses with all the skill, wisdom and integrity he possessed. They were lucky to have him and he damn well needed their money. Besides, it kept him smack in the middle of the horse racing industry, surrounded by the finest animals in the world, a world he understood just about as well as any man alive.

Frank circled the barn wanting to check on the turf pile in the rear and he heard the neighing and whinnying of the horses inside. The sound brought great joy and comfort to him, the strong and healthy sounds of animals he owned, a source of pride and gratitude that filled him almost every day as he set about his work with these beautiful creatures. Again he reminded himself of how fortunate he was and how his life filled him with happiness known to very few of the inhabitants on this gorgeous and terrible island. And he thought not for the first time, of the random nature of life and the small, indiscriminate things which could often dictate one's success or failure, one's opportunities or lack of opportunity, one's happiness or misery. He could claim no accomplishment in being first born son. It just fell to him. But with it fell the opportunity to join his Da in the family business as well as his claim to the family land. What else could a man want or need other than a viable and thrilling trade and a fine piece of land to raise one's family and luckily again, to house one's business? He did not need to look very far or to think too hard of what might have been if he had been born second or third or fourth son or if he had been born, God forbid, with a pair of tits. All he had to do was to think of his own family and he did so with a heavy heart. Both the second and third sons, his brothers Liam and John, had left Ireland long ago, Liam to America and John to Australia. Liam had died in a tragic accident in the New World while John had made it to Australia and had been working a small farm in the South but had not been heard from in many years. His only sister, Bridget, was a spinster living in a convent in Dublin where she worked in the hospital as a nurse. She was a sad and lonely woman with few prospects and enough resentment to fill a racecourse. But it was his youngest brother that most firmly underscored the difficult path his life may have taken had he not been blessed to be born before the others. Darcy Walsh sat in Mountjoy Prison in Dublin and had for the past three years, a twenty-two year old man who had fallen in with the paramilitary arm of Sinn Fein shortly after the Easter Rising and captured on a gun smuggling assignment bringing in weapons from mainland Europe. Darcy was Frank's youngest brother, younger by eighteen years and in some respects much further apart than the years would indicate. Try as Frank could, he barely remembered Darcy in his youth, recalling little more than a squabbling baby in a crib or a young child digging in the dirt of the yard. Frank was too busy learning his trade and working with horses across the country to pay much mind to another sibling, especially one so many years his junior. There may have been a few days here and there when he kicked the ball around in the yard with the little one, but it offered no challenge and Frank bored easily of the effort. But he could recall with some sweet melancholy hoisting Darcy, maybe about four or five years of age, onto a young mare and leading him about the track on his first ride and he remembered the boy, blond hair blowing in the breeze, a smile the size of the moon on his face, yelling for the horse to go faster and faster. But Frank worried about the danger and soon scooped the boy off the horse and Darcy screamed at him in protest running back to the cottage, tears of rage and anger rolling down his soft, young cheeks. It seemed to Frank that Darcy Walsh had never stopped screaming since. He had visited his brother in prison only once in the past few years. The conditions were far worse for the men in Mountjoy then Frank would ever allow for any of his horses. Filth, overcrowding, little food and cells packed with angry, violent men created an atmosphere ripe with tension, brutality and danger. Darcy had quickly absorbed the personality of the prison population, angrily accusing his brother of being part of the Irish problem, beholden to the Anglo-Saxon gentry, spoiled by their keen need of his talents and the compensation it commanded, and ignorant or unsympathetic to the Republican cause. Frank tried to reason with him, trying to get Darcy to see the way out of the struggle was by trying to build Irish owned businesses, beating the English Lords at their own game and sharing the small amount of wealth he had accumulated with the community around him. But Darcy would have none of it. In his bitter and angry way, he cursed his brother telling him to never return to Mountjoy as he wished never to lay eyes on Frank Walsh again. So Frank had honored that wish and stayed away but he did so with a heavy heart. He followed the news about the prisoners in the local papers, staying on top of the political climate which was growing worse and worse throughout Ireland. Many of the prisoners had begun a hunger strike but he did not know if Darcy was amongst them but he did know their tactic was garnering great attention across the Irish Sea, much of the British population appalled by the treatment of the prisoners. He had heard rumors of the possible release of many of the strikers on humanitarian grounds. He offered a quick prayer for his youngest brother and then entered the stable, anxious to get on with his work.

Chapter Four

Barreen, Kildare County – May 1920

O'Malley, the farrier, arrived the following Saturday. Mick was always thrilled when the old man came on the weekend. He loved watching him work with the horses and listening intently to the conversation between Da and the farrier, and he was anxious to see if Whish't Daddy would get a new set of shoes. Mick remembered the first time he'd met O'Malley shortly after his colt had been born. To Mick's tender eyes, the farrier looked to be at least a hundred years old and judging by the way he walked and talked and heard almost nothing said to him, Mick figured he must be close in his assessment. Two years later, the old man looked pretty much the same. He pulled up in a wagon drawn by a horse looking as old as himself, the rear of the cart loaded down with the tools of the trade - huge anvils, great big hammers for shaping and pounding, tongs that looked big enough to pick up a horse, a wide assortment of nails and clips, rasps of every size, a few knives of different shapes and mounted to the rear of the wagon, a large forge of black iron, scalded by years of huge and brilliant fires. The old man was hunched over but still as tall as Mick's father and despite his age, he unloaded the tools with relative ease, straining only with the largest anvil which he plopped down in the middle of the yard next to the barn. He had clumps of gray hair sticking out of a large, blocky head and his overalls were covered in dirt and grease and grime. A thin, brown cigarette dangled from his lips. He shook hands with Frank and they talked quickly about which of the horses required attention and then

Frank disappeared into the barn to fetch one of the stallions. O'Malley nodded at Mick and lit another cigarette. "How's that beautiful beast of yours, my boy?" the farrier asked with a grin.

"He's doing just fine, Sir," Mick replied enthusiastically. "I been checking his feet every day like you told me to do and I think he may be due for a new pair of shoes, he's growing like a weed." Mick added.

The farrier nodded. "I'll be sure to take a look, son. That beast has the hooves of champion and we need to make sure his shoes are just right, don't we?" He tussled the boy's hair and continued laying out his tools.

A moment later Da came out with the big gray, Chipper, and they cross-tied him to the fence posts. Mick hopped up and took a seat alongside the stallion, stroking his face, eagerly watching as O'Malley went about his business. Using a clawed hammer, he deftly removed the clenches on the old shoe and then slowly peeled the iron shoe away from the hoof with a pair of pliers. Da handed the old man a tool they called a nipper and O'Malley carefully clipped away the excessive growth of the horn of the heel, a process which his father would later explain was not unlike clipping fingernails or toenails for a person. Then the farrier selected a large rasp and pushing hard down on the horse's foot, he worked for several minutes on leveling out the hoof, careful not to damage the sensitive parts of the sole. With a very sharp knife, he cut away at parts of the foot, explaining softly to the boy that the foot needed to be smooth and properly positioned to assure a good fit with the shoe. Da had built a good hot fire in the forge and O'Malley selected a shoe from his store and using the big tongs, jammed the iron shoe into the blazing fire, holding it there long enough to make it malleable. The shoe turned bright orange with a blue tinge in the hot fire and it smoked and sizzled when removed from the flame. He held the smoking shoe up to the horse's foot, checking the size and shape and then he made a few adjustments with the hammer, smashing the shoe on the large anvil several times until he was happy with the result. Then he dipped the smoldering shoe into a container of cold water, the sound hissing across the yard in the morning sun. He used a combination of nails and clenches to attach the shoe to the horse and then made a few more adjustments, clipping and filing the nails, ensuring a smooth, well fitted shoe. He inspected his work quickly and then moved on to the horse's other feet. Mickey was intrigued by the process and he watched the farrier's every movement and listened to his every word. As he worked through the procession of horses, the subjects Da and O'Malley talked about changed as quickly and as often as the Irish weather. Much of the morning discussion centered around the horses, their health, the growth of their hooves, the way the shoes wore on their respective feet, which ones had the feet for a champion's run, which were mere plodders or more suited to stud. O'Malley thought Bellweather a better horse than he'd shown to date and questioned Da on his choice of rider, a young Monahan lad by the name of Killhane.

"He ain't got the feel for that big bastard, Frankie," the farrier stated in between blows with the shaping hammer. "Bellweather got to have his own way coming out; you can't be holding him back for down the road. The fecking horse loses interest if all he sees are other horses' asses in his way. I'd put Brian Grant up on that beast and he'd get him across the line, mark my words." Grant raced a good number of stallions, mostly jumpers, for Athy House, and he'd had his share of winners but of late Da seemed reluctant to put him up in the chains.

"Brian is a good lad," Da said to the old man softly. His eyes roamed around the yard for a moment and he looked Mick directly in the eyes. He held the gaze a few moments and Mickey felt his father was telling him that what he heard next he was to keep to himself and tell no one. Mick nodded slightly in acknowledgement. "But he seems a little distracted of late. His mind ain't always on the horse or the race I'd wager." O'Malley looked at Da for a moment and shrugged.

"Not surprising for a young lad about his age, is it Frankie?" the man asked with a smile. "It's either the ladies or the drink I'd imagine?" But Da just looked at him and said nothing. After a few moments the farrier understood. "Caught up in all of that crazy nonsense is he?" He shook his head and went back to his pounding and it seemed to Mickey he slammed the hammer down a lot harder than he had earlier in the day.

A little later the conversation came around to the racing game and Frank Walsh greatly valued O'Malley's opinions and insights into the state of racing in Ireland and the United Kingdom. He respected his judgments on the dominant stables and strongest horses racing in the various tournaments and championships across the land, always keen to understand the competition. The old man spoke for a long while, reviewing the field for each of the upcoming races in May and June, starting with the jumpers down in Cork and Kerry, covering the flats out in Clare and Galway, the five main races at the Curragh and a few races across the Irish Sea in England. Da asked a number of questions regarding the bigger races held at the Curragh, especially The Derby, The Oaks and the St Leger. Da was planning on running Bellweather in the Derby, thinking he might give the superb War Lord from Montgomery Castle a fair test. But he had his reservations.

"I don't want to run him unless he's got a real shot to win. Every time I put up a horse from Athy House, there seems to be more and more attention on the ownership of the stable and less and less attention paid to the horse. I'd rather keep things quiet as far as that goes for now," he said cautiously. The old man nodded his big, gray head in understanding.

"They'll hear nothing on that score from me, Frankie. As far as Bellweather's chances, I can't say he'd be the favorite. You know Montgomery will have their entries and I am sure they will be very competitive."

Da took in this information, nodding in agreement. Montgomery Castle had one of the longest and most successful records in the annals of horse racing in Ireland going back to the early seventeenth century. For hundreds of years, the various Lord Montgomery's had owned and bred some of the most famous of horses in all of the United Kingdom. The Castle was far out West, in Connemara, and Frank had been out to their land on a number of occasions, once to interview for a position on the Lord's team of trainers and once to watch a match race of two thoroughbreds, one owned by the current Lord Montgomery and one owned by a French businessman who dabbled in the sport of kings. The two three year olds that would most likely run in the Derby were Atlantic Wind, a filly with a pedigree almost as old as the Castle and the previous year's winner, War Lord, a stallion of incredible size and stamina, surely the favorite in any race he ran. Frank could not deny that Bellweather would be sorely tested. The Derby would field at least ten horses. Besides the two from Montgomery, there was certain to be at least two or three more horses with the ability to run with Bellweather. Still, he thought he'd take his chances.

When Da told Mick to bring Whish't Daddy from the barn the boy nearly sprinted to his stall. He fit him quickly with a bridle and checked the D-bit to make sure they could properly cross tie the big horse. He led him out to the yard and the farrier smiled at the sight of the two year old. He ran his gnarly hands down along Whish't Daddy's neck and across his chest and then gently down his legs, testing the elbow, knee, cannon bone, shin, fetlock and finally the hoof. He examined the hoof for cracks, measuring the angle of the shoe, ensuring its proper fit would reduce any stress on the ligaments and tendons of the horse's leg. He used a pick to clean a few pieces of debris and trimmed a little around the wall and then he examined the other legs and feet in a similar fashion. He patted the big horse on the shoulder when he was finished and smiled at Mickey, nodding in appreciation. "This beast is being well taking care of, son. That's good. But I think his shoes are fine for another month or two. Keep doing what you been doing and his feet are ready to fly." The old man paused and looked at Frank, a question forming on his lips.

Frank smiled. "I know what you are going to ask. We're getting close. Mick's got him so he can load and unload with no problems. He can break from the gate without a second thought. His stamina is incredible. Now we just need to do a few more things to maximize speed. We haven't tried to run him flat out and I want to make sure he can take the pounding. I'd say three or four months. Maybe we can run him for the Saint Ledger." He stopped and looked at his son who had a broad smile filled with pride and anticipation. "What do you think Mick?" Da asked.

"I say we'll be ready, Da. Whish't Daddy is ready now but I think your right, another few months and this boy will be ready to fly. Yes, Sir, Whish't Daddy will be ready to fly."

The farrier was packing up his wagon, meticulously placing each hammer, hasp, grip and assorted tools in their designated place, making some kind of order from the chaos of metal, steel and leather gear. As the late afternoon shadows lengthened, Fiona appeared in the yard carrying a small pail and two mugs and handed a glass to each of the two men. The farrier bowed in appreciation and Da gave his wife a gentle kiss on the cheek. She poured a frothy amber liquid into each man's glass, the beer's sudsy head overflowing only a small bit.

"You are a grand woman," the farrier exclaimed. Clinking his glass against Da's, he took a great big swallow, emptying half the glass. "Just what I needed," he said wiping some of the beer from his lips with the back of his hand. The men sat in the seat of the wagon and Mickey climbed onto the back, anxious to here what might be said next. Mother left the pail of beer and excused herself, returning to the kitchen and her dinner preparations. Da gave Mickey the same look of warning as he softly approached the next subject.

"Do you think the season is still in jeopardy, Shamus?" he asked quietly.

The farrier took another long gulp from his glass and shaking his head from side to side, hesitated before speaking. "Not sure Frankie, certainly things could be better. But no one liked cancelling the season during the war and the stables were all pleased as punch to be back in the game the past two years. Now the war on the continent is history but we seem to be coming damn close to another one right here at home." He looked at Da directly and Mickey's father nodded in understanding.

Thoughts of Darcy sitting in Mountjoy Prison flicked across Frank's mind and he scowled at the state of unrest that had settled across his beloved country over the past four years. The Easter Rising had been the work of a handful of fools in Frank Walsh's opinion and if the British government had just kept the lot of them in jail instead of executing so many of the Volunteers they would be long forgotten instead of turning them into heroes and martyrs across most of Ireland. And the last few years had seen a growth of the Republican movement. With that growth came violence and murder Frank could not condone. Surely he wished for a free and independent country, he held no allegiance to the crown and he abhorred their ruthless and unfair treatment of the Irish people but he did not believe all the killing would achieve any sort of positive result. It would only encourage harsh reprisals from the Royal Irish

Constabulary and from the British soldiers assigned to the country. The violence down in Cork was particularly ruthless, entire towns and cities burned to the ground and many small businesses ruined in the process. Frank Walsh fervently believed that only through strong commerce and private ownership of business and industry by the Irish people would they overcome the yoke of colonialism that had burdened Ireland for hundreds of years.

"The Republicans are gaining support as the reprisals grow worse and I am afraid the violence will continue to spiral out of control," Da said. "I am hearing Dublin Castle plans to bring in thousands more men to augment the Constabulary, rough men, war veterans, men as hard as nails." Da looked at the farrier who nodded in confirmation.

"Yeah, I am afraid it's true," the old man said sadly. "Another lot of them arrived by ship into the harbor in Dublin last week and I watched a fair bunch of them carousing around the town, razing a ruckus and terrorizing the population. And they are hard men, for sure. They ran out of uniforms for the RIC and these boys are outfitted in khaki pants and tunics and funny looking black berets and caps. Black and Tans the people are calling them, and the people are learning real fast to stay out of their way. A good beating and a few less bob in their pockets would be the price paid for anyone not heeding the warning." O'Malley drained the last of his beer and held out his hand to shake Da's hand. He gave the boy's head another gentle tussle as Mick turned back towards the barn, leading Whish't Daddy away.

The old man watched the horse and the boy disappear into the barn and he looked back at Frank Walsh. "That is quite a horse you have there, Frank. I think that big beast has steel, my friend. And he's got that twinkle in his eye to tell you he is going to be something special," the farrier said, readying to leave. As he turned the wagon towards the gate he hesitated, another question forming on his craggy face. "Who do you plan to ride that monster?" he asked curiously. Frank hesitated, a look of slight uncertainty coloring his eyes.

"I can't say for sure, man. As I said I am having some problems with Brian Grant and I am not sure the Kilhane boy could handle the job." He looked at the farrier wanting his reaction. The old man nodded a few times and then pointed his chin towards the barn where Mickey and Whish't Daddy had just disappeared. Frank moved his head in that direction. After a moment, he understood.

"The boy?" he saw the old man nod his head up and down. "I don't know, he's a little bigger than most jockeys and has never held the reins in any sort of competition. It might be too great a leap with such a horse." He squinted at O'Malley and waited. The farrier shrugged.

"That boy was born to ride that horse, Frank. But you'll do what's best, you always have." He nodded and with a wave of his hand and a gentle snap of the reins, the wagon, the old horse and the old man ambled across the yard and out onto the dirt road, heading west into the setting sun.

Chapter Five

Dublin Castle - May 1920

The mood in the castle reflected much of the sentiments found on the streets of Dublin. Fear, uncertainty, anger, outrage and sorrow mingled with the unmistakable scent of conspiracy leaving a heavy gloom hanging over the building and its inhabitants. Dublin Castle was home to the loyalist government responsible for the administration of Ireland and it was a government under siege since the Easter Rising four years earlier. Changes in personnel made less than two years before, both in the civil administration and in the military rulers of the occupying government, did little to alleviate feelings of ambiguity and indecision regarding day to day direction of the country. This ambiguity was compounded by the contradictory and confusing opinions, suggestions and dictates submitted by the government of Lloyd George in London, as well as the British Parliament. The Home Rule bill seemed to be sleeves from the vest as it seeded no real power to the Irish people and did not address the central question of a united or divided Ireland. Handling of the growing menace from the Irish Republican Army under its crafty and well organized leader, Michael Collins, was a major source of debate both in the castle and in London. The challenge of dealing with an increasing number of labor strikes by railroad and dock workers in Ireland had a rippling effect on unions and the Labor Party in the United Kingdom. Sentiment around the world focused keenly on the British government's treatment of the Irish people, mostly in a strongly negative manner. Collins was very adept at manipulating public opinion in favor of the Republican cause and he used every opportunity of reprisals by the RIC or the British Army to portray the English in the most abhorrent light. Pressure was mounting on the leaders in Dublin Castle to regain control over the country and all means possible were under consideration to do the job. Prime Minister Lloyd George's handpicked man to engineer this badly needed turnaround was a career police officer with vast experience, including a leading role in combating civil unrest during the coal strikes in South Wales. Eighteen months earlier, General Sir Nevil Macready, a man with a strong dislike of politics and politicians, assumed the duties of Commander of British Forces in the country, both the military and the Royal Irish Constabulary. On the civil side of the occupying government, a bluff and foolhardy career politician by the name of Sir Hamar Greenwood simultaneously took over as Chief Secretary to Ireland. The two men were faced with the enormous challenge of returning Ireland to some sort of peaceful and productive nation. The challenge had so far proved daunting. Both men had offices in Dublin Castle and retained large staffs, some who were loyalist to the core and others whose sympathies secretly lay with the IRA Volunteers.

As they did regularly, Secretary Greenwood met with Nevil Macready in the military leader's office, both men bringing along their trusted assistants, both men having grown leery of the other's positions and intentions. Macready's right hand man, a Scotsman by birth named Ian MacDermott, had a reputation for underhanded tricks and an overzealous dislike of the Irish citizenry. Greenwood's top assistant, Under-secretary John Harrington, was an Irishman from County Wicklow who professed loyalist commitment while employing a combination of brilliance and mirth to maintain his position in the hostile environment of the British rulers. This meeting was coming on the heels of a yet another series of raids and attacks by the Republicans and tempers in the room were running very high.

"I am bound and determined to root out these so called Volunteers and toss them all in the goal or even better, watch every one of them swing from the end of a rope," MacDermott began the conversation. He was sitting behind a large desk, both hands bunched in fists and nervously banging lightly against the desktop. His face was deeply flushed with exasperation and he smoked a dark, thin cigarette as if he might inhale the entire fag in one deep breath. Greenwood sat across from him; a large and sloppy man who looked much too big for the small chair he occupied. Sitting beside him, John Harrington appeared far more calm and composed. Macready sat near the unlit hearth and allowed his eyes to shift from one man to the next. He found the interchange between his assistant and the civilian leaders fascinating. Macready felt a chill pass through him. The late evening was cool in the drafty room and would have benefitted from a small fire for warmth but the hearth lay empty and cold.

"Aye," the Scotsman continued, "here in my hands alone are reports of near thirty-five raids on postal offices, income tax collectors and police barracks in the past week, all in some fecking recognition of their damn rising of four years ago. Why they burned the damn tax roles and destroyed barracks across Cork and Kerry and out as far away as Galway City! These so called Republicans are a growing menace and if we don't put a stop to them soon they will never be stopped at all." MacDermott tossed the papers on Macready's desk with disgust. He was a short, plump man, with thinning gray hair and the pock-marked, pale complexion of a sickly child. He stood and paced behind Macready's desk, occasionally looking out of the large window overlooking one of the busiest streets in Dublin. "A stern lesson is what these bastards are in need of, by God I tell you, a damn stern lesson."

Macready nodded in agreement while lighting a cigarette of his own. The ashtray was overflowing with butts and ashes and small bits of paper. Heavy blue smoke hung over the room. "What do you propose?" he asked the Scotsman.

MacDermott thought for a few moments and then laid out a long list of actions including mass arrests, destruction of personal property belonging to any known Volunteers or supporters of the Republican cause, seizure of all printing presses belonging to Irish Nationalist newspapers, public flogging and execution of leading IRA members and the immediate institution of martial law. "We clamp down like a mailed fist across the throat of this Godforsaken insurrection and we squeeze and we squeeze and we squeeze until the fecking life of it is drained away like so much milk from a teat. Let these bastards know that His Majesty's government is not to be taken lightly in any damn way."

Macready's eyes moved from the passionate Scot to his civil counterpart who was shaking his head from side to side across the table. "No, no, no," Hamar Greenwood began with deep conviction. "There have been far too many reprisals by the RIC already and all they have managed to accomplish is turning the sentiment of the Irish people in favor of the Republican cause and turning the outraged opinion of the world against England. The Constabulary is nearly depleted. We can barely get anyone in the country to join the RIC for fear of retribution; a good number have been killed or maimed already. We need to find a different path. Violence has only begat more violence and these attacks continue to spiral out of control leading to looting, burnings and in many cases harming the personal property of our Loyalist citizens and in some cases the citizens themselves."

"Oh rot on that," MacDermott hissed in reply. "These traitors only understand one thing, and that is raw, unrestrained power." He slammed a pudgy fist down on the desk and the big ashtray rattled about sending more ashes and butts across the table. Macready raised his hand to his aide and MacDermott reluctantly quieted down.

"What did you have in mind," he asked Greenwood cautiously.

The Chief Secretary motioned to Harrington and the aide handed him a sheaf of papers from the binder in his lap. Greenwood's eyes fluttered over the page quickly and then he cleared his voice, glancing overtly at the Scotsman. "We think there are a number of things we can institute that will have a more positive impact than more violent reprisals. The first and most important is to continue to work through the channels available to reach a cease fire with the Republicans." MacDermott began protesting in loud opposition but Macready silenced him again with a stern glance. Greenwood continued. "If we can achieve a workable cease fire than we may be able to negotiate a lasting truce, depending of course on the status of Home Rule and what comes out of Ulster."

"Figure on nothing but trouble from the North," Macready warned. Greenwood nodded and went on. "On a more local level, we suggest institution of a curfew beginning immediately requiring all citizens to be off the streets by nine at night and no one about before eight in the morning. Anyone violating the curfew will be subject to immediate arrest." He looked at Ian MacDermott and the Scotsman grudgingly nodded his approval. "In addition to negotiating a cease fire and imposing a curfew, there are a number of local activities we are considering banning or suspending for the time being until the hostilities come under control. Included in the list of activities are travelling circus acts which include large animals, theatre shows with any Republican content or sentiment, sale of alcohol in public houses or taverns after curfew, cancellation of all boxing exhibitions, football games and all horse racing matches scheduled for the remainder of the year." Greenwood put the piece of paper on the table and looked at Macready for his reaction. The military man smoked another cigarette while considering the list.

"Do you expect they'll just sit at home and tend to their knitting?" he asked sarcastically. Greenwood began to answer but Harrington jumped in ahead of his boss.

"Well, no sir, we really don't," he began. "I am quite certain there will be considerable backlash to closing the public houses early and shutting down the boxing, football and racing for the year. When it has been done in the past, the racing in particular was shut down for two years due to the war, quite often private matches were arranged with considerable interest. But they do not draw the large crowds like we have at the Curragh or down in Cork or out in Galway. And it is the crowds we are most interested in eliminating as they provide the best opportunity for trouble." He looked from Macready to Greenwood but both men looked unimpressed. "You must understand the average Irish person wants peace as well," he insisted softly. "I am sure there will be an acceptance of the new regulations over time if they're effective in combating all the violence. That is how it must be presented, not as a penalty but as a means to a more peaceful society."

The room was silent for several moments and then the Scotsman sighed loudly. "A bunch of rubbish you're proposing although I do agree with the curfew and cutting back on their appetite for drink. The rest is a load of manure. We need to control the streets and parks and towns, not limit their use. Let them have their damn plays and games and races.

Just have my boys standing by ready to apply the fist if things should get out of hand. That's what your society is all about Harrington, if they'll behave they'll have their peace but by God if they don't they'll feel the wrath of the Empire on their wretched backs." MacDermott strolled angrily from the room slamming the door in his wake, leaving Macready looking across the desk at his civil counterparts.

"I suggest we take these things under advisement for the time being, Hamar. Let's discuss it again at the end of the week. I need to speak with London before we finalize anything. Is that alright?" Greenwood agreed and the meeting ended abruptly. John Harrington followed his boss from the room shaking his head in disbelief.

Two hours later, in the same room, MacDermott and Macready shared a glass of sherry and discussed what had transpired earlier.

"I am quite certain that cancellation of horse racing will not sit well with a number of the members of the House of Lords," Macready stated softly. "Lord Montgomery has the ear of much of Parliament and I know he was very angry when the season was cancelled for the war. That man lives for his damn horses and with a stable like his, well I guess it should be that way."

MacDermott shrugged. "I don't really give a damn about any of that. They can cancel what they damn well please. My greater concern is the Constabulary. With all the murders and the resignations we are still lacking enough men. We can not bring the lads in from home fast enough. Another ship docked this morning and another five hundred boys came ashore. We need ten times that, maybe more, if we're to regain control over this Godforsaken place." Macready nodded in agreement and the Scotsman continued. "We are getting some damn fine men though, tough men, lads that have proven themselves at the Bourne and in Alsace-Lorraine. Tough men they are, hardened and happy to have a job of any sort. They'll take no gruff from this lot, of that I am certain."

"We are providing them with some rules around the use of force, I would hope?" Macready asked carefully.

"Don't you worry about that, Sir Nevil, leave all of their training up to me. This way you can report into London whatever you damn well please. I will let my men know there is a line and there will be consequences if they cross the line. But I assure you they will have plenty of leeway to administer the required justice before they come anywhere near that line."

Macready drained his drink and nodded at his aide. MacDermott had seen considerable fighting in France at the early part of the war and it seemed to Macready that the violence of war had consumed the man's heart and his soul. He was a walking wave of anger and hostility. For a small man MacDermott had the ability to intimidate and Macready watched as others shied away from the little Scotsman whenever the violence inside began to bubble to the surface. He had seen both Greenwood and Harrington back away on several occasions. It occurred to Macready that in MacDermott he had the right man for the job of bringing order to an otherwise disorderly land.

Chapter Six

Mountjoy Prison - May 1920

Darcy Walsh carefully removed the short letter from its hiding place inside his left shoe and quietly surveyed the crowded yard at the rear of the jail looking for prison guards or known snitches who would be far too happy to report his possession of personal correspondence. It was forbidden in Mountjoy but the letter had been carefully smuggled in to him by another Volunteer, a boy he had grown up with in Kildare, Brian Mahoney, now a prisoner himself. The yard was packed with many young men like Brian. Most of them had been arrested on suspicion of treasonous acts and held in the jail for as long as three years. Most had no idea how much longer they would remain at Mountjoy. Seldom did any of them get to speak with a lawyer and visitation by friends and family was very rare. The day was cool and damp but Darcy was grateful for the time in the yard, glad to be outside instead of locked in the cage he shared with three other men, a cage reeking of human waste, sweat and fear. Unfolding the precious piece of paper, he glanced once more around the yard then let his eyes fall across the page, reading words he knew by heart, words he had read a hundred times, words that burned deeply inside his soul.

Dearest Darcy,
You are in my prayers every morning and every night.
My father says little about you but I know you are never far from Da's thoughts. We hear many horrible rumors about Mountjoy and I can only hope you are being treated alright and that you are well.
I miss the feel of your hand in mine and the sound of your laughter.
Be strong dear Darcy. I await your return.

Love,
Maureen

He read the letter several times over, imagining her voice as she would pronounce the words, crisply and clearly and with a hint of sadness tracing her tongue. In his mind's eye he saw her beautiful face, her soft white skin, her long golden hair, her mischievous smile accompanying her lyrical voice, her lovely beauty apparent in every way. She was his brother's oldest daughter but Darcy did not see Maureen in that way. They had nearly grown up together, Darcy only three years her elder. In all practical purposes they were far more like brother and sister but Darcy could not deny a more powerful feeling, a deeper, more passionate attraction to Maureen than a man should rightfully feel for a sister or for his brother's daughter. As youngsters they had shared the same bathtub and were dressed and undressed in each other's presence more times than Darcy could remember. He could not recall when he started noticing the curves of her slim waist or the budding breasts across her chest. They had done everything together as children, playing in the fields, walking together to school, sharing meals and baths and books and secrets and laughter and tears. They often held hands as they walked through the woods and Darcy could feel her smooth fingers wrapped around his own and feel her shoulders rub gently across his arms. He had kissed her a few times, gentle, soft kisses across her lovely lips, kisses that would make him want so much more but he would always pull away, force himself to separate from her physically although he could see the same desire, the same want in her eyes. The night before his arrest they had wandered deep into the forest beyond the barn, walking arm in arm, Maureen telling him of her father's plan to send her off to school in London, adamant that she would not go. Darcy remembered protesting the plan, cursing his brother and his loyalist leanings. They had come to the old creek where they liked to sit on the big rocks and dangle their feet in the cold, rushing waters. The sun was setting over the tall pine trees and the sky was a mural of soft pinks and purples and streaks of orange and blue. He slid his arm across her shoulders and Maureen rested her pretty head in the crook of his arm. He told her of his mission the following day, knowing she believed in the Republican cause and her strong support for the Volunteers. He was careful to minimize the danger involved but she still worried for his safety.

"Darcy, you must not be captured. I hear terrible stories of the boys they take away and how they are treated. Some have even been hanged." She stopped, her voice catching with emotion. "I can't imagine if something were to happen to you. I don't think I could bear the pain." He squeezed her tightly, smiling down into her beautiful hazel green eyes. He could feel the passion and desire building within. He could smell the fragrance of her hair and her skin and her flesh felt soft and warm against his body. She slipped her dress from her shoulders, the fabric falling below her breasts, her thin slip covering her barely. He gasped softly and his hand moved slowly towards her slip, touching the smooth, soft fabric, gently slipping a finger inside to feel the supple, warm skin and the firm point of her nipple, hard and erect to his touch. His head bent down and gently kissing her lips he rubbed his fingers back and forth across her nipple, desire pounding through every ounce of his body, blood flowing hot and raging through his veins. She shifted her weight allowing the dress to fall further down, the slip now covering her waist and her legs and her groin.

"No," he said softly, fighting the raging desire inside his loins.

She took his hand and moving it between her legs she whispered "yes," and then moaned wantonly, clutching him tightly with her arms.

Just then a horse and wagon came juggling along the dirt road across the creek and hearing its approach they moved quickly apart, Maureen slipping the dress back upon her shoulders, Darcy sliding away from her side, painfully aware of the separation of their desire. It was their neighbor, Mr. O'Boyle, carrying a load of turf back from the bog and seeing the pair sitting on the rocks he waved, shouting a greeting.

"Come along, dear girl," he said with a laugh, "I'll give the pair of you a lift back home. I am sure your mother will be putting out supper any minute." They had little choice, not wanting to give O'Boyle any reason for suspicion or concern. They moved slowly from the rocks, Darcy holding her hand as she crossed the water, grateful for the feeling of her flesh, badly wanting so much more. They hopped into the wagon alongside the farmer and made their way back home.

Darcy slipped the letter back inside his sock and then put his shoe on, glancing around again looking for any danger. But the yard offered no threat and he smiled when he saw his friend Mahoney approaching.

"Reading it again, are you," Brian asked with a sly grin.

"Maybe I am, Mahoney, what's it to you, my friend," Darcy replied cordially. He liked Brian but was not sure he totally trusted the man. In the IRA it was a dangerous game to trust anyone too much. Brian nodded easily and sat beside Darcy with a sigh. He too inspected the yard before proceeding.

"I have had word from outside, from the Commander in Dublin," he began softly. Darcy's heart leapt with the possibility of an end to his incarceration but he only shook his head slowly, wanting to attract no unnecessary attention. Mahoney continued. "The campaign is beginning to draw great concern abroad and they think that with a little more publicity they can get much greater pressure to bear on the government for concessions, possibly even a break through on Irish Rule. The English parliament is in disarray on Ireland and Lloyd George is desperate to stay in power. America is clamoring for Irish independence and a good part of the continent is in agreement."

Darcy nodded again, unimpressed by the news having heard so much of it before. The world was always voicing support for the Irish and the English government was constantly nervous but normally it all translated into greater oppression at home with little promise of any real progress for the country. Darcy had heard promises for years and years before the Easter Uprising and more so ever since but all he had seen on the streets of Dublin were arrests, destruction of Irish owned businesses and the raw savagery of the English occupation. He wondered if it would ever change. Sentiment amongst the Irish people was still uncertain. Darcy thought of people like his brother Frank, landowners, business people, and men with far more to lose than the average Irish peasant. They wanted no bold strokes, no drastic measures to upset the current balance of power which leaned heavily in their own favor. Darcy thought of how much he hated his brother. Frank had the land, he had the family cottage, the barn, the horses and the brood of children and more than anything else Darcy could think of, he had Maureen. The unfairness of it all appalled him. How could the order of birth impact a person's life in such an inequitable way? That was why he had joined the Volunteers in the first place, to fight the English occupation yes, surely for that. But also he had joined to fight the injustice of his own country and his own family. As Darcy seethed with contempt for his brother, the next words that came from the mouth of his friend jarred him back to reality.

"They want us to join the strike, Darcy," Brian whispered conspiratorially. "They want another ten men and we have been chosen. They think adding more will bring the required attention to force some kind of change."

Darcy's mind went blank. He tried to concentrate on Maureen, on Frank, on the prison, on Mahoney but nothing would take hold. He felt the yard spinning faster and faster. His eyes could not focus on Mahoney or the prison walls thirty feet away. Panic welled up inside of him. He could not join the strike! To starve one's self to death was not something he had signed up for. He was willing to do whatever he could for the cause, for the IRA, for Irish independence, but killing himself was not part of the bargain. He just couldn't do that, not to himself and not to Maureen.

"No, Brian," he said desperately, "I can't do that. I won't do that. Please tell them to get someone else. I can not starve myself in this place. I can not do that at all."

Brian Mahoney looked at him sadly for several long, desperate moments. Gently placing his hand across Darcy's arm he spoke softly but with great sincerity. "You have no choice my friend. This is not a request from the Commander. It is an order. You know what happens to the boys that do not obey orders, right? You would certainly be dead tomorrow if that is what you say. At least with the strike you'll have more time and the hope of some reprieve. You have to agree, Darcy, there is no other way."

Darcy knew Mahoney was right. He had seen some of the boys in the yard with knives in their backs or their brains scattered in the hallways of the prison. Sometimes it was the guards to blame but more often than not it was their own kind. He did not want to die that way either. He turned his head to his friend nodding slowly.

"Okay," he said in a tiny voice of utter terror, "okay." As Mahoney walked away Darcy reached slowly for his shoe, removing the letter once again.

Chapter Seven

The Dublin Docks - Late May 1920

The pubs along the waterfront were mean and dangerous places. They were jammed packed with sailors and soldiers and dockworkers, pickpockets, con artists, prostitutes, murderers and thieves. Their appearance mirrored their clientele, rough and shabby taverns offering very little by way of comfort or atmosphere. They were small, crowded rooms with a few chairs and tables, a slab of wood or cement acting as the bar, paint peeling from the walls or unpainted walls splintering from age, dampness and neglect. Pipe and cigarette smoke permeated the tiny taverns, a thick, blue cloud hanging down from the ceiling inches above the heads of the patrons. The smell of smoke mingled with the aroma of stale ale, horse dung dragged in from the street, urine and rotten food. In some places the smell of death overpowered everything else. On this Friday night, crowds of dockworkers were spending their meager earnings having been paid earlier in the day and most of the criminal element was on hand to help relieve the workers of any sterling they did not spend on whiskey or ale. All along the row of pubs across from the docks, people spilled out from the packed rooms into the street, loud screaming, cursing and laughter bringing a hint of celebration to the seedy waterfront.

This kind of neighborhood did not bother Ian MacDermott in the least. He had spent the good part of the last fifteen years in places much like this and it was what he had come to expect from the pathetic Irish people, a nation of drunks and liars and disloyal bastards.

Watching them swill their paychecks, piss in the streets, laugh like hysterical school girls and sing awful ballads about their wretched history reinforced in Ian a great hatred of these people and steeled his determination to put them back under the thumb of the British Empire. It was that purpose which brought him to this dismal place a week after the meeting he'd had with his weakling boss and the absolutely despicable Hamar Greenwood and his Irish lackey, John Harrington. The meeting had annoyed McDermott greatly. He did not understand the equivocation of Macready or the liberal leanings of Greenwood. Neither man seemed to value the superiority of the British way of life over the rest of the world, the advantages of English culture, law and upbringing. MacDermott himself was a Scotsman, his father a soldier from Edinburgh, but his mother was thoroughly English, a lady in every way and a distant relative of the influential Lord Montgomery. Ian understood the British way deep in his bones. His boss however seemed quite ignorant of the superiority of his own race. It was either that or the man had far too much regard for the rights and privileges of lesser beings. He often referred to the savages in Africa as Negroes and called the natives of India by their tribal names. In Wales he had gained a reputation as one to prefer a lengthy negotiation to a quickly administered suppression. Macready had been asking him for a good part of the past week about the training regiment the newly recruited Auxiliaries would receive, anxious to make sure it included rules and regulations on the restraint of force, instructions barring violent reprisals against the general population and training on the general culture of the Irish people so the Auxiliaries might better understand the citizenry. All complete horse shit in the mind of Ian MacDermott. In his experience the only thing people really understood was raw power and the only way to control a disobedient population was to administer that raw power without mercy and with all the force and vigilance possible. He had learned this lesson early in life and he had learned it well.

After his mother's death when he was fourteen, Ian's father's soldierly career took him to various far reaching places and he witnessed first hand the power and force of the English Crown. In Kenya, his father led a group of soldiers working the streets of Nairobi enforcing a curfew the locals did not want to adhere to and he came home with many stories of bloody heads, violent beatings, street justice and the justification of all things necessary to bring about obedience, if not peace. When they moved to India it was much more intense. The Indian people were far less willing to submit to the will of the Empire than were the savages of Africa. Calcutta offered both the mystical call of the East as well as the sophisticated civilization imbued in the elite of English society. The natives of British India lived somewhere between these two worlds, demonstrating an intelligence and cunning which they leveraged to their advantage when intermingling with the ruling British class. Ian's father told him often of the deceitful nature of the Indian people. In the first decade of the twentieth century, the Indians were desperate to throw off the yoke of British oppression and the first stirrings of a violent uprising began showing its ugly head. Assassinations of British officers became commonplace after the partitioning of the Bengal Province and attempts on the lives of the Lieutenant Governor and the Viceroy underscored the deep unrest across the vast and crowded country. Ian recalled his father telling him one evening that it was time to take the gloves off, that these terrorists and assassins would feel the mighty power of the English army as they smashed the insubordination mercilessly, destroying any and all traitors daring to participate in the conspiracy. The occupying forces would rightfully restore the Crown to its God given place as benevolent imperial ruler. And smash the revolution they did. Ian recalled his father's words uttered long ago as they left India on a ship bound for home months after colonial rule had been restored. "Never, ever allow an inferior race or people to treat you or the King you serve with anything less than their complete respect and appreciation for the benefice of our great civilization. A dog learns to heed his master from the fear instilled by the whip. These people are no different Ian and be sure you treat them no differently."

In the years since, McDermott had finished his schooling in London and then joined the Army himself, serving at first in the Far East and then as a Corporal in a combat brigade fighting the Germans in the North of France during the Great War. The fighting was brutal, violent work and death filled the trenches on both sides of the battle. Hordes of men, both English and German, raced to their doom across muddy, bloody fields running headlong into relentless gun fire or into the sharp cold steel of a bayonet or sword. After fourteen months of fighting Ian's luck ran out when a bullet smashed his left knee, shattering the bone and sending him to the rear to convalesce. It was in a small town about fifteen kilometers west of Paris that he first met the man he had come to find on the waterfront in Dublin this night. The man's name was Arthur Butterfield and he too was recovering from an injury suffered in the fighting on the western front. He'd been hit with shrapnel in the right eye, the wound leaving a gaping hole in his face which had scarred over with a thick layer of hideous, purplish oozing skin, a gruesome sight in this giant of a man. Ian learned quickly that Butterfield was not to be trifled with, that he took offense at anyone staring at his disfigurement and that when he took offense he displayed a wrath and rage knowing no boundary. One evening during their convalescence, the two men were sitting together in a café in a quiet French town when a small boy, a street urchin no more than twelve years old, came up to them begging for food. The boy, noticing the gaping hole in the giant's face, started pointing at Butterfield's eye, laughing and making disgusting sounds and distorting his face mocking the big man. Butterfield sprang from his seat so quickly no one had time to intercede. In one speedy snatch of his tremendous hand he snared the boy by the throat and with a brutal twist with his other hand, broke the boys neck as simply as if he were breaking a chicken leg into two pieces. Then he violently tossed the boy back into the street, the child's head smashing into the cobblestone pavement, leaving a sickly trickle of blood coming from his ear. The boy was obviously dead. Butterfield sat back down and casually finished his glass of wine and then he left quickly, stepping on the child's neck as he walked away. There had been discussions of charges against the man but most of the others who had been in the café that night, including Ian, suffered a case of convenient amnesia and weeks later the violent giant returned to the front where he fought another six months until the end of the war.

Ian MacDermott had come to the waterfront on this night to find Arthur Butterfield because he had a job for the man and knew the giant to be perfect for the work at hand. He stepped into the last of the dingy pubs, a place called Con's, weaving through the crowd of drunken

Irishman and ugly whores, finding Butterfield sitting alone at a small table in the rear. MacDermott slid in on the other side and pointed to the big man's glass. He waved over the serving wench ordering a refill. MacDermott rarely drank himself and certainly wouldn't take the chance of drinking in such a shithole like this. Butterfield drained the fresh ale in one long gulp and then yelled to the girl for another.

"Go easy, man," Ian said softly but Butterfield only shrugged. "I am glad you finally arrived from London. I don't want you in any trouble on the first night you're in Dublin. These places don't take kindly to members of the RIC and hate the Auxiliaries even more. They've come to calling our boys Black and Tans. When you see your uniform you'll understand. We've run out of the regular ones and been issuing some khakis and black jackets and berets, should look smashing on you, Butterfield." The big man let out a loud belch and he stared at MacDermott with his good eye. The hole in his face still oozed a yellow, gooey liquid and Ian wondered why in hell the man did not wear a patch to hide such a horrible affliction.

"Your cable promised me a good rank, fair pay and a job worthy of my talents. All I ever been good at is breaking heads and killing. So which of the two are you in need of?" His voice was a deep, raspy sound and his words few and far between. The good eye never left MacDermott's face. Shifting nervously under this Cyclops's stare, Ian nodded in response.

"A little of both, I'd imagine. We are going to make you a Captain in the Auxiliaries and give you command of a regiment of about three hundred men. Your main responsibilities will be to maintain order in your assigned area and to make sure your men do not abandon their duties or in any way subvert the Crown by lending support to the Republican cause. So you need to keep our men in line and they need to keep these people," MacDermott paused, waving his hand towards the rowdy crowd with a look of disgust on his face, "from any more disloyal or violent acts against the Empire." The two men sat in silence momentarily, Butterfield sipping another beer considering his assignment.

"How much autonomy will I be granted," he asked, his one eye settling again on MacDermott's face.

"You will have nearly total control. You will report to me and only to me. If there are any complaints from the citizenry, I will handle them. I will run cover for you with Macready. I really don't want to know how you plan to keep these pathetic bastards in line or how you'll control your own men. I just want to know you are in control and that we have no, uhm, problems, coming from your zone."

"Fair enough," Butterfield said with a nod. "Where am I going?" he asked.

MacDermott leaned in closer lowering his voice. His shifty eyes scanned the pub searching for anyone trying to overhear their conversation. "We are placing you in Kildare County, just a short ride outside of Dublin. Republican activity has been minimal over the past few years, nothing like down in Cork or Kerry. But we have seen the signs of a growing presence in some of the small towns and villages. Just last week one of our battalion stations was over run and set ablaze. I want to stop this insurrection before it becomes a real problem. I want the IRA wiped clean from Kildare County. I want the populace to know you are the law in the county and that they are subservient to you and to the British Crown. Do you understand? Do you have any questions?"

Butterfield sat in gloomy silence for another while. He nodded a few more times and then pointed a long, bent finger towards MacDermott. "I got no questions for you MacDermott, but I do have one word of warning. If anything I do becomes any sort of problem for me than I am going to become a very big problem for you. I expect you have my fucking back in everything that goes on. Don't disappoint me, Ian. If you do you will be very sorry. I hope you understand me." With that said he raised his tremendous bulk from the table and pushed his way out of the pub. MacDermott gave him a few moments lead and then hurried away, glad to be away from both the crowd and the hideous Butterfield.

Chapter Eight

Barreen, County Kildare – Late May 1920

Mickey led his horse from the paddock towards the gate of the small course by the barn. The new day was already warm promising stifling heat later in the afternoon followed by a cooling shower some time in the early evening. The weather pattern had held steady for the past two months and the combination of glorious sunshine with evening rain left the countryside lush with vegetation, the grasses thick and full and every shade of green, thick moss spreading like a shadow across rocks and crags and roads and bridges damp from night rains or the morning dew. Searching for his Da, Mick looked back up towards the cottage, a low, stubby wooden structure capped with a grayish thatched roof from which a chimney poked up like a short ladder leading to the heavens. The yard surrounding the house was abloom with flowers, beautiful red and yellow roses, pink chrysanthemums, and blossoming globeflower bordering the vegetable garden which held the promise of a decent harvest. Behind the house, to the East, the rolling foothills of the Wicklow Mountains appeared in the distance as gentle waves against a brilliant blue sky. To Mick's left, heading to the West towards Blackwood, the plains and lowlands spread out like a lush green carpet, occasionally dissected by stone walls or shaded by small farm fields, all praying as well for a generous yield from the land. Mick took a deep breath inhaling the sweet aroma of the morning. He smelled the wet grass and the scent of hay clinging to his clothes, the pungent fragrance of the powerful stallion walking at his side, the gentle bouquet of the myriad of flowers in bloom floating on the gentle morning breeze coming out of the South. He loved this time of year and he loved this enchanted place where he lived. His earliest memories were of running and rolling with his sister Maureen across the fields and pastures of his home, of racing her through the paddocks and in and out of the big, gray barn, of hearing the whiney of the giant beasts as Da worked them in the yard or on the track. He recalled with special fondness the unique sound of a thoroughbred racing at full speed around the makeshift course, the pounding rhythmic thud of hoof on grass, the noise of the most beautiful animals in the world nearly taking flight. And it was in recalling this incredible and special sensation that he filled with a joyful, nearly unbearable anticipation. He had been working towards this day for the good part of twenty four months and he was nearly bursting with excitement and pride that the day had finally arrived.

He patted Whish't Daddy's massive shoulders as they walked casually towards the small course, his love and pride in this wonderful horse excruciatingly difficult to conceal. He could not believe all they had accomplished together. He marveled at how far they had come, the long days of training, practice, repetition, trial, preparation, success and failure all flipping through his mind like the pages in his school book.

Mick smiled fondly recalling what Da had called his "first day of higher education" and leading the wee, new colt into the pasture for the first time. As a mere weanling only a few months old they began Whishy's formal training. Da explained carefully to Mick that the important thing for a youngster was to get the horse comfortable with being handled and to be taught how to stand still, walk sideways and backwards, to calmly load onto a wagon for transport and to interact reasonably with the other horses, especially when in close proximity. For days on end, Mick would take Whish't Daddy into the paddock and with a short lead looped around his neck he would walk him around and around in the paddock, talking to him softly, teaching the colt the sound of his voice and the meaning of his commands, getting him to stop, turn, reverse field and move in step, neither lagging behind nor surging ahead. Mick quickly developed a deep rapport with the young horse. His intuition regarding the horse's moods and wants and desires came as natural to the boy as understanding his own feelings and emotions. Mick had no experience to compare with this incredible affinity to Whish't Daddy; he assumed it was the same for all horsemen and with all horses. But Da and Maureen and the few other hands occasionally working around the farm marveled at the boy's gift for handling the young colt. His hands moved gracefully and confidently along the horse's neck and shoulders and chest. He could feel the horse growing almost daily. He took extra care in examining the legs and feet, testing the muscles and tendons and ankles and hooves checking for inflammations, swelling, abrasions or excess heat. The horse quickly became accustomed to Mick's gentle touch and he often nestled his nose into the boy's neck as he made his inspection. It took Mickey less than a few days to accomplish the sometimes difficult task of loading and unloading the horse into the trailer Da used to cart the horses to the racecourse or to other farms around the country. Many horses shied from the climb up into the wagon or became nervous by the enclosure covering the vehicle. It often took weeks or even months to get the more rambunctious of the stable to cooperate with this process. Mick had worked his magic with the horse and Whish't Daddy was moving in and out of the wagon as comfortably as he moved from stall to paddock every day.

The boy spent hours with the horse grazing in the pastures, often leading him alongside of Chipper or Bellweather or one of the broodmares from the stable. Whish't Daddy had an easy going confidence with the other horses, spent parts of his afternoons nibbling flies from the backs and shoulders of the bigger stallions and meandering clumsily around the big yard alongside the gentle mares.

When Whish't Daddy became a yearling the training took on a number of different aspects as Da began varying their work outs and changing the routine. Da told Mickey that the horse was likely a year or more away from any sort of racing, teaching his son the importance of ensuring Whish't Daddy's peak physical development over that period of time. They would concentrate on introducing the colt to running and building his endurance, not caring anything about speed at this point in his life. It began with the horse galloping gently across the paddock or in the wide pasture, rider less with Mick urging Whish't Daddy on with gentle pats to his rear or by teasing him with a leafy branch across the nose. First they ran for only a few minutes with the growing horse loping about with long but moderate strides. As the length of these jaunts expanded, the camaraderie between Mick and the horse grew even closer with communication between them nothing more than a click from Mick's mouth or the easy wave of a hand. Da often laughed to himself when he saw the boy and the horse running about in the fields, unsure of who was training who. After every work out, remembering the early training, Mick was sure to check the horse's legs and feet, feeling the cannon bone and the long pastern bone and spending an inordinate amount of time on the horse's hooves. Mick could feel the beast's legs growing stronger, the mass of muscle and bone firmer and bigger with every passing week. Eventually these sessions stretched to thirty or forty minutes every two or three days and in-between he would turn out Whish't Daddy for some easy wandering about with the other horses. Da told him he was doing fine work and that he liked the look of Whish't Daddy in not only his build and his gait but also in the puckish and exuberant attitude the horse demonstrated during his work outs. These compliments filled Mick with pride making him keener to learn more and to teach his horse more. He spent every hour possible down by the stables either listening and working with his father or training the horse that had become the most important aspect of his young life.

As Whish't Daddy approached his second birthday Da introduced a variety of gear or "tack" into their daily routine, prepping the horse for the day in the not too distant future when he would take on a rider and begin the hard and fast lessons of a racehorse. Mick quickly learned the differences in various types of bridles and bits and how to locate the bits in such a way to ensure the horse was comfortable and controllable and when necessary, how to force his head up or down which he would need to do on the course. He learned the benefits of various bridles and reins and side reins and how to set bits and rings and yokes to encourage or discourage varying behaviors the horse would require. It was a big day when Mick first placed a saddle on Whish't Daddy's back and it took him a number of efforts before he could properly place it correctly as the horse grew skittish from the heavy weight. They had started with blankets of differing thicknesses but the saddle was clearly more than the horse cared to bear. But Mick was determined to saddle his charge and despite the aches and pains in his arms and back he persevered, pleading softly with Whishy to take the saddle and allow Mick to secure the leather girth beneath his big belly. After the first few days, Whish't Daddy graciously accepted the saddle and went about galloping with his usual exuberance and for the next days and weeks the horse galloped about with the saddle in place, quickly becoming accustomed to the weight and feel of it. Once acclimated to the saddle, it soon came time to place a mount on the horse and Da had warned the boy that this could get a bit tricky. Mick pleaded with his father to let him be the first one to mount Whish't Daddy but Frank was reluctant to let the young boy attempt such a dangerous task.

"You've had almost no experience in the saddle Mick and certainly none riding a monster like this. We'll have Rory Killhane break him first and then you can spend some time riding him over the next few months. I don't want you to get hurt, son. A fall from a horse this big is no bargain." The boy muttered several ill founded arguments on his own behalf but Da would not be swayed. Although disappointed, Mick did understand his father's position. Whish't Daddy had grown to over fifteen hands and was as broad across the chest as Mick could stretch one arm. When he felt the horse's shoulders and back and hindquarters they were as solid as the stone walls that dissected much of the Irish countryside. He imagined falling from the big beast and having Whish't Daddy land on top of him and he grudgingly went along with his father's plan. It was early on a May morning when he saddled up the beautiful thoroughbred and led him from the barn out to the yard where his Da and Killhane awaited. Rory was from Wicklow, a lad of twenty six years with some modest success in the saddle. He was of typical size for a jockey, slightly over five feet tall and barely six stone soaking wet. He had seen plenty of Whish't Daddy over the past two years as he worked alongside Frank Walsh with a number of the other mounts. But still his eyes seemed to widen at the sight of the massive beast saddled and needing to be broken. He'd been around horses long enough to know this could be a tricky and dangerous process. He tightened the helmet on his head and took in a number of deep breaths. He trusted his boss in all things related to horses and racing and he looked sheepishly towards Frank but the man only nodded, encouraging him to mount. As the sun continued its climb into a powder blue Irish sky, Rory made his first attempt to mount Whish't Daddy. Placing one foot firmly in the stirrup, the horse began snorting and rocking about. Frank held him firmly by the bridle and the colt seemed to resent this restriction but he steadied and Killhane boosted himself onto the colt and for a moment all was right in the world. Whish't Daddy held steady, almost frozen in place. Slowly Frank let go of the bridle and the colt turned his head ever so slightly, acknowledging his new found independence. And then with a great neighing roar he lifted himself onto his rear legs and reached up towards the heavens with his front hoofs, all but standing straight up, kicking furiously at the sky. Killhane went flying out of the saddle, landing a good number of yards behind the horse and taking the direct impact of the fall on his little rear end. Whish't Daddy bolted around the yard prancing and preening, looking quite pleased by his small victory. It took Frank and Mickey fifteen minutes to settle the horse again and this time Killhane approached his mount with something akin more to fear than slight trepidation. And rightly so as Whish't Daddy barely let the young man place his foot in the stirrup before he bucked and reared and sent the young rider scurrying away. The young man tried time and again to mount the spirited animal and after hours of no success it seemed to Mick that Whishy had taken this now as some kind of contest he was determined to win. Da went into the barn returning with a few more long reins which he slipped over the horse's head and a small chain attached to a thick spike intended to anchor the horse, preventing him from bolting and giving the rider time to get comfortable in the saddle. He secured the chain around the horse's left foot and buried the spike into the ground, banging it down hard with a steel shovel.

"Go on, try him again," he said to Killhane. The young man looked terrified, as if he'd rather swim the Irish Sea then try to mount this feisty stallion one more time. He shook his head slowly but went ahead. Stepping quickly into the stirrup he pulled himself on to the saddle in one rapid motion. Whish't Daddy held steady for a few moments and then he began to paw at the ground with his right front foot. The neighing began slowly but built like the sound of a locomotive coming around the track. Suddenly he reared up again, his powerful leg pulling the spike from the ground with unexpected ease, the rider again being deposited on his back and the horse racing away in victory, coming to rest on the other side of the yard. Frank looked at him with amazement and then checked on Killhane to make sure he was okay.

"I ain't trying him again, Mr. Walsh," the jockey said with obvious terror. "That horse is a mean son of a bitch, if you don't mind my language, Sir. I ain't going to try and mount him ever again." Walsh was helping the young man to his feet when he heard the horse whinnying in a much different tone. Looking across the yard, he saw Mick holding the horse easily by the bridle and stoking his face gently, almost like a lover's caress. The boy looked over to his Da and waved.

"Can I try," he asked enthusiastically. And before Frank could answer, before he could tell the boy, no, it was far too dangerous, Mickey slipped easily into the stirrup and plopped himself comfortably up into the big saddle. Leaning over he whispered into Whish't Daddy's ear, rubbing him gently along his long, dark mane. Slowly the horse began at first to walk, and then a gentle trot and then with a little encouragement from his rider the young colt began to gallop easily, prancing about the yard in long, loping strides, Mick holding tightly to the reins but looking as relaxed as he would if sitting by the fire reading a good book. He gave out a loud hoot and then deftly bought the horse back to a steady pace, walking him over to where his father and the astonished Killhane looked on in disbelief.

"I was going to tell you it was too dangerous, son, but I guess you proved me wrong," Frank said with a wide smile.

Mick bent down and whispered to his horse again. Then he looked up at his Da returning the smile. "Whishy is my friend Da. He's no danger to me. We are a team, me and him, and we will always be one." He jumped from the horse and led him away to the barn where he groomed him for a long while, all the time talking to his friend of championships to be won.

For the next eight weeks Mick and Whish't Daddy enjoyed a schedule including trail riding in and around Barreen, starting with only short trots no more than a half a mile, getting the horse used to climbing and turning and feeling the effects of wind and rain and animals racing about in the forest. Sometimes they rode alone and sometime Da or Rory or Brian Grant would ride along on Bellweather or Chipper or one of the mares, getting Whish't Daddy familiar with the feeling of another horse moving along close by. They took to the trails every third or fourth day and in between Mick would turn out his charge after checking him thoroughly for any signs of stress on his body, especially his legs and feet but despite the rocky terrain and the often wet and slippery trails, the horse held up extremely well and both Da and Mick grew more and more excited by his rapidly growing potential. They added swimming to the big horse's regiment and every few days Mick waded Whish't Daddy across the wide stream to the West of the cottage or took him down to the small lake Da had named Lough Walsh allowing the horse to splash and swim around for nearly an hour. Mick taught the horse how to jump and within weeks Whish't Daddy could effortlessly clear large rocky outcrops, big fallen trees and deep country streams ten feet wide. It took little time to bring the horse to a full gallop over a course of two miles and after maintaining this distance and occasionally a bit more for the good part of two months, Da pronounced Whish't Daddy ready for the next and final phase of his training, running for speed.

"Tomorrow we'll start testing him some, Mick, we won't try to flush him, not for another month or so, but I think he is developing way ahead of schedule so I think it's time to see what he's got. What do you think, son?"

If Frank Walsh could not tell by the smile on his son's face than he would have had to be blind as a bat. He knew the boy had been waiting for this for over two years and he knew the horse was ready as well. Maybe not to race just yet, they'd think about running him at the end of the season or maybe hold off until the next spring but either way Whish't Daddy was ready. All you had to do was look him in the eye.

The make shift course took up much of the grassy pasture behind the barn leading out to the rolling fields of Kildare. Over the years it had been improved from a rock strewn and craggy path to a smooth, wide grassy track a little more than a half mile in distance. Mick recalled the many summer mornings he would spend with Maureen picking rocks and weeds and sticks from the course or watching his Da or one of the other men cut it down low with the tractor or rake it smooth making sure to level out any holes or burrows that could prove dangerous to the horses. The course could easily fit five or six horses across but it was seldom that more than two or three would run at the same time. Da never used the track for racing in fear of attracting too much unwanted attention, and used it solely for training, knowing it would provide a good advantage to the horses in his stable. Mick moved down along the smooth track and approached the "starting gate" Da had made to teach the horses how to start the way they would at a real race course. Mick had worked with Whish't Daddy bringing him in and out of the gate many times, sometimes with Bellweather or Chipper alongside, again wanting the young horse to grow comfortable with the surroundings he would find in a real race. He was about to put his horse in the gate when he heard Da coming from the barn, chatting with Brian Grant. At first Mick thought they'd been working with Bellweather and his final preparations for the Irish Derby the following week. But suddenly he realized why Brian was walking with his father. With a sickening thud of disappointment he noticed Grant was ready to ride, dressed in his riding boots and gloves, goggles sitting on top of his head and a crop dangling from his wrist. The look of displeasure must have been clear on Mick's face as his father approached, holding up one hand, palm forward and shaking his head slowly.

"No, Mick," he said softly placing his hand on the boy's shoulder. "Not this time. When we start looking for speed we need a sure and experienced hand. Its dangerous work and I know you and this horse are of one mind but I just can't allow you to try this until you learn a lot more about working in the chains. Brian here knows what needs to be done; he'll be real good with Whish't Daddy. I want you watching and learning. Some day your time will come but we are a long way from that day." He patted Mick on the back and then ran his hands along the horse's withers. "He sure is a beauty, son. You got a damn fine horse here, you've done well." With conflicting feelings of pride and disappointment, Mick passed the reins to the jockey and stepped aside. He watched Grant back the horse away from the gate as he prepared to mount. Part of Mick was hoping for a repeat of when Rory Kilhane tried to break Whishy but somehow he knew that would not happen. And he was very curious to see how they would go about moving the horse from the full gallops he had been taking with the thoroughbred to the kind of speed required of a racer. Da took the large saddle off Whish't Daddy's back that Mick had put on the horse only a short while ago. He slipped on a much smaller and lighter saddle. He secured it firmly and then moved out of the way and nodded to the other man. Grant pulled himself up easily onto the big thoroughbred and steadied his mount as the horse nervously skittered about. When he was settled, the jockey calmly walked him into the gate and waited inside as Frank moved to pull the lever to open it. Whish't Daddy pranced through the opening quickly and horse and rider began an easy trot down the track. It seemed to Mick that Brian Grant was taking it slowly, gaining a feel for the big horse's tendencies and desires. Da had often told the boy that every horse was slightly different in how they wanted to run. Some were sprinters wanting to go flat out as soon as they were given the bit, others tended to run smoothly for a while and give bursts of speed varying in intensity as the race progressed. Still others saved most their energy for going full out in the stretch run to the finish. Grant was only twenty years old but he'd been riding for over four years and Da thought the boy had a good way with most horses although Mick remembered his comment about Brian being a little distracted of late. But he appeared comfortable on Whish't Daddy and as Mick and Da watched they could see Grant tighten the reins pulling the bit tighter in the horse's mouth, leaning a little more over the front of the saddle starting to rise up and down, sometimes nearly standing in the saddle. He looked to be talking into the big horse's ear and Mick momentarily felt envious as he watched Whishy begin to move from a trot to a gallop and from a gallop to a sprint. Mick watched the jockey's every move, noticing his hands were crossed over the horse's neck and each hand held both the rains and good handfuls of Whish't Daddy's thick, dark mane. He watched the rhythm and balance with which the rider rocked up and down, his short stirrups allowing him to stand and lean far over the horse's neck. He noticed he rarely used the whip at all, only gently tapping Whishy on the rear from time to time. The horse looked very comfortable as he came around the last turn heading towards Mick and his father. Whish't Daddy's chest was moving up and down slightly, almost in rhythm with his rider and his nose flared in and out, his breathing steady and strong and without difficulty. His long legs stretched generously before him, propelling horse and rider across great swaths of the course, sending chunks of grass flying behind him, the sound of his hooves pounding on the ground, his ears cocked slightly back but not with alarm, muscles moving gracefully back and forth. As he passed by completing the first lap, Mick could almost swear the horse was grinning. Grant took him quickly around for a second pass and as they reached Mick and Da a second time he slowed the horse back to a gallop, finishing up with a final easy trot around. Bringing Whish't Daddy back without any sign of strain, his breathing back to normal and a playful look in his eye told Mick his horse liked the speed and would love to do it again. Grant slipped easily from the saddle and Mick quickly took the reins. He ran his hands along Whishy's face kissing him gently and congratulating him on his first real run.

"That is quite a horse you have their Mick," Grant said, removing his gloves and goggles. Looking towards Frank he nodded. "I think he gave us a wee taste of what he can do. It felt like he had so much more in the tank, both in terms of speed and endurance. I'm not even sure he felt me up top. And I didn't have to ask him for much, he just seemed to know what he was supposed to do." Da nodded with a smile. Returning his gaze to the boy, Grant continued. "You're training yourself a champion, there Mick. Whatever you been doing, I say keep it up. That beast was born to run."

Mick was beaming with pride as he led the horse back towards the barn. He was thinking about what Grant had said about training a champion when he heard a loud commotion coming from up by the cottage. Turning to look he was surprised to see a group of men in uniforms all riding down the hill heading toward Da and Brian Grant. The uniforms were all a mix of black and tan. Mick had heard stories about men dressed like this. They were part of the RIC or the Auxiliaries. A sense of dread filled him. He hurried Whish't Daddy into the barn, tying him up in the last stall in the back. He hurried back to the yard feeling scared to death.

Chapter Nine

Barreen, County Kildare – Late May 1920

Frank Walsh stepped out across the track to meet the men in uniforms. He froze momentarily at the sight of the huge man in the front of the column. He had seen the man in town the previous day and having him here now, on his own property, filled Frank with dread. Sitting high on his large horse made Butterfield look gargantuan. He walked his mount up close by Walsh, sneering down at him from above. The leaky, putrid hole where an eye should have been still managed to bore into Frank and the queasy feeling in his stomach churned, growing worse. On his massive head the man wore a black beret and it tilted over his forehead covering his face in shadow. It seemed only the missing eye lived in that darkness. His head moved from side to side, taking in the cottage, the gardens, the barns, the paddocks, and the green fields rolling away into the distance.

"Who owns this place?" he asked with disdain.

"The cottage is mine. My name is Frank Walsh. What business brings you here?" Frank was trembling inside but determined not to let the man intimidate him.

"Damn fine piece of land to be owned by a shanty peasant," Butterfield replied and as he did so he spit a big gob of green gook towards Frank's feet. Walsh did not flinch but could feel his heart pounding in his chest. "And a barn with horses, too?" he sneered.

"The barn and horses are owned by Athy House. I'm their head trainer," Frank added hoping to fog the issue of ownership from this nasty giant.

"Very nice," the soldier commented sarcastically. Then his one eyed glare rotated slowly settling finally on Brian Grant. He stared long and hard at the diminutive jockey. Frank could see Grant growing more and more uncomfortable as the moments passed. He dropped his eyes letting his chin fall and stared long and hard at his riding boots. "We been looking for someone in these parts rumored to be part of the insurrection against the crown. One of the "Volunteers" as your people so affectionately refer to them." Again the words were laced with bitter sarcasm. "I am told he is a very little man, one of about your size, jockey." Brian Grant shuffled his feet but did not raise his head. Butterfield reached out with one of his massive boots and kicked the young man viciously in the shoulder. Grant fell hard to the ground and looked up in terror. "What's your name, boy?" the giant asked.

The jockey hesitated, looking towards Frank Walsh for either help or advice. With none forthcoming he answered softly. "Grant, my name is Brian Grant."

"And tell me Brian Grant, would you be one of the rebellious bastards who set fire to the post office in Kildare town Tuesday night of last week?" Butterfield moved his horse closer to the jockey who lay sprawled on the course. The young man tried wiggling away to a safer distance but Butterfield continued maneuvering the horse close upon him. Fear lined the jockey's face, his eyes bulging from their sockets, his lips frozen in terror, unable to speak. "Well, answer me damn it," the giant roared. He looked ready to stampede the horse over Brian Grant's trembling body. Grant remained frozen either unsure or unable to speak. Just as Butterfield readied to raise the horse over him Frank Walsh interceded.

"Brian was with me last Tuesday all day and all night. We were out in Galway looking over some stock. He helps me evaluate the yearlings. He was nowhere near Kildare."

Butterfield turned the horse slowly, moving towards Walsh. He looked down at him long and hard but said nothing. Then he noticed Mick standing back by the barn door. His head moved ominously in that direction. "Maybe this lad is the one we're looking for," he said to Frank with a nasty grin. Frank moved slightly towards his son, positioning himself between Butterfield's horse and the boy. He looked up at the RIC Captain trying to hide the terror building in his heart.

"That's my son Michael. He's just a child. He was with me as well last week out in Galway," he lied. Frank hoped the tremble in his voice did not betray him and as best he could he held the hard look of the gruesome Captain glaring down from above. After what seemed an eternity, Butterfield finally backed off the horse, turning back towards his men. With a bit of jostling around, the seven other riders fell into a rough formation behind their leader. He turned back towards Frank Walsh who was helping Grant up from the ground.

"If I find out you're lying about the jockey being in Galway it will be your head, Walsh. Have no doubt of that, peasant. And Grant, just know we will be watching you. Your little rebellion will be short lived in these parts. Kildare County is my own now, let that be known." He stared at both men for a long minute and then turned the horse beginning the slow trek back up the hill. About half way up the small hill, the door to the cottage opened and Frank's daughter Maureen walked into the yard, curious of the commotion down below. She wore a pretty yellow dress and her auburn hair shined brightly in the afternoon sun. Butterfield stopped his horse. Moving his head in her direction he stayed focused on the young woman for a very long time. Then he turned and looked back down the hill towards Frank Walsh once again.

"Hey Walsh," he yelled, his gravel filled voice booming a vile warning. "I will certainly be back and when I come you can introduce me to this fine young lass." And then he started laughing a loud, hideous, horrible laugh that trailed behind him as he and his men road away into the noon time sun.

That evening Frank sat by the fire smoking his pipe and Fiona sat with her knitting, one eye on the needle work and one on the pensive look of her husband's face. Frank was not an exceptionally handsome man, his eyes bunched a little too closely together and his ears stuck from his head like two potatoes, a little misshapen and very fat. But his eyes were a vivid blue and held a fiery intensity which burned even brighter in times of difficulty or strife. The set of his strong jaw as he drew on the smoky pipe confirmed to Fiona that he had much on his mind.

"A penny for your thoughts, my good man?" she asked in her soft, soothing tone. Frank looked at his beautiful wife and smiled. She indeed was a beauty he thought looking upon her lovely countenance. A rare beauty, radiant in every way, physically, emotionally, spiritually, beautiful on both the inside and the outside, he would tell anyone that would listen. And she knew him very well, and looked after him carefully. He followed his smile with a shrug but she insisted. "Come now; tell me what it is that's on your mind, love. That man frightened you today. Is that it?" she asked.

Frank shifted in his seat drawing again on his pipe. He nodded his head slowly.

"Yes, yes he did," Frank admitted to his wife. "He is a very terrible man and the stories of the terror he is raising across the county are many. I did not believe them myself, well not until I had a first hand view of what the man is capable of, and then I started to believe."

"What do you mean?" Fiona asked with great concern.

Frank hesitated again but then plunged ahead, glad to get the thing off his chest.

"He's the new Captain from the Constabulary barracks down in Kildangan, no more than a half hour ride from our front door. He is a very bad man, Fiona, a very bad man." He drew on the pipe again exhaling a great plume of smoke into the small cloud gathering in the thatch above. "I was walking down the street in town heading from the feed store to the market. A little ways past the market a young boy was walking a small dog and the dog was yipping and barking up a storm. A small band or RIC Auxiliary troops stood in the middle of the street, maybe seven or eight of them. They were checking identifications of any young lads and giving them a rough time. This Captain, his name is Butterfield, a hideous looking giant of a man, stepped away from his men and crossed the street to where the boy was walking with the dog. He yelled something to the boy but I could not hear what he said and then suddenly he pulled his gun from his belt and fired three shots into the dog killing him on the spot. The lad started to scream in protest and Butterfield smashed his face in with one mighty blow, sending him sprawling into the street, blood gushing from his nose and mouth, several teeth lost in the road. A few people standing in the vicinity moved to help the youngster, I started towards him myself, but that bastard Captain pointed his gun towards anyone coming close and told us all to back away. After a few minutes the boy managed to get to his feet and he picked up the dead dog and hurried away, his tears mingling with the blood and puss coming from his face. I was horrified, my dear. I had never seen such a callous, brutal and cowardly act and this is the man charged with maintaining the law in our area. I am appalled by the man and his actions and frightened by what it could mean in the weeks and months ahead." Fiona took Frank's trembling hand in her own, holding it close to her stomach, offering reassurance in her gentle touch.

"And there is disturbing news from Mountjoy as well," Frank added slowly refilling his pipe. His eyes met Fiona's briefly and she could see the fear they held. "I spoke with O'Connor in the feed market and he told me word from Dublin is not good. He said more and more of the boys are joining the hunger strike and more than a few are close to death already. He did not know who might be the ones in the worst shape but it could be any of them, I'd guess." Turning his gaze back to the fire, he stared into the flames for a few minutes, his mind churning at all the possibilities, Darcy foremost in his thoughts. "O'Connor said there are rumors of a concession by the Castle and that the boys may all be freed. But that might just be conjecture; no one really knows what is happening. We've heard it all before."

"But you don't even know if Darcy is among the ones starving themselves," Fiona added hopefully. Frank shrugged again.

"Not something I'd think Darcy would sign up for but he may not have had a choice. These Republicans are becoming more and more aggressive. They know they have the ear of the world and that the Crown is under great pressure to improve the situation. There are more and more incidents both in the city and across the country. O'Connor wouldn't say anything directly but he hinted more and more Volunteers are being recruited right here in our own town. I have a strong feeling he is right about that. Brian Grant has been greatly distracted of late. He's missed work several days in the past few months and when he is here he seems preoccupied and jumpy. He did fine with Whish't Daddy today but nearly fell off of Bellweather during a training run last week. Told me he hasn't been sleeping well of late and when I asked him why he just shrugged and walked away. And a couple of the lads working in the stables at the Curragh have been overheard discussing raids on the barracks up in Maynooth. They don't know what they're getting themselves into these young fools. As the IRA builds its forces, the Royal Irish Constabulary is bringing in thousands of veteran soldiers to augment their own strength. And from what I saw yesterday, these are very dangerous men. Having that horrible man show up at our doorstep today scares the devil out of me."

Fiona squeezed his hand tightly and kissed him on the cheek. "We will find a way to deal with this monster, just as we have figured a way to deal with all the other challenges the good Lord has sent our way over the years. We have a two year old child and I am hoping and praying she grows up in a better world than the one we have been living in for most of our time together." Fiona hesitated a moment, unsure of how much she wanted to share with her husband regarding their daughter. "Perhaps a year in London with my sister might be best after all for Maureen," she said added softly.

Frank nodded but said nothing more. Fiona knew that meant he would think about it. He stood and turned feeling the heat of the fire on his back. He kissed his wife on the head, hiding the tears gathering in the corners of his eyes. He feared all their children would soon be living in a world of violence and terror and that the wonderful life they had worked so hard to provide might be rapidly slipping away. He could feel the violence building in the counties and towns around Kildare and he could smell the hatred gathering in the homes, streets, and people of the villages across the beautiful and terrible land of Ireland. Ireland, his home, his beloved home.

He shuffled into the dark church late Saturday evening and kneeled for a few minutes on the hard wooden kneelers at the back of the small, silent church. An elderly woman working her beads and mouthing a Hail Mary occupied a pew in the front by the statue of the Sacred Heart. Otherwise he was alone. He made his way into the narrow closet confessional pulling the heavy drape behind him, dropping himself into near total darkness, much like a coffin, he thought. The small window grate slid open and the figure of a man's head could be seen vaguely behind the thick gray screen.

"Go ahead," said a familiar voice. Father Dunn's gruff, curt tone pronounced the mass every morning and twice on Sunday, his reading of scriptures monotone and unenthusiastic, his sermons laced with fear and foreboding, the promise of the hell fires of eternity a most common theme. Frank had not been to confession for nearly a year but he knew the routine.

"Bless me father, I have sinned. It has been ten months since me last confession," he began, knowingly shaving a few months off the interval. Still he heard the priest grunt his disapproval. He confessed a small laundry list of offenses from missing mass twice and using foul language far too often, to a feeling of hatred for the forces of oppression and a disgust in his own lack of charitable activity on behalf of the community. He paused for a few moments, wrestling with the words to express the real reason he had come seeking the forgiveness of God Almighty, even if it had to be through His intolerable and dislikeable advocate.

"Anything else," the priest demanded.

"Yes, Father, there is one other thing," Frank replied, still struggling to find the right words. "I lied to my wife, Father," he said but then quickly corrected himself. "Well it wasn't exactly a lie; it was more in what I did not say to her then in what was said."

Father Dunn waited a few moments and then asked in an exasperated tone, "So what did you not tell the woman? Come on, out with it, my supper is waiting."

"Father, I told her I am worried about our country and I told her some of the why but I didn't tell her everything for fear of upsetting the poor woman. And she has enough on her mind caring for all the young ones. She is a strong woman, so strong, but still I could not bring myself to tell her what I had seen."

"Go on, what was it," the voice said impatiently from the other side of the screen.

Frank took a deep breath and then spilled it all at once. "Father there is a new Captain for the RIC, a man named Butterfield. He is a vicious and mean man. I saw him shoot a dog dead in the street and smash a young boy across the face."

"That's it? That's what you've seen that you did not tell your wife?" he asked in disbelief.

"No Father, that's only part of it and that part I did tell my wife. But I could not tell her about the young girl. She was a pretty thing, no more than fifteen or sixteen years old, maybe a few years younger than my own Maureen. She was walking down the street in Kildare town and it appeared she was doing a little shopping, maybe for her Mom. She had a bag of groceries and a small parcel of wool. It may have been one of John Murphy's lasses, I really can't be certain. But this Captain, he's the size of a door frame and with the missing eye, he came upon this young girl and stood in front of her on the street and would not let her pass. She excused herself a number of times and tried slipping around him but the giant just laughed and stayed in her way. He began pawing at her, first knocking the parcels from her hands and then fumbling with her clothing. She began to cry and tried pulling away and that's when he grabbed her. He took her by a huge handful of her strawberry blond hair and began dragging her down the street. A number of us began to protest and move towards him but he drew his firearm and fired at our feet sending us all scattering about. He kept dragging the poor girl back towards the buildings in the rear of the town, out by some of the old stables. He harnessed his weapon and grasped tightly to her hair with one hand and tore at her clothing with the other, sending her garments scattering in the road as he went. You could hear the poor child screaming and crying as they disappeared behind the stable walls. A few of his men formed a line blocking anyone from approaching. After a while her screaming stopped and then she sobbed no more and the Captain reappeared fixing his own clothing and he started shooting again, in the air this time telling his men to disband the small crowd that had gathered. He threatened us all, roaring in a voice of anger and hatred I hope to never hear again. But I fear I will Father, I fear I will. And I could not tell my dear wife that story for she will fear him terribly as well." Frank fell silent, a slight relief to have the story told, but shame still clutching at his heart at his inability to find the courage to try and save that poor, young girl.

"Is that it then," the priest asked. "You lacked the nerve to tell you wife that you lacked the courage to help this young girl." His voice was full of accusation and contempt.

"Yes, that's it Father, that is it exactly," he said in a whisper of defeat.

"Four Hail Mary's and Four Our Father's," the priest responded. "Now quickly, say your Act of Contrition." Frank recited the words without feeling, the darkness of the church closing in around him.

Chapter Ten

Dublin Castle – Early Summer 1920

The Castle nearly quaked with tension. The hunger strike was now in its fifth month with more and more prisoners joining the protest every day. Two had died and it was rumored that several others hovered near death's door. Dispatches from London came in daily almost always reversing the instructions provided a day earlier. The outcry from around the world was united in its support for the Irish people and in its abhorrence of the cruelty of the British military and police. American Senators and politicians arrived on ships daily, pleading the case of the Republican hunger strikers and lobbying for Irish independence at once. Across Ireland IRA activity rose to new heights. British military barracks and RIC garrisons were attacked with impudence. Soldiers and the Constabulary were shot and killed, maimed and kidnapped from Mayo to Wexford and from Donegal to Cork. Post Offices, banks, tax offices and government buildings were burned and looted in broad daylight with armed Volunteers growing bolder with each passing week. Reprisals were brutal and swift. Homes of those thought to be involved were destroyed, the families left homeless in the streets with little more than the rags on their backs. Young men found guilty of nothing more than looking suspicious soon found themselves swinging from the end of a rope, their lives cut short by the violence of the times. Entire towns and villages were burned to the ground, businesses ruined, homes wiped out, hundreds and thousands of people displaced and the mood of the country edging towards the breaking point.

"You wanted to see me?" MacDermott said as he entered Nevil Macready's smoke filled office. Hamar Greenwood sat opposite the military Commander and in his hand he held an official dispatch. He looked both nervous and slightly relieved.

Macready pointed to another chair and the Scotsman took a seat. "Let him read it," he said to Greenwood in a voice of resignation. The Chief Secretary handed the papers to MacDermott and the little man read them carefully, his squinty eyes only inches away from each page. When he was done he tossed the dispatch across the desk, slamming his hand down hard in protest.

"No," he exclaimed angrily. "No, damn it." His face turned bright red with anger, his small eyes bulging from his head in disbelief. "Release the prisoners? Are they daft? We can not possibly do that. It will be an embarrassing sign of weakness. It's tantamount to surrender, Nevil. Don't you see that? Please, you can not allow this to happen."

Macready shook his head slowly fighting desperately to find the right words. "I don't know, Ian. London is adamant. Perhaps it is for the best. Maybe it will calm things down a little. Maybe the people will take it as a sign of compassion. Many of those men are close to death. After what happened when the first two died, we do not need any more martyrs. That I know for sure." He looked up at MacDermott but could not hold the man's horrified stare.

"Yes, I quite agree," interjected Hamar Greenwood in his arrogant, self serving tone. "The people have had quite enough of this strike. It provides them something to hold against the Crown. By letting the men go we take away their cause. We silence them in a way we never could while their boys are in our prison." He looked at MacDermott briefly but quickly looked away from the fiery glare of the Scotsman. Slowly Ian rose from the chair and began pacing across the room. Both Macready and Greenwood followed him from the corner of their eyes, uncertain of what he might do next but certain it would be full of rage and fury.

He surprised them by starting quite calmly. "We take away their cause?" he questioned softly, letting his angry eyes rest upon Greenwood's diverted face. "Men who have willingly and knowingly committed crimes against their King, men who have destroyed property of the British Empire, men who have murdered and assassinated the King's forces in cold blood, men who have been captured and imprisoned, men who are now close to death, now we free them to return to the loving arms of their families and the warm embrace of their grateful citizenry? This is how we take away their cause?" He let the quiet words float across the room and the desk and towards his boss and his civilian counterpart. And when the silence in the room was total and it filled the room with discomfort and anxiety, he returned once again slamming his bunched fist with all his might onto the desktop, making a loud bang shaking the room to its core. "No," he screamed in protest. "We take away NOTHING!!!" His small head strained noticeably with the effort of his expression. "We give them victory, damn it, Greenwood. How the hell do you not see that, man? We give them exactly what they have wanted and hoped for. We give these guilty bastards a pass and we let them go and we encourage every young boy who sees these men return as heroes the idea that what they are doing is a good and noble thing and that they too can take up arms against their King and get away with it and return to their home and hearth as heroes as well. We take away nothing Greenwood," he hissed. "We give them victory and I for one will not be a party to that." He sat down again crossing his arms and staring at Macready expecting some kind of explanation. After an interminable wait, the military Commander offered little more than what he'd been told from his bosses in England.

"The pressure on Lloyd George is unbearable. And it is not just what they are hearing from America and other places overseas. The Labor party is promising a general strike across the United Kingdom if something isn't done to stem the tide of death from Mountjoy. The Prime Minister is convinced that a strike of this magnitude will put a strangle hold on the already fragile economy. Things have pretty much degraded since the end of the war and a strike will only make it worse. The trains and ports will shut down, ships will not unload, mining will come to a halt, and goods will not be made or shipped or sold. The economy will dry up completely and all hell will break lose across the United Kingdom. There is a crazy man named Hitler taking advantage of a like situation in Germany and Lloyd George is desperate to avoid a similar fate back home. They have thought this one through a number of times and their decision is final, Ian. As much as you and I wish it could be done another way, they want the prisoners in Mountjoy set free and we have little choice but to do exactly as they have suggested." He shrugged his shoulders and lit another cigarette, awaiting a reaction from his assistant.

"Okay," Ian replied making an obvious effort to keep himself calm. "Who am I to argue with the Prime Minister?" he said with a disingenuous smile. "We will let these killers and murderers and kidnappers and insurrectionists go. We will clear the halls of Mountjoy of every last one of them. We will send them all home." MacDermott stopped momentarily and then pointed to Greenwood with his pudgy little finger. "But I won't send them home alone, that I will not do. Each and every one of those prisoners will return home with a pair of eyes glued to their back. One of my boys will follow every one of them. Oh, at a discreet distance to be certain, but follow they will. And they'll watch their every move and listen to their every conversation and know their every friend or brother or fellow Volunteer. And should any of them, any of these disloyal bastards step even the slightest bit out of line, I will tell my boys to shoot to kill and to not give a second thought. And you've met a few of my boys and you know they will not hesitate a moment." He stood and walked across the room. When he got to the door he turned, offering the other two men the most evil of smiles. "Perhaps the Prime Minister is right this time. Those men should be released from prison. We have a much better chance of eliminating the whole lot of them once their back at home. Once they think they're safe and sound." He quietly closed the door behind him leaving the other two men in gloomy silence.

Chapter Eleven

Mountjoy Prison – Early Summer 1920

Darcy Walsh knew this was the day he would die. He was no longer in pain. The terrible and vicious sensation of his stomach liner being torn out a strip at a time had given way weeks earlier to numbness, a cold and empty feeling in his gut, a feeling that matched his melancholy seeming appropriate for his last day in this hellish world. He could not remember exactly how much time had passed since he'd last eaten but he knew it was more than six weeks. He knew that because he'd been counting the days in his cell and marking the weeks as they went by on the wall with a simple scratch from a small stone he'd found in the yard. He recalled scratching a sixth small line but shortly after that they'd taken him from his cell and placed him in the infirmary. He could not remember if that had been a day before or a month before. All sense of time lapsed and his existence dwindled to a blur of terrified sleep punctuated by haunting dreams and fitful and frightening awakenings in a room full of other men suffering the same appalling reality. The men were allowed to drink a little water every day and the doctors tried to encourage them to take some juice or a piece of fruit but the Republican leadership had forbidden any life sustaining substance other than water. In his dreams the water rushed along in cold, rock strewn streams, hurrying on with a gurgling sound, cascading over and around boulders and crags and lapping up against silt lined shores. From time to time Maureen appeared running alongside the stream, her long blond hair bouncing across her slim shoulders, her smile enchanting in the sunlight, her tiny wave beckoning him closer, calling him to the shore. But as Darcy climbed the boulders and rocks, clambering to get across the river he would invariably slip and fall in the rushing rapids, unable to reach his beautiful girl. Then she would be gone but he would hear her voice calling from a distance, pleading loudly, calling for his help in a frightening tone, begging him to come and save her. He would awake suddenly in a fit of panic only to find the squalid room full of other men like himself, all wasting away before his tired eyes. The flesh on their faces had been reduced to the thinnest layer of skin pulled tightly across their skulls, eye sockets sunken deeply below foreheads bereft of hair, cheekbones swollen; lips stretched tightly hiding mouths that had barely any teeth left in their blackish gums. Their arms and legs pointed awkwardly from their emaciated torsos, brittle sticks lacking any semblance of muscle or excess flesh. The few that still bothered to open their eyes radiated only resignation and a desperate hope for the end. Three men had already died. Two from the initial group of hunger strikers, one more lad that had began at the same time as Darcy. As he absentmindedly let his eyes scan pointlessly across the filthy room he wondered how many more of them would die and how many more would die this day.

He knew he would. And he didn't care. His life had been short, difficult and thoroughly disappointing. He could think of no single accomplishment to be proud of so perhaps dying in the hope of gaining a true and lasting independence for his country would count for something, if in fact his death would count for anything at all. He had his doubts. He owned nothing. He had no skills beyond the ability to pull potatoes from the ground or milk a willing teat. His mother and father were dead many years, his brothers and sisters all gone away with the only exception being a brother he hated nearly as much as he hated the British soldiers and their lackeys spread across the countryside. He had little use for a God that left an entire nation in such desperate condition that the only ones who prospered were the ones that left Ireland or joined the forces of oppression. The priests were likely to pronounce a great reward awaiting them all in heaven for their suffering but Darcy had heard enough over the years of things getting better and they never did. And they never would, not here or in the hereafter, wherever the hell that might be. He was beginning to welcome the thought of death. It could only be a relief from the misery of his current circumstances and from the dismal life he'd lived for twenty-two years. Again he started drifting into a fitful sleep.

This time the water did not rush along the stream as much as it howled furiously along in huge, deep and dangerous currents, wave after wave of angry violent surges smashing against the rocks and crashing loudly along the river's shore. Try as he might, Darcy could not maintain his footing in the wild stream, slipping over and over below the speeding surface of the water, swallowing great mouthfuls of the brackish river, fighting desperately for breath, anxious to gain a foothold to rise again above the surface. Managing to secure his footing against a slick and slimy boulder he hoisted himself high enough to see the shoreline and there she was, his beloved Maureen, only this time she was not alone. Her father was beside her, the two of them running full out, Maureen in the lead and Frank frantically chasing behind her, hand outstretched but unable to reach his daughter. The frantic runners took turns taking frightened looks over their shoulders in fear of whatever or whoever chased them from behind. Darcy lost his footing and fell again below the surface of the raging waters and struggled mightily to stand, his lungs filling with water, knowing death was only moments away, wanting but another glance of his beautiful Maureen before he left this painful world. A powerful rapid raised him from the water's depths and he gasped as he saw a huge man in a black beret riding a big horse bearing down upon his brother and his love. It was hard to see the monstrous man's face but from the coursing river Darcy thought it somehow ugly and deformed. The man was reaching down with a tremendous hand trying to grab either Frank or Maureen. As his hand grew closer to the girl, Darcy slipped again below the surface and thought for sure he would never rise again, swallowed up for all eternity by the rushing waters of the stream. But again he found a foothold and raised his head from the river but this time it was not a monstrous man riding the horse and reaching for his beloved. Now it was his nephew, Frank's boy Mick, dressed in the crimson and gold of Athy House, riding a huge and beautiful chestnut thoroughbred, reaching down, gently sweeping Maureen off her feet, settling her carefully on the saddle in front, brother and sister riding off safely into the distance. Frank clapped from behind, glad to have his children safely away from harm. Then he turned to the water beckoning Darcy with the wave of his hand, calling him to shore, pleading with him to come to safety. Darcy wanted to wave back but for some reason he could not. He could not let the resentment slip away. Instead he took his foot from its safe perch, allowing himself to be swept away by the speeding water, slipping quickly below its surface, opening his mouth purposely now, swallowing huge mouthfuls of the cold, dirty water, drinking it in greedily, wanting the stream to fill his lungs one final time, wanting the water to take his breath away, wanting the last of his miserable life to be washed away in the cold, dark waters, welcoming the blackness quickly closing in around him, knowing death had finally come and anxious to feel its final cold embrace.

A voice spoke very loudly. He thought the words must be coming from an angel or a saint. Could it be Saint Peter? Or more likely, the words were from Satan, welcoming Darcy to the hell he so well deserved. Either way, the words were faint, distant, difficult to hear, at first a whisper but then a growing sound and soon nearly a shout and a shout of many men.

"Pardoned!" he heard one faintly exclaim. "We're free," another said with as much voice as he could muster. "It's over, the strike is over," a third whispered hoarsely. Then a loud and more definitive voice of command sounded through the room. With disbelieving eyes he saw the Captain of the Mountjoy Prison Guards unfurl an official piece of paper and after first clearing his throat, the man spoke in a deep, sonorous tone, taking his time to pronounce each and every word precisely.

"By the order of the Prime Minister, Lloyd George, and the concurrence of the British Parliament, all current prisoners of Mountjoy Prison arrested on charges of political insurrection, treason, disloyalty or sedition are hereby granted amnesty and released by the British government and are free to return to their homes and families. It is strongly suggested you refrain from contact with any know revolutionaries or enemies of the state or you will again be subject to incarceration, trial and punishment including death by hanging. You are free to go." With that he turned and left the room, leaving behind a group of thirty or more men all near death, all with barely a bit of energy left to properly celebrate their unexpected new lease on life.

Darcy closed his eyes and this time the only thing he saw was Maureen's lovely face. She was smiling and he could not wait to touch her.

Chapter Twelve

Connemara – Summer 1920

Lord Montgomery left the small group of men standing by the stables and walked back towards the castle. It was a very warm and sultry morning, humidity was high but the ocean breezes brought some measure of relief from the heat which had settled on the island over the past two months. He much preferred London, although the weather there could be even more dismal than in Ireland, but for the racing season he would put up with Ireland's lack of culture, the absence of theatre and opera and the near impossibility of finding a suitable glass of wine. During the summer months he excused all of the island's many failings, accepting them as the price to be paid for the unmatched quality of the horses raised in this beautiful and pathetic part of the world. He took no credit for selecting this obscure and sparsely inhabited section of the country, knowing full well that the decision leading to the placement of Montgomery Castle a short distance outside of the tiny fishing village of Cleegan on the Atlantic Coast had happened many generations earlier and made by someone far wiser than he. It was an odd place to build a castle although Ireland was littered with castles of every shape and size in many unusual places. And as with most castles, a small village had grown up in and around the sturdy walls that encompassed the numerous stone structures that formed Montgomery Castle. Along with these buildings there were accompanying stables, a large racecourse and a vast plethora of champion horses the various Lord's Montgomery had produced over the past hundreds of years.

Most of Connemara, ancestrally known as the Clan of Cormack by the Sea, was a collection of mountain ranges, connected lakes and their corresponding sandy beaches. The original Lord Montgomery had an eye on the lucrative fishing trade which was a huge part of the area's economy and when awarded this province by the British Crown it included the fishing rights to Lough Corrib and the Atlantic Coast from Kilkeiran Bay to Killary Harbor. From the late sixteenth century to the present day, Castle Montgomery had been the focal point of the region, providing a marketplace for the fishermen to sell their catch, for goods to be bought and sold by cobblers, farmers, linen traders, tool smiths, and herders. Innkeepers kept travelers housed and fed inside the castle walls and taverns filled their appetite for drink while the castle guards ensured their safety and in some cases, their incarceration. A wonderful if unlikely byproduct of the region was the fine horses for which its reputation had grown steadily over the past centuries. Legend had it that the first of these great speedy beasts had sprang forth fully formed from the crashing waves of the mighty Atlantic Ocean and was the first sire of the long list of champion racers to follow. In the narrow strip of land between the Maamturk Mountains and the sea, the Maam Valley offered enough flat, grassy earth to place the horses, build vast stables and barns, place a race course and hold a number of seasonal races. A job in the stables with the Lord's horses was much preferred to work in the fields or on the fishing vessels which often failed to return from the sea. And much like in the other areas of Ireland where horse racing approached religious status, the position of trainer in Lord Montgomery's Castle was a highly sort after one and one that bought with it considerable prestige and income. Over the centuries the craft was passed down generation to generation and currently the Master Trainer for the Castle was one Michael Cleary, a tall waif of a man with a crooked grin and a generous laugh, a man well schooled in his trade and dependable as nightfall. Cleary oversaw six assistant trainers, four veterinarians, sixteen stable hands and if you asked him he would say he also held sway over the six jockeys that rode for Castle Montgomery, although they would be loathe to agree with him on that point.

Lord Montgomery glanced back at the group of men he had been talking with and could see Cleary pointing out chores and hear him shouting orders to the staff. The hustle and bustle around the stables quickened as the hands fetched clean straw, water and blankets and carried them in and out of the stalls while the trainers took turns marching horses back and forth from the barn to the course, stopping to have them groomed or checked over by one of the vets. Montgomery watched with satisfaction, pleased by the diligence, efficiency and effort of the team. The stable boasted twenty-two racers in all, every one of them capable of winning any race in which he chose to enter them. Cleary was doing a damn fine job and it was showing in the results.

1919 had been an outstanding year for the Castle and its stable. The Blue and Red Montgomery colors had been raised as champion in twenty-one different races including the King's Plate in Galway held at nearby Ballinrobe, the Cork Royal Jump, and in the prestigious Irish St. Ledger held in the fall at the Curragh. An additional thirty entries from the stable had placed second or third throughout the season in various races, contributing handsomely to the Lord's coffers. And it appeared to Lord Montgomery that 1920 would prove even more successful than the year before. The stable's best horse, War Lord, had won a hard fought victory at the Irish Derby only a few weeks earlier and his prize filly, Atlantic Wind, had taken the Irish 1000 Guinea's inaugural run. It brought the Lord considerable joy to win any race at the Curragh, wanting to show the Kildare racing aristocracy and the equestrian community in that region that his stable in the West could best any colt or filly they placed in the gates. To win two of the premier events held at the bastion of Irish racing gave him great pride and much satisfaction. Many other championships and seconds and thirds had been won around the country throughout the season but Montgomery's energy now clearly focused on the final premier event to be held at the Curragh, hoping to take a third championship in the running of the St. Ledger in September. He strolled through the streets inside the castle nodding now and then to one of the shopkeepers and smiling at the ladies busy buying cloth and linen. His mind wandered back to the Derby in June and the fine performance of the majestic War Lord. The monstrous stallion had burst from the gates with his usual enthusiasm. Moran, the jockey, had him in full stride by the first turn and the horse maintained his speed throughout the first three legs of the race and it appeared he would run away from the field as he had in many of his previous races. But coming down the stretch the big thoroughbred from Kildare, a mighty colt with massive shoulders by the name of Bellweather, closed ferociously, the two horses running neck and neck as they came to the wire and only Moran's experience and poise enabled War Lord to thrust out his big head and take the championship by a nose. It had been an outstanding race with an incredible finish and Lord Montgomery's joy in victory, although great, had been slightly diminished by the nerve wracking last few strides, the two horses pounding the turn in stride, almost mirror images of each other, both wanting the wire first, War Lord fortunate to best his rival by the smallest of margins. And it was not so much the splendid competition that concerned Montgomery. Often his horses were sorely tested down the stretch and often they were beaten, it was part of the racing game. No stable won every race and rare was the horse that went unbeaten. War Lord currently held that notoriety and the Lord hoped he could close out his three year old season with such distinction. But Bellweather worried him. He was not concerned that the horse could upset him in the St. Ledger although it was possible. What worried him greatly was not the horse itself but rather its ownership, the stable from which he hailed. Lord Montgomery grew up in the Irish racing game with friends and contacts across all of the United Kingdom. He was extremely familiar with the more well know stables situated in Kildare. Lord Langley flew the green and white colors of Castledermot and had managed a few champions from his moderate stable. Newbridge housed the more powerful Farrington Stable and they were always in contention, especially in the jumps. Stables in Naas and Maynooth owned by British families that had not seen Ireland in more than a century still trotted out solid competitors and had their share of victories. But Bellweather was owned by none of these. Over the past three or four years the name Athy House and its crimson and gold colors played a more and more prominent role in Irish racing. He knew the head trainer, a very capable man named Frank Walsh who he had once tried to hire, and he knew that more and more the small stable was producing horses with great potential. They had claimed a number of titles in smaller races around the country and the showing in the Irish Derby warned of a talented new competitor which Montgomery Castle would need to consider. What the Lord knew nothing about was the stable's ownership. Quiet inquiries in both Kildare and Athy had found out nothing more than the trainer's name and that the stable was small and of limited means. Montgomery had accessed some land titles and horse registrations but all the paperwork led to was a confusing circle of corporate ownership rumored to be based from either Scotland or America. No one in London seemed to know anything more about Athy House then he did and the few contacts he had in America provided no information at all. It was a mystery Montgomery wanted solved and he was a man accustomed to getting what he wanted. He made it a point in all of his business dealings and especially in horse racing circles to know his competitors and adversaries as well as he knew his own business. It was critical to understand the alliances, networks and capital at the disposal of any stable in the Kingdom. He demanded knowledge on any and all resources, financial, technical, or otherwise, insisting he understand when a great deal of funds could purchase a superb sire or lure away a top notch jockey. He knew next to nothing about the ascending Athy House. They were a riddle in many ways and his next appointment might prove useful in getting him closer to solving that riddle.

He entered his quarters, handing his gloves, hat and cane to the servant at the door.

"Mr. MacDermott is waiting in the parlor," announced the elderly butler as he handed the Lord his smoking jacket and slippers. "I will bring tea and scones as soon as you have been situated." The man slipped off quietly towards the kitchen.

Lord Montgomery hesitated before heading into the parlor. This MacDermott fellow he found very disquieting. He was a distant relative on his wife's side, a nephew or second or third cousin, something of the sort. He'd met the man once before when he was at a dinner party in Dublin earlier in the year. The host, Lord Gallagher, had strong ties to the Foreign Minister in London and when he came to visit with Greenwood, the Irish Secretary, a party was thrown in his honor and most of the provisional government responsible for ruling Ireland had been invited to the affair. It had been a boring evening with few of Montgomery's friends in attendance and most of the conversation centered on the ineffective nature of Home Rule, the rising peril of the Republicans, and the devastating effect of labor strikes across all of the UK. Much to the Lord's disdain, not one word was spoken about horses. The roast had been cooked far too long and the wine a mediocre Burgundy from one of the lesser houses in that region. Montgomery was anxious to leave when he was approached in the foyer by a small man with a limp, squinty eyes and the scent of fury cloying to him like bad perfume. MacDermott introduced himself with a handshake trying far too hard to impress and quickly explained the distant relation, spending too much time and energy trying to get Montgomery to acknowledge a form of kinship. He then went on to describe the critical nature of the job he held, claiming responsibility for all police officers, constabulary and auxiliaries in the country. He alluded to some control over the British soldiers in Ireland as well but left Montgomery only confused and disinterested with his exact role. The Lord was trying to make his excuses and get away from this tiresome fellow when the man landed on a small bit of news to pique his interest.

"They may cancel the remainder of the racing season, Lord Montgomery. Is that your understanding as well?" MacDermott had asked, squinting his eyes more tightly.

Montgomery held the man's stare momentarily, thinking the little Scot was searching more for a reaction than confirmation. Montgomery had heard the banter back and forth between the fools in Dublin Castle and the bigger fools back in London but his own sources assured him the season would continue without interruption. He'd fought bitterly against shutting down the races during the Great War and he would do everything in his power to make sure the stupidity taking place across Ireland by a handful of misfits and criminals would do nothing to affect his livelihood or the great sport on which it depended. "They can try all they want, MacDermott. It will never happen."

The little man shrugged looking slightly uncomfortable discussing such an important issue with a member of the House of Lords. But still he pushed ahead. "It might. We tried both a curfew and restriction on the sale of alcohol but the enemy continues to grow its forces and insight disloyalty and insurrection. We can handle the every day events;

the normal activity both in the cities and the countries, but it's the crowds and large gatherings that have proven difficult to control. The Volunteers move freely about in these huge groups, trading weapons and information, making plans and recruiting more lads to join the uprising. The thinking is if we can eliminate the big crowds than we can eliminate a great deal of their activity. I'm sure you'd support such an approach?" he asked the question with a small, sly grin, bating Montgomery.

The Lord eyed him momentarily, slipping on his hat and gloves. "I will support no such thing and don't you dare presume to put words in my mouth," he said sternly. "Horse racing is as much a part of this country as green fields, potatoes and rolling pastures. It's a fair amount of our economy and one of the few things in this wretched land that provides a reason for celebration. Over my dead body will anyone cancel the remainder of the season," he said. Then hesitating, he pointed a finger in MacDermott's face and continued in a voice laced with fury. "Do your damn job policeman, and let me do mine. Do you understand me?" He waited a good, long moment before the little Scotsman nodded his head and stood aside, allowing the Lord to pass.

Now the little policeman was waiting in the parlor and Montgomery needed his help. He did not think their previous flare up would give MacDermott cause to object to his request. Montgomery had spent enough time in the House of Lords to know that difficult and angry conversations one day could easily give way to pleasantries and accommodation on another. He actually was quite efficient at manipulating his colleagues in Parliament and he had a certain reputation as one who could find common ground with his most ardent adversary. Besides, MacDermott reminded him of every military man he had ever met – anxious to please their superiors, especially those that could help a career and desperate for acceptance by the ruling class. The Lord looked at the upcoming discussion as an opportunity to hone his skills at gaining agreement and to demonstrate the art of flattery. He stopped momentarily at the door and then entered the parlor with a flourish.

"My dear Ian," he said jovially, extending his hand quickly, "I hope I have not kept you waiting very long. A problem down at the stables requiring my attention, still no excuse for one to be tardy, my apologies." They shook hands quickly, MacDermott's grip not quite as aggressive as in their initial meeting. "My man is bringing tea and scones shortly; can I interest you in anything stronger, possibly a sherry or a dram of whiskey?" He could see the man was both surprised and pleased by his warm greeting. No doubt he had been bracing for another difficult encounter.

"Oh, uhm, no, tea will be just fine Lord Montgomery, fine indeed." MacDermott shifted awkwardly in the sitting chair, his small feet barely making it to the floor.

"I am so glad you could come out to Connemara, Ian, I trust you had a good journey?"

"Yes, very pleasant, Sir. It is a lovely part of this country although I must admit I'd be very happy to catch the next boat across the Irish Sea."

"Well I certainly understand that young man but I must say, we need good men like you here in Ireland now. I have done some asking around about you and your name is held in very high regard at many levels of our government. We can't have you running back to London, not when you are needed so desperately right here." MacDermott was nearly beaming with pride as Montgomery lavished him with praise. He was quietly wondering just who in what part of the government had paid him any sort of compliment.

"Your Aunt Ethel sends her regards. She was quite thrilled to know I would be meeting with you and wished she was here to spend time with her favorite nephew. Unfortunately she does not take very well to this climate and much prefers the finer things London has to offer. I may never get her back to Connemara!" he said with a laugh. MacDermott eagerly joined in the laughter and then the servant came in and placed the tea and scones on the table, pouring a cup for each man and putting plate, saucer and spoon in front of each. He bowed expertly and quietly left the room. The two men munched a moment on the scones, sipping their tea in silence.

"I do feel the need to apologize for my abrupt behavior in Dublin, Ian," Lord Montgomery said, hoping the sincerity in his voice was far more than he felt in his heart. "It was a particularly dreadful day for me, including the necessity to put down one of my favorite fillies, broken cannon bone, terrible really, quite terrible." He hesitated momentarily, allowing the sadness of the situation the moment it deserved.

"I am so sorry to hear that Lord Montgomery. I did not know," the Scotsman offered.

"No, no one would have known, Ian and please do call me Andrew, we can do away with all the formality, what, being family and all." He watched as MacDermott nearly burst with unrestrained pride. He nodded his desire to operate on first name basis and Montgomery continued. "The remainder of the day was a tragic blur. When I arrived at Lord Gallagher's party I felt depressed and anxious to be alone. When you told me of the plans to suspend the remainder of the racing season, it just bought back the sight of that poor horse lying broken in the yard. It does not excuse my rude behavior but I did want to apologize and let you know it will not happen again."

MacDermott stood from his seat and came around the table to the Lord's side. He placed one of his tiny hands on the back of Montgomery's neck and patted him gently on the arm with his other hand. "Andrew, you do not have to apologize to me for anything. I should be the one apologizing for my callous disregard. I should have seen the disquiet in your face and allowed you to leave without interruption. For that, I am sorry."

Lord Montgomery gently removed the man's hands and nodded his acceptance. If he only knew how the Lord loathed his touch things might have gone far differently. "So we can put the entire incident behind us and move forward as friends, yes?" Again he held out his hand and MacDermott grasped it like a life raft in a storm. After a moment acknowledging their new found friendship, Montgomery proceeded on the path he had intended to pursue all along. "So now, is it all resolved? I heard from Hamar Greenwood that a decision was made to suspend the boxing and circus events but that the horse racing and football would continue. We only have a few months left in the season. It makes sense to complete the year."

MacDermott braced at the mention of the idiot Greenwood's name. The arguments in the Castle had been frequent and very ugly and in the end they agreed to split the list of suspensions with racing and football surviving, much to Ian's disdain. He knew the decision was all but irreversible, still he saw an opportunity to take some advantage of the situation. "Well, it looks very much like that is the case as long as I concur. My superior, General Macready, leaves those decisions to me. And although I am inclined to deny the racing for the next few months, I could be persuaded if I can find another way to thwart the growing army of Volunteers hell bent on destroying the British Government in Ireland."

Lord Montgomery nodded, giving himself a moment to think. MacDermott was most likely lying through his teeth about the horse racing. Macready would never delegate a decision so monumental to an assistant, not at this time with all the turmoil in the country. Still, he knew the Scotsman wanted something and he would use that something to get what he needed in return. Give and take was a game he played very well. "What did you have in mind?" he asked.

MacDermott rubbed his chin for a moment and then dove right in. "We know the racing business is heavily infiltrated by the enemy. We have arrested many stable hands, trainers, jockeys and bookies with ties to the Republican cause. Some we get useful information from about raids, other members, shipments of weapons, that sort of thing. But nearly all of our contacts in the racing business are down in Kerry and Cork with a growing presence in Kildare County. We have no one out here in the West. What I could use your help with, My Lord, I mean Andrew, is recruiting a man or two that could give us a view into the Republican activities out here in Clare and Galway. That would be of great assistance." MacDermott watched now, hoping he had not overstepped his position, imposing on a Member of Parliament for assistance in clandestine work.

Montgomery thought for several moments and could find no negative to agreeing to the request. He generally disliked the Republicans and would be more than happy to assist in their demise - as long as it did not interfere with his enterprise or his horses.

"I think I could help you with that Ian. I have a few ideas on how we might find the right man. Let me give it more thought and talk to a few of the boys and I will let you know. Anything I can do to help rid this scourge is nothing less than my duty." He left it at that and after an uncomfortable minute of silence MacDermott rose to leave. He shook Montgomery's hand and as he got to the door the Lord stopped him.

"Wait, Ian. There is one other small thing that perhaps you can help me with." MacDermott could not nod his head enough times to underscore his desire to help.

"It must be kept absolutely quiet. Any inquiries must be made with the utmost of discretion." MacDermott kept nodding and Montgomery continued. "There is a stable of horses down in Kildare; I think its right outside a town named Barreen. The name of the stable is Athy House. They have been a growing presence in the racing game but I have not been able to find out much about them. I was hoping maybe you could help me with that." He waited on MacDermott's reply, knowing it was a simple enough request.

"What type of information do you need, Andrew?" he asked, pleased again to use the Lord's given name.

"Anything you can find out at all. How many horses they have, what kinds of horses, how big is their operation, who are the important trainers, that kind of thing. But I am also very interested in understanding who owns Athy House. Try as I may that still remains a mystery. And it would be information for which I would be very grateful to obtain." He let that hang in the air, watching pound notes forming in MacDermott's mind.

"Let me look into it, Sir," he answered quickly. "I think I should be able to find out everything you need to know." He put his hat on his head and shook hands with Lord Montgomery once more. As he left the room, his new found friend closed the door softly, a smile of satisfaction playing slowly across his lips.

Chapter Thirteen

Barreen, Kildare County – Mid-Summer 1920

Mick was down by the barn when he saw the men coming up the road. A rickety wagon was being pulled by an old draft horse with one driver. On each side a man rode beside the wagon and Mick thought he recognized the younger of the two, a lad a few years ahead of him in school. The back of the wagon was flat with low sides with a tarp covering it completely. He saw his father come out of the cottage and head down the hill to greet the men.

"Good afternoon," he said taking a good look at both the men and the wagon. He was relieved to see they were not with the Black and Tan but still his instinct for danger remained on high alert.

"Mr. Frank Walsh?" the older one enquired. He was a man in his forties, a hard looking man, a man who knew violence and violent ways.

Walsh nodded. "I'm Walsh, how can I help you?" He was eyeing the youngster on the other horse, fairly certain he was one of the lads from a nearby farm.

"We have something for you. I think you have been waiting for this for a few years now." With that he dismounted from the horse and moved towards the wagon. He slowly removed the tarp covering the vehicle and it took Frank a moment to figure out just exactly what this thing was that he was to receive. In the back of the wagon a makeshift bed had been laid of burlap tarps and old rags. A distinctive and unpleasant odor came wafting from the bed. Lying in the middle of the tarps, with only a head and one thin, bony arm showing was the most emaciated and horrible sight Frank had ever seen. The head was little more than a skull with the thinnest covering of skin pulled over the face and nearly hairless head. The ears looked turned in and grossly disfigured. The arm sticking out from the bedding looked the size of the wee babe lying up in the cottage, in fact it looked thinner. At first glance, Da thought he was looking at a corpse.

Mick had managed to make his way up from the barn and moved close enough to look into the wagon. He almost choked from the stench and nearly vomited at the sight of the man in the coffin like structure but he refused to allow himself such a childish luxury. Looking more intently at the emasculated face, he saw something in the eyes that was not only familiar but very near and dear to his heart. He reached down to touch the man and the famished limb moved only a fraction, a bony finger touching Mick's elbow ever so lightly. Mick smiled at him and he thought he saw the skull try returning the smile.

"Da, it's Darcy," he said looking up at his father in amazement, and then louder, "its Darcy Da, he's finally come back to us. He's finally come home." With that he gave a loud whoop of immense joy they could have heard in Dublin and raced off towards the cottage.

Da watched him go and wished the boy had stayed right where he was. He moved closer to the wagon himself and looked down at his youngest brother. The mix of emotions running through his mind covered a spread wider than all of Ireland. Yes, he was relieved to see Darcy out of harm's way and glad the boy had not perished in the goal. He was saddened horribly by his condition and alarmed he would not live to see the next morning. But more than anything else he was greatly frightened by what Darcy's arrival portended for his family, his lands and his business. He'd known for a few years before his brother's incarceration that trouble followed Darcy Walsh around as surely as night follows day. And why had the boy been put away in Mountjoy in the first place? Because he'd gotten himself tied up with the Republicans and their great, stupid struggle which was destined to end for Darcy nowhere but at the end of a rope. He could see in Darcy's eyes that his brother was reading his every thought. He looked away, turning towards the older of the two escorts. "I assume you are some kind of Republican official? Is that why you are here? What is your name?"

The man nodded holding Frank's stare. He did not blink. "My name is Riordan but you're better off forgetting you ever heard that." His tone was matter-of-fact and his face showed no emotion.

Frank grunted upon hearing it. "And what the hell am I supposed to do with him now? Can you tell me that? You bring him to my door, nearly dead, most likely wanted and with more trouble trailing in his wake than I have ever known. What in the name of God do you propose we do with him now?"

"He's not wanted. He was just released from Mountjoy and pardoned for his so called crime. I would think as his older brother you'd want to take him in and nurse him back to health. That is what any decent man would do."

Frank held his temper in check but it was not an easy thing to do. "Don't you dare preach to me about decency and obligation! Your kind knows nothing of either. If I am to take this pathetic soul into my house," he turned quickly glancing at Darcy, "I put my entire family in danger. Why the Constabulary has been here on a few occasions already and the last thing I want to do is give them another reason to return. Those Black and Tans are savages, man, don't you understand? All I need is to give them cause to enter my home and the carnage they will cause has no end. I think you are going to have to take him somewhere else." Frank was surprised to feel a hot tear sliding down his cheek as he said these words. He was truly a man conflicted but his first responsibility was to Fiona and the children, not to his long lost and troubled brother. He looked again at Darcy and to his surprise he saw the young man nodding slightly, apparently agreeing with Frank that the situation was too dangerous. He limply waved his fleshless bone in the air, indicating they should move on. A dead silence followed for a long minute as Riordan considered his options. He was about to mount up and take Darcy somewhere else when a loud group burst out of the cottage and came running down the hill, most yelling and laughing, all shouting the name Darcy over and over. Frank turned and grimaced, knowing full well that this would change things none for the better.

Maureen was in the lead, her golden locks bouncing behind her with Deidre racing stride for stride with Mickey. Walking slowly behind them was Fiona carrying the wee little one. Maureen arrived quickly, looking directly into the wagon. Darcy's ghastly appearance brought her up short and her hand flew to her mouth, a desperate, broken sound escaping into the afternoon breeze. Tears formed quickly racing down her cheeks but she stiffened straight away, reaching into the wagon letting her hands cup his face gently, her fingers caressing the deep hollows of his cheeks.

"Oh Darcy, you poor man, you poor, poor man! What have they done to you? Oh my sweet Lord, what have they done?" The bony hand moved again from under the covers, touching the slender hands holding his face with the lightest, gentlest gesture imaginable. And now the bony face did smile. It was a sad, disfigured and desperate smile but still the joy on his face was apparent. The other children arrived and after a moment of adjustment they all took turns touching the broken body in the wagon and covering him in words of welcome and encouragement. A moment later Fiona arrived and looking at her young brother-in-law, she managed to hide the horror in her heart and smiled, welcoming him home, thanking God for his return.

Da cleared his voice and spoke softly but all had turned to him to listen. "I think it's best if they take Darcy elsewhere," he said desperately, making sure his eyes avoided both his oldest daughter and his wife. "It's far too dangerous to have him here. I'll help these men find a more suitable place."

"No!" Maureen cried in dismay. "You can't do that Da. You must not send him away. He needs us, he needs his family. Can't you see that? He's a broken man. He'll certainly die if you send him away. Please, Da, please, you have to let him stay." Maureen had pulled herself up on the side of the wagon and had one arm wrapped around Darcy's head in a loving embrace. Tears were running down her face, falling into the wagon making a wet circle on the burlap around his head.

"Maureen, I can't," Da replied in agony. "I can't put you and your sisters and your Ma in any more danger. You saw those damn Black and Tans, they'll be here in no time if they know a Republican is in our house. They may have pardoned Darcy but they'll never forgive him nor will they ever forget him. They'll destroy this place. You know it. You know I'm right," Da insisted.

"So is that what you've become, Da," she asked, sniffling back her tears and holding her head up high, accusation filling her eyes. "A coward, is that what you are? A man that would send his own flesh and blood away to protect his precious land and his damn horses? Is that my father?" Da looked at her as if he had been slapped across the face.

"Don't speak that way to your father, Maureen." Fiona's voice cut through the building tension. She looked from one to the other, her eyes filled with love and pity for both as she weighed the awful options in her mind. She looked back at Frank, seeing in his eyes a silent plea of desperation. Fiona raised her hand gently, holding Patricia tightly with her other arm. "Frank, we can not send him away in his condition. If we did and he failed his death would be on your hands and you would never forgive yourself as long as you live. I have known you all my life and it would eat away at your soul." Maureen half smiled in sad triumph hugging Darcy carefully, afraid of breaking his brittle body in half. "However," Ma continued, "as soon as he is strong enough Darcy has to leave. Your father is right; his presence in our home is a danger to us all. He has chosen his path and it is one of great peril. But it is his choice. With God's grace we will heal him quickly and then only the good Lord can watch over him moving forward." She turned to Deidre. "We will put him in your room. Patricia will move in with Maureen and you can sleep in the loft with Mickey. Now go quickly and ready the bed and heat a pot of water. We'll clean him up and feed him some broth and then he will need to rest." With that she turned abruptly, walking back towards the cottage.

Frank took a deep breath, resigning himself to the plan, knowing full well his wife was right. He hated Darcy for bringing this trouble to his home but he loved him as a brother and he could not willingly send him to his death. He looked at the wagon driver and pointed down the road. "Take it up a little further and it will curve around to the front of the cottage. It will be easier to carry him in from there." Maureen slipped off the wagon and the others backed away as the reins snapped and the draft horse plodded along. The girls headed back up the hill to mind their chores, Maureen anxious to help carry Darcy inside. Da and Mick stayed below with the Republican officer and his young associate.

"I will put some of my men on watch around your place, Walsh. We'll protect you from those Black and Tan bastards. We always protect our own," he said with some pride.

Frank Walsh watched the wagon disappear around the corner and looked up the hill as his girls disappeared into the cottage. He looked at Mick and then down towards the barn and the horses grazing in the paddock. He shook his head and sighed. Then he turned towards Riordan, pointing a finger right at his chin. "You get the hell off my property and don't come back. We're not your own kind. Me and my boy will protect our own land. When Darcy is better he'll come find you, I am sure he knows where to look. Take your men and your guns and leave us alone. I wish to hell I never heard anything of your kind." With that he nodded towards Mick. "Come on son, we got work to do." They headed down towards the barns where Frank always found solace and a place to think. The Republicans moved up towards the house and a little while later Mickey heard them galloping away.

Chapter Fourteen

Dublin – Late July 1920

The two men sat on opposite ends of the park bench watching the children kicking a ball in the field across the walking path. It was late on a warm, sultry July afternoon and both men had removed their jackets. One was dressed as any Dublin business man would be attired, with coarse black woolen slacks, a white shirt yellowing from time, a thin black tie and shoes that were very old and tattered in places. The other man drew quite a contrast. His slacks were of off-white linen and his shirt lightweight cotton with thin blue stripes. He wore no tie but on his head he sported a straw hat with a blue band to match his shirt and his shoes were white, gleaming in the sunlight. He had a big, round, red face and he was smiling broadly in the Irish sunshine.

"I wasn't expecting sunshine on this trip, my friend," he offered casually. "Every time I've been here before you folks have worn the gray out of gray. And I usually go back with a suitcase full of soaking wet clothes. To whom do I have to thank for the beautiful weather, John?" he asked. He took the hat off his head and raised his face into the glorious sunshine.

The other man hardly moved. He grunted in response acknowledging what had been said. He shifted uncomfortably on the bench. "Harry, you have the envelope, I trust?" He let his eyes roam both ways along the path before letting them settle on the man sitting beside him.

"Oh yes, my friend, no worries on that account. American green backs, and a fair stack of them to be sure. You tell Michael Collins we do not renege on a commitment and his American friends are a hundred percent in support of the fight. The release of the hunger strikers only strengthened our resolve. You have public opinion swinging firmly behind Irish independence not only in the States but all around the world. How do you see things from your unique perspective, John? Do you think the people support the struggle? In the end, it is the Irish people that need to embrace the Republican cause. Without them, all the greenbacks in the world will do you little good." He let the sunshine bathe his pale face in a warm embrace while keeping one eye on the other man.

"Yes," the Dubliner replied, "I sense a greater resolve from the common man. I feel our time is at hand. Even though the hunger-strikers have been pardoned and some of the rules have been loosened, it seems the citizens grow wearier of the English occupation every day. The lads are signing up with the Volunteers in record numbers and the British are bringing in more and more of the Black and Tans to take the fight to them. Home Rule is on again off again thing and we'll never get agreement from the North so either we settle for partition or all hell breaks loose. You can see the factions taking their separate positions and one of my greatest fears is a civil war here in the South which will inflict as much damage as the damn British."

"Well," said Harry, "you can fight only one war at a time and right now that means fighting the British and getting them out of Ireland. Back in America we don't have a great understanding of the inner political workings of the Irish people. We just want you to have your own country and to be free like we are. That's where the money comes from, its people who remember the heel of the British in their back or the emptiness in their stomachs. Its people who wish they never had to leave Ireland but are damn glad they will never have to come back." He popped the hat back on his round head and stood up glancing both ways as he did so. He pointed with his chin at a newspaper he had left of the bench. "There is a second envelope in there as well. It's a letter for my friend. I can count on you to get it to him, I trust?"

The Dubliner nodded, scooping the paper and its contents into his hand. He folded it in half and placed it in a worn, leather satchel. "How are you holding up, John," the man with the straw hat asked. The other man shrugged.

"The danger is greater for the lads in the field. They are the ones doing the difficult work," John said with a sigh. "I am merely a conduit for information and funds. I wish I could do so much more."

Harry smiled a sad smile and tipped his hat. "Don't sell yourself short, my friend. The work you do is every bit as important as the guys with the guns, and even more dangerous. If your found out you'll swing from a rope quicker than most. So please be careful, John. Your people need you." He nodded towards the Dublin man and then moved away, walking slowly in the sunshine, carrying his jacket over his shoulder.

Commander Riordan watched carefully as the man from Dublin approached their secret rendezvous point. He wondered not for the first time how this gentle dandy of a man survived in such a back stabbing and dangerous world and how he seemed to do the things he did with an ease and grace Riordan found admirable. The meeting place was a long, low building at the end of a street in the South side of the city, most of the surrounding buildings and structures serving a large linen factory. This particular shop housed a number of large machines designed to press the finished linen and the Commander stayed tucked behind one of the big presses, keeping one eye on the window with a view of the street and the other on the door. The Dubliner knocked using the preordained code and Riordan replied in kind, then the door slid open and he slipped in quickly. He placed his satchel on a small table and shook hands with the Republican soldier.

"I trust you weren't followed?" the Commander asked. The other man just stared at him in reply, shaking his head. "I'm sorry but you know we can't be careful enough. Did he arrive?"

John opened his satchel and tossed the thick envelope full of money across the table. The American dollars stuck out in places and Riordan looked pleased by what he saw. "That should buy you enough powder to blow up half the city," he said in a voice laced with sarcasm. He shook his head as the cash disappeared into the soldier's pockets. "Please show some discretion in how you use the funds. We are winning over the court of public opinion and we do not need any stupidity to shine a light on the wrong side of this argument," he said bluntly.

The Commander grunted. "We are not in an argument my friend; we are in a god damn war." He stared down at the Dubliner but the smaller man was clearly not intimidated.

"Every war is an argument where those that think with their balls instead of their brains expect violence to produce a better answer than discourse. What it usually produces are lots of dead bodies and no answer to the original question but I do not expect you to share that view."

"What else can you tell me that will help our cause? And please, spare me any further philosophy. You can discourse all you want but the god damn British only understand a loaded gun staring them in the face. But I don't expect you to share that view either."

"Fair enough," the Dubliner replied. "They are using the Black and Tans to follow all the poor lads that were set free of Mountjoy. They mean to learn their where-abouts and then follow them after they've healed, hoping to find Volunteer strongholds and weapons caches. The pardons are just gist for public opinion. They mean to hunt all those boys down and kill them as sure as I am standing here. After all they have been through nearly starving to death; they'll soon be hunted like dogs once more. Only if they're caught again, they'll never see the inside of the goal." Commander Riordan nodded in understanding, unsurprised by what he'd heard. He had a lifelong and well earned distrust of the British government, its soldiers and constabulary puppets and that they meant to do his men harm was a given for any in his line of work.

"Okay, we will take precautions. Anything else?" the Commander asked.

John nodded. "Yes, you need to be more careful with your operations executed in large crowds. They know plans and guns and other weapons are exchanged in the big gatherings, especially the racing, the football and the circus shows. I'd be particularly careful at the Curragh in September. I think the place will be crawling with spies, soldiers, and the Black and Tan. You may want to spread the word that nothing should be ventured at the Saint Ledger, it is most likely a trap." Again the Commander nodded, appreciating this bit of advice. The Dublin man slipped the other thin envelope from his satchel and handed it to the soldier instructing him where it should be delivered and asking that it be done quickly.

"We're not exactly welcome on his land but I will find a way to get the letter to him. I am surprised he has a part in any of this," Riordan said.

"He does not. It's a private matter and I'd appreciate it if you let it remain so." He held the soldier's eye for a good, long minute and then turned and left the building. The big soldier gave him ten minutes and then took off in the opposite direction.

Chapter Fifteen

Barreen, County Kildare – August 1920

Speed! Now it was all about speed. Save Bellweather's close finish at the Derby, it was all Da talked about, it was all he thought about and it was all he pushed Mick to deliver *now*! They were careful to run Whish't Daddy only every fourth or fifth day but over the past six weeks the transition from fast galloping or galloping with bursts of speed to full, flat out velocity had been successfully completed. Brian Grant did almost all the riding with Mick taking the reins only if Grant was away racing Bellweather or one of the other horses. Brian worked the horse hard but always came off his mount shaking his head and grinning from ear to ear.

"He handles it like a stroll in the park. I don't think he's even trying very hard. He switches leads so naturally, almost like a ballroom dancer. He can power out of the turn working his right side and then switch effortlessly to his left and fly down the stretch without a hitch. Look at his ears; they're perked up like he's prancing in the paddock. My God, that is a lot of horse there, Mick. I don't know what you've been feeding him but he feels like a great, flying beast of some kind, he does." Mick beamed at the jockey's lavish praise, stroking his horse's face with loving care. Grant was right, Whishy had filled out tremendously. Standing at a full eighteen hands, he weighed over eighty stone and every inch of the magnificent animal was pure muscle. His chest and neck and shoulders were wider than Mick could spread his arms and his flank and legs bulged in rhythmic ripples as the horse moved gracefully around the yard. His deep brown eyes showed an intelligent curiosity and whenever Mick began to saddle him, the intelligence was joined by a twinkle of passionate confidence and competitive fire. In the beginning, Da had showed Mick how to maintain a detailed chart on the horse's physical development and progress and Mick had carefully recorded every hand of growth and every stone of weight with the pride of a beaming mother. He'd kept detailed records on the horse's health, his legs, his muscles, his hooves, his illnesses, his recovery time, his feeding schedule and of course his running distances, time and rest in-between. Da would occasionally check the records and he would always smile and compliment his son on both the record keeping and Whish't Daddy's steady progress on the road to becoming a champion racer. And the road was approaching a point Mick had been waiting now for two and a half years.

"We'll let him run his maiden race next week, in Punchestown down in Naas, the County Cup, we'll have a go at it and see how he does." Da spoke the words casually but the look in his eye told Mick his father was as anxious and excited to get Whishy on the track as he was, but maybe for different reasons. Mickey just wanted to see the horse run. He was certain beyond any doubt the horse would win his race. He was a champion. Of course he would win. But Da had changed a lot since Darcy had come home. He barely ever laughed or smiled any more. His brooding eyes constantly searched the borders of the family lands, looking for trouble, always on edge, hardness had crept into his gentle personality and everyone in the family could feel it. In the cottage things were very tense. Da checked in on Darcy every night but barely a word was shared between the two brothers. It seemed to Maureen and to Mammy that he was more interested in Darcy's healing so he could make plans on getting rid of the man than any concern he had for his brother's health. Da did not allow any of the girls to go into town without him and told them to leave the house only if accompanied by another or by Mick or Mammy. Conversation around the table or the hearth had always been lively and full of laughter in the Walsh home but now meals were muted and single words or sad looks prevailed. Every night Da sat smoking his pipe by the fire, staring into the flames, as silent as a stone. Even his approach with the horses had changed.

"I thought we weren't going to run him until next spring," Mick asked, pleasantly surprised by Da's announcement. Although he was elated by the change in plans and confident of Whish't Daddy's ability, it was very unlike Frank Walsh to diverge from plans concerning his stable. Da stroked the horse along the chestnut withers and shrugged.

"Sometimes things change, Mick," he said and again his eyes looked off down the road. "You never know when you'll have another chance to do something. Things could happen and most likely none for the better and then we'll be kicking ourselves in the backside for not taking the chance when we had it." He stroked the beautiful horse for a few minutes, deep in thought, and then he looked at his son, trying to smile. Mick thought he saw a tear in his father's eye but in an instant it was gone. "You think he's ready, don't you Mick?" The boy nodded, patting Whishy on the face.

"He was born ready, Da. He's a champion I tell you, that much is for sure." Da found a real smile for his son and ruffled the boy's hair. Mick smiled a great big smile in return.

"Okay, take him in and get him groomed, clean water and hay as well. Off you go." Mick hugged his Da for a moment and then led Whish't Daddy back to the barn, his step light and full of anticipation.

The week passed in a blur. Da had Mick run the horse only one more time early in the week and then ordered plenty of rest, a fortified diet with added barley and corn for additional protein and plenty of fresh, clean water. Mick groomed Whish't Daddy several times a day, wanting the horse to look the part of a champion as well as to run like one. He meticulously picked over every inch of the horses legs and hooves, picked and cleaned even the smallest bit of dirt or grass from his feet, checked the fit and stability of his shoes and carefully monitored his breathing, sleep, energy and attitude.

On the night before the Kildare County Cup, Mick was in the barn standing outside Whish't Daddy's stable double checking his notes, making sure he had not missed anything relating to the horse's care, fitness or preparation. He heard a noise behind him and turned to see Da walking down the barn holding a bag with great care. Much to Mick's surprise, Mammy walked beside him and there was a wee hint of mischief in her eyes. She almost never came down to the barn and certainly not late in the day when she was normally up in the cottage preparing supper or tending to the girls. Da came alongside his son and gave him a gentle hug. He bent and kissed Mick atop his head and then without a word handed the boy the cloth bag. Mick took it carefully, looking up sheepishly at his parents.

"Go ahead," Da said, "open it." Mick carefully opened the sack and looked into it. He slid his hands in gently, slowly taking out bright, colorful linens from inside. As he removed the items from the bag his eyes lit up like they often did on Christmas morning. The first item was a large square of cloth in brilliant crimson and gold checks. Mickey knew it was the saddle cloth that would be slipped over Whish't Daddy's back before the race and his saddle would sit upon this cover to make the saddle more comfortable for the horse. The second piece, made of the same cloth and colors, was the racing blinkers Whishy would wear over his head for the race. It too had brightly colored checks and there were two large holes that would allow the horse to see and two smaller holes which would allow his ears to fit through the head covering. Two straps on either side would be used to fasten the blinker underneath his neck. Mickey gently rubbed the cloth between his fingers feeling the smooth, satin like finish and he rubbed it against his own cheek imagining what it would feel like against Whishy's big face. He looked up at his parents with something akin to amazement, smiling a broad, loving smile.

"It's lovely, Mammy," he whispered, knowing full well that she would have been the one to make such beautiful things. He hugged her tightly and she laughed, tussling his hair in response.

"Go ahead, Mickey, put it on your horse," she said. "Let's see how it looks." Mick hopped up on the fence alongside the stable and quickly slipped the blinker over Whish't Daddy's massive head, making sure the eye and ear holes were properly situated and that the straps fastened snugly underneath. He stepped back and Whishy turned his head slowly, preening for his owner and his wife and the trainer who he loved so much. Mickey nearly cried with happiness as he watched the big horse turn from side to side, nodding every now and then as if to say he approved of the head gear and would run like hell while wearing it. "He looks wonderful, son," Mammy said with pride.

Mickey shook his head vigorously in agreement. "He sure does Mammy. He looks like a champion." Carefully he removed the blinker and the saddle cloth and placed them safely back in the bag. He knew Brian Grant would be clad in a matching jersey and he could not wait to see how splendid horse and rider would look as they moved towards the starting gate. He handed the bag back to his father and his parents slipped away, leaving the boy with his horse and his dreams.

They left the homestead early the next morning. Mick had loaded Whish't Daddy into the covered wagon and cross tied him carefully to make sure he could not fall or bolt from the big cart. The horse did not seem to mind, familiar with the wagon from the many times Mick had led him in and out and from the short trips around the yard they often took for practice. Da sat in the front of the wagon holding the reins and Mickey sat beside him trying desperately to contain the excitement bursting inside. Brian Grant rode alongside on one of the mares and they were all glad to get an early start. The race would not be run until well into the afternoon but Da wanted to get the short trip over, stable the horse and make sure all the paperwork allowing him to run was properly filed and approved. He also liked to spend a few hours scouting out the competition, assessing the fitness of the other horses, understanding who would be their mounts and taking some time to evaluate the course conditions. A light mist was falling as they pulled away from the farm and the roads glistened with moisture, small puddles forming in some of the road holes and alongside in some of the ditches. Mickey didn't think much of it until he heard Da ask Brian Grant about running the horse in the rain. Brian didn't answer straight away so Da asked him again. Grant looked up, clearly distracted and it took him a moment to collect himself and reply.

"It won't be a problem, sir," Brian said softly. "Whish't Daddy won't mind the wet grass. As long as I can see the course we'll do just fine."

They ambled south leaving Barreen travelling on the main road that ran down through Naas and into Punchestown. Despite the mist, it was warm and the air fragrant with the scent of cut grass and damp moss. They chatted now and then about the horse, the race course, the neighboring villages but mostly an uneasy silence surrounded the three men as they made there way through the larger towns of Clane and Naas. They stopped for a few minutes and Mickey went to fetch clean water for Whishy while Da checked in with a friend working in the feed store. They'd been riding for nearly two hours and had another hour to make it to the Punchestown Race Course. Da looked even more worried pulling away from Naas, his eyes squinting together and his jaw firmly set.

"What is it Da?" his son asked. Da looked at the boy and shrugged.

"A bigger field than I'd expected, Mick," he replied. Then turning towards Brian Grant he continued. "You'll have your work cut out for you, Brian. I was hoping Whish't Daddy's maiden would be a smaller field. But they'll be at least ten in the County Cup. Farrington Stables has three entries and Castledermot will have another two. I suspect a horse from Celbridge Farms and most likely a few others will run."

"How about Montgomery Castle," Grant asked riding a bit closer to the wagon. "Will they have their big stallion in the gate?"

Da shook his head. "No, War Lord wouldn't be running in a race of this stature but they may have a new filly in the race. She's not to be taken lightly either." He rode on in silence for a few moments. Mickey could see Da's mind working hard, most likely considering strategies and options and possible obstacles to be avoided. "Hopefully we're not on the fence," he muttered to the jockey. "If we are the first thing you have to do is get him to the outside. If he gets jammed in his maiden he may not know how to find his way out so that is your first priority Brian, get him some room to run. You know he's got plenty of stamina so you don't need to push him early. Let him find his legs and get comfortable with the crowd and keep him where he can see the leaders. If he's the horse we think he is he'll let you know when its time to make your move. But watch for the others. I don't have to tell you some of those bastards will do anything to take home the cup, especially the ones running more than one horse. They just want their colors to fly and they'll work as a team to make sure it happens." Brian shrugged indifferently. He grunted his agreement and wandered a little further from the wagon alone with his thoughts. Mickey's excitement quickened again but he was unclear by what Da meant that the other jockeys would do anything to win. Other than riding their horses what else could they do?

They arrived a little after noon and the Punchestown Race Course reminded Mickey of a huge country fair Da had taken him and Maureen to in Dublin a few years back. There were people everywhere. Large colorful tents were set up outside of the course and hawkers sold everything from cold jars of lemonade to warm pastries to horse heads fashioned out of cloth with long poles sticking out of their necks and a tremendous array of aquiline paraphernalia including pictures, pillows, blankets, mirrors and clothing all adorned with the likeness of a horse or the race course. Smaller booths were scattered about and most had a board displayed with the listings of horses and their odds for each race. Mickey marveled at the coins and bills being exchanged by men manning these booths and shouts of displeasure or argument came from a few of their customers as Da made his way across the big lot and back towards the entrance for the horses and course workers in the race.

If outside Punchestown Race Course resembled a town fair, inside, on the backside of the course, convinced Mickey that it was the busiest horse stable in the world. The level of noise and activity was unlike anything he'd ever seen in his life. The stable area was separated from the grandstand and clubhouse by the long, wide oval track and it was made up of a series of low lying buildings, long, tattered barns with separate stalls every five or six paces and a number of smaller facilities providing storage for feed, manure, old equipment and other tack. Walkways and worn paths meandered randomly from the main dirt road which was now a muddy mess stretching endlessly as far as the eye could see. Trainers, handlers, veterinarians and stable boys filled the backside, all acting in various capacities to lead horses in and out of their stalls, to check on their health, to carry feed or muck out stables, washing down their charges or grooming them when needed. The aromas of manure, hay, sweat and anticipation mingled together filling the misty afternoon with a rich, powerful scent Mickey would forever connect with his first race. Da instructed him to keep the wagon out of the way of the comings and goings of the other men and horses and instructed Brian Grant to stay close by if the boy needed any assistance. He stepped down from the wagon and headed off towards one of the official looking buildings, nodding and shaking a few hands as he made his way through the crowd.

Inside, Frank met with the Head Stewart and reviewed his registration form and payment of all fees which had been made in advance. He verified the colors Athy House would wear and presented Brian Grant's certification as a jockey. Satisfied, the Head Steward assigned Whish't Daddy to an open stall and shook Frank's hand, wishing him luck. Returning to the wagon, he saw Mickey standing on the bench searching about the crowd. Grant was no where to be seen.

"Brian said he was going to say hello to an old friend, Da, but I lost him in the crowd." Frank looked about momentarily, concern creasing his brow but he decided Grant would have to wait, they had more important things to tend to for the time being. They found their assigned stable, unloading the horse quickly. Mickey held the reins firmly, watching as Whish't Daddy took in the circus like atmosphere surrounding him. The din of voices yelling, horses braying, the crowd milling about inside the course and the occasional rumble of thunder was disconcerting but the big colt did not seem to mind. He sniffed at some of the other horses as they walked by and shuffled his steps a few time but otherwise seemed content and unbothered by the vibrant atmosphere. The first race would not be run for another hour so Da took the time to get the horse acclimated to the surface. He and Mick led the beautiful animal down the crowded road along the backside and through the access gate onto the course. As they moved past the other stables and trainers and course personnel, a low hum of commentary could be heard concerning the young horse, his build, his gait and his impressive beauty. A few whistles of appreciation followed them as did the customary questions on who the horse was and where he hailed from. Da's eyes roamed the backside and the track searching for his jockey but Grant was nowhere to be found and Frank's concern grew with every step. Once on the course, he handed the reins to Mick and told the boy to allow the horse to walk at a healthy pace, to get him used to the feel of the wet, grassy course and to the sounds of the crowd around him. Again a series of whistles and cries of appreciation came from the patrons around the track and up in the grandstand and Mick could not help beaming with pride. He made a full loop around the course, knowing the race would be a little shorter than one time around, eight furlongs in total and he made a point of showing his horse exactly where the finish line would be.

"Right here, Whishy, that's where you must get to first, boy. I know you will. I just know you're going to win." He ran his hand along the horse's nose and felt the moisture on his skin. It felt tingly and warm, his excitement hard to contain. It was a long way around the course, nearly twice as long as the one Da had built at home. But it was a distance Whish't Daddy could run without even trying. Mick had run him further than eight furlongs a number of times and the horse did so without effort. If Brian Grant handled him correctly, Whishy would win going away. With that thought, Mick returned the horse to his stable and let him rest in the dark, moist barn. He wondered if Da had found the jockey.

Frank was at his wit's end when he came around the last of the small buildings towards the end of the backside and found Grant standing with a small group of men all in deep conversation, a few of them race course personnel and others looked like strangers to the sport. Frank was about to yell to the jockey when he recognized one of the men in the group to be the IRA leader, Commander Riordan, who had returned Darcy to his doorstep. The man had a box in his hand and he was handing something to the others around him. Frank remained at the side of the building, watching closely as this exchange took place. He could not tell from the distance what the man was handing to those around him. He contemplated interrupting their meeting but hoped to see what was in the box before making his move. Grant stuck something into his waistband behind his back and Frank thought he saw a flash of metal. Their conversation appeared to be ending and one of the men had taken a few steps from the group when suddenly from the other side of the building from where Frank stood, a loud commotion erupted and a group of soldiers charged towards Brian Grant, Riordan and the others in the circle. The soldiers wore the Black and Tan of the Auxiliaries and it was not hard for Frank to spot the giant Captain with the one eye leading the charge. Punches were exchanged and a few of those in Grant's group were thrown to the ground but Riordan managed to pull out his pistol and shot one of the auxiliaries through the chest. More gun fire erupted and soon many people were screaming and running about. As Frank watched, he saw the Commander escape into the crowd, hiding his weapon and melting into the melee around him. Brian Grant was not so lucky. Frank witnessed in horror as the Black and Tan Captain grabbed Grant and another man each by the throat, choking them until they gave up all resistance. He dumped them on the ground in a heap and then the Black and Tan soldiers began tying up the small band of Volunteers, taking away the revolvers from their pockets and waist bands, the guns they had received only minutes before. A moment later, a small man with a pronounced limp and a small moustache appeared alongside the hideous Captain.

"Nice work, Butterfield. I knew these race courses were rife with conspirators and traitors. Take these men up to Dublin and throw them in Mountjoy. They won't be shown the same leniency as their predecessors. And station as many men as you have around the outside of this race course. I'd like to find that Republican officer and beat a few answers out of him. Or have you do it for me," he said with a slight chuckle. Butterfield looked at him with disdain, his one good eye full of malice and hatred.

"Don't tell me what to do, MacDermott," he answered with a nasty snarl. He leaned over and punched Brian Grant in the back of the head and then stormed off into the crowd slamming people as he moved away.

Frank Walsh looked at the bloody melee and his jockey and knew for sure the man would never again ride atop a race horse. He wondered if he would even walk again. He slipped back quickly down the road towards the stables and Mick and Whish't Daddy, wondering if he could find another jockey to ride the big horse.

Chapter Sixteen

Punchestown Race Course – August 1920

"Please Da, I can do it," Mick begged his father. "I know I can do it. I've ridden him more than anyone else, even Brian, Da, please, please let me try."

Frank shook his head. "Mick I can't take the chance. Sure, you've ridden Whish't Daddy around the track at home and through the fields around Barreen but riding him in a race is a completely different thing, son. You could be badly hurt. There will be a dozen other horses bursting out of the gate and every one of them hell bent on pushing their way to the lead. You don't know anything about steering him through traffic or how to absorb the bumping and shoving that goes on. Why, you're liable to be killed, Mickey. I just can't take the chance." Walsh looked up and down the backside of the course once again. After Grant's arrest he had worked his way up and down the stretch of stables and buildings looking for an available jockey he could trust with Whish't Daddy. The few that were to be had were a combination of drunks and thieves, men he knew to pull their horses up to benefit by a few sterling from another owner or stable. There was a man named Riley from Cork he thought might do but when the man heard it was the horse's maiden he declined, saying he preferred riding only seasoned thoroughbreds. Frank was weighing his options and leaning towards packing up the wagon and heading back home, willing to wait for another opportunity. But Mick persisted.

"Da you told me only a few days ago that we never know when we will have another chance to do something. You said yourself we never know what might happen next that could take our chance away. Well we're here now and Whish't Daddy is as ready as he'll ever be for his maiden race and I am ready for mine! If we don't do it today something could happen and we may never get him on the course and never give him an opportunity to win and if ever there was a horse that deserved that opportunity it is this one. Please Da, I am begging you, please let me do it."

Frank looked at the boy and for the first time realized he wasn't a little child anymore. He had to think a moment to realize his son was now almost sixteen years of age and he saw maturity and purpose in the boy's face and eyes he had never noticed before. He also saw a determination and a measure of confidence in Mickey's presence that would not be easily dismissed. He thought of the Captain of the Black and Tan's and Darcy and Brian Grant and the bitter turmoil infecting his country like an awful sickness and he knew that sickness likely would spread sooner than later and might destroy all he held precious. And Mickey was right, they were here now and the horse was ready to run. His eyes roamed the backstretch one more time and then he looked at the beautiful horse, taking in his stature, his build, his rippling muscles, his clear, intelligent eyes. The horse surely was ready. Then, looking at his son, he knew in his heart the boy was ready as well. Although it scared him to death to let Mick take the huge beast on to the course against a legion of seasoned riders and a field of powerful thoroughbreds, there was something even more daunting about denying the boy this chance. Frank felt he would lose something in the bond the two shared, a bond between father and son, formed in the past twenty-four months of training and sharing the unique and wonderful feeling of watching a magnificent race horse come into form. If he packed up the truck and took Mickey and his horse home, there would forever be this thing that lay between them, this lack of confidence or trust between himself and his son. Silently praying for the boy's safety he made his decision. He put his hand on Mickey's shoulder and looked him squarely in the eye.

"Alright, son. I want you to ride to win, Mickey," he said softly, emotion filling his voice, a tremble clearly discernable in every word. "But I want you to be very careful. If it gets too crowded and you're unsure of what to do or if you feel at any time you're in danger from the other horses or from the speed or from the chaos of the race, I want you to pull him up and come in gently. Do you understand me, son? I want you to run the race the best you can but most importantly, I want you safe to race another day. Will you promise me that, Mick? Will you promise me you'll put your safety first?"

Mick smiled a wide and beautiful smile and placed his hand atop the hand his father had on his shoulder. He gave it a gentle squeeze. "Don't worry, Da. I'll do just fine. Me and Whish't Daddy will be okay. We're a team and we know how to take care of each other so we'll be just fine." Da nodded, looking away hoping to hide the tears of pride and fear forming at the corner of his eyes. Taking a deep breath he looked back at the boy and returned the smile.

"Okay then. We have a lot of work to do in the next hour. I'll tell you how I think best to work him and what to look out for on the course. Then you need to get him ready to go and get yourself dressed. Brian's shirt and cap are in the wagon, they may be a little tight but they will have to do. I need to see the Stewart about changing riders and make sure everything else is in order." He was about to turn away and head for the Stewart's office when he looked back and smiled again at his son. "I love you, boy. I hope you know that." As he walked away quickly Mick just smiled and turned to his horse.

"Time to run, Whishy, finally time to run."

Two hours later Mickey sat on the seat of the wagon with tears streaming down his cheeks and an ache in his heart he thought would never go away. He could hear Whish't Daddy in the back of the wagon neighing occasionally and he thought he heard the same sadness and disappointment from the horse that he felt in his own broken heart. The two hours were mostly a blur. The time had passed so quickly and so much had happened. The range of emotions spanned an incredible spectrum providing a wild ride to rival the incredible moments atop Whish't Daddy for the first time in a real race. It started with him saddling the beautiful animal with the saddle cloth his mother made laid carefully across the horse's broad back and with the special, smaller racing saddle fitting perfectly and buckled up tightly under his belly. He fitted the Athy House blinkers carefully over Whishy's ears and eyes and secured it under his big head. Then Mick had dressed for the race. He proudly put on the matching silk jacket with the crimson and gold colors, a pair of tight white pants, Brian's leather boots which were snug on Mick's feet and the leather cap on his head designed for minimal protection in the event of a spill. He had a pair of goggles and a light racing crop to complete the outfit and when fully dressed he stood besides his horse beaming with pride.

"Don't we look swell, Whishy," he said to the horse with a chuckle. He patted the thoroughbred on the neck and then ran a brush along his sides and cleaned his face with a soft towel. "You have to look just right for the winner's circle," he told the horse, kissing him on the nose with affection. Whishy nuzzled his muzzle into Mick's neck, kissing him in return. Da came back and told the boy he had to report to the Stewart's office to be weighed, assuring Mick that it was just a routine procedure, explaining every horse was assigned a certain weight to ride and knowing full well that Mick, slightly larger than most jockeys, would do just fine. Da had to lay out a few shillings for the boy to ride in the race and he told Mick in time they would need to secure a proper certificate to ride in the bigger races around the country. Mick wandered around and found the Stewart's office and got on the scales and after some good natured ribbing by a few of the elderly Stewards, he was told to be ready to load at the gate in fifteen minutes time.

Da spent the precious few minutes reiterating his instructions for the race one last time. Get out of the gate as cleanly and quickly as possible, avoiding any congestion at the start. Find a lane a few paces off the rail and keep in sight of the pace setters. Da expected it would be the number five horse in the green and yellow of Farrington Stables, a pace horse with blazing speed but quick to burn out. Try and stay two or three lengths behind him and when he starts to fade, take the inside and hug the rail. Don't let him go full out yet. Watch who comes up on the side and if it is either the slim, dark, thoroughbred from Farrington or the white horse named Knight Rule wearing the blue and black of

Celbridge, than stay within striking distance but hold on until you hit the far turn. As you make your way down the homestretch let him have his way. He should make up any separation quickly and no horse in the field could stay with Whish't Daddy when he had it turned all the way up. Mick listened intently and he knew the plan.

They marched the beautiful horse down the backstretch and through the pass into the course. The whistles and cheers for Whish't Daddy reignited, a murmur of anticipation rolling through the crowd. Mick proudly mounted his horse and could not describe the joy and excitement running through his veins as they trotted along, passing folks lining the white fences and then along the grandstand where the people with a few extra pounds could sit in comfort while watching the races. He followed the other horses circling the track at a gentle trot, some accompanied by their trainers, others just with jockey aboard. Da stayed back by the starting gate, taking full measure of each horse as he arrived to be placed for the start. Mick noticed the white horse from Celbridge and he thought the jockey riding aboard was glaring at him with disdain. He had no idea why but it was slightly unnerving. None of the horses looked nearly as impressive as Whish't Daddy although the sleek sprinter from Farrington Stables had a beautiful gait and a twinkle of mirth in his eyes. Whishy had been taking his own inventory of the competition and it seemed to Mick his horse was not impressed. He neighed once or twice nearing the other horses and when he passed by the big white from Celbridge Mickey thought Whishy looked at Knight Ruler the same way the horse's jockey had looked at Mick. Up to this point Mick remained very calm and relaxed. He'd been taking in the spectacle of his first real horse race, looking at the pageantry of the event, the cheering crowds, the smell of the other horses, the freshly cut grass and the heat of a humid Irish summer. He'd thought little of the actual race beyond his father's instructions. But as they began loading Whish't Daddy into the gate at position number eight, a sudden, utter and complete terror grew inside Mick like a wild weed in the summer sun. His mouth went completely dry. His head pounded. The noise was cataclysmic. He was surrounded and locked in and paralyzed by the fear of having no idea what was about to happen or what to do when it did. A second later the bell went off, the gate opened with a jarring clang and Whish't Daddy sprang from his position but Mick had not been ready for the burst from the gate and instinctively pulled on the reins to keep from falling. The split second reaction put him exactly where his father told him not to be, at the back of the pack, watching thousands of pounds of equestrian muscle, bone and sinew pound the grassy track in front of him, sending big chunks of green grass flying into his face and his horse's face. His goggles fogged up and grew harder to see out of and Mick hated himself for putting them in this position. Fear began filling his mind and his body. It was not so much a fear of being hurt by the chaos of horses, hooves, bodies and rail, all flying past him at a terrific speed, but it was more a fear of failure, of causing the terrific horse he knew raced beneath him to be denied the right to run the race the way he was capable of running, to run like a champion. As this sense of failure nagged at him he had the sudden realization that Whishy was trying to tell him something. He leaned a little further over the horse's neck, standing up just a little higher in the stirrups, holding tight with only his ankles and a handful of mane and rein. He listened hard and after a moment he knew what Whishy wanted. He calmed himself and slid the big horse closer to the rail where he noticed the other horses were beginning to avoid. It was most likely due to the wet grass, soggier closer to the rail, harder to maintain traction and provide real speed. But it did not seem to bother Whishy. Mick could feel him pulling harder with each tremendous stride, passing first one horse and then two more and then another and finally he could see beyond the mass of horse flesh that had blocked his view. As they maneuvered through the first turn his goggles cleared slightly and he could see the backstretch of the course laying before them as clear as the road to Dublin. He noticed for the first time that the sprinter his Da had said would set the pace was indeed at least four lengths further along and there were two other horses racing between the Farrington Stables pacesetter and Whish't Daddy, one of them was the big white stallion from Celbridge. Mick bided has time as Da had instructed, feeling a little better about things as his horse found his stride and the two raced along in relative calm. As they made the far turn Knight Rule closed the gap and the sprinter began losing momentum. Soon only the big white horse raced in front of Whish't Daddy and a second entry from Farrington Stables came up, running stride for stride with Mick. They raced liked demons around the far turn and then made for the home stretch, three thoroughbreds pounding down the course taking immense strides, nearly flying, each of them covering much of a football pitch in but a few strides. With three furlongs to go the horse from Farrington Stables closed quickly on the outside of Knight Rule and the two went along in tandem but at the quarter pole Mick gave Whishy his head and the big beast responded. Mick felt his gait change as the horse lengthened and quickened with each stride and as he closed on the white horse on the inside Mick knew he had them both beat. He was set to fly past them in a burst of speed with Whish't Daddy exploding towards the line. And then without warning, seeing nothing by way of danger as he passed, a vicious slap across the nose and mouth from some kind of lash or whip or crop hit him very hard. The surprise and pain and shock of the attack caused Mick to tighten on the reins ever so slightly, bringing Whish't Daddy up at precisely the wrong moment, allowing the two other horses to race by quickly with no chance to catch up with only two lengths to run.

Mick crossed the line with his horse a solid third, blood running freely from both his nose and mouth. Da raced out on to the course to grab the reins as the big horse galloped along cooling down from the race. Da noticed first the boy's face and then the horse's lack of heavy breathing or exertion. He asked the boy what happened but Mick was unsure.

"I don't know Da," he said fighting back the tears as he slipped from the saddle. "I know we had a lane, we were going to blister our way to the line. But something hit me out of the blue; I am not sure what it was. It hit me right across the face." Da handed the boy a towel to wipe away the blood and took the horse leading him back to the backside and the stable assigned for the day. He told Mick to wash the horse down and give him a little something to eat and then to wait for his return. He was going to see the Stewart to place an inquiry, although he was not certain about just what. He returned thirty minutes later, obviously angry and fit to be tied.

"Someone said they saw Knight Ruler's jockey, a real bastard by the name of Cowen, lash out at you with his crop just as you moved to pass him. But the man denied it and unfortunately there is no one to verify the story. So the Steward refused my inquiry and said the results stand. I'm sorry Mick. You ran one hell of a race son, and so did your horse. I am very proud of you both." Mick could only nod, the tears continuing to flow as he scrubbed down his horse and ran the brush along his side. The disappointment he felt was beyond anything he'd ever known. "Get him ready for the ride home, Son. I have to close out with the Steward and I want to find out about races down in Carlow for the next few weeks. We'll have another chance, my boy, don't you worry about that." Da's words cheered his son only a little bit, the disappointment of the day far too fresh in his mind.

Frank read the riot act to the head judge one last time and then went looking for the jockey or trainer of the white stallion, Knight Ruler. But he found only a few stable boys and grooms around the horse's assigned place and no one knew or would say where the other men had gone. Frank decided it better to leave that conversation for another day and to head back to Barreen as soon as possible. With any luck they'd make it by nightfall. As he made his way along the backside towards their wagon he saw a familiar figure walking towards him. The man's height and elegant dress gave him away and as he drew closer to Frank, he smiled, stopping to talk.

"Lord Montgomery," Frank said, extending his hand politely.

"Mr. Walsh," Montgomery replied casually. After shaking hands, he looked around quickly. There was no one within earshot and he spoke softly. "Your man was fouled; I could see it clearly from where I was standing."

Walsh nodded his head in agreement. "I think it was clear from any vantage point. The only one who seemed not to notice was the patrol judge. Would you care to set him straight on my behalf?" He looked Montgomery in the eye, waiting for his response.

"It's not my place, Mr. Walsh. I did not have a horse in the race, as they say."

Walsh was disappointed but not surprised by the Lord's answer. He had expected the man would do little to help. "That is quite a horse you have there," Montgomery continued. "Without the interference from Knight Ruler he may well have lapped the field." He made the statement with admiration but Walsh knew there must be more to come. "Bellweather was his sire, is that correct?" Montgomery asked, knowing clear well the horse's lineage. "And the mare?" he asked.

"With all due respect, I doubt the name would mean much to you, Lord Montgomery. She's a little known lady by the name of Queen of the Isle. Athy House purchased the mare several years ago but as I understand things, her parentage is unknown, perhaps from Scotland or Australia. I really am not sure." Frank hoped the equivocation was not too blatant, quickly switching the subject. "I was surprised Montgomery Castle did not enter your young filly," he bated Montgomery. The Lord smiled knowing Frank's intentions.

"She will run in one of the more important maiden races, Mr. Walsh. But back to your colt, Whish't Daddy, right?" Walsh nodded. "I would like to buy the horse and I am prepared to offer quite a large sum. Would you be interested in such an offer," he asked.

Frank shook his head sideways. "That's not up to me, Lord Montgomery. The owners of Athy House would have to decide on that. I am quite certain they want to hold on to him. We expect great things from this horse." Montgomery eyed Frank carefully, his face showing both mirth and suspicion.

"Athy House is quite a difficult entity to unravel. How do I contact the ownership to make my offer," he asked.

"You would have to make the offer through me and then I will make sure it gets to the correct people to entertain the decision. I am prohibited from sharing that information. All the proper forms for registration are on file if you'd like to have them reviewed." Frank was growing uncomfortable with the discussion, hoping the man would leave quickly. "We need to be heading back to Bareen, my Lord. The daylight is already fading. So if you will excuse me," he said and made towards the stable.

"One more thing, Walsh, before you go," Montgomery added. "The jockey, the young boy, I have not seen him with the reins before. Who would the man be? Or is that another closely guarded secret of Athy House?" he asked with a chuckle.

Walsh shook his head again. "No, no secret about that, Lord Montgomery. The rider is my son, Mickey. It was both his and the horse's maiden ride. I thought they both did very well. Would you agree?"

Montgomery nodded. "Very well indeed," he replied. "He did well to free the horse from the crowded pack and had impeccable timing when he asked the horse to move. Very impressive for such a young man, you must be very proud." Walsh nodded briefly, anxious to end the conversation. "I will send a formal offer to Athy House through your stable in Barreen. I trust you will discuss the matter with your, uhm, partners, or is it your superiors?" he chided Walsh.

"I just work for Athy House, Lord Montgomery. I will make sure they receive the offer. Good Day," he added quickly, walking off to find his son.

The soft velvet light was fading from the Irish sky as the old wagon bounced along the bumpy road close to Barreen. Mick's tears had subsided and now he only sniffled every few moments, gamely trying to forget the heartache of the race. Frank slipped the wagon's reins into one hand and threw his other arm around his son's shoulders.

"Buck up, now, Mick. We don't want your Mammy and the girls to see you in such sad shape. You ran a damn fine race and you finished third. There's no shame in that." Mick shrugged, remembering the sudden smack across his face and the uncontrollable reaction to pull Whish't Daddy up. He could not deal with the injustice of his defeat.

"It's just not fair Da, that's what's bothering me the most. I can take losing in a fair race, that's all part of the game, but to lose on such a lousy foul, why that's just not fair at all." His father laughed a soft, sad laugh and hugged the boy a little tighter.

"Well Mickey, then you learned a very important lesson in life today, one that we all come to realize sooner or later." The boy looked at him quizzically. "Life is rarely fair, son. I take no pleasure in being the one to tell you that but it is true. More often than not things work out in a way that benefit less the deserving than the unscrupulous or the lucky or those in a position of power. It's not just horse racing I am talking about. Just look at our country, son. Many a man breaks his back with long days of hard labor and they have nary enough food to feed their family or improve their lot in any way. People who have worked to build their own businesses see them destroyed by the insanity gripping our land. Women are abused, men are hunted and hung or shot and often the wrong ones are punished for the sins of others. No Mickey, don't count on life being fair, you will only be disappointed." The boy sat contemplating his father's words as the wagon approached the family farm. All was quiet and he could see some of the horses grazing in their paddocks in the falling light.

"So will every race go like today," the boy asked with great concern. "Do I have to expect to be fouled and hit at every turn?" Now it was his Da's turn to shrug.

"No son, not every race will work that way. But you surely need to be ready for anything once you're up in the irons. Horses will crash into you and Whish't Daddy, riders may pull at your saddle blanket or your riding crop or at your arms and legs. Sometimes the other stables will run a pair of horses and one of them will be assigned the task to make sure the competition has a very rough road to travel and usually that competition will be you because they'll pick the best horse and go after him and try to knock him out of the race. So you will need to be ready when we get down to Carlow next week. We're going to enter Whish't Daddy in the Carlow County Plate and I like our chances. So be ready, son. You may have lost one on a foul today but the lessons learned will pay dividends down the road." He hesitated a moment and then gave Mickey one last squeeze of the shoulder. "I am proud of you, son. You'll have your champion. Just give him time." Mickey took a deep breath and exhaled, all the disappointment falling away as it can only for a lad of fifteen years. His mind began mulling over the race in Carlow and how much better he'd manage Whish't Daddy along the way.

Chapter Seventeen

Barreen, County Kildare - Late Summer 1920

Maureen held Darcy's hand carefully as he struggled out of the bed and onto his feet. Six weeks had passed since his return and under Maureen's constant and diligent care the young man felt his health and strength slowly returning. Some flesh and muscle appeared on his bony frame and the skeletal look of his face retreated daily, replaced by soft, pink tissue across his forehead, under his eyes, filling out his cheeks and chin. The first days had been the hardest when he could barely choke down the thin broth Mammy made daily or swallow even the smallest morsel of bread or meat. He'd slept most of the day and long into the night, waking up with violent dreams or seeing ghosts of various descriptions teasing him from across the small room. Sweat bathed him and the bedcovers were soaked nearly every morning but Maureen did not care. She gently washed down his face and neck and shoulders and back. When she cleaned his stomach and moved her hands playfully towards his crotch he would always slink away and whisper to her to stop.

"Not in your father's house, Maureen, please," he insisted with as much vigor as he could muster. "He wants me out of here as soon as can be and if he catches you doing that, it will be this evening at the latest." He smiled thinly, patting her hand as she gently rubbed his cheeks.

"Da is down by the barns with his damn horses," Maureen replied bitterly. "How a man can care more about the animals than his own flesh and blood is a mystery to me, Darcy. But I am very proud of Mickey.

Da says he's done all the training on Whish't Daddy and nearly won his maiden. Only a vicious foul kept him from victory. He's quite a young man, my little brother! As are you, Darcy Walsh, and you are not going anywhere just yet. Why you've just barely made it to your feet. You're still mostly skin and bones. I don't think you could hold a bucket of water in your hands, my dear. We've got a long way to go before I will allow you to leave this home," she said forcefully, "if I ever let you leave at all."

Darcy tried to smile but he could not. "Your Da is right. My presence here is a danger to you all. I need to find someplace else very soon. I'd feel terrible if I caused you any harm or if anything happened to the others or to the wee one. I'll be okay, Maureen. In a few more weeks I will be strong enough to go and then I will have to leave. I won't give him any more chance to resent my being here. If I never see him again it will be too soon." The few steps in the small room and the short conversation tired Darcy greatly. He sat back on the bed, his thin body barely making a sound or an impression on the matting.

Maureen sat beside him, stroking the few hairs away from his forehead. "Maybe I will go with you when you leave, my dear. We can run away together. Maybe we can go to America. I hear stories in the village all the time of people taking the chance, of them boarding the big boats and heading across the ocean to a new world, a new life. We could do that Darcy, couldn't we," she asked, trying to hide the excitement in her voice.

Darcy took her hand smiling weakly. "We'll see, dear Maureen. There is a lot to be considered. We have no money and I do not know anyone that could help us arrange the voyage. And there is the work I have to do here," he added with little enthusiasm.

"What work?" Maureen asked pointedly.

"The Volunteering, Sinn Fein, our fight for independence from the damn British," he said the words without enthusiasm, as if repeating a stock phrase he had been provided.

"Sinn Fein?" Maureen asked incredulously. "Are you joking? They damn near killed you in that prison and now you want to go back to that life again? Is that what you are saying? Is it really all that important to you? For what? They have done nothing to make your life better. And what about me? Do you just leave me here on my own? So my Da can send me to London or some other dreadful place to do dreadful things for the rest of my life? Is that what you want?" Her voice had risen far higher than she had wanted and after a moment there was a light knock on the door and Mammy popped her head in.

"Is everything alright," she asked looking at her daughter and her brother-in-law sitting much too closely on the bed. Maureen shifted away and then stood, moving across the little room. "I heard the yelling and I thought perhaps something was wrong," she added, looking anxiously towards her child.

"It's fine, Mammy. I was just trying to talk some sense into this man. But I don't think he has even a wee bit of it in his thick skull." She looked accusingly at Darcy. His head was facing towards the wall behind him, avoiding the stares of both women. After a moments silence Maureen stomped passed her mother leaving the room with a sad, angry look in Darcy's direction. Mammy's eyes followed momentarily betraying great concern.

"Do you need anything, Darcy?" she asked softly. He shook his head from side to side, embarrassed by the compromising situation. She closed the door quietly and crept away, her mind cluttered with painful thoughts.

A rider came through the pasture and handed an envelope to Mick, quickly speeding away without revealing his identity. He was a young man, only a few years older than Mick but no one he recognized. The rider had asked if he was on the Walsh farm and when Mick told him yes, he'd drawn the letter from his satchel and left without another word. Mick found Da in the barn and gave him the letter, Frank's name written neatly on the envelope. Da moved off to the small cubby hole in the back of the barn he used for doing paperwork. A makeshift desk formed by placing a panel of wood over several empty feed crates was covered in papers and a collection of bits and reins and old horse shoes. Da collapsed into a rickety wooden chair, opening the letter just as he had read many such letters before. He knew by the handwriting who it had come from and he was anxious to learn its content.

Dear Frank,

We're glad to learn you feel Whish't Daddy is a horse of rare ability. We know you will train him to be the champion only you and your boy could develop and we have complete faith and trust in your decisions regarding how and when he runs and who rides the horse. However, given the worsening political climate and the general unrest spreading across the country, we would like you to consider shipping the colt to a safer realm, perhaps in England or here in America. We can assure you he will be well looked after, receive the attention of our best trainers, grooms and stable hands. He will only be raced on a schedule you feel appropriate. Of course, all winnings will continue to be split as in the agreement defined and we are ready to assume all costs of transport and care during the journey. We would hate to see anything impact the horse's future and want to see no harm come to Athy House, its stable or its people. The normal funds have been deposited per the usual procedure and we are ready to augment those to a reasonable extent should you agree to this request. Please respond at your earliest convenience. You and your family remain in our thoughts and prayers.

Sincerely,
Friends of Athy House

Frank read the letter over several times trying to decipher any hidden meaning or implied warning in the words but he could see none, telling himself to accept the communication at face value. He moved towards a large iron barrel filled with water just outside the barn and reaching for a match in his pocket, he set the letter and envelope ablaze, watching as the charred ashes fell harmlessly into the cool water with a soft hiss. As the paper vanished, his mind mulled over the strange alliance that had helped forge Athy House and the clandestine partnership that kept it alive. No one else knew of this association and it was paramount no one ever learn.

Fifteen years earlier Frank's talents were working their magic in several stables in the South and one in particular down in Cork. The stable just to the North of Kinsale, Old Head Farms, boasted twenty-two stallions, seven fillies and a record that was the envy of nearly every horseman in the country, bar Montgomery Castle. He'd trained the winner or the place horse in seventeen events including the Derby, the One Thousand Guineas, the Cork Plate and stakes races in towns from Dundalk to Tralee. Job offers rolled in from Farrington Stables and a dozen other competitors including Lord Montgomery himself. In May of that year, Frank was in Dublin for an interview with an owner who had arrived from Edinburgh and he was staying at a small boarding house south of the Liffey. After returning from his meeting he was met in the parlor of the house by a tall man with a broad, round, red face and a deep, baritone voice. He wore white shoes and in his hand he held a straw hat. He suggested they go down the road to a pub close by where they could talk in private. Frank agreed and few moments later they were sipping Guinness in a cozy snug away from the pub's noisy patrons.

"My name is Harold Fitzgerald but my friends all call me Harry the Horse on account of my passion in life is for horses. I don't know if the name Brady means anything to you but I work for a man named James Brady or Diamond Jim as he is referred to by the American press. He is very prominent in American racing. Only recently he invested considerable sums of money in a race course in Saratoga, New York." Frank nodded slowly wondering where in the world this unusual man was going with their mysterious conversation. "Mr. Brady is greatly indebted to you and the reason I am here is to present a business proposition on his behalf."

Frank sipped his beer, eying the man carefully. "Why is this Brady fellow indebted to me if I do not even know who he is?" he asked.

"Your brother Liam saved his life," Harry the Horse announced directly. "And in the process he lost his own. It was an accident down on a pier in lower Manhattan. Your brother was unloading a cargo ship carrying bales of linen coming in from Manchester. Mr. Brady had an interest in the cargo and he was walking the dock watching the operation. A cable on the crane assisting in the unloading snapped and six hundred pounds of merchandise dropped from seventy feet in the air and was set to land directly on top of Mr. Brady's hat but your brother bravely dashed from his post and shoved the man out of harm's way.

Unfortunately, he could not escape the weight of linen himself and the entire crate crushed him, killing him instantly."

Frank received this news with a mixture of sorrow and surprise. Liam had died many years earlier but he had known nothing of how it happened other than receiving a short letter from his brother's neighbor saying he'd been killed in an accident. To learn he had died a hero sacrificing his life for another made Frank proud but the horror of the way he died left him empty and sad. He also was very curious on why this man was telling him all of this now.

"So, what does this all mean to me, Mr. Fitzgerald? Why are you telling me now when my brother died so long ago?"

The American nodded, his big head bounding up and down as if on a pole. "Mr. Brady has long wanted to show his gratitude but quite honestly it was very difficult to track you down. For years we tried to reach a brother in Australia to no avail and I have been personally searching for his next of kin here in Ireland for quite some time." Frank was unsure if he believed this tale but found no reason to doubt the man's honesty. "Anyhow, here we are now and if you'd like to hear it, I'd like to relate Mr. Brady's proposition." He waited until Frank nodded and then continued. "Mr. Brady is a firm believer in the cause of Irish independence. He is pursuing that goal on many different fronts, using his wealth and influence wherever possible and in many different ways. He strongly believes that the best way for Ireland to stand on its own two feet is through enterprise and industry and Irish ownership of businesses across the country." Frank smiled at these words, having felt the same way for so long. But he did not want to let on just yet until he understood more about this man, his boss and their intentions. Instead he began to protest, citing the many laws restricting ownership of land, property and businesses by Irish citizens. Harry the Horse held up his hand, nodding in agreement.

"Yes, yes, Mr. Walsh, I am very well versed in the legal issues as is Mr. Brady. We are also very experienced in helping people like you to, how should we put it, work around these challenges? Mr. Brady has helped numerous Irishman to "own" property and businesses through a series of legal instruments and entities which will somewhat smoke up the actual facts around the true and real equity holder in a particular business or transaction."

Frank was unsure of what the man was saying and still unclear on what he was talking about "owning" as Frank had little more than the small cottage to his name. But the American seemed to know all of that.

"When Mr. Brady wants to make a proposition it is well researched and thoroughly understood. You currently own the plot of land on which the cottage stands, the small barn and two plow horses you occasionally rent out or use for transportation. Your current income is derived from your training work and occasionally you are given a bit of the purse but seldom does it happen. You do better than most of your neighbors and can make ends meet but little more than that at this time and little prospect for improvement in the future." Harry said all of this matter-of-factly and sat quietly waiting Frank's reply.

"That is all true," he said softly.

"Well that is all about to change," Fitzgerald said with great enthusiasm. A moment later he launched into a vision which Frank could only have dreamed about let alone believe could ever be reality. "We would like you to begin to build your own stable," he began. "You can acquire the accompanying lands both to the South and to the West of your property today, lands that formerly were part of Castle Longpond as you know. You have a tremendous ability to spot a talented horse and you are as skillful as any trainer in the land in developing top racers that can challenge across Ireland and the United Kingdom. You will have to build a much larger barn and paddock area and in time put in a rudimentary course for training. Over time, your stable will become one of the most famous in all of Ireland." The man sat beaming with pride over the things he foresaw for Frank Walsh. He drained his pint, calling out for the barman to send another round.

Frank was stunned. He was unsure on whether to trust the man at all. His vision seemed too far fetched to be believed. He waited until the Guinness arrived and then began peppering the American with a laundry list of questions. Most centered around how all of this, the land, the barn, the horses, the equipment, the required help and other necessities would be funded and how would he own this imaginary stable of horses and racers. Harry patiently took him through how it all would work. A corporation would be formed in Ireland but it would be owned by two other companies in Australia which in turn would be held in partnership by two American companies with a few other entities taking partial equity stakes and limited partnership roles, all designed to keep both the government and any other interested parties in the dark regarding the truth. Harry reached into his jacket pocket and spread a series of documents across the table. One listed out a budget of costs and expenses for building and running the stable, one provided a list of potential races, purses and anticipated winnings; one was a bank draft with a figure written across its face that made Frank gasp in surprise. Finally, Harry handed him a sheet of paper listing out five different businesses, a hat maker, a dairy farm, a law firm, an importer of fine art and a book store. Each listed a name to contact with an address.

"I am sure you feel this might all be a sort of swindle, Mr. Walsh. I assure you it is not. These firms are all part of Mr. Brady's Irish investment. If you reach out to them I am certain they will vouch for our legitimacy as well as for our honesty in how we work together. It is in our best interest for you to succeed."

Frank looked over the mass of paper work, reviewing the names on the list of references one more time. It was all very overwhelming. But in the back of his mind he could not help the growing excitement coming to the fore – to own his own stable!!! It would be a dream come true. And he knew it was something he had the skill and energy to do very well. He knew more about horses than any man in the country and he was aching to prove it.

"How do we get started, Mr. Fitzgerald," he asked nervously.

"Please call me Harry," the man replied with a loud laugh. "Think of a name for your stable, my friend. When you have the name we will update all the paper work and make the first deposit in the bank in Dublin. You will be listed as an employee of the corporation but in fact you will own the business in its entirety. The deposit will cover all the costs of building and buying your first stallions and mares. Then you get started. I don't think I need to tell you anything about horses or barns or paddocks or courses. Do I?" he asked.

Frank shook his head. "No, that I know plenty about but you do need to tell me why, Harry. Why all this just for me? What did I do to deserve any of this?"

Harry shrugged. "Well, it's not all for you, Mr. Walsh. It's for your brother Liam, God rest his soul, and it's for an Ireland we all have dreamed about for a long time. An Ireland owned and run by Irishman, a land where we can succeed or fail on our own merits. And it's also a bit for us, Mr. Walsh. We know a good investment when we see one. We are counting on a certain return we know you will provide. The figures are all listed in those papers. It will take time but we believe eventually you'll deliver on your potential and we think that it is going to be huge." He raised his glass to toast their new venture but Frank held up his hand and cut him off. Raising his glass slowly a smile came to his lips.

"To Athy House, Harry, we will name our stable Athy House. That's for my Mom. She would like that." The two men happily clinked glasses together, a partnership was born.

And over all these years the partnership had survived and flourished. All the promised funding for raising the barn, building the stables, putting in the paddocks, buying the horses, hiring help and getting the myriad of supplies over the many years had always been waiting in the bank for Frank to spend. With their meager winnings, he had deposited the agreed upon commission to which his American partners were entitled in another bank in Dublin and their communication was very seldom, strictly by mail and usually through a third party intermediary. Even the death of Diamond Jim three years earlier had not ended the unusual arrangement. Investments continued, letters arrived occasionally and Frank assumed they came from Harry the Horse. Every now and then the man appeared out of nowhere to ensure Frank of their continued commitment. Sometimes he made a few suggestions on horses or racing techniques being tried in the states but for the most part he seemed to show up only to bolster Frank's confidence and to share a pint or two. Now, years later, the future of Athy House never looked better but the warning tone in this latest letter regarding the political climate in the country registered deeply with Frank. He worried every day over the plight of his brother, the threat

Darcy bought to his home, the presence of the horrible Black and Tans and their despicable Captain, the growing resolve of the Republican cause and the rippling chaos spreading across Ireland. Fires, bombings, murders and looting happened every day both in the larger cities and across the countryside. Frank wondered if Whish't Daddy would be given the opportunity to become the champion race horse Walsh knew he was born to be or would that opportunity be dashed by the terror and bloodshed between the Volunteers and the British or worse, in a civil war many spoke of now as the greater threat. One thing Frank Walsh knew for sure was that right now he could not and would not ship the horse out of the country. He'd toyed with the idea of sending both Mickey and Whish't Daddy across the ocean to America but he knew the loss of a son would be far too painful on the boy's mother and not any easier for himself. And as a man who had dedicated his life to raising and training thoroughbreds, he could not ship away his greatest chance at true majesty. The horse was very special and Frank hoped to see that special talent and form run many times over and win championships by the bushel load. Only time would tell if that would happen. He watched as the ashes of the letter disappeared in the large barrel of water and then he returned to his chores checking over his horse's feet.

"Bless me father for I have sinned," he began. Again the church had been empty save one elderly woman praying to a statue of the Virgin. He heard Father Dunn shifting about in his seat on the other side of the screen and he was certain the man was anxious to get to his dinner and a few glasses of wine. He decided to do away with the preliminaries and get the one major sin of lying off his chest but he was somewhat uncertain on how to parse his words. "I have been propagating a lie regarding personal ownership of property for many years, Father. For this and all my past sins I am greatly sorry." He sat in silence hoping there would be no inquiry regarding the details and he grew uncomfortable as the silence lengthened, broken only by Father Dunn's occasional grunting which indicated little in terms of his feelings.

"Tell me more," the whiney voice commanded from the darkness. Again silence hung in the air.

"Well, Father, there is not much really to tell. I own some property and due to the laws from the past I have hidden my ownership in a complicated web of paperwork, much of it based overseas but all of it intended to keep people from knowing the extent of my ownership." Frank bit his lips, wishing he had resisted the temptation to cleanse his soul of this tricky and somewhat justified lie. He thought he heard Dunn humming from the other side.

"More," the priest spit out. "You are in the confessional man. You do not tell our Lord and Savior part of your lie; you tell him all of it." Now Frank really regretted coming to the confessional.

"I am in a business that is primarily the bastion of the wealthy and in many cases the Lords and Dukes of the land. I am just a humble man from a humble place and I have built a small business which allows me to share some of my abundance with my neighbors and friends and certainly the church, Father. But I am afraid that in being less than truthful about the ownership I have sinned and for that reason I have come to ask for forgiveness." Dunn let him stew for a few more minutes, Frank desperately hoping there would be no more questions.

"Well, what about taxes, man? Have you been paying your share of taxes to the crown or have you been cheating Caesar of his fair share of your uhm, abundance?" The priest laced his voice with feigned concern but Frank knew he was far more interested in what came to the church than what made its way to the coffers in Dublin or London. Frank assured him all fair taxes had been paid over the many years and that other than concealing the ownership of his property no other sins had been committed.

"Well then, say ten Hail Mary's and ten Our Father's and now repeat the Act of Contrition." Father Dunn mumbled his absolution while Frank gratefully ran through a speedy version of the contrition prayer. He thought they were done and thanked the priest and was standing to leave when Dunn's whiney, conniving voice stopped him short. "And Walsh, you have been forgiven. But it may be wise to keep your little horse and buggy operation quiet for a while longer. The laws may be changing but attitudes are trailing far behind. Not that I care what happens on the race course but this parish needs a few parishioners with greater means than scratching potatoes from rocky soil on a tiny parcel of land." Frank was taken aback by the priest using his name and openly stating he knew the concealed ownership meant Athy House and the racing horses. He hoped the man could be trusted; he was a priest after all. He thanked him again but still Dunn was not finished. "And I will expect a sizeable donation arriving at the rectory over the next few days. Remember Our Lord's command, Give to Caesar what is Caesar's and to God what is God's. Either coin or considerable produce will do nicely. Good night." Frank blessed himself absently and then raced away from the small church.

Chapter Eighteen

On the Road to Carlow – End of August, 1920

Michael Cleary took great pride in leading his caravan of wagons and horses from Connemara across most of Ireland and down to County Carlow. It was a sultry day at the end of August but luckily no rain had fallen while they'd been travelling throughout the past week. The sky boasted milky white clouds smeared across a light blue background, the sun climbing in the East shining over a patchwork of greens and yellows and blues as vivid and varied as anywhere on the planet. The sight of rolling fields and low hills in the distance brought a smile to his broad face, increasing the enthusiasm building in him for the coming day. Behind him in covered wagons were six anxious horses he planned to run in different races in Carlow's Gowran Park. Two fillies would run in two different claiming races and he felt quite positive they would both best their rivals. A two year old colt would run his maiden in a race of like horses and Cleary felt it would provide a good opportunity to see what the horse had inside. He'd trained well but one could never be sure until they were stuck in the gate with no other choice but to run. The remaining three horses would all race in the course's premier event of the season, the Carlow Plate, which in addition to a fine gold plate would also put 300 Guineas in the treasury of Lord Montgomery should things go as expected. The trainer new from past experience a few quid would surely find its way into his own deep pocket as well. He had little or no concern they could lose. He knew his strategy and he'd seen it work in countless races. He knew his three horses each knew their role and each of their jockeys understood the plan perfectly. Trinidad, a blazing pace setter, would burst from the gate, quickly separating himself from the pack. Any horse trying to keep pace with this splendid specimen would surely fade on the backstretch, just as Cleary knew Trinidad would do himself. That was fine. Depending on position at the gate, his aptly named colt, Strong Bow, would get off with the pack and then go hunting for the strongest competitor, trying gamely and within the rules, to crowd the other horse either close against the rail or outside to the wide side of the track. The horse was thick and blocky and his jockey very adept at the maneuvering required in making things difficult for another horse and rider. Should Trinidad and Strong Bow be successful in their assignments, he had no doubt of the race's outcome. Because the third colt bursting from the gates wearing the Blue and Red colors with the Montgomery Crest would be the finest horse he had raised or watched run in the thirty-five years he had been involved in the Sport of Kings. War Lord was a monster in every way. His physical presence was astonishing. At a full seventeen hands to the withers and seventy plus stone, the mass of muscle and tendons and bones fused with an attitude, determination and a cocky sense of predestination forming a horse that would not be denied. He was a bastard to train. He kicked and bit and stomped and reared and tossed rider after rider, chased more grooms and stable boys out of the business than Cleary could count and generally just made things far more difficult than they ever needed to be. But when you have a horse of that pure ability and attitude you deal with the issues and focus on the prize at the end of the wire. The horse was beautiful to look at and beautiful to watch run. Cleary had told more than a hundred people that if he had found a girl with an arse half as beautiful as War Lord's he be a married man instead of a happy bachelor. Watching War Lord break free from the pack and take the bit, flying over chunks of grass the size of most Irish gardens, was thrilling to anyone in the business. He was one in a million and Cleary felt blessed to have had such a horse to train at any time in his life. If the game plan was followed, War Lord would win going away. He'd watched him blow away the field in race after race over the past two years and when Bellweather, the big horse from the obscure Athy House, had challenged him in the Derby earlier in the year, War Lord had shown him just what kind of grit it took to be a champion. No other horse in the land could match his speed, tenacity, strength and desire. The Carlow Plate would be theirs.

One of the grooms rode up to Cleary and told him Lord Montgomery wanted a word. He abandoned his reverie concerning War Lord, trotting back towards the ornamental wagon carrying the Lord. He maneuvered alongside the carriage drawing close enough to chat with his employer. Montgomery looked very relaxed sitting on satin pillows and smoking a gray pipe, blowing mouthfuls of pine smelling smoke out the window, nearly right into Cleary's face.

"Pardon," the Lord offered casually as he tapped the pipe in a tray beside the pillows. "Lovely day for racing Mr. Cleary," he added.

Michael smiled broadly nodding in agreement. "Certainly is My Lord. Should be a dry, fast course and that will make our chances even better, not that I think we need any help. He's in great shape and loading him up this morning you could see he is very eager to run." Montgomery nodded approvingly.

"Do we have any word on the size of the field?" he enquired. Often the smaller tracks were unable to announce the fields in advance and if they did word did not always make its way to distant places like Connemara.

"Nothing definite but we expect about nine or ten in total. The stables around Carlow will certainly participate as it's close to home. Kildare will send a few I am sure and we know Kilkenney Farm is sending a small delegation."

"Who from Kildare?" Montgomery asked pointedly.

"Farrington and Castledermot are rumored to be coming but I have not had that confirmed," Cleary replied uncomfortably, knowing well where Lord Montgomery was taking the conversation.

"And Athy House," he questioned, "have you found out anything about that beast I saw race in Punchestown? Do you know if he is running? Whistle Daddy or something like that, I think," he added. Cleary shrugged in the saddle moving his head from side to side.

"Whish't Daddy," he corrected. "Very little have I heard about that one. I spoke with a few of the trainers from around Dublin and they know Frank Walsh to say hello but not much more. No one saw this

Whish't Daddy run before the race you watched and you saw first hand the kind of horse he is. They say had his regular jockey not been pinched just before the race he surely would have won. That poor kid had no chance against the likes of Jimmy Cowen. But rest assured War Lord is up to any challenge. This Whish't Daddy might be impressive in a claiming race with a field full of grazers but wait till he gets a hold of our guy. Then let's see what he can do." Cleary did not feel as confident as he hoped to sound extolling the virtues of War Lord over this new rival. He had known Frank Walsh most of his life and knew the man to be every bit as good a trainer as himself or any man in Ireland. Athy House had produced a few winners each year over the past decade but did not appear to have the resources to expand its farms, stables and horses. However, he'd learned that Bellweather had been Whish't Daddy's sire and he knew from the recent Derby that the father had challenged his beast and almost beat him across the line. Montgomery had told him the horse had every bit of his father's size and then some. If he had as much heart and just a little more determination than the battle would be drawn. The thought of it filled Cleary with a mixture of excitement and worry. But he was interrupted in his thoughts by Montgomery's next question.

"Have you made any progress on the other matter we discussed? You mentioned Walsh's jockey being pinched down in Naas. He was receiving guns from a Commander in this "Volunteer" movement. I need to be sure Montgomery Castle does not suffer that same fate in any of our races, not to mention the shame it would bring upon the Castle and the name."

Cleary considered his reply. He had been surprised when the Lord had come asking him about any involvement the trainers, grooms, jockeys or stable boys might have with the Republican cause. Although he knew Montgomery held a place in the House of Lords, it seemed to Cleary his politics centered around the economy in general and the racing game in particular. The Lord expressed a need to gather any information regarding recruitment, gun running, kidnappings, burnings, bombings or any other Republican activity committed by anyone associated with the racing business, be it within Montgomery Castle or other stables in Connemara or neighboring counties. Cleary was no gossip and he tried to mind his own business but one would have to be either dumb or deaf or maybe both to know nothing about the growing presence of the Volunteers across all of Ireland. He knew a good number of the lads he tipped pints with down at the tavern had some involvement of one kind or another and he knew a few of the jockeys acted as couriers, racing messages and dispatches across the land. But he sure as hell wasn't going to share that information with his boss. People that told the wrong thing to the wrong people often wound up with a bullet hole in the back of their head and Michael Cleary was enjoying life far too much at the moment to tempt fate.

"I have heard some things about a small cell down in Clare. I don't have anything specific just yet but from what I hear they're planning some kind of an attack on a garrison or a postal office in the fall. I don't have any names yet." He left it at that and looked at Lord Montgomery to gage his reaction. The man nodded slowly and Cleary thought he saw a small remnant of a smile cross the Lord's lips. Perhaps he knew Cleary was selling him a pile of manure or maybe he was considering the possibility of catching a group of Volunteers in an act of treason. Either way, he dismissed his trainer with a small wave and then drew the silk curtain closed across the carriage window.

Ten miles to the north Frank Walsh and his son formed a far smaller caravan making their way to the very same race course in Carlow. Frank handled the wagon reins with Whish't Daddy standing patiently in the covered section behind him. Mickey rode alongside the wagon on one of the new ponies Da had purchased a few months back. His mind kept flickering from one thing to another and he found it difficult to concentrate on the race later in the day. He kept replaying the race at Punchestown and wondering what more he could have done to get Whish't Daddy passed the white stallion and avoid the cowardly slash of Cowen's crop. He'd replayed the moments over and over in his head wondering if he should have bounced his horse back towards the rail or let him bump hard into Knight Rule or ducked under the unsuspected blow. He'd discussed it with his father and with some of the boys at school and also with Rory Killhane. Mickey had feared his Da would ask Rory to ride Whish't Daddy now that Brian Grant was in the goal but Rory laughed at the suggestion when Mick mentioned it one day.

"You're Da knows that horse and he knows you and he knows the two of you go together like tea and toast. He told me you run a hell of a race down there in Punchestown. A damn shame about the foul but now you know what to expect. Most riders are good and honest men but you'll come across your share of scoundrels over the years. Best you learn the lesson early, Mick, can only help you down the road." Since the race at Punchestown, Mick had spent a great deal of time picking Rory's brain, learning more about technique, how and when to stand high in the irons, when to use his heels or his knees, how to lay flat out along a horse's neck, what to do in heavy traffic and how to bounce to the outside or to tuck into the rail. Rory loved sharing his expertise and gladly demonstrated on his different mounts how to ride in traffic, how to get through an opening as narrow as a cat's arse, how to bump and grind and how to let the horse fly. Mick absorbed it all like a sponge in the kitchen sink, taking his turn to imitate the more experienced Killhane, deeply grateful for the crash course in competitive racing. Rory had never gotten over his fear of Whish't Daddy and he had great respect for the boy's magical manner with the tremendous beast so he gladly tutored him over the weeks between the races.

O'Malley had come earlier in the week and re-shod Whishy, telling Mick he was fitting him with Champion's shoes, winking at the boy as he nailed down the silver plated iron onto the horse's solid hooves. Mick listened intently as the farrier told Da what to expect down in Carlow.

"Montgomery is bringing his team with an aim on taking home the Plate. You know the drill they like to employ - a pacesetter, a blocker and their tremendous closer, War Lord making for the wire. Will not make it easy on this fellow right here," he concluded, finishing up on Whish't Daddy's shoes. Da nodded and asked the old man about others in the field. "Usual cast of characters but they'll be of no concern. War Lord is the horse to beat." He looked Mick directly in the eye. "You won't need to worry about any gamesmanship from that stable. They don't do it and they don't need it. They got a hell of a lot of horse and they know how to get him across the line, you understand?" Mick nodded, thinking he understood their plan and hoping he had the goods to best it.

"We got a hell of a lot of horse, too, Mr. O'Malley," the boy said with some pride and both his father and the farrier laughed heartily at this reply.

"Any word on any expected interference from the authorities?" Da asked quietly, his gaze automatically going first up the road and then up towards the cottage.

The farrier shrugged. "Yuh never can tell. After what happened down in Naas you should know those damn Black and Tans will be all over Gowran Park hoping to find more trouble. And seems anywhere you look these days trouble is standing there waiting. So I'd be careful if I was you, Frank. After they nabbed your man Grant, they may be keeping a close eye on your comings and goings as well." Da nodded and Mick noticed the tight set of his jaw and the worry in his face. The farrier left wishing them both luck and safety and Mick hoped both would make the trip to Carlow with them.

"You alright, son?" Da asked as they made their way into Carlow County on the rocky county road. "You look like you got the weight of the world on your shoulders, Mick. Anything you want to talk about?" Mick laughed a shy, uncomfortable laugh, wanting to cause his father no more worry or grief than he already carried.

"I been thinking about the race, Da. I don't want to let you down again. And I don't want to let Whishy down either. You both deserve a lot more from me than I gave you last time. We should have won that race and it's my fault we didn't."

Frank looked at his son and felt so much love and admiration for the boy he nearly burst. "Mick, you done wonderful son, please don't blame yourself for what happened. It was your first race and you ran it just fine and if that bastard Cowen hadn't slashed you with his crop you would have won going away. So don't feel it was your fault because it wasn't. You did just fine. And you'll do even better today."

"Do you think we can beat this War Lord, Da? Mr. O'Malley said he is quite a fine horse." The boy was genuinely concerned and anxious to hear his father's opinion.

"He is a damn fine horse, Mick and it won't be easy to beat him. You understand how their team works so you know what to watch for. And you got a hell of a horse underneath you as well. So just do your best and I think it will be plenty good enough." Mick nodded in agreement and moved closer to the wagon. He pulled back the cover, peaking in at Whish't Daddy who stood nearly sleeping in the back of the wagon. The horse turned his big, beautiful head and looked Mick right in the eye. He nodded up and down twice and Mick understood the horse to be saying he was ready and that what Da had said was right and true. They'd do their best and Whishy thought that would be plenty good enough too.

Unbeknownst to Frank Walsh or his son they were being followed. Half a mile to the rear Arthur Butterfield and his patrol of Black and Tans galloped at an easy pace, taking care not to be seen by the men they followed. Butterfield was in a sour mood, as usual, and he kept thinking about the conversation he had with Ian MacDermott the previous night. MacDermott had summoned him to Dublin and they met once again down by the city's waterfront and strolled along the near empty pier as the weather was wet and damp. MacDermott seemed anxious and more angry than usual, his pink complexion turning back and forth to bright red as their conversation ebbed and flowed.

"These damn Volunteers continue to grow in number and in veracity," he started in his thin, whiney voice. "Kildare County is no different Arthur," he added with exasperation. "Last week we had a bombing of the postal office in Newbridge and a soldier was assassinated in Cellbridge Township. A cadre of rifles was stolen from the barracks outside Naas and we have absolutely no knowledge of who was involved. I put you in charge to stem exactly this kind of activity," he said, his voice laced with accusation.

Butterfield wanted to reach out and squeeze the little man's head until it exploded in his hand but he knew that would lead to all kinds of trouble. And as much as he disliked what MacDermott had said, he had to admit the man was right. His command was working hard day and night and they were sparing no effort to uncover new recruits and leaders of the bombings, murders and weapons theft occurring over the past weeks and months. They'd been fortunate to stake out the race course in Punchestown and capture eight Volunteers and Butterfield personally interrogated each of these men trying to uncover additional information. He killed two of them in the process but reported they'd been shot while trying to escape. The interrogation of Brian Grant had proven the most frustrating. He had the slight man tied to a chair with his hands behind his back and his head fastened tightly to a pole. Grant watched in terror as Butterfield interrogated another Volunteer before him, beating him into unconsciousness, waking him with pails of water only to be beaten again to within inches of his life. Butterfield saw the fear in the jockey's eyes and felt certain he would break quickly and blabber out all he knew about other Republicans and their organization. But the jockey had proven tougher than expected. After a barrage of punches, kicks, nicks with a blade and severe whipping across his hands and back, Butterfield took the barrel of his revolver and jammed it into the man's mouth threatening loudly to blow a hole in the back of his neck if he did not begin to talk. Still, somehow Grant found the courage to remain silent. It was widely speculated by the forces of the Crown that these Republicans feared reprisal by their own leaders more than the wrath of the British forces. Butterfield screamed in the man's face, jamming the gun in deeper but the fear in Grant's eyes only turned to sorrowful resignation. In exasperation Butterfield moved the gun from the back of the man's throat, jammed it into his cheek, pulling the trigger and blowing a hole through the jockey's face which later in life he'd be able to poke his finger through. Grant pissed himself and then feinted in response and Butterfield gave up on him and moved on to terrorizing the next in line.

When he told MacDermott that the interrogation had yielded little by way of new information the small Scot's consternation boiled over. "Are you losing your fucking touch, Butterfield? I bought you here to suppress any and all rebellion in this county and now it is as dangerous a place as any in this Godforsaken land. We have these damn Republicans causing havoc across the land and each day the Crown loses more and more control of the situation." His loud whining turned the heads of a few passersby along the docks and Butterfield told him to pipe down before he incited more trouble. In a lower tone MacDermott continued. "Well, at least we confirmed the connection to the horse racing with these damn Volunteers. This Grant fellow is a jockey for Athy House, one of the smaller racing stables in the county. And it turns out their head trainer, a man named Frank Walsh, is brother to one of the Republicans that we foolishly released after the hunger strike." Butterfield nodded at this information, having already known most of it. He had visited the stable in Barreen and warned Grant that he was under suspicion. And he'd had one of his men follow the wagon carrying Darcy Walsh back home from Mountjoy Prison. But Butterfield's overriding memory of the Walsh home was not the stables or horses or jockey or even Frank Walsh himself. It was of the pretty, young daughter with the strawberry blond hair that stirred his longing. Perhaps another visit back to the Walsh home was in order. His reverie was interrupted by the whining of his superior.

"Are you listening, Butterfield?" the man asked sharply. "I said we need to keep a closer eye on anyone involved in this racing business and an especially close watch on this Athy House. There are a number of matters that raise concern. Not only do we know this Darcy Walsh is a certain problem, you have the link to their jockey Grant and we have strong suspicions regarding the ownership of the enterprise. I have done considerable investigation into this but continue to become entangled in a confusing web of paperwork and international corporations that lead only in circles. It is very possible Athy House is helping to fund this Republican insurrection. It has become a matter of great concern to some members of our government and it is something we need to sort out quickly." MacDermott thought it best to keep secret Lord Montgomery's interest in the ownership of Athy House but he wanted Butterfield to understand the importance of the situation, hoping the big, dangerous beast could figure out a way to untangle the web or maybe tear it to pieces.

Butterfield easily convinced himself a visit to the Walsh home was definitely warranted and when they arrived early the next morning they were just in time to see the wagon and another horse and rider heading away from the farm and out towards the road that would take them down to Carlow. Butterfield quickly decided to follow them, overcoming a powerful urge to pay a visit to the young girl inside the cottage. That it would take him out of his jurisdiction was of no concern, MacDermott would cover for him. And he'd been told to keep a close eye on both the Walsh family and the racing business. A nagging certainty grew in him that the two were closely related and if he followed one it would bring him answers to the other. And some day down the road it would lead him back to the Walsh home and to the beautiful lass with the long hair blowing in the breeze. He kicked his horse a little harder galloping up a small hill from which he could see Frank Walsh and his son in the distance.

Chapter Nineteen

Gowran Park – Late August 1920

Despite the two day trip, the inviting atmosphere of celebration and festivity in Carlow greatly surpassed the joyful first impressions Mick felt on their trip to Punchestown a few weeks earlier. The sheer size of the race course and the surrounding grounds along with the many canvas and linen tents, wooden stands and benches stretching along the front side of the course left Mick overwhelmed and dazed by the breadth of it all. Colorful flags and pennants waved from the course's ramparts in the late morning breeze and several bands were competing for the crowd's collective ear as they rang out race tunes, military marches and lusty ballads of love and loss. People milled about playing games of chance, drinking from large mugs of ale, eating the wide array of country fare from delicious cheeses and sausage to lamb served on flinty skewers and handfuls of gooseberries, loganberries and blackberries, the juices from the tasty fruits running down chins and cheeks and into a few greasy beards. Several fist fights flared up as Mick and Da made their way towards the backstretch. Everywhere Mick looked book-makers were busy taking wagers and an overriding air of anticipation hung over the large crowd and the big race course. Many in the crowd had come to see the great War Lord, his reputation and fame well known in racing circles across the land. Whish't Daddy remained an unknown, having run only one previous race, but Mick was certain his tremendously talented horse would be a secret no more by the time they left Carlow County.

The backstretch covered a huge swath of territory with a training track located in the rear, and barns and stables running in numerous rows between the training track and the main course. Huge piles of hay covering the muck and manure of the past weeks were piled over ten feet high and a wafting, visible steam rose from the piles like barn fires spread across a campground. Grooms and hot walkers went to and fro leading horses and ponies out from their stables to the front side and back and Da and Mick rode past countless stalls before arriving at their assigned place. The routine was much the same as it had been at Punchestown with Da searching out the Stewards to ensure all their paperwork was in order while Mick got Whish't Daddy into the stable along with his pony and began prepping for the race. They would not go off until late in the afternoon but Mick wanted to make sure everything was perfect so they could concentrate on the strategy and execution of the race. He passed the time checking over Whishy's legs and feet, grooming him carefully and supplying him with plenty of clean water. Da returned with a mysterious grin on his weathered face and Mick asked him what he was smiling about.

"I'm not really smiling Mick," Da replied. "I guess I just am happy we are going to find out a few things today. War Lord is going to be in the gates with you. I thought to put you and Whish't Daddy in a claiming race but when I heard that big bastard was running in the Carlow Plate I couldn't resist making the change. It cost me a few bob to get him in but I got a feeling we'll do just fine. And then I will be smiling all the way back home!" Da ruffled his son's head, his tone quickly turning serious and businesslike. "Surprisingly, they have both horses running at the same weight. I would have expected a lighter load as we have no wins under our belt and War Lord has plenty. But I am sure Lord Montgomery's influence had something to do with it. Anyway, we are going to have to be very careful on the course as I have watched their team a few times over the years and they know their game very well." Da went on to explain one more time the way Montgomery Castle would employ a big horse to crowd out its most dangerous competitor leaving War Lord sitting just a few lengths off the pace horse to grab the lead with a burst of speed towards the wire. Mick thought back to Punchestown and the slow start which led to being trapped behind a herd of horses in front. He told himself he needed to be alert at the gate and to get Whishy into a position from which he could stay with War Lord and then battle down the stretch. Da pulled out the racing form with the list of horses in their race, the ninth, showing Mick the three horses that would be wearing the colors of Montgomery Castle. He pointed to the number three horse, Trinidad, the pacesetter. "He will probably hold it until the seventh pole and then begin to flag. Don't try to stay with him, lay a few lengths back. I am sure War Lord will give you company." He hesitated a moment reviewing the form and then nodded and pointed again to the paper, this time at the number nine horse. "Strong Bow's only job out there this afternoon will be to cause you problems. We've drawn a good position as the number four horse so he will come at you from the outside and look to crowd you into the rail. Whatever you do, Mick, you have to get our boy away from this hunk of lard. I can't tell you how to do it. You'll have to feel it and I know you'll figure it out when the time comes. Once you get to the far turn, War Lord will start to move. You do the same. And then it's the two of you down the stretch and may the best horse win." He looked Mick in the eye and his son nodded.

"I won't let you down, Da. We are getting to that wire first," the boy exclaimed with quiet confidence.

"You never let me down, son. And regardless of what happens today, I'll still feel that way on the road back to Barreen." He left to get some food from the wagon for them to eat and he told Mick to try and get some rest. But the boy knew he'd never sleep waiting to get up in the saddle so he spent the time dressing in his colors and whispering to his horse.

Cleary carefully watched the jockey, Quiney Moran, ease War Lord down the backstretch and through the small pathway leading out onto the front side and the main track. He was a beautiful sight to behold. His near black coat glistened in the afternoon sunshine and his chest, shoulder and neck muscles rippled in harmony as he pranced along the course. His saddle cloth matched Moran's shirt and cap, the crimson red and dark blue wrapped carefully around the eagle crest of Montgomery Castle. The crowd applauded enthusiastically, whistles and shouts of admiration cascading from both the stands and the large groups lining the white fences stretching from the finishing pole back down the home stretch. Many in the crowd had followed War Lord's career over the past two seasons and they knew they were watching greatness unfold before their very eyes. Many in the crowd had at least a few quid riding on the majestic horse and the prospect of a few pints or a nice meal compliments of the champion encouraged their fervor even more. Cleary nodded to Moran, acknowledging his understanding of the game plan and when the jockey gave him a slight wave he moved towards the stands, hopeful to find a seat in the Lord's booth affording a good view of the entire race. As he made his way up the stairs and through the stands a low rumble from the crowd grew into a considerable roar and Cleary turned to see another horse, a chestnut colored monster with a white stripe and a small white circle below running down his elegant head. Cleary ran back down the stairs pushing his way through the excited crowd making his way to the fence where he could get a very close look at the horse from Athy House. He had never seen a thoroughbred bigger than War Lord but this beast walking the track a few paces behind was at least a full hand taller and looked larger across the chest and through the shoulders. His legs were sturdy and graceful and his gait rhythmic and long, the exact step and pace Cleary looked for in a champion. The jockey was a mere lad. Cleary thought he could be no more than fourteen or fifteen years of age but he rode atop his mount with confidence and ease, a slight look of wonder twinkling from his eyes as he took in the cheering crowd. The boy turned the horse back towards Cleary and as he moved past the trainer, the horse turned his head slightly, looking him right in the eye. Cleary would swear later to anyone who would listen that the damn horse had actually winked at him as he passed by. The crowd kept cheering and yelling out the big horse's name, Whish't Daddy! Whish't Daddy! Whish't Daddy! He heard over and over. Cleary felt the first bit of discomfort in the pit of his stomach as the horses made their way towards the gate. He raced back through the crowd and up the stairs of the stands and found Lord Montgomery sitting comfortably in his box, chatting easily with another wealthy man at his side. Cleary excused himself and interrupted.

"You said he was quite a horse my Lord, but yuh didn't tell me he was a beast as big as that!" Cleary babbled like a young child who'd just seen a ghost or a fairy in the woods. "My God, he's the biggest thoroughbred I have ever seen! And he looks like he's got that special something in him, Sir! I must say I hope our guy is ready!"

Lord Montgomery excused himself to the man on his left and then turned back to his trainer with a wry smile. "Our GUY had better be ready Mr. Cleary," he said pointedly. "That is what I pay you a handsome amount of coin to ensure. And it was just a few hours ago that you did just that. I warned you this would not be easy. But War Lord is a champion and Moran a proven rider. The youngster is very wet behind the ears and his horse quite new to this as well. I like our chances. For your sake, I hope I am right." With that he waved his hand dismissing the trainer, sending Cleary off to find another place to watch the race. Montgomery turned his attention to the track where the final horses were being maneuvered into the gate.

War Lord sat in the two hole with Whish't Daddy two gates over in the number four position. The sprinter, Trinidad, was between them and Mick let his eyes roam momentarily down the gate to the number nine horse, Strong Bow, noticing the jockey eyeing him as well. Mick knew he would be coming at him and his mind mulled over a few ways to react. He leaned over Whish't Daddy's neck, whispering quietly into his horse's ear.

"Okay Whishy, this time we're ready. I feel your strength and speed and heart beneath me and I know all I have to do is get you in the right spot and you will do the rest. But when we break, follow my lead boy, I got an idea. Just trust me on this one." He patted the horse's neck and Whishy nodded in reply. Then the gates swung open.

Mick felt Trinidad explode from the spot beside him but he felt he was out quickly as well. Expecting the large crowd of horses jostling for position this time, he let his horse move deftly around the course, finding a hole from which the action could be seen from every angle. Hooves pounded the spongy track; dry grass flew up and around Mick's head and eyes, flying across his goggles and blowing away just as quickly.

He heard the laboring breath of the beasts around him and the curses and shouts of encouragement from the other jockeys and somewhere far off in the distance he heard the din of the crowd bouncing around Gowran Park. At the first pole he remained in the middle of the pack and could see the blackness of War Lord a pace or two ahead on the inside. But that was no concern to him yet, he would see War Lord further down the road. Out of the corner of his eye he saw the glint of red and blue edging its way towards him from the outside and knew this would be Strong Bow, trying to box him in. With just the gentlest of encouragement he moved Whish't Daddy to the right, pointing him down the track but on a slight angle heading right at Strong Bow's nose and with a click of his tongue and a gentle snap of the reins he felt his horse accelerate instantly, moving rapidly towards the oncoming blocker. In two strides Whishy had covered the space required and bolted right in front of the other horse nearly grazing him as he flew by. Mick could not help but feel elated as he sensed Strong Bow pull up behind him, knowing he'd never catch up with Whishy now and that he had foiled the horse's mission. Now the race was truly on.

The pack flew around the first turn with Trinidad in the lead taking the slight rise in stride. As they hit the back stretch three horses separated Whish't Daddy and the leader. One wore the colors of Farrington Stables and a small gray wore a yellow and white cloth Mick could not identify. They were going stride for stride in the middle of the course. Slightly to the inside, War Lord raced along showing no signs of stress or strain. His jockey dropped his chin and Mick knew the man was searching the field for him and his horse. He did not have to look very hard or very far as Mick sat no more then a half a length behind but further to the outside. Along the backstretch the din of the crowd grew fainter but the sound of the horses pounding down the track, snorting and groaning filled Mick's ears. He watched War Lord carefully as they made the far turn and he saw Moran slide a little lower in the saddle, stretching himself along the horse's slick, black neck. In two tremendous strides he passed the unknown horse in yellow and quickly passed by the entry from Farrington Stables as well. Mick kept in stride with him, knowing Whishy would be patient but feeling him readying himself to let go. Trinidad began to flag and War Lord took the lead as they turned towards the final stretch with Mick and Whishy a full length behind. The temptation to give him the bit and let him go nagged at Mick but he had decided before the race to wait for the next to last pole to make his move. It would only give Whishy two furloughs to catch up but Mick thought it would be plenty. The roar of the crowd returned, sounding like an oncoming locomotive and Mick let the cheers wash over him and his horse, feeling its energy and strength growing along with them. He saw Moran take another peak, most likely surprised they had yet to make their move. He saw the quarter pole coming up quickly and he stretched himself along Whishy's neck clucking loudly and patting him gently with the reins. Mick felt the horse shift gears beneath him, the easy gait expanding, the rhythmic breathing getting deeper and longer, the strides half again as long, the head bouncing towards the wire with an explosiveness Mick knew they would only find under the most intense of competitions. It seemed only a stride or two or three and they grew even with the dark beast on the inside. Then they were racing together, two horses, two riders blending almost into one, a stride and Whishy was out in front by a head and another stride he was behind by a nose and so it went down to the wire, fans screaming, hooves thundering, bodies extended, hands gripping reins, snorting, panting, grass flying, War Lord unwilling to give way, Whish't Daddy pushing himself to the wire, Mick begging him for more, feeling there might be nothing left to give, both horses pounding the last few strides, both extending their heads at the wire, both unrelenting, both certain of victory, both across the wire and listening to the delirium of the crowd, both running another quarter then slowing, slowing, slowing to a trot. The jockeys raise themselves up and look towards each other; both smiling at their adversary, both unsure of who had won but both certain it had been one hell of a race. They slowly turn and make their way back towards the finish line and looking up they see a steward at the finishing line waving a red flag, indicating a photo finish. To close to call, it would be up to the camera to decide.

It took almost twelve minutes by Da's pocket watch before the word came down from the Head Steward – Dead Heat, a tie, no winner or two winners depending on your point of view. The crowd went crazy knowing having backed either horse would make for a payday and another round of cheering and applause went up for the two great horses and their gallant riders who had put on such a tremendous show. Mick had stayed atop of Whishy, waiting to hear the decision, hoping to trot the horse into the winner's circle. Da held the reins and when the announcement came he looked up at the boy and smiled. Mick smiled back but Da could tell his son was not completely pleased. They shared the winner circle with War Lord and Lord Montgomery and a tall, funny looking man that Da knew and that must have been the other trainer. He shook Da's hand and they shared a quick word. Lord Montgomery nodded towards Frank Walsh and then the jockeys dismounted and unsaddled their rides. Moran came over to Mick extending his hand. The man was almost as old as Da and he seemed surprised when Mick removed his helmet and goggles, letting his long blond hair fall in front of his face.

"You run a hell of a race, son," the man offered with a smile. "That's a hell of a horse you have there. No one's ever caught us from behind, never!" Mick shook his hand, returning the smile and thanked Moran for his kind words.

"I was hoping not just to catch up to you," he went on without any conceit or overconfidence but with the ease of a child. "I wanted to pass you and win the race. But you have a fine horse too and Whishy just couldn't get by." The older jockey laughed, squeezing Mick's hand again.

"You'll win plenty of races with that monster," he said. "There's no shame in a dead heat. You come in first now didn't yuh?" He laughed again and handed the saddle to a groom and then patted War Lord on the face. With a respectful nod towards Mick's Da he walked away with the other trainer, shaking his head in disbelief.

Whish't Daddy was washed down, watered and fed and tied off safely in the wagon as the sun began its descent and they readied for the long ride home. Mick was about to mount the pony as Da had taken his place on the front bench of the wagon. But before they pulled away the tall, gawky looking trainer from Montgomery Castle walked towards them holding up his hand.

"Mr. Walsh, if you have a moment just a brief word?' Da nodded, jumping from the wagon and the two men moved a distance away. "Lord Montgomery wanted to know if you presented his offer to the owner's of Athy House. He has instructed me to ask you to name your price for that magnificent animal," he said quietly. "It seems the Lord is quite smitten with him." Cleary looked slightly embarrassed to be asking the question.

Frank shook his head from side to side. "Please tell Lord Montgomery I am flattered but the horse is not for sale. Tell him I enquired of my ownership and they politely refused. We are expecting great things from Whish't Daddy and he will remain with Athy House."

Cleary nodded having expected the response. "Can't say I blame yuh," he offered with a wry smile. "He is an extraordinary horse." He hesitated momentarily, looking around the backstretch carefully. "It's just that Lord Montgomery is very used to getting what he wants and he is normally able to go to whatever lengths necessary to get whatever it is that he wants. And he wants your horse." He looked Walsh square in the eye and nodded. Frank hesitated a moment and then shook his head in understanding. Cleary was not threatening him but rather warning him of things to come. Walsh extended his hand and meant to leave but Cleary grasped it tightly, leaning in closer he continued in a soft voice. "They're taking a damn close look at the racing game in search of Volunteers," he said. "Your man Grant being pinched in Punchestown puts Athy House under suspicion. They may very well use that against you Frank. If I was you I'd be very careful." He turned his eyes towards Mick and then looked back at Frank. "Keep the boy out of harm's way too. It would be a shame to see such a talent wasted." Letting go of Frank's hand, he waved to Mickey before moving quickly down the backstretch, disappearing in the vast jumble of stalls and barns.

It was dark and a soft rain had been falling for the past three hours. They'd been on the road for two days and now Barreen lay only another hour to the North. Both Mick and his Da were weary. Mick kept reliving the race in his mind wondering what more he could have done to beat War Lord to the wire. Perhaps he had held Whishy back too long? Maybe he had taken him too wide to avoid Strong Bow?

Maybe he had let War Lord get too big a lead? He had asked Da all these questions and Da assured him he had run a flawless race but Mick was unconvinced. With a horse like Whish't Daddy you should win every race, of that he was certain. Surely War Lord was a formidable foe but Whishy would learn to beat him and Mick would learn how to get it done. He bounced around in the saddle feeling every hump and bump in the road. He could not get over the excitement of the race, the atmosphere, the people cheering, the sound of the stretch run and the smell of the horses and the feeling of flying towards the wire. But the tiredness dulled his enthusiasm and he worried about Da. Ever since the trainer, Mister Cleary, had spoken to him, Da seemed very quiet and withdrawn. Normally after such a race he'd be very enthusiastic but they'd rode most of the two days in silence, Da alone with his thoughts.

Frank Walsh headed towards home with a heavy heart and head full of worries. He wanted to remember the elation and joy he felt watching his son and his horse race down the home stretch, giving all they had to get to the wire. He wanted to revel in the sizeable first place purse he'd shared with Montgomery Castle for tying in the Carlow Plate race. And he wanted to share nothing but joy and happiness with his beautiful boy who had raced so very well. But he could do nothing of the sort. Cleary's words of warning hit squarely home and as he road the last few hours across Ireland his fears and worries grew as big as the land they traveled. There was no way he could hold off the coming onslaught if Lord Montgomery set his mind to taking Whish't Daddy away. Once upon a time Frank believed that the veil of secrecy constructed by Diamond Jim Brady and Harry the Horse would serve to keep Athy House safe, preserving his ownership in the business and protecting the investments made to improve the stable and bring more champions to Barreen. But he had neither the resources nor the contacts to fight a member of the House of Lords. Montgomery was too powerful and too well connected both in the government and in the racing game. If he truly wanted Whish't Daddy he would take him away one way or another. Frank knew it would devastate his son like nothing else ever could. The thought of explaining to Mick that his horse had been sold, stolen or cheated away brought tears to his eyes. And the whole mess with Brian Grant and Darcy and the damn Volunteers only made matters worse. He spent a long stretch of the trip contemplating what he would say to get Darcy to leave their home as soon as he returned. It was growing more dangerous by the day for him to be there along with Mammy, Maureen and the young girls. Darcy had not recovered completely but he was well enough to move to another place and Frank decided it would have to happen soon. Darcy's influence on Mick was to be considered and Frank was bound and determined to keep his boy away from all the Republican nonsense tearing the country apart. He was thinking of ways to keep Mick occupied, thinking of races to put him in and other horses to have Mick train and even the possibility of sending him abroad when suddenly out of the darkness of the night a rush of horses and riders descended on them, surrounding Frank, the wagon and Mick riding on the pony. There were eight or ten soldiers, all dressed in the now familiar tan trousers and black shirts and hats. In the front of the wagon holding a rifle and looking down at Frank from his solitary eye, Arthur Butterfield appeared as the angel of death. Frank reached out to grab hold of his son but the boy was too far away and one of the Black and Tans pulled up close alongside of Mick and held a revolver by his side.

"We want no trouble," Da said directly. Butterfield spat on the ground in front of the wagon and laughed an evil, dark laugh.

"Maybe trouble come looking for you," the ugly monster replied. He moved his horse up closer to the wagon and looked inside the covering into the back where Whish't Daddy stood quietly. "Nice horse," he added loudly, "and pretty damn fast from what I seen in Carlow." Frank tensed wondering if Butterfield would take the horse, unsure of how Mick might react. Cleary's words of warning raced through his head over and over. Butterfield let go of the covering, moving over towards Mick.

"Please," Frank said quickly, "leave the boy alone. He has no part in all of this."

Butterfield pulled up to Mick and slapped the boy easily across the face. It was not intended to hurt but left a slight sting none the less. "Be my thought that the boy got a great big part in all of this. He raced the damn horse didn't he? Done a damn fine job from what I could see."

Mick tried to look Butterfield in the face but the sight of the leaking, puss filled hole was too gruesome to take so he looked away into the distance. Butterfield laughed harshly then pulled alongside the wagon and dismounted. He stood beside Frank Walsh waving his rifle in the air. He let loose a loud shot that split the night and Whish't Daddy whinnied in fright from the back of the wagon. "This here is a toll road, Walsh. Don't you know that?"

"No, I did not recall this being a toll road. It wasn't as of a few days ago," Frank replied loudly. His words belied the fear seeping deep into his bones. Butterfield and his men could kill them on the spot and take the horse and everything else and no one would ever know the difference.

"Well things have changed since then, now haven't they?" Butterfield said in reply. Frank looked up at him and shrugged, unsure of what to say. "Well now, when you went down this road you had a horse running in a race, right? But now you're coming back this way and you have a horse that won a race, ain't that right?" Frank nodded in agreement, Butterfield's intentions beginning to take shape. "And when you win a big race like the Carlow Plate you also win a fair amount of money, true?" Frank looked at the big man but said nothing. Butterfield stuck the end of the rifle in his face and laughed again. "It would not do very well for this young boy to win his first horse race one day and lose his father a day later. That would be terrible." With that he cocked the rifle. Mick made a move towards his father but two of the auxiliaries grabbed him firmly, keeping him away. Slowly Frank nodded his head and his hand slipped behind the bench and he came out holding a small canvas bag. He handed it to Butterfield, watching the man carefully. The Captain took the parcel, opened it quickly and looked inside. Pulling one coin from the bag, he looked it over closely. "The King's currency, excellent," he said. Then he looked over towards Mick and tossed the coin in his direction. It fell at the feet of Mick's pony. "Man's got to be paid for a day's work, right?" he said with another horrible laugh. Then he backed away from the wagon, mounted his horse signaling his men to form up to the rear. When they were ready to go he spat again towards the wagon, pointing the gun at Walsh. "Best regards to the women at home, Walsh. Tell 'em I'll be seeing them real soon." And with that he raced off into the night, his evil laughter echoing in the darkness.

It was well after midnight when they arrived in Barreen. Mick helped Da get Whish't Daddy down for the night and they pulled the wagon inside the barn and put away the tack and feed. Barely a word had been spoken between them after the Black and Tans raced away and Mick had a million questions but he knew the time was not right to ask his Da any of them. As they moved up the hill towards the cottage, Da threw his arm over Mick's shoulder pulling him tightly towards him.

"I am sorry about the way this all worked out, Mick," he said softly. Mick began to protest that it was not Da's fault in any way but Frank stopped walking and looked gently into his son's face. "I guess this is another one of those difficult lessons, son. You won the Carlow Plate today, well at least half of it. And we got almost nothing to show for it. Lord Montgomery took the Plate explaining that it should go to the horse that led most of the way, as if that has ever had anything to do with a horse race. And then those bastard Black and Tans took all our coins, half of which were rightly yours."

Mick fished the coin the Captain had thrown at the feet of his pony and offered it to his father. Da smiled and shook his head. "No Da, the money don't mean nothing to me," Mick said quickly, not wanting his father to feel badly for what had happened. "I just want to keep riding Whishy. I know we will win plenty more down the road." He went to move on up the hill but his father stopped him again gently tugging at his arm. When Mick turned Da reached into his side pocket removing a gold medal on a blue ribbon. On the medal was an engraving of a horse's head and its inscription read *"Carlow Plate, 1920 – First Place."* Da slipped the ribbon over his son's head; the gold medal lay across Mick's chest glistening in the moonlight.

"I managed to talk Lord Montgomery into giving you the medal. Congratulations, Mickey. You ran one hell of a race. I could not be more proud of you." With that he hugged the boy very tightly and they walked up towards the cottage arm in arm, weary but not defeated.

Chapter Twenty

Barreen, County Kildare – Early September 1920

Maureen walked briskly a few paces ahead of Darcy, carefully skirting the small stream which ran heavy from the recent rains. Every few moments she stopped to check on his progress, watching as he slowly limped along the wooded trail. For the past two weeks she had dragged him from his bed, taking him away from the house, leading him through the wooded trails and along the many streams and ponds scattered in the countryside not far from the cottage. It had been very slow going the first time or two but after a week and then ten days, his legs began adjusting, growing stronger, his balance returning and his stride longer and more stable. In their first walks, they could barely cover a mile before the fatigue stopped him cold but now they could cover quite a distance and although he limped, stumbled and tripped, stopping often for deep breaths, it was obvious his recovery had come a very long way. As they approached a small waterfall where the stream banked and then cascaded along a series of boulders and large rocks, Maureen slowed and waited and then took Darcy by the hand. She carefully guided him along the side of the falls, slick with blue green moss and then much to his surprise she ducked her head and slid behind the waterfall, disappearing into a damp cave, tugging him inside behind her. He slipped into the glossy, small grotto, bending his tall frame to ease into the tiny area half the size of the kitchen in the cottage. Maureen pulled him down onto the wet, cold ground and kissed him on the lips as he moved beside her.

"How did you find this place?" he asked looking around in awe.

She laughed a tiny laugh looking at him playfully. "Surely you don't think you're the only boy I've ever walked these woods with?" she teased. He looked a little surprised but answered her with a shrug and a small laugh of his own.

"It's nice," he said softly.

"At least it affords us a little privacy," she replied. While Darcy slept over the past weeks, Maureen had walked the woods often searching for just such a place. The deep forest provided many secluded areas and hidden glens where they might be alone but surely this tiny wet den under the falls would be found by no one and the noise of the water would cover any conversation or sounds coming from the cave. She knew their time together was growing short. And there were things that needed to be said and discussed and things that needed to be done before she allowed him to leave Barreen. Da had returned from Carlow angry and scared and informed Darcy he wanted him gone within the month. Something had happened; Mick admitted as much but would provide nothing of the specifics. But she saw in her father's face and the set of his jaw that this time no one would persuade him otherwise. Even Mammy seemed to agree. Over the past few weeks, ever since she had come upon her and Darcy sitting closely together in the bed, Mammy had cooled towards her husband's brother and grew stern with her daughter. Maureen had overheard her mother asking her Da about London and did he really think they could send her there for schooling. When Maureen asked her about it she only responded that it would be in her best interests to get very far away from Barreen as soon as possible.

But Maureen did not want to go to London and she did not want Darcy to leave without her. And she did not want him to return to the Volunteers and wind up back in Mountjoy or hanging from a noose in Dublin Square. She wanted him to take her away, to leave together for America or Australia or Scotland or even to the North where no one would know them and they could start their lives again. She knew what had to be done. They were safely in a place to do it. She slipped her fingers inside his and put their two hands gently on his chest. They were half sitting and half lying on the wet stones of the cave, the rhythmic sound of the water cascading above them, the air filled with the thick scent of moss and dirt and stone.

"Do you still plan to go back to that life?" she asked softly, knowing he would say yes. "They'll be shipping me off to England just as soon as you're gone and Lord knows when we might see each other again, if ever." She sniffled softly moving her head onto his chest, sliding their entwined hands down onto his stomach.

"Aye, Maureen, you know I have little choice in the matter," he replied weakly. "They come after deserters with all the same fury as they go after the British, of that I am certain. So does it matter much whose bullet winds up in my back? Dead is dead, so I'd just as well fight for the cause as much as run away." He used his free hand to stroke her face and then let it caress her long, beautiful hair. He thought it felt like silk as his hands slid through her curls, letting his fingers twist them into circles, smelling the flowery fragrance of her head on his chest. For the first time since leaving Mountjoy he felt the longing stir in his loins and he told himself to ignore it and maybe it would go away.

"So you have no choice but to go and get killed and leave me alone in this God-forsaken land with no hope and only a future as a seamstress in the factories of Manchester or London?" He could only grunt in reply. "Is that what you want for me Darcy Walsh, to rot away in some sweat shop across the sea, alone and sad with no one to hold on to? Is that what you want?" She lifted her head slightly from his chest and turned to look into his eyes. Pain and anguish lined his face and he twisted his mouth in and out trying to find the right words to reply.

"I wish it could be different, Maureen. I truly do. But I have nothing to offer you. I am a poor man with nothing, no land, no position, no skills, why I don't even own a horse to ride away on. Besides," he said looking away from her, "I am your Da's brother. We shouldn't even be here together." His voice ended in barely a whisper, the words silenced by the rush of the falls. Maureen slid her hand underneath his shirt and let it wander across his chest and over his stomach and back up along his nipples, feeling them harden from her touch. He moaned, shifting slightly beneath her, feeling his passion rising, trying desperately to keep the heat from consuming him. She raised her head again and kissed his chin and then his cheeks and then her lips were upon his and he spread his mouth and her warm, wet tongue was inside his own, exploring his own tongue and teeth and gums and he felt her hands sliding below his waist and a meager protest uttered from him before her small, soft hand closed around his bulging manhood. The water racing over the falls seemed to grow louder and the small cave closed around them, its strong scent mingling with the flowery fragrance of her hair and skin and then somehow, in moments obscured by the sounds and scents and passions, she was suddenly naked above him, her beautiful white skin barely visible in the darkness of the grotto, her small pink breasts floating before his eyes, his hands finding their softness, caressing their pointed tips, her lips back upon his mouth, now feeling their naked skin touching, pressing, searching and finally his last unspoken protest vanished in the ecstasy of their protective cave and the majesty of her warm embrace.

They walked back towards the cottage holding hands in the gloaming. Darcy had said nary a word since leaving the cave, a look of guilt and anguish covering his face. Maureen did not care, she had expected this reaction. She felt the wetness between her legs and could not help but smile a wee smile considering the possibilities.

"A penny for your thoughts," she enquired softly.

He shook his head in dismay, stuttered a few times before finally being able to speak. "What we did was wrong, Maureen, sinful even," he exclaimed with sorrow. "It's bad enough us not being man and wife but me being your uncle to boot. That is a terrible thing I done." He shook his head over and over as if shaking it enough times might chase the memory from his mind.

"It was a beautiful thing *WE* did," Maureen countered squeezing his hands tightly. "Surely you could not have done it by yourself," she said with a small laugh. "Or at least it wouldn't be as much fun," she added poking him in the ribs gently.

He tried to smile but it was only a sad, pathetic attempt. "We can't let your Da find out, Maureen," he said, desperation seeping into his voice. "Surely he would kill me and he'd have all the right in the world."

Maureen stopped and turned towards him. She took both his hands and held them firmly raising them up between them as if in prayer. "At least we agree on that dear Darcy," she said softly looking into his eyes. "So we will make sure they never find out. For now you will have to leave and find a good, safe place to stay. Perhaps you can find our cousins out in Limerick and stay with them for a while. Is it Gerry out that way with Aunt Olive?" she asked. He nodded. "You leave in the morning and go find them, Darcy. I am sure they will take you in. Give me a month or two to see where things stand. At the right time I will come and meet you and we will get away together, we'll start our own family somewhere else, somewhere safe from all this madness."

Darcy looked at her and no words would form in his mouth. Too many thoughts swirled about in his head. He still had her scent and the tantalizing feeling of her flesh against his own fresh in his mind. He heard what she was saying about escaping out towards Clare but he was not sure if he could do that but unwilling to admit it to her. Had she mentioned starting a family? Could they do that? Where would they go? His Sinn Fein brethren would not be so willing to let him leave and the Black and Tans were out there somewhere looking for all the Volunteers. His brother's face formed in his mind and his shame and embarrassment returned in full strength. He looked first at the beauty of Maureen's lovely green eyes and then turned away, filled with disgust for his own actions, his own cowardice, his own being. What had he become? Then he realized she was still talking.

"For now, just go down towards the barns and stay there for a while. I will slip into the house and tell Mammy I went off for a walk alone. In a while come up to the cottage and say you'd been down with the horses. Mick and Da have been in town so they won't know. Don't hold your head down, Darcy Walsh," she commanded. "You're a fine man and you need to act like one. Tomorrow starts a new day and new life. Everything will be alright as long as we are together." With that she kissed him gently on the lips one more time and turned, walking down the path that would take her towards her home. Darcy watched Maureen walk away, desperately wanting to call to her to tell her things could never be the way she envisioned. Instead he stood paralyzed by his anguish and his fear. She was long gone and it was almost dark when he finally worked up the courage to make his way down towards the barns and the horses, hoping he would not have to look his brother in the eye.

Chapter Twenty One

Dublin Castle – Early September 1920

Ian MacDermott entered Sir Nevil Macready's office and was very surprised to find Lord Montgomery sitting with his boss by the fire sharing a glass of brandy. The evening had turned cool and damp, a light drizzle fell softly in the Dublin streets and an air of uncertainty hung like a cloud over the city. The Irish Republican Army under the astute leadership of Michael Collins continued making the lives of British soldiers, the RIC, the auxiliaries and the men charged with ruling the country miserable and dangerously in peril. Assassinations of officers took place in broad daylight, kidnapping of soldiers, administrators and those suspected of spying happened almost daily. Recruitment of more and more Volunteers encouraged by the Republican success allowed for more bold and daring attacks on barracks, post offices and civil offices of the British Government. Reprisals by the Royal Irish Constabulary aided by the Black and Tans ramped up mercilessly including vicious acts of violence, burning of homes, public hangings of untried suspected Volunteers, confiscation and destruction of personal property and the ongoing relentless harassment and derogatory treatment of the law abiding citizenry. The atmosphere of Dublin and most of the country wavered amongst fear, hopelessness, anxiety and distrust. The Home Rule Bill was generally considered a joke as was the independence declaration made by the Dail earlier the previous year. The average Irishman prayed for an end to the hostilities while harboring the aching desire for a free state. And those tasked to maintain British rule in

Ireland and return the country to a peaceful, productive colony of the Empire, felt a prideful duty to the Crown while secretly admitting the hopelessness and moral uncertainty of their assignment. Everyone lived nervously on edge, uncertain of what a walk in the city might precipitate or when the next attack from either the Republicans or the British might bring tragedy or destitution to their homes and family. And through all of this chaos and disruption life went on.

"Ian, please pull up a chair and join us," Sir Nevil said with a slight wave of his hand. Lord Montgomery nodded to his distant cousin but did not bother to stand or offer a handshake. MacDermott clumsily dragged a heavy chair from near the desk and tucked it into a corner by the fire, welcoming the small bit of warmth it offered. "Lord Montgomery was just telling me how disappointed he is that there is still no knowledge of the ownership of this Athy House," he said with a hint of disapproval in his voice. MacDermott stiffened at the criticism but tried to hide his embarrassment. "I would think the question well within your capabilities and resources to ascertain," Macready continued, waving his hand in a cavalier manner. "Am I missing something about this Ian? That damn horse of theirs, Wishing Daddy, or something like that, has been all over the newspapers, seems to be the biggest thing in the racing game right now, him and of course, Lord Montgomery's champion, War Lord. I would think everyone would be talking about the horse and where he came from and who owns the damn animal. What am I not understanding," he asked, looking exasperated and confused.

MacDermott stuttered and stopped and started for a few moments before collecting himself and addressing the question. A quiet fury built slowly in his heart as he considered Sir Nevil's audacity in discussing a subject with Lord Montgomery of which he was completely ignorant. Macready read dispatches from London and sent responses based on other reports he read and the man knew absolutely nothing about what actually happened outside the walls of Dublin Castle. But rank had its privileges and Ian had lived with many a superior that spoke more with their balls then with their brains and he'd cleaned up many a mess because of it. This one he would try to nip in the bud.

"It is rather extraordinary, Sir Nevil," he began, slightly nervous but determined to make his point. "A very intricate weave of deception has been put in place to hide the actual ownership of the enterprise. There exists a partnership here in Ireland, with papers registered right here in Dublin, made up of three foreign entities, two of which are corporations in Scotland and one of which is yet another partnership in America. When looking further into the foreign entities, one learns that they are also owned by foreign organizations in far off places including Africa and in the Far East. Almost all of these corporations, partnerships and companies register a Postal Box as their address and the few that don't have proven to exist only in theory," he said, warming to the subject. "I have sent enquiries to personal acquaintances in both Scotland and the United States requesting additional information but in all cases any further knowledge is protected by laws in those countries and so we gain no further information from these contacts. Whoever set up this masterful and impenetrable web of dead ends knows considerable about corporate and international law. It certainly was nothing done by a horse trainer in a bog outside of Dublin." He smiled slightly at his small joke, hoping his explanation proved sufficient. But it did not.

"Thank you, MacDermott," Lord Montgomery replied irritably. Ian felt terribly abused by the use of his family name. Had they not agreed to a first name basis when he visited Montgomery Castle? What happened to Ian and Andrew? Hadn't my Lord suggested they move forward as friends? And now it was only MacDermott? Ian hoped the flush he felt rising in his face was not apparent as Montgomery continued. "My own people researched the equity concealment months ago and I knew you would find nothing more if my solicitors were stifled in their efforts." Ian thought perhaps there was an insult hiding somewhere in that statement but he let it go. "My expectation was that you would use the other tools at your disposal. Tools not available to someone in my position," he said with pointed intent. MacDermott began replying but Sir Nevil cut him off.

"You know the kinds of things to which my Lord alludes," Macready added, pointing towards the obvious. "With our contacts on the ground, as they say, one would think you'd have cracked this nut in little more than a few days. I am sure there is more than one man of qualified interrogation skills reporting through the ranks to your office, Ian. We need to be certain we are exploring all avenues possible." Now Ian was bristling with indignation at the suggestion that he may be derelict in his duties. And here was Macready, the bastard, suggesting they use "qualified interrogation skills," surely a euphemism for the kind of thing he had warned Ian against many times in the past.

"We continue to scour the countryside in an effort to solve this riddle," the Scot replied evenly, hoping his temper would hold. "It is all together possible that no one is in a position to know the true ownership of Athy House other than the owners themselves, whoever they may prove to be." He looked from his boss to Lord Montgomery and found both of them looking at him as one would look at an odd insect trying to determine its origin.

"Certainly someone in this Godforsaken country knows their little secret," Lord Montgomery said with a wry smile. "I think perhaps you have not looked under the appropriate rock or scoured as you say, the right barrel of rotten apples." He looked at Sir Nevil hoping for translation.

"Ian, I think Lord Montgomery is exactly right. Have we looked into all the brothels and bars in the area to see if perhaps this Walsh character let the secret slip to a whore or a barman after a few too many? Have we insisted strongly enough with his employees? If I recall correctly we arrested one of them for Republican activities and another family member had some involvement in all that as well. How about the newspapers, have we uncovered what they may know? And these people tell everything to their local priests and teachers so we surely should be checking in with the schools and rectories in the vicinity of Athy House."

"Yes, duly noted, Sir Nevil," Ian replied icily, furious at the implication he did not know his job. Surely they had tried to beat the information from Brian Grant but the little jockey proved impossible to crack. Even a bullet hole through his cheek did nothing to make the man talk. He was opposed to the release of Darcy Walsh and the other hunger strikers from the beginning and he planned further scrutiny of that man very soon. The newspapers had been of no help and the local riff-raff across Kildare County and much of Dublin were interrogated thoroughly but no one knew a damn thing about Athy House. Walsh drank very little and never went with whores, those things proving to be dead ends. He had to admit to never considering schools or churches and made a mental note to address that shortcoming very quickly.

"Lord Montgomery is fairly confident he can return our efforts with a favor of his own," Sir Nevil interjected, pouring both himself and Montgomery another glass of sherry. He did not offer any to Ian. "He is gathering information on a cell of Volunteers out in Clare and hopes to be able to provide us with some names in short order. Certainly we will want to be in a position of quid pro quo for his fine efforts," Macready added.

Ian nodded. His exasperation knew no bounds. It had been his idea to have Lord Montgomery look into Republican activity in the racing game and out west and now it was presented to him as if Montgomery had come forth with the information on his own. And this coming from his own flesh and blood. Feeling taken aback and insecure, Ian responded with a great deal of information, blabbering out things he would have normally kept to himself far longer.

"It's not just the racing game we are learning, my Lord," he began. "My men have infiltrated the footballers and a few of the larger circus shows. The footballers are rotten with Volunteers. We have had our eyes on Croke Park for a while now and we believe men are being recruited, guns are being distributed and plans being laid for more assassinations throughout Dublin and some in other cities as well. Collins has his hand prints all over this. The circus shows are lower key and we have shut down most of them anyway. But the racing game and footballers provide prime suspects at this point. Any help Lord Montgomery can provide will of course be greatly appreciated. And certainly we will obtain the identity of the owners of Athy House with speed and diligence." He looked from one man to the other, much like a child looking to his parents for approval or compliment. Neither came.

"That will be all, Ian," Macready said in a dismissive tone. "We will review the resource allocations and the incident responses in the morning. Thank you." Ian looked again from one to the other, glancing longingly at their glasses of sherry and then he stood up slowly and nodded. He raced from the room in a furious rage and as he barged into the hallway, he slammed into John Harrington standing just outside the door.

"Get out of my way," he said angrily to the Assistant Secretary of State. He pushed past him with a shove and hurried down the hall. Harrington righted himself, returning his attention to the conversation on the other side of the door.

Hours later in a dimly lit inn on the edge of town the Commander of the Kildare Brigade of the Republican Army met with his Dublin contact. The thin man wore his customary black suit and looked tired and drawn. Riordan drank from a dark pint of lager but the Dubliner sipped a strong cup of tea with two big spoonfuls of sugar.

"I had warned you about transacting business at the races but still you went ahead. How many men did we lose down in Punchestown," he asked softly.

"Seven in total," Riordan replied with a shrug. "We had little choice. With the barracks raid in Naas planned for the following week we needed the guns distributed in time for the boys to learn to use them. I didn't want any of them shooting off their own damn foot."

The Dubliner shook his head slowly. He knew the goals of Dublin were filling rapidly with young men and he knew most of those boys had a good chance of ending up swinging from a rope. The violence in the streets and surrounding villages frightened him daily. He wondered if it was all worthwhile. "So you continue to take the fight to the British and where does it all end?" he asked in an exasperated voice.

Riordan shrugged. "It ends when the British get the hell off our land and go home. It ends when we are free," he added.

"And if they leave us alone but stay up in the North, is Ireland still free?" the thin man asked softly, placing his fingers beneath his chin.

The Commander shrugged again, this time a shadow of uncertainty covered his face. "The North is not my problem, John," he said evenly. "Surely I'd like to see all of Ireland as one and the whole damn country free. But if partition means the English get the hell out of the rest of Ireland, leave my home down in Kilkenny alone and I don't have to pay a tax on my crops to the Crown I despise, then I can live with it."

"They'll be plenty a Republican that thinks otherwise, I am afraid," John replied. "And if there are those that think the fighting has to go on 'til all of Ireland is free then we'll be fighting each other soon enough and what the hell's the difference if you die from a British bullet or from one of our own?" The Dubliner ran his hands through his hair. Covering his face he shook his head again in dismay. "Forget I asked the question," he said in disgust. "More importantly, remember what I said about the racing matches and especially the Curragh. With the St. Leger coming up in two weeks the place will be crawling with Auxiliary and a fair number of spies. Don't fall into the same trap again. And we've recently learned the British are concentrating a good number of their resources inside the Gaelic Association and the footballer teams. You'd be smart to keep your boys away from the stadiums and the pitches around Dublin and the surrounding counties. Croke Park is surely a target for them. Why, I heard two companies of Black and Tans tore up half the seating under some feigned search for weapons. So you're forewarned Commander." He slipped another small bag of coins across the table and the soldier whisked it away quickly. "Enough in there to feed the lads and buy some shoes and boots and a coat or two, winter is on the way," he said standing quickly. "The other letter I left with you last time, I trust it was delivered?" Riordan nodded twice. "No reply?"

"Not yet," he answered, "but as I told you, Walsh don't care for the cause all that much. Why should he? With that nice farm and all those horses I might not care either." The Dubliner nodded in understanding and then slipped quietly away through a rear door.

Father Dunn soaked up the rest of the brown gravy with a large chunk of bread stuffing it in his mouth with relish. The gravy dripped slowly down his stubbly chin and he wiped it away with the back of his hand, staining his dark cassock in the process. He slurped down a large swallow of wine and let out a loud belch in satisfaction. The roast had been excellent, maybe a bit on the rare side but that was how he liked it and the roasted potatoes were soft and buttery. The wine was an excellent burgundy given to him by a parishioner who had confessed a particularly unsavory sin and Dunn was certain the woman in question wanted to assure the sin would stay within the confines of the confessional. The priest considered the gift an absolutely unnecessary one as he normally maintained the confidentiality of the confessional box but still, it was appreciated, assuring a certain level of silence on his part. He rang for the cook, Mrs. Fitzsimmons, and she quickly cleared his plate and then brought him tea and a small sweet scone she had baked earlier in the day. He went to the press and found a small bottle of whiskey and poured himself a small dram, a habit he enjoyed at the end of a good meal. He was surprised to here a loud knock on the front door and a moment later Mrs. Fitzsimmons poked her head into the dinning room.

"Sorry to bother you, Father. There is a man asking to see you." She sounded uneasy as she told him of the visitor and looked a bit frightened. "Actually he's not asking, he's demanding. Soldier he is, one of them Black and Tans, an officer I think." She closed the door and the priest heard her scurry back to the kitchen. He swallowed the remainder of the whiskey and then made for the parlor at the front of the house. He assumed the soldier had some interest in the mass schedule or perhaps wanted confession, he only wished they would come at a more respectable hour. He swept into the parlor but halted abruptly taking in the size of the man waiting for him and the soldier's hideous affliction. He was easily the biggest man the priest had ever seen and the gaping, leaking hole in place of his right eye sent shudders down Dunn's spine.

"Yes," he asked meekly, "you wanted to see me?" He inched his way behind the large desk occupying the middle of the room, wanting to put a barrier between himself and this frightening man.

Butterfield looked at him curiously for a few moments, staring with his one good eye. The priest was a sloppy excuse for a man with a filthy frock, unkempt hair and with the smell of booze wafting in his wake. The soldier could see the fear in his small, beady eyes. "Have you no manners, priest?" he asked in a scornful voice. "You do not offer me a drink or a spot of tea? I am an officer of his Majesty's government, a visitor to your home and you show me no courtesy?" He enjoyed watching the priest squirm as he waited for a reply. Dunn slipped around the desk avoiding Butterfield as much as possible and called out to Mrs. Fitzsimmons, asking her to bring tea and drink for his visitor. He slinked back behind the desk and tried smiling at Butterfield but the smile disintegrated into a worrisome frown. Butterfield looked about the room and then dragged a large chair over by the desk. He sat down abruptly, grunting as his massive frame filled the seat. He waited silently staring at the priest until the cook arrived with tea and a bottle of brandy. She had a glass in her hand and made to pour out a measure but Butterfield yanked it from her grip and drank greedily from the bottle. Mrs. Fitzsimmons all but ran from the room. When he had drunk his fill of the brandy, the soldier sipped his tea, settling his one good eye on Dunn.

"So tell me priest," he started in a bating tone, "have you a good little bunch of Catholics here in your parish?" The priest nodded in reply, surprised by the question. "And do they do all the little things your fish eating faith requires?" Father Dunn looked at him quizzically, unsure of his meaning. Butterfield snorted. 'You know what I mean, priest. What do you call them, sacraments, is that the word? I been long away from any kind of church but even a long lost Lutheran like myself knows something about those things." He took another long swig from the bottle, eyeing the priest some more.

"Yes, uhm, yes, my parishioners all take the sacraments regularly," Dunn sputtered in reply quite sure he had no idea what the man was talking about. "We baptize all the wee ones and communion is given daily, the older ones we confirm and most we someday marry," he added trying to be helpful. Butterfield nodded.

"You forgot one at least," he said directly. The priest began to speak but the soldier interrupted. "Do you hear all their confessions priest?" he asked with a sneer. "Do you listen to their pathetic little sins, their common thievery and lies and the occasional fornication, do you, Father?" he asked, lacing the last word with sarcasm. Dunn nodded, managing to reply in the affirmative. He waited for the next question, wondering if perhaps someone had learned of the excellent bottle of burgundy and the sin which had brought it to his table. Butterfield continued.

"I am wondering if it might be considered a sin to tell lies about the things you own or the things other people own," he mused with his one eye on Reverend Dunn. Still Dunn was mystified by the statement. "You know it's been all but illegal for years for your peasants to own much more than the tiniest parcel of property and surely they can not have their own business. You do know that, don't you priest?" he asked.

"Many of those laws have been changing, Captain Butterfield. It is Butterfield, am I correct," Dunn added, nearly certain he had heard the name from several parishioners over the past months. The stories surrounding his name were never less than frightening and usually horrible to recall. The soldier nodded, offering a half smile.

"So your peasants have told you about me, have they, priest?" he said with a short laugh. "Good, then you know I am not to be trifled with," he added. "I don't give a damn what laws have changed and what laws have not. I want to know the name of the man or men that own this horse stable in your town, this Athy House. Can you tell me that, kind Father?" he said, sarcasm lacing his words. Dunn instantly recognized the name Athy House and it took him only a moment longer to recall the confession of a man named Walsh regarding the deception in place to hide his ownership of the stable. He considered blurting out this information to the frightening soldier but something told him to wait. He shook his head from side to side.

"Of course I have heard of this Athy House," he replied carefully, "but why would the ownership of a horse stable be of any interest to me or to the Church?" He hoped he sounded more convincing then he felt. Butterfield's one eye bore down on him like a laser. "The trainer is one of our parishioners, a man named Walsh, Frank Walsh. Perhaps you should be talking to him, Captain. Surely he would know far more than me about such things."

Butterfield took another long swallow emptying the bottle; he let it fall to the floor with a crash. Broken glass scattered across the wooden floor. He stood and Dunn could hear some of the glass crushing beneath his feet. The soldier leaned over the desk breathing his hot, brandy soaked breath into the petrified man's face. "If I find you been lying to me priest, I will come back and kill you. Do you know I will, Father? I'll rip your balls from your ass and stick them down your throat and watch you choke on your own nuts. Do I make myself clear?" The priest was shaking uncontrollably now but he was able to keep his hands and arms hidden behind his back as he nodded several times, convincing Butterfield it was time to leave. When the big soldier got to the parlor entrance Dunn spoke in a whisper and Butterfield turned to listen.

"I'll try to find out about Athy House mark my words," he said, "but I'd expect there might be something in it for the church if we can be of assistance," he said slyly, hoping not to overplay his hand. Butterfield looked at him for a few minutes and then nodded.

"I am sure we could come to some accommodation," he replied grudgingly.

The priest summoned all the small courage he possessed, saying the next words in hope they would not incite Butterfield's terrible wrath. "Perhaps you could send your superior in a few weeks. Hopefully then we can have a chat, just he and I. Would that be alright?"

Butterfield stared long and hard through his one working eye. He considered tearing the man's arm off and beating him with it but it would not do to harm a parish priest in this God forsaken land. And he had to admit, he appreciated the priest's guile. What would it matter if he sent MacDermott to learn the truth about the ownership of Athy House rather than find it out himself? They'd have what they needed to keep Lord Montgomery happy and hopefully he would share more information regarding the growing presence of the enemy. That would work just fine. Butterfield nodded to the priest one more time and then stormed quickly from the house, slamming the front door in his wake. Father Dunn left the parlor instantly, returning to the press in the dining room and poured himself a very large glass of whiskey. It took him thirty minutes to stop shaking.

Chapter Twenty-Two

The Curragh, Naas - Mid-September 1920

It was the grandest race course in all of Ireland and the stately pageantry and spectacle were only surpassed by the riotous excitement of the huge crowds. Mick had grown slightly accustomed to the circus atmosphere and the slew of carnival tents, vendors and hawkers of every kind seen in Punchestown and Carlow but the grandeur of The Curragh - the rolling grassy surface, the miles of white fence around the course, the huge clubhouse and grandstand and flower laden grounds far surpassed anything his imagination might conjure. The backstretch housed more barns and stalls and horses than he thought could be held in all of Ireland. The hustle and bustle of activity had steadily grown from their early arrival shortly after dawn throughout the cool morning and peaking just before the first race would begin. Horses and ponies moved back and forth from stable to the course snorting and whinnying with abandon, hot walkers cooled down those finished with their exercise or those testing the surface of the course. Harried grooms raced about carrying buckets of water to dump on their charges or filled their time brushing, washing and primping with care. Trainers carefully assessed their horse's performance, checking their legs and hooves and eyes and teeth, searching for any imperfection, anything that might cause concern while running or affect their attitude when placed in the starting gate. Nervous jockeys fiddled here and there with their saddles, synching the straps under their great beasts, first looser than tighter than looser again, looking for that perfect fit. They adjusted bits and bridles and saddle cloths and blinkers until fully confident their mount would run his best race. For today was not just any day at the Curragh, not just another day at the races. Today would be the last of the season's great contests, the last of the classics that would be discussed and dissected and revered for many years to come. It was the third leg of the triumvirate in Irish racing that included the Two Thousand Guineas, the Irish Derby and today's race, the St. Leger. Horses that won these races went down in history as the greatest of their time; their performances recalled in great detail and marveled at by knowledgeable punters from one end of the country to the other. Wagering would hit a total only matched by the most important football contests or the Derby held earlier in the year. The crowd was the biggest Mick had ever seen and the din of shouting hawkers, cursing gamblers, anxious bookies, and excited visitors blended with the loud bands and the booming of the loud speaker announcing races, odds, pole positions and colors, creating a cacophony of sound rolling across the grounds. Mick had been out walking the course to get a feel for the grass surface and returned to their stable confident and pleased.

"It's firm and fast Da," he reported. Rain earlier in the week had been a concern but a few days of sunshine and cool temperatures combined with the morning's close cropping, left the track hard but not brittle or dry. "Whishy likes it a little softer but I think he will be fine with the way it feels and it will make for a good run." Da was sitting on a bale of hay reviewing the racing form and making calculations in his head while taking notes with a pencil as short as his little finger. He nodded, looking up at his son.

"Good, Mick," he replied with a smile. "I been to the stewards and again we'll be riding with the same weight as War Lord. I argued that his win in the Derby should add a few pounds but the head man just refused to listen.

"So we'll have our work cut out for us again. It looks like Montgomery Castle will employ the same strategy but this time they have a pacesetter named Ghost Trail. Strong Bow will try to box you again and you know what you're up against with War Lord." Mick nodded but he did not say anything. Da looked at him carefully, sensing some question or concern. "You alright, son?" he asked.

Mick looked at him quizzically. "I have an idea," he offered cautiously. He waited for his Da to nod and then continued. "I know we have been trying to avoid the blocking and then sit a few lengths behind the pace setter and try to duel War Lord down the stretch," he started carefully. He thought it very bold to question the strategy of a man who knew horses and racing as well as his father but he knew Whish't Daddy better than anyone and he had a hunch. "I want to go right to the lead and take them by surprise and go wire to wire for the win!" He was standing next to the big horse and patting him on the cheek with a loving tenderness Da found endearing. He let the boy's words sink in and then shook his head around a few times, first up and down, then sideways and then he just looked up at the boy and smiled.

"You know this is a long race, Mick?" he questioned. "The longest Whish't Daddy will have run. I am concerned he'll get gassed coming down the stretch and finish out of the money all together. War Lord has been formidable for over two years and Quiney Moran is very experienced at picking his spots. I have my doubts on that strategy son." He saw Mick's face fold into a disappointed frown and the boy's mouth opened slightly but whatever he was going to say he decided against. Da stood up and slipped his arm around his son's shoulders. "I said I have my doubts, Mick. But you are the one that has trained this horse and you are the one that will ride him and you are the one that will win or lose with him. So I will leave the strategy up to you. It's chancy, but that's why they run the race." He ruffled Mick's blond hair and then told him to get dressed. The race would start in an hour. Da was going to look around and Mick knew he was worried about the Black and Tans, remembering the purse of coins they filched after the race in Carlow. Da told him he'd leave the purse with the stewards if they won and claim it another day when he knew things would be safe and secure. Still he looked worried. Mick watched him go and hoped Da was not angry with his idea.

Lord Montgomery approached Frank Walsh as he passed by the grandstand and moved towards the finish line. Montgomery was decked out in a knee length sporting jacket, wore an ascot around his neck and had on boots worth six months of Frank's income.

"A word, Mr. Walsh?" he requested. Frank shook his hand and they moved slowly together along the stands full of people. "Your horse looks very good," he began, "you must be very confident." It was more of a statement than a question but Frank nodded.

"Yes, I am always confident in Whish't Daddy. He is an extraordinary horse. But I know your horse is every bit as good my Lord, so we never get too cocky." Walsh looked at the other man and could see some doubt moving across his face.

"Not sure," Montgomery replied with a shake of his head. "War Lord seems a little cranky today. Perhaps a cold or a bad night's sleep or a problem with the leg, he feels slightly warm around the shin on his right side." Da nodded, wondering why his adversary was sharing this information. "I thought to maybe scratch him but it seems such a shame to disappoint the crowd," he said looking up into the overflowing stands.

Frank looked at him with some surprise. "Surely if the horse is ill he should not run. Your first responsibility is to the horse, not the crowd." Frank could not believe he had just spoken such words to a member of the House of Lords but his devotion to the equestrian kingdom ran deep in his veins.

Montgomery shrugged. Clearly he did not consider Frank Walsh to have a valid opinion regarding where his responsibility lay but he took a different tact. "Perhaps an agreement to split the purse?" He asked. "Surely we know one of these two horses will win the race. Should we have an agreement I will tell Moran not to push War Lord and your boy can cruise home and into the winner's circle. This way we both finish ahead of the game," he added with a smile.

Da shook his head from side to side. "I will not be a party to any such bargain, Lord Montgomery," he said. "First of all it is not fair to the people betting on the race, clearly if he is not ready than you should scratch. Besides, why would I agree to split the purse if your horse may be sick or injured? It is not at all to my advantage."

Montgomery stopped and turned, looking Frank directly in the face. "I said he *may* be sick or injured, nothing is definite. I was just trying to ease the load for us both." He stared at Frank for a moment longer and then changed tact again. "How about we race for the horses, than?" he asked with a face more solemn than death. "If War Lord prevails, your horse is mine. If Whish't Daddy wins than you take War Lord back home with you to Barreen. An interesting and exciting wager, I think. What do you say?" Frank looked at the man like he was crazy. He recalled with some trepidation, Michael Cleary's warning that Montgomery would do whatever necessary to get what he wanted, Surely such a wager would prove somehow very costly.

"No, no thank you. I do not accept the wager and do not know what game you are playing at, my Lord. First you say your horse is ill, then you want to make a deal to split the purse and now you want to wager for the horses? I do not understand. I do know we will run the best race we can and give the customers a good and honest show. I do hope you will do the same." With that he turned and walked away quickly leaving Montgomery smirking in his wake.

The bugle sounded and Mick felt the acid in his stomach and the clenching of his gut. It was not fear. It was anxiousness and the desire to have the race underway. He moved Whish't Daddy down the backstretch and through the small path connecting them to the main course. He could feel the eyes of the other trainers, jockeys and grooms watching their procession and he heard a mixture of comments of praise with some jealous claims of the horse being overrated. But the attention was on him and his horse and would be for the rest of the day. When they entered the small stretch of course where the patrons lined to view the next contestants, the crowd exploded with applause. Mick had not been privy to most of the newspaper coverage over the past two weeks but he knew since the dead heat in Gowran Park the racing world was smitten by this tremendous, beautiful, powerful horse and its young rider and embraced the unexpected rivalry with the far more celebrated War Lord. Da told him the papers in Dublin were full of pictures and stories about Whish't Daddy and retold in detail the two races he had run. Some claimed the race in Carlow to be one for the ages and other writers had hinted that Whishy would prove far superior to the outstanding War Lord and raved about the coming battle at the Curragh. In the recent weeks, walking through the small village of Barreen running errands with his Da, Mick heard time and again words of encouragement from men in the streets and the ones working in the shops. "Go get 'em, Mick," they would say, "you and Whish't Daddy are going to leave him choking in your wake!" One old man told him he was the pride of the county and his horse the finest animal in the land. Da reminded him over and over that it had just been two races and warned him of overconfidence in the St. Leger but Mick did not feel over confident. He just knew his horse was a born champion and no other horse would ever deny him.

But the explosion of cheering and applause still caught the young man off guard. He looked up into the sea of wild, screaming fans and watched in awe as they waved small pieces of cloth matching the crimson and gold colors of Athy House. He had never seen so many people before and to have them all screaming and yelling for him and his horse was incredible. He leaned over his mount whispering in his ear, "They love you, Whishy. They know you're going to win and they want you to know it too." He patted his horse gently on the neck and Whishy turned his head a bit to let Mick know he agreed. They galloped slowly back and forth along the grandstand and then made their way across the course to where the gate waited for loading. Da was down by the gate with one of the grooms and they took the bridle moving Whish't Daddy closer to load. They were in the third position and Mick felt confident of a clean start. Da patted him on the leg.

"Be careful, son," he said softly. "They may be up to some trickery. I am really not sure. But keep your eyes open and as always Mick, your safety comes first." He patted him again and then slipped away towards the stands. War Lord loaded two horses later and in another moment they were ready to go. The gates flew open and the race was on.

Mick had but a split second to make his decision and he went with his gut. Sliding low over Whish't Daddy's neck he clucked into his ear twice and prodded the big horse gently with a squeeze of his knees. The horse seemed to explode beneath him and with three or four furious strides past the other horses they were out in the clear, nothing but race course ahead and the sound of hooves fading in the rear. Mick felt the power and the rhythm and the strength beneath him and he let himself ease into the same rhythm, rocking gently with Whishy's lengthening strides, feeling the splendid and peaceful connection to this beautiful beast he'd first felt riding him through the leafy glens and along the rocky trails of Kildare. Although he heard the roaring cheers from the grandstand, they sounded far away and muffled, almost as if he were dreaming. He was aware of the horses behind them, heard their snorting and the pounding of their hooves, heard the cajoling of their jockeys and the occasional crack of the crop across a horse's flank. He smelled the earthy grass and the pleasant scent of his horse and even his own sweat, rolling down from beneath his arms. But it all seemed surreal. He felt disconnected from the race, from the crowd, from the gentle breeze blowing across the Irish afternoon and all he did feel was the sheer wonder of the beautiful animal running, gliding, flying beneath him. Exhilaration filled his mind and body and he held the reins loosely in his hands intertwined with the horse's rough mane as he looked out from his goggles at the huge swatches of track disappearing behind them and the rapidly passing white fences and posts indicating their progress over the course. Later Da would tell him that at one point they had opened a lead nearing ten lengths and as they turned towards the grandstand and down the stretch to make for the wire it looked for all watching that Whish't Daddy would win going away. But then something frightening happened. Mick was unsure of what or why or how but he felt the magical horse beneath him begin to slow, he felt the strides shorten and the pace falter and he begged his friend for more, urging him on, pleading with him to get to the finish. He recalled his father's warning that the race would be long and that Whishy might run out of speed if he ran full out the entire race. Now he could here the crowd's roar building and he could feel the approach of another horse and he need not peak behind him to know it was War Lord closing the gap in great, huge strides of his own. They were no more than two furlongs away from the wire when out of the corner of his eye Mick saw the big, black horse gaining and a moment later they were abreast, moving stride for stride, length for length, towards the finish line. Later on Mick would tell his Da in a tone of wonderment and disbelief of those final frantic moments of pure magic.

"I swear Da, he just slowed down to take a look at War Lord. He had plenty left, I tell you. He just wanted to look that big black boy right in the eye. And that's what he did, Da, he looked him right in the eye," Mick exclaimed with the unmitigated joy of a child. Continuing, he said, "he turned his beautiful head towards War Lord and when the other horse looked back, Whishy looked him dead in the eye and I swear I heard that other horse whine. And then Whishy put his head down and dug for that wire with all he had left and I knew we were going to win, I knew it wouldn't even be close." And it wasn't. Whish't Daddy's last strides would become legend in the Curragh and the people who witnessed his finish would never forget what they had seen. One man claimed the horse's feet never touched the ground over the last furlong and another claimed the horse had leaped the least thirty feet and could have cleared a ten foot hedge in the process. The noise from the crowd was ear splitting. The Winner's Circle was packed with well wishers and back slappers and the Stewards were beaming with pride as if they had run the race themselves. They slipped a wreath of flowers over Whish't Daddy's head and Mick took him up and down the grandstand a few more times to the hysterical cheers of the wild crowd. When finally he slipped down from the saddle Da was waiting and he hugged his son with all his strength, nearly crushing him in his loving embrace.

"You did it Mick," he said with tears racing down his cheeks. "You knew what you wanted to do and you did it, son. You ran a tremendous race, a race to be remembered for all time. I can't tell you how proud I am of you boy, that was something special to behold." They held onto their embrace for a very long moment and then Mick stepped away smiling brightly for his father.

"I didn't do much Da," he said with a laugh. "I just let him run. And there is no other horse in the land that can run like Whishy. I told you he'd be a champion. I told you he was going to win." He hugged his father again and then turned back to his horse and laid his forehead on top of Whishy's long nose. They remained like that for a long time and when they finally separated, tears of joy ran down the young man's face. He led the winner back through the small path and along the backstretch to the loud cheers of all the grooms and jockeys and trainers looking on in awe.

Chapter Twenty-Three

Across Ireland – October 1920

The hand gun exploded loudly and Darcy felt the strong kick causing him to recoil although he had been expecting the reaction. Commander Riordan gave him a disgusted look and when the man next to Darcy fired towards the target he held his hand and arm steadier, drawing a nod of approval from the leader. They had been at the pistol practice most of the morning as they had for most of the last ten days. Twelve Volunteers formed their unit and they came to calling themselves the Apostles. The Commander drilled them daily in target practice, hand to hand combat, climbing ladders and walls and jumping from lofty perches to the hard ground below. Riordan was relentless in his drilling, demanding accuracy, awareness, preparation and stealth. Often the target would move a moment before Darcy fired and the Commander would yell at him to adjust more quickly. The in-close fighting always included a dull knife or a sharp stick which he taught them to thrust and jerk and slice accurately for the most effective manner of killing. Ladders were pushed away from their position in the middle of a climb necessitating a quick and acrobatic leap to safety. Landings required a difficult silence and a neat, soft roll absorbing the shock. They drilled from morning to night and when they weren't drilling they were cleaning weapons, sharpening knives or studying maps indicating the terrain, streets and buildings in all of downtown Dublin. The Commander spoke no details of their mission, saying only that when the time came, he was damn sure the Apostles would be ready. Darcy did not know the exact location of their training camp, only that they'd all been piled in a covered wagon near the hideout in Naas and driven for several hours over hill and dale, moving again in the dark of night to a barracks in the middle of a forest somewhere in the countryside. He fired the pistol several more times trying for a steadier hand and was glad when Riordan told them all to break for lunch. He took a plateful of the watery stew and a chunk of stale bread, making his way down to the rocks running alongside a small stream. He found a comfortable spot to eat.

Nearly six weeks had past since he walked alongside another stream with beautiful Maureen. As it always did now, thinking of her brought a terrible shame to his mind and an inconsolable sense of loss to his heart. He was ashamed of what he had done with her, knowing deep in his bones that it had been a terrible sin, an incestuous deed he could never undo and his shame was multiplied by the cowardly way in which he had left her. He did as instructed, hiding down by the barn on that fateful day weeks ago, taking care to avoid his brother when Frank and Mick returned from town. He hid under a pile of smelly blankets listening to his brother and his nephew ready the horses for the coming night. He heard fresh water being poured and the horses being brushed and the easy exchange between father and son as they went about their chores. He was greatly relieved when they closed the barn door, knowing they'd be moving up towards the cottage for the night. He considered following them, thought about walking into their home and looking at his brother's face and at his sister-in-law's face and at the beautiful woman he had deflowered only hours earlier. He knew he could never do it. He knew the shame and guilt and remorse would betray him and his brother and his wife would know the terrible thing he had done and he would be vilified in their hearts forever. He could never bring himself to face them again. He thought of finding a way to tell Maureen of his decision, possibly slipping into the cottage late at night and leaving her a note or waking her to tell her of his plans. But he could not take the chance of being caught so he just burrowed deeper under the horse blankets trying to sleep, waiting for the dead of night and the chance to run away, to escape from his brother's glaring indictment and the sheer hatred that would follow. He tried freeing his mind from thoughts of

Maureen but their time together beneath the waterfall returned over and over, renewing both his longing and his shame. He thought of her waking to find him gone but knew he could do nothing to change that. They could never be together, they could never have a family, and they could never see each other again. So in some ways he felt he was doing what was best. He was going away, disappearing and if there truly was a God in Heaven, than he would be killed by the British or by the Black and Tans and receive the terrible things he deserved, both in this life and beyond.

Sometime in the night he awoke from a difficult sleep and slipped from beneath the blankets and out of the barn and ran quietly down the road leading away from the family cottage and the woman he would always love. He took the fork down by the glen leading to Naas where he knew the Republican barracks was hidden on the edge of town. It took him most of two nights to get there and he was careful to stay hidden during the day, hiding from both those he hated and those he loved. He was received in the barracks coolly, knowing some amount of suspicion always clung to those who'd been away for a while, whether away in prison as he had been, or returning from the unknown which often could be worse. It took weeks to work his way back into the trust of the other men and when Commander Riordan told them he was looking for volunteers to accept a very difficult and dangerous mission, Darcy's hand was the first in the air. The next day they loaded into the truck and now, almost two weeks later he hoped he had done the right thing. They were being taught to kill, they all knew that. Who they would kill no one could say, the British of course they all assumed. But could he do it, he wondered? Could he fire a gun at a man's heart and shoot him dead? Could he thrust a knife inside another's chest and rip him apart, watching him bleed out and die? Or would he run away scared and cowardly, just as he had done to his beautiful Maureen? He did not know how he might act and he was terribly frightened to find out.

Maureen slipped from the cottage and walked briskly away towards the forest. She knew she would be sick again, at least the third time in the week, and she wanted to hide any signs of illness from her mother. Mammy had already started asking questions about her lack of appetite and her sudden need for napping in the middle of the day. Her eyes seemed to bore holes through Maureen's belly when she sat sipping tea by the hearth at night. Maureen could not help but feel Mammy knew everything. She knew about the tiny baby growing inside her daughter's womb and she knew how it got there and who was responsible for the deed. Their conversations were short and tense, Maureen quick to assure her nothing was amiss, that she felt fine, had nothing on her mind other than completing her chores and doing some shopping in town. Mammy often brought up Darcy's sudden disappearance, questioning Maureen on why he left without saying good-bye and where he may possibly have gone. Maureen told her mother she knew nothing of his whereabouts or why he left making light of his absence, speculating he would return any day with a good tale to share on where he'd been. Mammy didn't believe any of it, Maureen knew.

She stooped behind a big tree and threw up the small amount of food she'd been able to swallow for breakfast. A spoonful of eggs and a bite or two of bread were all she'd managed to get down and she wondered again how long this morning sickness would last. She would be unable to hide it from Mammy too much longer and in another six weeks she'd begin to show, a small bump surely all the confirmation her mother would need. But she did not plan to be around the cottage or Barreen or maybe not even in Ireland if things worked according to plan. She was certain Darcy would come back. He loved her, she knew that. Surely he had had just been too scared about what they had done to return to the cottage, too frightened of what he might say to his brother or to his brother's wife. And maybe he thought it best to get away sooner rather than later, to make his way out to their cousin's place in Clare and await word from Maureen. Perhaps a letter would arrive any day now and advise her of his plans and how they should proceed and where she should meet him. She sat on a fallen log and wiped her mouth with a small cloth she kept in her sleeve. She pinched her cheeks hoping to return some color and let her mind wander to the day when she would be with him again and they would be sailing across the ocean to a new life in America. She had decided it should be America. England and

Scotland were too close and she did not want anyone chasing after her and bringing her back. Australia was so far away she thought the journey might be far too much for the wee child growing inside of her. But America would be manageable. She and Darcy would go to the New World and start a new life and no one would ever know of their relation and their child would not be looked upon as some freak of nature. In America they would be free to live the life she dreamed of, to be in love together and to have a big family and to never be afraid of the secret that they shared. She rubbed her hands across her belly as she found herself doing many times throughout the day wondering if the child would be a boy or a girl. She was partial to a boy, hoping he would be tall and handsome like his Da but she would take whatever the Good Lord felt appropriate and she would be glad either way. The thought of leaving Barreen made her a little sad. She would miss her sisters but mostly she would miss Mickey. He was growing so rapidly from a boy to a man she could barely keep it straight. In the beginning of the year he seemed a child. But now, as a successful trainer and jockey, her father's equal in some ways, he seemed to grow into manhood over one summer. She hoped it would not change him too much. Mick had always been bright and joyful and fun. Now she saw a more serious side, a little more like her Da, but of course the responsibility and fame accompanying his success with Whish't Daddy was sure to have some affect. He was in all the papers after the tremendous race at the Curragh, everyone in town knew his name and called after him in the streets. She was so proud of her little brother and happy for him and Da, even if Da seemed to care too damn much about the horses. In reality she would miss them all, even Mammy and the cottage and the barn and the horses just a wee bit. She wiped a tiny tear from the corner of her eye and took a deep breath, readying herself to return home. There was mending to be done. Hopefully she'd be able to manage a bit of the soup Mammy had cooking on the hearth. And soon she'd hear from Darcy, of that she was certain. She smiled at the thought of seeing him again.

After the St. Leger Whish't Daddy ran three more races. At the end of September he crushed the field in Tipperary winning by nine lengths and Mick told his Da that the horse had barely broken a sweat. They went west to Galway in early October picking up another easy win in the Galway Cup running against a weak field. After the race, Da purchased a chestnut filly that had run second to Whish't Daddy, telling Mick he liked the way she pranced and that with proper training she'd be a good addition to the Athy House stable. They ran the last race of the season towards the middle of the month back in Punchestown where it all began and again Whishy took the gold medal although Mick thought him a wee bit fatigued. He only crossed the line a neck ahead of a big, clumsy gray from Farrington Stables. In none of those races did War Lord run and in fact they saw nary an entry from Montgomery Castle after the besting at the Curragh. Gossip among the racing community was that Whish't Daddy had broken his competitor's spirit and that the horse would never run again. Da dismissed such talk, assuring Mick that Michael Cleary was an excellent trainer and the horse a proven champion and he was all but certain they would cross paths down the road. When they returned to Barreen after the last race Mick was sad to see the season end but very proud of his horse and what they had been able to accomplish together. He could see the pride beaming from his father's eyes and although he knew there was still much about Ireland and the stable and his family Da worried about every day, he was glad they had given him a few moments of pure joy watching them race across the finish far ahead of the field. Da told Mick that a percentage of the winnings were being kept in a safe place for Mick when he got a little older and he made sure that every medal they won went to his son. They kept them in a small tin box with a tricky clasp that tended to stick. Mick told his father that neither the money nor the medals were necessary but Da insisted.

"You done a man's job, Mick. It's only fair you get a man's pay," he said when Mick protested. "And we would have never won those races without you training him and you taking Whishy around the course. It's high time that a man gets paid properly for his labor in this country. And I'll be damned if I steal from my own blood."

"Alright, Da," his son replied thoughtfully. "But could you give me just a couple of coins now?" Da looked at him with surprise. "I want to buy a new blanket for Whishy, a nice thick, warm one for him to have over the winter. He earned it just the same as I did, Da, don't you think?" Frank smiled a great, broad smile and put his arms around his son hugging the boy very tightly. October was drawing to a close and the two men had worked most of a Saturday cleaning and storing the tack, mucking out and washing down the stalls, floors and walls of the barn, closing up any cracks or loose boards and readying the place for winter. The sun was beginning to sink below the horizon as they walked up towards the cottage. Da stopped half way up and reached into his back pocket.

"I forgot to ask you about these," he said to his son with a mischievous grin. Handing a small envelope to the boy, he watched him open it carefully and remove two tickets. Da could not help but laugh loudly when he saw the look on the boy's face. "You think you'd like to go with me Mick, it should be quite a game."

Mickey nearly jumped into his father's arms so filled with excitement and joy. "The footballers, Da, really, we going to the game, just me and you, Da, really?"

Da smiled, nodding his head. "Yup, Mick, just you and me. At Croke Park in Dublin the third week of November, Dublin against Tipperary, what do you say?"

Mick let out a loud hoot and a louder holler hugging his father tightly. "I say let's go Da, I can't wait. We'll have a swell time. Dublin's going to kill them, Da, just you wait and see. It will be an old fashion blood bath!" Frank Walsh laughed along with his boy and the two turned, walking arm in arm back up towards hearth and home.

Hamar Greenwood listened restlessly as the small Scotsman briefed the three men sitting in Nevil Macready's office. The little man's voice irritated the Chief Secretary and he wondered how Macready listened to him every day. Greenwood's assistant, John Harrington, however, was very engaged, jotting down notes as MacDermott droned on.

"So you're saying this Cairo Gang has infiltrated the Republicans across Ireland and set up a network of spies that can bring the entire IRA to its knees?" Harrington looked at Ian MacDermott with a look of incredulous disbelief. The Scotsman nodded with obvious satisfaction.

"We are talking about some extremely bright and very brave British officers, Under-Secretary," he said with a tone of derision. "Most of these men have served the Crown in dangerous assignments across Egypt and Palestine both as soldiers and intelligence agents. They are crafty and cunning and do not back away from a good fight. I assure you these are exactly the kind of men we need to crush this rebellion."

"Yes, sounds like the kind of agents we can count on," Sir Nevil added easily. Greenwood nodded in reply, secretly wishing all of these soldiers and secret agents would go home and let him administer this Godforsaken country in a more gentle and effective manner. All of this killing and murder did little good in his mind and men like Sir Nevil and Ian MacDermott made him very nervous.

"Are we protecting these men somehow?" Harrington asked casually. "This Cairo Gang, I mean. Obviously these agents are of great value to the government and risking their lives in doing so. Do you want me to assign some of our civilian staff to find them safe houses or more secure lodging? We can also provide them with transportation in the event of an emergency."

MacDermott scoffed at the idea. "Your secretaries and clerks are going to help protect some of the finest officers in the British Army? Not likely, I think they are quite capable of caring for themselves."

Harrington nodded. "Yes, surely I see your point. But at least I should prepare letters of transit for these brave men in the event they need to leave the country quickly." He left unsaid the reason why these agents may need to flee Ireland in haste but the others all understood the violent nature of their assignment.

Sir Nevil piped in. "Yes, I think that would be of use, John." He looked at his assistant and could see the disagreement on the man's face. "Ian, it is very possible these men may need to get away very quickly. Provide the names of the agents to the Under-Secretary and he will prepare the necessary paperwork. It goes without saying that this information is top secret, John, so please do not share it with anyone but yourself."

Harrington nodded again, jotting down more notes. "Of course, Sir Nevil," he said. "It will never leave my sight."

MacDermott's tried putting aside his superior's interference and the civilian's instigation but an element of irritation remained stuck in his craw. Would they never let him do the job he did better than anyone else without some kind of unnecessary meddling? Still he plodded ahead.

"We continue to focus on the racing game, the Gaelic Athletic Association and the few associates we have linked to the Republican leadership. Michael Collins continues to evade capture and his top lieutenants have gone underground although the Cairo Gang has a few names they are pursuing. Stemming the flow of guns coming in from America and the Continent continues to challenge our resources. Footballers across the country have been caught hiding weapons in their stadiums and dressing rooms and jockeys and trainers continue acting as couriers of important messages and military orders. The enemy becomes more organized and sophisticated every day and it is imperative we stem the tide sooner rather than later or it will be beyond salvageable."

Sir Nevil let out a long, defeated sigh. "Yes, Ian, quite right, I am afraid," he said sadly. "The international community continues to rally around the Irish Cause and discount the murder, kidnapping and bombings by the IRA. Our soldiers are more exposed every day and I am afraid it is beginning to show in their morale." Greenwood shook his head in agreement and scowled.

"We should send those boys home and take our chances with the civilian population. I don't see how things could be any worse," Greenwood said. Harrington nodded in support of his boss but Ian MacDermott flashed his angry temper once again.

"That is ridiculous and insane Mister Secretary," he nearly shouted. "Without the army and the Auxiliary to keep the peace this country would descend into absolute chaos. And you and your administration would be hung from every lamp post in Dublin. My men are doing their very best and I dare say, Sir Nevil, they have not lost one bit of their grit or their determination. They are here to defend the Crown and they will do so with all their resources or they will die in the trying. Their morale is fine. And they will be victorious." He banged his small, bunched fist on the table for emphasis, looking about with a challenging glare. No one replied. "In the coming weeks we will turn the tide. The Cairo Gang will help us turn the tables on these rebellious bastards. Our network is in place and we will soon move to wipe out the leadership of the Republicans. Then you will all thank our brave soldiers and agents for their daring and their steel." He looked for a long moment at Greenwood with particular disdain and then turned to his assistant. "I will have those names to you by end of day. Please forward the letters of transit by tomorrow night. You are right in saying we may need to move quickly, as a matter of fact I am certain that we will." With that he nodded to Sir Nevil and walked briskly from the room.

Out in Connemara, Michael Cleary watched the young groom walking War Lord from the course to the barn, taking care to let him saunter and tarry along the way. The workout had been very good. Although they hadn't raced their champion after the St. Leger, Cleary maintained a scaled down training regiment including course work every six days. War Lord seemed fit and ran beautifully and his practice sessions showed no after effects of the stinging defeat at the Curragh. Cleary had mulled over the race time and again in his mind. He was convinced that Whish't Daddy had won more because of their surprising strategy than anything to do with the quality of the horses involved. He had watched War Lord winning race after race without trying very hard and sometimes giving only half an effort. He had seen his prize pupil lay waste to many a field and he had seen him use speed, technique, endurance and cunning, whatever was necessary whenever it was necessary in every race over the past two years. He would not believe that one race changed anything. Where they had been beaten was in letting the other horse get out too far ahead. He did not necessarily blame Quiney Moran for this error. The man was an excellent jockey and had steered many a horse first over the line. And it was quite a shock to everyone seeing the Athy House entry speed right out of the gate and go to the lead. He had not done that at Punchestown or in Carlow. He did not think a horseman like Frank Walsh would take such a chance. Surely the odds of a young horse with a young rider being able to maintain the lead in the longest race of the year were unthinkable. When Cleary saw the horse go out front he smiled, thinking for sure War Lord would run him down on the homestretch. But he did not. Their strategy had worked. Moran waited too long to make his move but when he did his horse chased the leader down and almost overtook Whish't Daddy. And that was what bothered Cleary the most, that War Lord had caught the big beast and still the other had enough left to make it first to the finish line. Extraordinary, Cleary knew, for a horse to have that kind of reserve. Still, he felt his horse could beat Whish't Daddy now that they knew their strategy and he wanted badly to have the chance to prove it. His employer did not feel the same way. The trainer saw Lord Montgomery walking towards him and he met him along the track.

"How does our Champion look?" Montgomery asked, his eyes watching War Lord disappear into the barn.

"Excellent, my Lord," Cleary answered trying to sound confident and upbeat. "We could run him a time or two more before the season ends if you see fit." Montgomery shook his head from side to side.

"I don't think so Michael. I think he needs a rest. He's had a fine year. Both the Derby and the Two Thousand Guineas in the same year is a smashing success. We can shut him down and rest him over the winter and be ready to go again in the new year." Montgomery saw the disappointment in his trainer's face.

"The St. Leger does not sit well with you does it?" he asked Cleary with a small grin. "I feel the same way. But not to worry. By the time the new season rolls around that horse will be one of our own. Montgomery Castle is the finest stable in all of Ireland, maybe in all of the British Isles and I intend to make sure it remains that way." He looked at Cleary but saw no reaction. "Athy House will return to its humble roots, where it belongs. Whish't Daddy will be here soon, count on it. So you will need to make sure his accommodations are fitting for the horse that he is. I want you to move War Lord to the smaller stable in the front of the barn and set up the larger stable with new walls and flooring and clean mats and blankets. I am hoping to have him here soon, by the middle of December at the latest."

"Do you really think Frank Walsh will let his prize horse go to another stable? He is a very astute horseman, my Lord. I think he will want to hold on to Whish't Daddy." Cleary eyed Montgomery carefully, anxious to hear his answer.

"Don't worry about things out of your control Mr. Cleary. That is mine to worry about. There are things in motion already which Frank Walsh is unaware of that will bring his beautiful beast to my door. Your worry is to make sure he becomes the greatest champion in the history of Irish racing. If you don't do that, you will suffer the consequences. Do I make myself clear?" He stared at the other man for a long moment and then turned and walked away. He stopped abruptly, saying over his shoulder, "I am still waiting for those names of the men involved with the Volunteers down in Clare. I need them very soon." He did not bother waiting for an answer and made his way slowly back towards the castle. Cleary watched him go feeling angry and insulted and very worried. Threatening to fire him was one thing but making him move their wonderful champion to a smaller stable seemed so terribly unfair. And if the horse from Athy House came to Montgomery Castle they would never race against each other again. And despite Montgomery's demand, he was in no way ready to provide names of those involved in Republican activities in the area. That would only hasten his own demise. Cleary pondered the dangerous situation as he made his way up to the barn to give War Lord the bad news.

Chapter Twenty-Four

Dublin – November 21, 1920

Darcy crouched behind the wagon besides the gray, wooden building and watched his prey. His heart was pounding in such a way that he thought it might rip right through his chest and go bouncing down the narrow Dublin street. Despite the cool morning, sweat covered his forehead and he felt it running along the side of his face and dripping from his armpits. His mouth was completely dry and he could barely breathe. It was sometime around nine in the morning, Sunday, and in the distance he heard the peeling of church bells and for a fleeting moment he wished he was in church. He wished he was anywhere but where he was and he wished he was doing anything but taking part in the mission that had brought him and the other Apostles to Dublin late the previous night, arriving under the cover of darkness.

Their training completed, their weapons at the ready, Commander Riordan told them they would be briefed regarding targets, locations and escape plans in the morning. Darcy spent the night convincing himself not to sneak off from their safe house, certain that if he tried he would be shot as a deserter before he reached the outskirts of the city. Thoughts of Maureen filled his mind as did the horrible days in Mountjoy Prison and images of the British Army and frightening members of the Black and Tans scouring the city and countryside. He knew once the mission was accomplished he would be a condemned man as would be all of the Apostles. When dawn finally peaked through the windows, he was surprised to see the Commander had been joined by the IRA Chief of Intelligence. Collins was taller and broader than Darcy had imagined. The man's enthusiasm and commitment to the cause and his pride in these twelve Volunteers filled him with eloquent praise and admiration for their bravery and he instilled in them the critical nature of their mission.

"Your targets, this Cairo Gang as they refer to themselves, could have destroyed our organization and crippled our ability to accomplish our ultimate goal of self-rule," he said. "They are dangerous men who have infiltrated our ranks and know far too much about our leadership, our recruits, our resources and our plans to remain alive. It is critical each and every one of these targets be eliminated. They planned to kill many of us so we will kill them first. You must ensure that your assignment is completed in full. Wounding these agents or letting them escape is unacceptable. You must be certain they are dead and dead completely. If you shoot them in the heart or in the stomach or in the leg, shoot them again in the head to make sure they are dead. If you use a knife make sure it finds their heart at least twice or cut across their throat and watch them bleed out. There can be no mistakes. Your mission today is the most important one our cause has ever known. You will go down in the history of the Irish Republic, yes the Irish Republic, as true heroes, as twelve men whose bravery and courage faced the most difficult odds and carried the day. Heed my warning men, these agents are very smart and very brave and very cunning. Do not take them lightly. Kill them quickly and then kill them again. Be careful and be brave, the Republic needs you!" The men responded with wild applause and shouts of bravado. Daring promises were followed by much slapping of backs and hugs and more than a few tears. Riordan laid out each Apostle's target and provided an address at which to engage. An escape plan was provided in detail and each man repeated all the information several times over until the Commander was certain they had it all committed to memory and an understanding of how to approach their target. It had all sounded very straight forward at the time.

Now Darcy Walsh did not feel so sure. As a matter of fact he was scared to death. His target, a British Officer by the name of Wallace, stood no more than thirty yards away, a tall, burly, bear of a man with a thick brown beard, a barrel chest and the set back shoulders of a military man. He was dressed in a brown woolen suit and wore a dark brown derby on his head, making him look that much taller. He was smoking a cigarette and talking to another man, a smaller fellow who had just delivered the morning newspaper. Darcy could overhear a few words about the football game to be played later in the day and the two men seemed to agree the team from Dublin far superior. The little man waved goodbye and walked away and when Wallace finished his cigarette he tossed it in the street and went into the house. Darcy waited a moment and then made his way to the backyard where he'd been told a staircase ran up the back of the four floor structure. According to his information, Wallace was renting a room on the third floor. Darcy reached into his pocket and felt the cool steel of the revolver against his fingers and his heart pounded even harder. He slid his finger through the trigger guide and imagined himself pulling the trigger. He hoped he had the strength to do so when the time came. He made his way up the stairs, cautiously and silently creeping towards Wallace's floor. On the landing a back door led to a small hallway with doors on either side. The target rented the room on the right. Darcy sidled up alongside the window, peaking in carefully, making certain he could not be seen. At first he saw only an empty room but then there was movement on the left and Wallace came from another room into this one, which appeared to be a small parlor. A sitting chair and a small table lined one wall and a small sofa faced it from the other side. Wallace sat in the small chair and opening his paper, began to read. Darcy watched him for several minutes and thought about aiming the revolver through the window and shooting the man from outside on the porch. But he did not know if the glass window pane might deflect the shot and he knew he must be certain to hit his target straight away. He inched back towards the rear door painstakingly, trying to remain silent. Gripping the round knob he turned it slowly and to his great relief the door opened. But it made a distinctive click and Darcy instantly froze, holding the knob tightly and listening intently for any sound or movement coming from within. He tried looking back towards the window but from this angle he could see only the empty side of the room. He remained still for more than five minutes and then convinced himself Wallace had heard nothing. Pushing the door open slowly, he slipped into the narrow hallway and flattened himself against the wall on the right. The door to Wallace's apartment was only a step away and again he listened intently but heard nothing from the room. On one of the floors below he heard a loud conversation, a man yelling at a woman, most likely his wife and she sobbed in reply. The enticing aroma of frying bacon wafted up from the floors below. He listened again at Wallace's door but still there was no sound. His fingers slipped around the revolver as he took it from his pocket, noticing with dread that he could barely hold the gun as his hands and fingers were shaking terribly with fear. He considered abandoning his mission and racing back down the stairs and running out of the city and into the country and running as far away as he could, running to the sea and throwing himself into the water and hoping the waves would swallow him up and the sea would take him away to the depths of hell he so well deserved. But he remembered his cowardly flight from his darling Maureen and he told himself that this one act would be penance enough for his terrible sin, that in killing this enemy of a free and united Ireland he would be leaving a legacy behind for Maureen and the others to admire. He could not run this time. He had to stand tall and be brave and complete his mission. He pictured in his mind's eye gripping the door to the agent's room, pushing it open quickly, stepping into the room with the revolver raised, turning towards the chair and table where his prey would be reading and then firing the revolver several times into the man's body and his head and watching him fall and die. Then he would escape. He took a deep breath, grabbed the doorknob, yanked the door open and moved quickly into the room. Nearly dropping the gun as he turned towards the chair, he managed to recover his grip, suddenly realizing the parlor was empty. Wallace was nowhere to be seen. He heard movement from the other side of the wall and stepped quickly into the other room, leading with the gun extended, trying his hardest to keep from shaking and dropping the revolver. Coming into a large bedroom, he again found it empty but before he had a chance to turn and look behind him Wallace slammed into his back sending Darcy crashing to the floor. He dropped the gun and smacked his head on the wooden frame of the bed, momentarily dazing himself. When he managed to roll over to his side he saw the military man frantically reaching into his coat pocket, no doubt grabbing for his gun. Darcy looked down, finding his gun half way underneath the bed and he reached for it but managed only to spin it further out of reach. He scrambled to his knees and dug under the bed frame, his fingers finally grasping the gun, his head spinning quickly to see Wallace holding his own revolver and the big man turning towards Darcy with hatred in his eyes. Darcy pulled his hand and the pistol from under the bed, aiming it towards his target but Wallace already had his gun trained on his attacker and with a hideous smile of revenge he pulled the trigger. Darcy inhaled deeply, expecting the piercing of his heart with a lead filled bullet and the sudden death he knew he had coming. But he felt nothing. The soldier's gun just let out a loud, distinctive click and the surprised look on Wallace's face would stay with Darcy for the little time he had remaining on this earth. As the soldier looked at his gun as one might look at flaming ice, Darcy raised his own weapon and found the strength and courage to squeeze the trigger, remembering to hold his arm straight and to brace for the recoil. The sound in the small room was deafening. A great, tremendous roar exploded in his ear and the gun bucked a little and he watched the big bear of a man stagger backwards until he smashed into the rear wall. His eyes were wide with shocked disbelief and Darcy thought it almost comical to watch the man slide slowly down the wall, his hands grasping towards the middle of his chest, the look on his face changing from surprise and disbelief to acceptance and regret. Darcy remembered his instructions and fired the gun one more time, aiming squarely between the man's eyes, watching with an odd curiosity as the man's face erupted into a bloody mess. Darcy looked upon his work with shocked disbelief and then gathering his wits, stood and raced from the small apartment out onto the porch and down the rickety steps, taking them two at a time, sucking down deep gasps of air, feeling both invigorated and amazed by the success of his mission. He heard screaming coming from the building and as he ran through the yard out into the streets loud yelling and shouting followed him. He did not stop to look behind, racing to the end of the block and turning right, he moved quickly then slowed to a brisk walk, eager not to draw any unwanted attention to himself. He tossed the gun in a large pond along the road and then pulling his hat from a rear pocket, he tucked it down low over his face and moved along the street, avoiding other pedestrians as much as possible. He was heading towards Grafton Street where he was to find transportation from the city to a hideaway in the countryside. As he moved more deeply into the city he saw more and more soldiers appearing on the streets, both RIC and the Black and Tans. He slipped closer towards the buildings along the road, ducking in and out of the shadows to avoid the soldiers. He thought he saw the giant Black and Tan Captain looking towards him as he crossed Grafton Street. He disappeared behind another building, planning to hide for most of the day, waiting for the cover of night to aid his escape. As he slipped behind a pile of old wagons and other debris he could still feel the pounding in his chest and the sweat dripping from his face. But he had completed his mission. And that made him feel better on some sad and lonely level.

Frank considered turning back and leaving Dublin only moments after entering the city. The military presence was overwhelming. On every street military vehicles crammed intersections and soldiers, RIC and Auxiliaries took terms harassing and intimidating the citizenry. For years they'd treated the common man miserably but the level of animosity and disdain on this day reached a new level. Wagons were thoroughly searched and many destroyed as the soldiers ransacked belongings, overturning vehicles and arresting their drivers. As Da and Mick crept slowly across Dublin the number of soldiers built steadily. Everywhere they looked young men were being pushed against walls, searched, interrogated and in many cases beaten savagely. Bloodied men staggered away in fright and women screamed in fear as they scurried from the scene.

"What's happening, Da," Mick asked with a look of disbelief on his young face. "Why are all these people being beaten up? What could they have done?" His eyes were wide and bulging as he watched the mayhem in the road. Ahead a soldier was waving them forward, indicating they should stop when they reached the other side of the intersection.

"I am not sure, Mick," Da replied, "but we may be about to find out. Something very bad must have riled up the troops. I have never seen them so out of control. Try to stay calm and let me do the talking." Mick nodded, gripping the side of the wagon tightly as they pulled up to the soldier. He was very angry and began shouting.

"Step off the wagon, right away. Come on, move," he yelled in a voice laced with hatred. He reached up grabbing Mick by the shirt and pulled him down to the ground. The boy scrambled to his feet to join his father behind the wagon. "Where are you coming from and where are you going?" the soldier demanded.

Da chose his words carefully. "We are heading to Croke Park to watch the footballers, Dublin against Tipperary. We're coming in from Barreen in Kildare. What is all of this commotion about?"

The soldier pulled the canvas cover from the back of the wagon uncovering an old saddle Da wanted to drop off to another farm on the way home. There was a mixture of bridles and reins and other tack scattered across the wagon. The soldier tossed the equipment back and forth searching for weapons or other contraband. Satisfied that nothing or no one illegal hid in the wagon he turned his attention to Frank and his son.

"What do you know of the Republican activity across Dublin this morning?" He demanded, looking at Da momentarily but letting his eyes settle on Mick, holding his stare firmly on the boy.

"He knows nothing about such things," Da answered. The soldiers eyes remained fixed on Mick.

"I didn't ask you so keep your trap shut," he snarled. "I want to hear it from him. Answer me boy, where have you been all morning?"

Mick licked his lips, trying to hide the fear in his heart. Speaking softly he replied. "Like my Da said Sir, I know nothing about that stuff. I am just a horse trainer and well, a jockey too. I'm here to see the match. That's all." The soldier stared at him a few more moments and then spun him around and told him to put his hands on the wagon. Patting him down roughly starting with Mick's arms and torso, he worked his way down along his legs, poking into his boots. He grunted as he stood up and then turned and looked to Da as if asking himself should he search the father as well. He decided not.

"Okay, you can go. But I am warning you. If we find anything tying you to those murderous bastards from this morning we'll come after you and hunt you down like dogs. Now get the hell out of here before I change my mind."

Da tossed the heavy cover back into the rear of the wagon and he and Mick jumped quickly back on top of the vehicle. Da grabbed the reins and cracked them once and the horse pulled them down the road heading towards the park. Soldiers and Black and Tans watched them proceed and Da winced when he saw Butterfield glaring in their direction. He hoped they would not be stopped again and held his breath until they were a few streets away and nearing Croke Park, home of the Gaelic Athletic Association and Dublin's mighty team.

Dublin Castle literally buzzed with chaotic activity. Military men, government officials, police officers, couriers and newspapermen raced from office to office giving orders, shouting obscenities, calling for assistants, demanding any new news on the outrageous attacks of the day. Racing up and down hallways and stairwells, they searched for more clarity and understanding of how such a terrible assault could have been perpetuated on the finest fighting men the British Empire had ever known. The last tally Ian MacDermott had was of fourteen agents of the infamous Cairo Gang dead, murdered by the Irish Republican Army, some shot several times over, some with their throats sliced through like pumpkins and one with his head mercilessly bashed in with a hammer as he lay sleeping in his bed. Most of the assassinations had taken place in the morning, between eight and half ten on the South side of Dublin. The operation had been carefully planned and nearly perfectly executed. Only one of the murderous bastards had been caught and none were killed. Ian had his men rounding up every young man coming into or leaving Dublin, interrogating them without restraint, desperate for a clue of how the attack had been planned and where the wretched criminals to blame might be hiding. He had little doubt of the man responsible for the mission. Michael Collins' murderous finger prints were all over this disastrous enterprise. His cunning and attention to detail were revealed at every murder scene, most of which Ian had visited personally. No traces of weapons or footprints were found. Not one witness had yet to come forward. Ian knew the Irish, normally reluctant to speak to the police, would under these circumstances be far more afraid of Collins and his men as anything the RIC could muster. His men had struck quickly under the cover of a quiet Sunday morning and they had vanished along with the morning mist. Fourteen brave and brilliant agents were dead and another half dozen wounded, the heart of the spy network so close to destroying the IRA had been wiped out in a single, brilliant and treacherous maneuver, a maneuver MacDermott knew could not have been planned without considerable assistance from someone on the inside. He had a few ideas on where to look for these traitors but he would leave that work for another day. Now he had only one thing on his mind and it was vengeance of the most brutal kind. He thought again as he often did of his father's admonition, the dog learned from the fear of the whip. And now the dog had severely bitten the hand that feeds it, the great benefice of the British Crown had been terribly wounded by this dog known as the Irish people. Well, that dog would regret this day for years to come Ian swore to the Almighty. He was about to bring the whip down with a terrible vengeance and he was nearly giddy with the thought of watching Irish blood spill in the streets. He left his small office heading outside the Castle where he expected to find the beastly Butterfield and his unit of Black and Tans. He would loosen the beast upon the people of Dublin and rejoice in watching them get the comeuppance they so keenly deserved.

Butterfield and his men were manning the intersection closest to the Castle. They had inflicted their fair share of fear and loathing onto the Irish citizenry. A growing pile of broken wagons, discarded wheels, torn blankets and a wide array of tools, clothing and household goods stood witness to the intensity and violence of their search. Even a few of the new automobiles had been confiscated from the wealthier citizens. They had arrested nearly twenty men of varying ages and sent them to the goal bloodied and broken. Butterfield was bellowing orders to his unit and directing their efforts with great tenacity. The hole in his face oozed more grotesquely as the combination of physical action and the swirling, gritty winds drew out more of the ugly puss and slime from the unsightly wound. He saw MacDermott's small frame waddling towards the corner and he met the Scotsman in the middle of the street. MacDermott looked around at the piles of debris, nodding in appreciation.

"Yes, good, excellent work," he commented enthusiastically, looking up at the huge Captain. "But enough of searching for these despicable bastards. Those responsible are long gone, vanished into the countryside or well hidden in this Godforsaken city. That's alright, we'll find them soon enough. Now it's time to teach these pathetic people a hard lesson on the consequences of their actions today and that a crime committed by any Irishman will result in the punishment of *ALL* Irishman." The small Scot pounded a fist into the palm of his hand several times over, glaring at the one-eyed Captain with bitter hatred in his eyes. "I bought you here to crush this rebellion under your heel, to grind them into the ground and spit on their heads. Well, today you'll have your chance, Captain Butterfield; today we take the gloves off!" He was almost shouting now and Butterfield nearly laughed at the somewhat comical sight of the little man working up such a huge hatred.

"What did you have in mind, Ian?" he asked. "I can take my boys down to Sackville Street and loot and destroy every shop and building along the way. We'll burn the area to the ground and take away every bit of merchandise we can load into the wagons. We'll leave them broken and without a halfpence to their names."

MacDermott shook his head from side to side, smiling a cruel and contemptuous grin as he spoke in a venom laced tone. "I don't want their things Butterfield. I want their blood!" Then he pointed towards the other end of Dublin and laid out the plan for Butterfield and his men. When he'd given precise instructions he told the man to hurry. "The British Army will be coming to the park from the other end. You and your men need to get there first. I don't want any interference from some officer hack lacking the necessary spine to do what is necessary. Get moving and remember we seek justice for the brave British agents that gave their lives today for the Crown." Butterfield nodded tuning back towards his men. With a few shouts and considerable swearing he had the regiment together and moving quickly towards Croke Park.

Mick's eyes were wide with both excitement and fear. The crowd in Croke Park, over five thousand strong, felt much the same way. The football match had been long anticipated and the stands were filled with men and boys wearing the light blue and navy combination of the Dublin team. Fewer were clad in the navy and gold of Tipperary but they had some representation to be sure. The crowd sang songs favored by either county and a few what Frank Walsh thought of as revolutionary ballads decrying British rule and yearning for Irish independence. Given the events of the day, he was quite certain that such patriotic songs could only pour fuel on an already out of control fire and that the British authorities would need little additional motivation to strike back against the Irish citizens. He had spoken to a number of other men in the park and rumors were growing more wild and unbelievable as the clock ticked towards game time. Some said that over a hundred British soldiers had been killed in a vicious attack on a barracks on Pembroke Street and others claimed that the number was less than ten and that the killing had been spread across the South side of the city and was the work of a single deranged man who had lost his wife and children when his house was set ablaze by the Black and Tans. Most agreed that the IRA had been involved and that a large number of British agents had been killed in a coordinated attack earlier that day. Across the crowd tales spread of recriminations by the British Army and Auxiliaries and of the arrest of brothers, sons, and cousins throughout the day. Most worried of more attacks by the government troops and the crowd shared a widespread uneasiness and a general sense of unrest as the whistle blew for the game to begin. Mick was thrilled to see the footballers clad in their brilliant uniforms race onto the pitch and for the ball to be tossed to start the battle. He searched the Dublin team and found his favorite player, Michael Hogan, and watched excitedly as Hogan skillfully rushed the ball towards the Dublin goal. As the Tipperary defenders halted his charge he managed to flip the ball behind him to keep the drive moving. The teams fought hard throughout the opening minutes of the game and the crowd roared with approval or moaned its displeasure as the match ebbed and flowed in the early going.

"This is great fun, Da," Mick yelled to his father and Frank turned and hugged his son tightly. Mick thought for the briefest of moments that everything was right in his world. He thought of his wonderful horse and the incredible season they had shared over the past months. And now here he was in Dublin, watching his favorite player on his favorite team in the greatest game in town. And he was with his Da and could anything ever be more perfect? Two younger boys sat on his other side and they too were with their father and Mick felt a brief, blissful interlude of perfection. A second later his magical moment was shattered by the unmistakable sound of gunfire followed by a panic that spread across the crowd faster than the Irish wind. The first shots sounded like they came from the Canal End of the Park and the crowd's eyes moved from the action on the pitch to the South end of the stadium. The loud boom of gunfire continued and moments later a line of Black and Tan soldiers poured out of the tunnel and spread across the field continuing to fire their weapons into the crowd and across the pitch. Da's arms pulled Mick towards him and the boy watched in horror as the young child sitting next to him cried out in pain, clutching his chest before falling off the bench and onto the floor. His father was trying desperately to pick him up as the crowd around them began stampeding down from the stands and across the field, heading towards the North end away from the oncoming soldiers. Mick wanted to help the wounded boy but the huge flow of people pushed him along like a powerful wave and he felt Da's strong hand holding him tightly by the back of his collar. As they raced across the field he nearly stumbled over the blood soaked bodies of two of the players and looking down he saw quickly that the man in navy and blue with the red stain in the middle of his chest was Michael Hogan. He looked quite dead. Again the crowd surged and they were swept further along. Still the guns boomed and people screamed and children were crying while bodies fell to the ground and chaos swallowed up all of Croke Park. Mick could smell the gun smoke in the afternoon air and felt the pushing and shoving of the petrified crowd as they neared the North exit. A collective scream of absolute fear deafened all in the Park. Da dragged him closer to the exit and they moved into a long queue trying to get out of the playing field. Once they squeezed their way through the tunnel and out into the street, row after row of British soldiers with guns drawn were randomly selecting men or older boys to be searched for weapons or taken away for interrogation. The gunfire finally stopped and everywhere Mick looked he saw shocked faces, tear filled faces, angry faces and faces destroyed by tragic loss. A soldier approached Mick and his father but Da quickly turned them in another direction slipping back into the crowd, skillfully avoiding the man, finally making their way to the outskirts of the angry mob. Da told him to just keep moving and they nearly sprinted to the wagon parked in the lot behind the Park. They were one of the first to get out of the stadium which made it easier to avoid the chaos that would soon follow. Da took the reins and they raced away from the chaotic scene. Within twenty minutes they were out of Dublin and heading towards Barreen. It was only then that Mick realized his shirt and pants were splattered with the blood of the young boy sitting beside him who had been shot in the chest by the Black and Tans. He fought hard to hold back the bitter tears of anger and fear building in the back of his eyes.

Chapter Twenty-Five

Barreen, County Kildare – Early December 1920

Ian MacDermott sat in a small public house that was part general store, part eatery and part pub. The tavern owner was busy selling a bolt of cloth to an elderly woman and MacDermott sipped his tea and nibbled on a sandwich as he waited for the arrival of Butterfield and his unit of soldiers. The town was little more than a row or two of small buildings, a few pubs and of course, a Catholic Church sitting in the middle of the small village with its pointed spiral topped by a cross and visible to the surrounding countryside from a long way off. Ian had just come from the church, or more accurately from the rectory nestled beside it, home to the pitiful pastor, Father Dunn. He thought back to the brief visit he had paid on the wretched priest and wondered again how any person could put the smallest bit of faith is such a despicable man. He had arrived at the rectory early in the morning, surprising the priest and his housekeeper shortly after the morning mass. The housekeeper said Dunn was eating his breakfast so Ian waited patiently in the parlor, promising himself the man would never keep him waiting again. When finally he arrived, they exchanged pleasantries then Father Dunn asked how he could be of assistance.

"You had a visit from one of my men a few weeks back, a Captain with the Auxiliaries, a rather large man with one eye," he offered. Dunn turned a pasty white remembering the gruesome and terrible beast that had enquired about Athy House.

"Yes, yes," he replied quickly, "I remember him very well, a frightening man, to be honest, Mister MacDermott, smashing things, making all kinds of threats. He demanded I reveal confidences shared in the sanctity of the confessional. And while I understand certain things may be necessary, I could not abide such conduct." Dunn, hesitating a moment, feigned indignation, and continued after a brief pause. "But he did indicate the potential for some accommodation for any information regarding the ownership of this Athy House, the stable with the growing notoriety for this Whish't Doggy or Whish't Daily or something like that."

MacDermott could not help but grin. "It's Whish't Daddy, Father and yes, I think we would be able to come to some kind of arrangement. It depends on what you are able to share with us. I know some of what you may know, is what, how do you say - privileged information?" Ian knew full well the man would give away the whereabouts of Jesus' shroud for the right amount of sterling but he wanted the priest to feel at ease so he would spill his guts.

"What kind of uhm, arrangement are we thinking about if indeed I have the information you seek?" Small beads of sweat were beginning to form across the pastor's forehead despite the cool morning chill. He hoped Mrs. Fitz was nowhere near the office. He suspected she had a bad habit of listening in on his conversations but perhaps he only expected the worst from most human beings.

"You tell me what you know of Athy House Father and I assure you the arrangement will be far more than you could imagine." Ian looked the priest in the eye holding his gaze until Dunn grew uncomfortable and looked away. A few moments later he responded.

"The man owns the entire enterprise by himself," Dunn began matter-of-factly. MacDermott looked at him harshly, uncertain of his meaning. He continued. "They've built an intricate web of deception, Mr. MacDermott, one intended to fool the likes of you and I, of most common men to be sure. A series of foreign corporations and partnerships and entities that are loosely aligned in some other dealings and a veritable sea of contracts and other paperwork obscure the facts. The trail runs from this wee town of Barreen across the Irish Sea and the Atlantic Ocean and I think it may also dip its toe in the South

Pacific around Australia. But no matter how far it is stretched or how complicated the ruse may get, in the end of things, Frank Walsh owns Athy House from top to bottom; the whole kitten caboodle is his. Ah, surely he pays a few quid to some so called partners here and there and no doubt there is more paperwork to keep up the charade but make no mistake Mr. MacDermott, Frank Walsh is Athy House and Athy House is his and his alone."

"Are you quite sure?" MacDermott asked directly. The priest gave him a long, hard stare.

"Yes, I have that on the most intimate of levels. What I am not sure about is our previously discussed arrangement," he replied, letting the words hang in the air. MacDermott fussed in his pocket. He produced a small bag of coins and placed it in front of Father Dunn with a plop. The priest lifted it briefly, no doubt calculating its heft and value in the same measure.

"Again, I have to ask Father, are you sure about this?" the Scot enquired.

The priest hesitated a moment and then took the bag of coins in his hand again. He tossed it gently from hand to hand, nodding to himself as he did so. Finally he put the bag in his lap and looked at MacDermott and smiled. "The man confessed it to me, Mister MacDermott, not normally where one would discuss a business deal but it was something he wanted to ease from his mind. Athy House is owned by Frank Walsh and no one else, Sir. And how that violates Irish law I have no idea, but I suspect you do. So if we are done here than I will ask you to leave. And please remember, everything we talked about needs to remain private. I hope I can count on you for that."

MacDermott gave the priest his hardest and coldest smile. "Of course Father," he said, "as sacred as the confessional in every way." He bowed politely and left, leaving the priest with one hand on his money and the other scratching his chin.

He poured himself another cup of tea and added a healthy dose of sugar and cream while considering the next steps regarding Frank Walsh and Athy House. The man had clearly broken the laws regarding ownership of private property. The Irish citizenry were limited by the

Ashbourne Act to ownership of small parcels of land, a law passed with the intention of maximizing the number of Irish peasants that would be granted the chance to own land. Walsh's clever ruse of international ownership allowed him to circumvent the law and expand his ownership to include far more acres of land on which he had built the barns, stables and training course on the outskirts of Barreen. Now the man would have to be arrested and charged for his crime. But that was only the most obvious reason Walsh needed to be punished. There were others. Ian was almost certain Frank Walsh was involved in Republican activity and involved in a very substantial way. Hadn't he made his home available to his brother, Darcy Walsh, to convalesce after the Republican hunger strike at Mountjoy? Wasn't it only logical that if the younger brother was a soldier in the Republican Army that his older brother provided support to the organization? Hadn't Butterfield told him he thought he'd seen both Darcy Walsh and Frank Walsh in Dublin on the morning of the attacks on the Cairo Gang? Darcy was thought to be a part of the assassination team as he was seen in close proximity to the murder scene where Officer Wallace had been killed. And it was far too great a coincidence that a few hours later the older Walsh and his son were spotted in a wagon moving across town. Most likely they were in Dublin to pick up the murderous Darcy and some of his cohorts. It was a damn shame they'd been able to escape in the confusion at Croke Park. Walsh and the boy were part of the racing game and one of their jockeys, Brian Grant, had been caught red handed receiving weapons down in Punchestown. Now they'd been linked to another hot bed of Republican activity, the Gaelic Athletic Association. When you added up all the parts and pieces one could only conclude that Frank Walsh was as much a member of the rebellion against the Crown as his brother Darcy. No doubt much of the winnings produced by Athy House went to fund the enemy's weapons and their dastardly plans. The venom in Ian's throat still tasted very raw when he thought of the assassinations of the members of the Cairo Gang ten days before. He was convinced that one Walsh had been a direct participant and the other a major contributor to its planning and funding, an equally vile crime. So the man needed to feel the whip and Ian planned to bring it down hard. And in the process he could accomplish another objective that would portray him in a very positive light to Sir Nevil and his friend Lord Montgomery. His distant cousin's desire to acquire ownership of the champion horse Whish't Daddy had been made quite clear. And it was well within his authority as second in command of the British forces in Ireland to order not only the arrest of a known enemy of the Crown but also to confiscate his property as compensation to the Empire for his treachery. So he would let Butterfield and his men loose on Athy House and crack the whip with a ferocity that would echo across the Irish countryside. The death of his agents would be avenged and as an added bonus he would deliver the much coveted horse to Montgomery Castle and bask in the Lord's gratitude and appreciation. He finished his lunch, draining his tea with pleasure. Hearing the arrival of the Black and Tan's out on the road, he left the public house quickly, eager to provide Butterfield and his men instructions regarding the raid on Athy House.

Mick was mucking out one of the stables when he heard the soldiers approaching. The pounding of hooves was accompanied by a mixture of men whooping and hollering in words Mick could not understand. Da came running from the back of the barn and looked down the road at the pack of horses and uniformed men making towards the cottage. A cloud of dust surrounded the approaching herd and Mick could see the fear clearly etched on his father's face.

"Jesus, Mick, they're coming for us now. I feared it would not be long," Da voice was trembling and Mick felt the fear spreading in his own stomach and his hands began to tremble. Da turned, grabbing his son by the shoulders and looked him firmly in the eye. "Listen to me son like you never listened before and do exactly as I tell you, do you understand?" Da's voice was bold and direct but laced with something close to panic. Mick had never seen his father like this; the man was always totally in control. Mick nodded his understanding and Da continued. "I am going to run up to the cottage and try and get Mammy and the girls out of the way. I do not want you to come up there, son, do you hear me?" Mick nodded again, the knot in his throat growing thicker and beginning to choke him some. "Whatever you hear up there, you don't come up. And if you hear any gunfire or if you see any smoke or fire coming from the cottage I want you to start letting the horses out, get them all out of the stables and barns and clear the paddocks and chase them away. Do you hear me, son?" Da asked shaking the boy firmly.

"Yes, Da, I do, I do, don't worry. But what are those men going to do? What are they going to do to Mammy and the girls? Why are they here?"

"We'll know soon enough, son, but I assure you they are not here for anything good. If it is what I think than you get the horses out of here quickly and then you take Whish't Daddy and you get far away as fast as you can. I want you to go out to Clare, to Mammy's cousin Olive and you stay with her until you hear from me, and you hide the horse, Mick, you make sure you and Whish't Daddy stay well hidden." Looking down the road they could see the soldiers getting near to the gate of Athy House. Their faces were wild with rage and they were screaming like banshees in the night. Da looked back at the boy. "I got to get up there Mick, remember what I said. Okay?" Mick looked at his father and could not help the tears beginning to roll down his cheeks. His father grabbed him tightly, hugging him dearly and kissing him on the head. "I love you, Mick. Remember, do not come up to the house." With that he turned, sprinting up the hill towards the cottage.

Frank reached their home only moments before the Black and Tans arrived. Mammy had Patricia wrapped in a blanket, holding her in a protective grasp, a petrified look covering her lovely face. The three year old howled loudly in protest while Maureen held Deidre in a tight embrace, trying to comfort her to no avail. The child was scared to death. They all were.

"What is it all about, Frank," Fiona asked softly. "Why are they here?" Before Frank could answer the door slammed open with a loud bang and the massive form of Arthur Butterfield filled the doorway. Behind him were ten men in uniform, all of them eager with anticipation for the destruction ahead. Frank moved quickly towards his wife, pushing her and the child behind him. Maureen moved away from the door towards the back of the room, herding Deidre towards the hearth.

"What is the meaning of this?" Frank asked, his voice filled with indignation. "Why are you men here and what gives you the right to enter my home without my permission?" His fear was turning to anger, his face flushed with rage. Butterfield took three huge steps towards Frank, smashing him hard across the face, sending him crashing into the table and knocking over two of the chairs. When Frank stood up a line of blood ran from his right eye and his nose bled heavily.

"I am here by the authority of the British Government and you are hereby placed under arrest for criminal activity and subversive actions against His Majesty's Empire. You and your Republican friends are going to pay Walsh for your wicked deeds and you're going to begin paying right now." The room had filled with eight of the Black and Tan soldiers, two remaining outside on guard. Butterfield grabbed Frank by the throat and smashed him hard with his other huge hand. Frank fell to the ground again, a deep, painful groan escaping from his gut as he dropped. The girls were screaming hysterically and young Patricia cried with abandon. Fiona tried putting herself between her husband and his assailant but Butterfield just swiped at her with his massive arm sending her crashing into the hearth, nearly dropping the little girl as she did so. Frank scrambled away from Butterfield, moving to help his wife but Fiona scurried further away, rolling into a ball in the corner, protecting her youngest with her body and her arms. Frank looked to the side of the fireplace and saw his shotgun leaning against the wall. He thought momentarily about grabbing it and shooting the horrible Captain but he knew he could never kill all the soldiers before they began killing him and his family. But he wanted to warn Mickey and tell the boy to get away fast. These hard men were here to wreak havoc and Frank wanted at least someone to get away safely. He stood quickly, grabbing the old gun and pointing it towards the roof he fired a blast through the thatch, hoping it might also be heard across the countryside, bringing some much needed help. A moment after the loud shot rang out Butterfield was back on top of him, tearing the gun away and smashing its butt into Frank's side. He felt a searing pain tear deeply into his ribs and collapsed into a heap near the small fire. Butterfield told two of the men to grab hold of him and they did so, dragging Frank to his feet. The Captain slammed him hard three times with his tremendous fists, breaking his nose, cutting both eyes, smearing his face with blood and ooze. Mammy whimpered in the corner trying to soothe the screaming child and Deidre buried her face in Maureen's side, crying and shaking with uncontrollable fear. Maureen watched the attack in silence, hot tears streaming down her petrified face, secretly wishing Darcy would suddenly arrive with some men to stop this terrible assault. When Butterfield tired of beating Walsh he stopped, turning and surveying the room with his hideous face. He walked towards Mammy and kicked her viciously in the side and the loud thud was followed by a piercing howl as the pain registered in Fiona's brain. She turned further away trying desperately to shield her child from the madness. Butterfield laughed and turned back towards Frank and the bloody mess that was his face. Walsh tried holding the Captain's putrid stare but his head was swimming in agony and he felt at any moment he might black out. Butterfield woke him quickly from his trance.

"I am going to give you the chance to choose, peasant," he said to Da with a voice laced with terror. "I must admit to having a fancy for the pretty one with the long, golden locks. She looks to me to be a very sweet ride," he said with a nasty laugh. Some of the other soldiers joined in nervous laughter, knowing what was coming. Frank eyed the man with hatred but no words could form in his head. "But if you prefer I'll take the old lady here and give her the fecking of her life. Sure you been at her a good long time yourself with this brood of wee ones but maybe she never felt the stiffness of a real man?" Again the horrid laugh filled the room and Maureen began sliding her young sister further behind her, much as Da had done with Mammy and the baby. Butterfield noticed and stepped towards her, fiddling with the belt on his pants as he crossed the room. Maureen tried to shy away but in a moment he was in front of her and his big hands began pawing at her hair and then her face and then he let them fall across her frock. Groping around, he found her breast and gave it a horrific squeeze. Maureen shuddered with fear and a small scream escaped from her lips. Da tried to stand, wanting frantically to get to the man and tear him away from his daughter but the two soldiers held him tightly, one producing a small, sharp knife which he tucked in tightly under Frank's throat. Da closed his eyes, howling in protest, the scream letting the blade dig a little into his skin and he felt hot blood trickling down his neck. Butterfield looked back towards Frank, fixing him with his horrible leer.

"You going to watch peasant as I feck your daughter?" he asked with a vile laugh. Then he tore Maureen's dress from the neck down, the material making a sharp sound as it ripped apart in the suddenly silent kitchen. Only Deidre's soft sobbing and Patricia's tired cry filled the room. The soldiers stared at Maureen's body, her ample bosom on display as both her frock and her undergarments were torn away. Maureen moved to cover her breasts but Butterfield reached and pinched her nipple viciously making her cry out in pain. He breathed his hot, putrid breath in her face and the green ooze from his vanquished eye leaked in small drops into her hair. She nearly gagged and tossed but she knew that would only entice his rage. "If you don't behave yourself, lassie, I might just have a go at the wee one behind your back," he whispered into her ear with a short, nasty laugh. At this Maureen stiffened and used her elbows to push Deidre further away. She felt his hand go between her legs grabbing roughly around her thighs but soon enough he found what he wanted and his massive hands and fingers began poking and exploring around her pubic hair and into her crevices, searching wantonly for her womanhood. Then he moved his hands away and fiddled again with his belt and then his pants dropped with a clang and he was holding his massive erection and pulling her towards him. Maureen thought of the baby growing inside of her and thought it best if she let him have his way or perhaps he would hurt the child somehow. As Butterfield began sliding inside of her, Mammy registered the same thought.

"Stop," she yelled hoarsely from across the room. She placed Patricia behind her on the floor, managing to get to her feet despite the relentless pain in her side. She was leaning on the table, her face a mask of anguish and grief. Butterfield looked back over his shoulder, hesitating momentarily. Mammy's voice was little more than a whisper. "Stop, please, please you must stop. She's a wee one growing inside of her. You can't do this, you may hurt the baby." She looked at Maureen tenderly, her eyes expressing understanding and forgiveness tinged with terrible desperation and regret. Frank uttered some unintelligible noise and she looked at him with sorrow. He looked back at her, his face a mask of confusion. "Take me if you have to, man, but please leave that child alone," Fiona begged, tears flowing freely down her petrified face.

Butterfield seemed to consider the offer for a moment and then he just laughed wildly and went about his business with Maureen. The young woman felt him enter her and she felt a great spreading pain and then some tearing and then she fainted, collapsing against the wall of the cottage. Butterfield held her long enough to gain his satisfaction and then let her slide to the floor with her sister dropping down beside her to either protect her or gain her protection again, who could say. Butterfield quickly dressed himself and then moved back towards Frank Walsh.

"A delightful young lady, your daughter, peasant," he said with a vicious smirk. Frank looked at him with pure hatred and pictured the death he would one day bring to this terrible man. Then Butterfield turned to Mammy, "I'll be back for you another day, lady. You might not be a ripe as she is but you got plenty of fight in you and some days a man wants a little fight." With that he leaned over and kissed the poor woman directly on the mouth and then laughed again his hideous laugh. He told the soldiers to take Frank into custody. And then he ordered the place burned. "To the ground men, every last bit of it. Burn the house, the barns and the stables. Bring me the horse with the white bar down his head, this Whish't Daddy. Do not harm the horse in any way. If you find the boy take him into custody as well." He ordered one soldier to take a picture of the building once it was ablaze so they could put it in the paper as a warning to others that would support the Volunteers. The men dragged Frank Walsh from his home and some of the soldiers sprinted down towards the barn. As the men fixed their torches, Mammy revived Maureen and then gathered the girls together along with a few meager belongings before leaving their home for the safety of the countryside. Within minutes the cottage was ablaze.

When the shotgun blast rang out Mick nearly jumped out of his skin. He was saddling Whish't Daddy in the event he needed to leave quickly and the horse spooked at the loud noise, skittered nervously, rearing up slightly on his back hooves. Mick held him firmly, whispering comforting words, settling him down. The boy did not feel very settled himself. He wanted badly to sprint up the hill towards the cottage and get inside to help Da and make sure Mammy and his sisters were safe from these frightening men. He remembered with a shudder the horrendous captain and the way the huge man had slapped him painfully across the face on the road back from Carlow. The soldiers had all seemed riled up and ready for trouble and now with the gun blast bouncing around in his head Mick was torn by the urge to help his family. But his father's admonition that he not come up to the cottage kept him from heading up the hill. He reminded himself of his responsibilities towards the horses and to keeping Whish't Daddy safe. He tied Whishy firmly to the fence in the paddock and raced back into the barn. Methodically he went through the building, loosening the restraints from each horse and leading them out to the pasture. He slapped each horse on the rear, the brood mare, the big Gray Chipper, Bellweather, the two show ponies and the filly Da had just purchased, shouting at them to scatter. They all galloped a short distance away but hesitated on the edges of the property, unsure of what was happening. Mickey ran back through the barn towards the paddock to get Whish't Daddy but stopped suddenly, moving quickly to the back of the barn where most of the tack was kept along with the blankets, water bottles and other supplies. He moved the pile of blankets and dug through the straw and loose dirt, unearthing the dented metal box he opened it slowly. The small pile of shining coins winked back at him as did the medals he'd won with Whish't Daddy over the past months. He had his small notebook in the box and decided he would take the whole thing. Something told him this might be his only chance. He raced back to the paddock and stuffed the box into the saddle bag along with a thin blanket and some hard biscuits. As he was mounting the horse he heard a ruckus coming from up by the cottage. Two men were running down the hill towards the barn and two others came out of the house dragging someone behind them. It took him a moment to realize it was his father and from afar he looked pretty beaten up. Again the urge to intervene filled him but from the hill he heard Da's raspy, desperate voice imploring him to go, to get away, to take the horse and run. He secured himself in the saddle, slipping his feet firmly in the stirrups, turning Whishy towards the paddock gate. One of the soldiers running towards him came very close and tried grabbing Mick by the ankles but the boy maneuvered the horse deftly and Whish't Daddy hit the man straight on sending him flying onto his back. The other yelled at him to stop but Mick whispered to his horse and a moment later they were a ways down the road and Mick slowed to look back towards the cottage. Da was being tied into a wagon and the big Captain was bellowing at his men to go after Mick and get the horse. A moment later he saw Mammy and his sisters come out of their home, huddled together and looking very frightened. He thought he could hear the girl's desperate cries reaching him on the evening wind. He wanted terribly to race back to help but the echo of his Da's plea remained in his ears and he fought the impulse hard. A moment later he saw three soldiers mounted on horses and heading his way. He pointed Whishy down the road, begging him to speed away. The horse felt as if he was breaking from the starting gate as he bolted down the lane heading towards the village. Mick looked behind him and saw Bellweather and the other horses scattering into the pastures and the countryside, racing away from the commotion. His three pursuers chased hard but Whish't Daddy's furious strides put great distance between them and within a few minutes Mick could no longer hear their hooves pounding the road behind him. But he took no chances. He veered off course and into the wooded dale to the South, knowing the terrain like the back of his hand, reminding himself of days that seemed so long ago when he and his horse learned to run like the wind, sailing over stumps and clearing streams with hardly any effort at all. He ran the horse hard for thirty minutes more. Coming to a small hilltop he stopped and looked behind him. There was nothing but the approaching dusk chasing them now. Mick thought he could still smell smoke coming from the hearth but after a few moments of looking back towards home he realized that the smell was from a fire and he knew with great certainty it was the cottage, the barn and the stables going up in flames. As he turned back to the South he could not stop the steady stream of tears sliding down his ashen cheeks.

Chapter Twenty-Six

Limerick – February 1921

Mick kicked the ball with his cousin Gerry but found it very hard to concentrate on such a trifling thing. He thought his time in Limerick boring and he missed his family terribly. The past two months had been the most difficult of his young life but he constantly reminded himself that he was lucky to have a roof over his head and at least a morsel of bread and the occasional bit of beef to fill the pit of his stomach. During that horrible time back in December it had taken him more than ten days to cover the distance from Barreen to Limerick. He rode only at night, too frightened to be seen by the British soldiers or the Black and Tans scouring the roads in search of the Republican guerillas responsible for what the papers were now calling Bloody Sunday. He worried also that thieves and ruffians might try to steal Whishy so he took great care every day to find a safe hiding spot deep in the woods or in high fields of hay to secret himself and the horse far from harm's way. Mick found clean water and some food for Whish't Daddy and groomed him as best he could given their nomadic existence. They wandered first south towards Waterford hoping to throw any would be pursuers off the trail and only when he was sure they were not being followed did they turn west towards Limerick. He worried constantly during the journey. Remembering the men dragging Da from the cottage, he wondered if any harm had been done to his mother or his sisters. The strained sound of his father's voice telling him to go kept repeating in his head. Upon arriving in Limerick, it took him several days and a hundred inquiries to locate Aunt Olive and her son who lived on the outskirts of the town in a small thatched cottage bordering a large field with a good sized pond to the north. Olive was very surprised to see him. Her admiration for her nephew's new found fame and concern for his haggard appearance changed quickly when Mick told her the story of the Black and Tans burning Athy House to the ground. He could see the woman grow instantly uncomfortable with his presence in her home. Mick assured her he would find a suitable hiding place for the horse at the back of the big field and pleaded with her to say nothing of his presence or that of his famous horse to anyone in town. He knew full well that any gossip in Limerick regarding her now famous nephew would quickly bring the soldiers looking. He spent three days building a small shelter out of tree branches, thatch and rope to seclude Whishy and every night he made sure the horse was well hidden and well fed, hoping to keep him calm and settled and drawing no attention. He rode him every few days but stayed hidden in the trees and the glen, barely allowing the big horse to break a sweat.

Christmas was particularly sad for Mick. His thoughts took him quickly to memories of holidays past with Mammy and Maureen and his younger sisters. He worried himself sick that they'd been harmed by the soldiers who burned down their home. He terribly missed having them all together at this special time of year. He thought of the previous Christmas before all the trouble. The family shared a wonderful meal of mutton, potatoes, carrots and parsnips followed by a delicious mince pie. Da smoked a dozen pipes by the hearth and Mammy sang the hymn about a child being born in a manger and he remembered so intensely beautiful Maureen hugging him tightly by the fire and telling him he was growing up too quickly. It was a very happy memory but it only served to make him worry that much more about them all. He admonished himself once again for escaping alone rather than rushing to their defense. He knew it wasn't what Da had wanted but after dwelling on it for months he'd come to the conclusion he should have followed his instincts and gone to help. Now he was just lonely, worried and bored. His cousin Gerry was a kind enough boy and although only a year younger than Mick, he seemed so much more a child. All he wanted to do was kick the stupid ball in the yard. He had very little interest in Whish't Daddy or horses or racing or any of the other subjects Mick brought up to discuss. Mickey worried not only about his family but also about Whishy and would his majestic horse ever be able to race again. His father's admonition to take the horse to safety left Mick uncertain of what to think. Da had obviously believed Whish't Daddy to be in certain danger which Mick knew was somehow related to Lord Montgomery. He believed Da would not have told him to escape with the horse and to hide him well unless something else he did not understand was in play. He often lay by the hearth in the straw bed close by Aunt Olive's kitchen remembering the feeling of blasting down the backstretch, letting Whishy take the bit, the two of them flying in a way no other person could imagine. He missed that feeling almost as much as he missed Da and Mammy and the girls. He hoped these idling days would not take that special, magical gift away from his tremendous horse. He hoped even more that it wouldn't be much longer before Da would appear and they'd start training again, then have a race or two in one of the courses down around Cork or out in Tralee. He was anxious to move on and he could tell Aunt Olive was keen to have him on his way soon, wanting to avoid any trouble the boy and the celebrated horse might bring. Two days later, in the middle of the second month of the year, word finally arrived from Da.

The man who brought the letter was a rough looking man, tall, square shouldered with leathery skin and squinty eyes that looked everywhere at once. It took Mick a few moments before recognizing him as the IRA leader that returned a terribly thin and sickly Darcy to their home in Barreen after he'd been released from Mountjoy Prison. Mick remembered Da treating the man very coolly and not wanting to take Darcy into their home. Now with the cottage burned to the ground along with the stables and barns, he thought that Da had been right and he wondered why this man would show up in Limerick claiming he had news from his father. He'd knocked on Aunt Olive's door late in the evening and spoke to her urgently. He produced a letter which she scanned quickly and then handed over to Mick. He looked it over carefully and then read it a second time.

To my dear son Mick,

This man is Commander Riordan from the Republican Army. He is going to help you. Take Whish't Daddy and go with him. I will come and find you soon enough. Your mother and your sisters are alright. I hope you are too. I love you son. Please listen to Commander Riordan and things will be okay.

Da

Riordan asked Aunt Olive for something to eat and water for himself and his horse. He instructed Mick to get Whish't Daddy ready, explaining they would leave soon and travel under the cover of darkness. He spoke quickly, using very few words and Mick asked him no questions. He packed his few belongings, walked through the field and around the lake to his make-shift stable where the horse was hidden. He saddled Whish't Daddy and moved quietly back through the field to meet the Commander.

"I don't know where we're going now, Whishy," he whispered to the horse. "But soon Da will be back and then Mammy and the girls too and we'll all be together again, just like it used to be. And then me and you can start racing again, Whishy. I know you been missing that something bad. But we'll be back at it soon, just mark my words." He patted the horse on the face, saying a small prayer that everything he'd promised would soon come true. An hour later he followed Riordan down the dark streets and away from the sleepy town of Limerick.

Darcy Walsh watched from the shadows as the Commander and his nephew entered the Republican camp. It seemed very odd to him that Mick would be with the rugged soldier and he wondered how on God's green earth the two of them had joined together. A part of him wanted to race across the grassy field and grab his nephew and hug the boy and ask him about his darling Maureen and how she may be fairing. But he remained hidden in the tree line, unsure of what Mick might know of his relationship with his sister. Darcy had always liked the boy and the two had gotten along well, often spending time together down by the barn or walking in the fields behind Athy House. But Mick had grown up very much from those earlier days and his success with Whish't

Daddy might have changed him from the innocent and carefree boy Darcy remembered. If the young man knew anything about him and Maureen then there could be trouble. Darcy had learned of the Black and Tan's attack on Frank's property and had returned to Athy House to survey the damage. There was nothing left. The cottage, the barn, the stables and paddock were all burned to the ground and destroyed. An ugly, wide black scar covered the countryside where he had lived with his brother and his family. The smell of smoke still clung to the land and walking through the greasy ashes filled Darcy with conflicting emotions of terrible loss and a bitter sense of justice that his brother had been served his comeuppance. Days later Commander Riordan told him that Frank had been arrested as a supporter of the Republican cause and was being held in the same prison where Darcy had spent almost a year of his life. Darcy did not know what to think about that. His brother no more supported the cause of Irish independence then Darcy supported flying cows. But he did wonder about Maureen and her mother and the other girls. Riordan knew nothing of their whereabouts or their condition. He told Darcy that Frank had the right people working on his behalf to free him from Mountjoy and this came as no surprise. Frank always managed to be on the right side of things, even when he was in the goal. He watched curiously as Riordan and Mick dismounted and heard the Commander tell the boy where to take the horses. He followed at a distance, wondering again why his nephew was staying in an IRA hideaway and why he was not with his mother and his sisters. It occurred to Darcy that if the right people working on Frank's case freed him, his brother might also appear in the camp looking for his son. Darcy slipped back into the shadows wanting time to think about his options and hoping for the opportunity to address Frank's son alone.

"He will be released?" Ian MacDermott asked incredulously. He was in Macready's office with his boss and Lord Montgomery. A bright fire burned in the hearth and the small room was very warm and smelled of smoke. MacDermott's complexion waffled from a bright pink to a raging purple as he hopped from one foot to the other, shuffling around full of anger and nervous energy. "The man is a supporter of this Republican insurrection and you are prepared to let him walk out of prison a free man?" He was nearly screaming at Macready, who was trying desperately to maintain his patience.

"Ian, please," Sir Nevil interjected, "there is no proof of Walsh's involvement with the Republican Army in any substantial way. And he has hired very powerful counsel, a firm with strong ties to America and the government in Washington. This is our only option. We need to release him immediately."

"Oh damn the American government," Ian replied angrily. "Our responsibility is to the Crown and not to any foreign power. This man is a link to this horrible conspiracy, to the bastards that assassinated our brave agents and I'll be damned if I stand by and watch him walk…" Before Ian could finish his rant Lord Montgomery cut him off completely.

"Stop it, MacDermott, right now. Say not another word," he commanded, his voice laced with cold, blue fury. "If it weren't for you and your damn men we would not have this situation on our hands. By what authority did you send your vicious Captain and his pathetic unit to Walsh's home to beat and rape and destroy his property? How could you condone such behavior? This man is a business man. He is a horse trainer. He is not an assassin or a soldier or a threat to our government in any way," Montgomery angrily admonished the little man, pointing a finger directly in MacDermott's face. "You had no right to do the things you did. You were instructed to serve a summons and to take possession of certain property. I saw your orders, man. In no way were you to have the place burned to the ground. We are lucky they have agreed to Walsh's release as their only stipulation. And you will release him, make no doubt of that. And if I learn that his magnificent horse has been harmed in any way, so help me, you will be punished and punished in full." Lord Montgomery stood and looked around the room with contempt. "I am beginning to understand why the Irish people hate us the way they do, gentlemen. We have earned their revulsion. The only thing of any value in this Godforsaken land is the quality of its horses. We should give them back everything else. We would be no worse off in the end. Sir Nevil, I'd like to speak with you for a moment in private." With that he stopped, lighted his pipe and then strolled out of the room in disgust.

A moment later Sir Nevil followed him into the drafty hallway and they moved towards the end of the corridor where they would not be overheard.

"I want him followed," Lord Montgomery said abruptly. He saw the confusion on Macready's face. "Walsh, Frank Walsh, have someone follow him discreetly once he leaves the prison. And don't have that savage Captain do the job. I don't want Walsh to know he's being trailed. I am quite certain he will lead us back to his son and wherever the son is the horse will be there too. So please, let's make sure this time there are no mistakes. Can I count on you?"

Macready nodded his head slowly. He was used to dealing with the ruling class and familiar with their demanding ways. Montgomery was much the same as every other Lord or Lady, Duke or Duchess he had encountered over his many years of service. But he wanted Montgomery to understand he was not anyone's errand boy.

"Of course, my Lord, we will have the man followed. But honestly I don't give a damn about this horse or any other horse," he told Montgomery matter-of-factly. "I will have him followed because he may well lead us to his son who may very well be with his brother. If we find the brother, Darcy Walsh, I am certain it will lead to other Republicans, possibly a number that were involved in the Cairo Gang murders. I am here to serve the interests of the British government, not the whims of Montgomery Castle."

Lord Montgomery nodded in understanding. "At least we know where each stands," he said. "By coincidence our interests are aligned. Please let me know if the horse is found. And please make sure he is not harmed. I hope I can count on you. That, Sir Nevil, is in the best interests of us all." He turned and walked away. Macready watched him go and shook his head in dismay.

The Dubliner was the first to arrive wearing his customary black. He had been careful to watch for followers, doubling back along the city streets several times checking for any tail. Content he was alone he took the stairs to the second level and entered through a rear door. The room was small and there was no hearth so a chill filled the air. A tiny window allowed a view of the street to the north and he peeked out every few moments watching for the arrival of the others. Ten minutes later the American was pounding up the stairs. He wore his customary straw hat which the Dubliner found to be odd for this time of the year. His face was pink with exertion and he smiled his broad, toothy smile as he shook hands vigorously.

"You look tired, John," he said in his odd, Yank accent. "I do appreciate your assistance with this matter. We could never have had Walsh released from Mountjoy without your help." The Dubliner nodded in acknowledgement but said nothing more, uncertain of the purpose of this meeting. A few moments later another knock came and two men slipped in quietly. Frank Walsh looked exhausted and drawn from his ordeal. Dark half circles lined the bottom of his eyes and deep wrinkles had formed across his forehead, at the corners of his eyes and around his mouth. He'd lost weight and seemed stooped over, his short stature diminished even further. The man with him looked anything but drawn. He was nattily attired in a crisp, white shirt, blue coat and top hat with well shined black leather boots matching his valise. He looked every bit the solicitor. His name was Patrick Barry.

"I don't think you have met my client, John," the man said to the Dubliner. Frank Walsh reached across and shook John's hand, noticing as he did so that the man's eyes danced around the room, taking in everything, looking him in the eye while at the same time checking the door and the whereabouts of the others in the room.

"I regret your inconvenience," the Dubliner said in a soft and thoughtful voice. Frank nodded but said nothing.

"John was very instrumental in gaining your release," the American added, grasping Frank's hand and hugging him with familiar ease. Before his arrest, it had been several years since Frank had seen Harry the Horse but the man had changed hardly at all. His pink complexion and toothy smile reminded Frank of happier times. He nodded in thanks to the tall, thin man dressed in black. With the pleasantries out of the way, Barry continued.

"Do we know if Mr. Walsh's letter has reached the boy?" he began. John nodded affirmatively assuring them it had. "And do we know if the boy is still in Limerick with his Aunt?"

The Dubliner looked directly at Frank Walsh. "Your son is safe. And so is the horse," he began. "They are safely tucked away with uhm, with friends," he added after a moment's hesitation.

Frank exhaled a sigh of relief and smiled. For the past two months he had worried about everyone and everything. The first few days in Mountjoy were a terrible blur. The injuries sustained from Butterfield's brutal beating caused him to pass out from time to time, the pain so intense, the head wounds throbbing, the constant ache in his abdomen and his ribs ceaseless, sleep fitful and of little good. They had placed him in the infirmary under the watchful care of a nurse named Bridget. He healed slowly but with each day he showed slight improvement. Once the pain no longer overwhelmed him, memories of the attack in the cottage flooded back, tormenting Frank. Shuddering, he relived the thud of Butterfield's boot finding purchase in his wife's ribs and the dreadful sound of Fiona's cry as she tried shielding her child. He heard the recurring petrified screams of his younger daughter Deidre and the small howls of the wee Patricia. With near fatal anguish he relived the horrible rape of his daughter Maureen. He could vividly see the resignation on her beautiful face and the horror in her eyes but mostly he repeatedly relived the helplessness he felt at being able to do nothing to stop her terrible violation. These visions haunted him every day. Two weeks after his arrival at Mountjoy, Harry arrived with legal representation. Somehow Frank was not surprised. The man in the straw hat had a knack of showing up at the most needy times in his life. The first thing they did was locate Fiona and the children, finding them living outside the village of Barreen with a friend. They too suffered the constant reliving of the attack of the Black and Tans but the solicitor assured Frank that no permanent damage had been done to Fiona or Maureen. They would be alright. Frank insisted no one come visit him in prison and Barry assured him no one would be allowed in on any account. Next their attention turned to locating Mickey. Patrick Barry arranged for enquiries to be made in Limerick but it took weeks before any acknowledgement of the boy's presence was received. Surely the boy was trying to maintain a low profile, Frank thought, certain Mick had been smart enough to hide his famous horse. Frank wrote the short letter to his son, giving it to Harry to insure its safe delivery. The American turned to his friend John, the Dubliner, to find a way to get the letter to Limerick and through his secret channels the correspondence safely arrived. While they waited to hear word back from Limerick, Barry developed a strong case in Frank's defense and Harry worked his contacts in Washington, Dublin and London to pressure Dublin Castle for Frank's release. Now, with the end of February approaching, the court ruled for his dismissal and the terrible nightmare of Mountjoy Prison began to fade. And thanks to these good men, Frank knew now his son was safe and Whish't Daddy was too. Knowing his whole family was secure, despite the horror of the Athy House attack, gave him strength and encouragement. But he knew much work remained to be done.

"When can I see my son?" he asked. The Dubliner looked at the other men and shrugged.

"As soon as you feel well enough to travel, Mr. Walsh," he said. "I will arrange for a guide to take you to the boy. He is out west but I am not at liberty to say where. But he is safe. As a matter of fact he is with your brother Darcy. You can see them both very soon." Frank felt an odd twinge at the mention of his brother's name. There was much about Darcy that left Frank unsettled. Although he'd been greatly relieved by his brother's sudden and silent departure from Athy House, it bothered him on a primitive level that Darcy had slipped off, saying nothing, thanking no one, disappearing like a thief in the night. And Frank had no doubt that his sheltering of his convalescing brother had contributed to the Black and Tan's motivation for raiding his home and attacking his family. There was something else that bothered him about Darcy, something he may have heard or felt in his deepest, darkest soul, but he could not put a finger on it. He could not place it. Perhaps it was something about the assassinations of the British agents? Was his brother a murderer? Could that be it, he wondered. Somehow he thought it was more than that. His brother had been nothing but trouble these last few years and Frank was in no great hurry to see him again. But he could not wait to see his son. They discussed plans and contingencies for the journey and left it that word would come through the solicitor, Barry, when Frank would be ready to go. Before they ended the meeting he ventured one more question.

"Do you think we can race Whish't Daddy again?" he asked anxiously. He looked at each man hoping for a sign. "I know Mickey will be chomping to get him running again. The Derby is not far away and I'd love to see if we can have him ready for that. What do you think?" The American looked at Barry and the solicitor shook his head.

"There still might be a problem with ownership of Whish't Daddy, Mr. Walsh," he said carefully. "The court left open the whole issue of contracts, corporations, partnerships and who in the end owns the land and the horses," he added.

"Why?" Frank asked angrily. "I own all of it - the land and the horses and I want to run my horse in that race and I plan on doing exactly that."

Harry frowned. "It's not going to be that easy, Frank," he said. "To be honest I think we'd be able to do it bringing some pressure from across the Atlantic but that would take considerable time. And there will be push back from on high. The only reason ownership of the horse is still an issue is due to Montgomery Castle," he said with a sigh. Frank looked at him questioningly. "Oh come on, Frank," the American continued. "This is no surprise. Tell me you didn't know Montgomery wants your horse and he is ready to do whatever it takes to get him. And that man is very fond of getting what he wants."

Frank shook his head in disbelief. "And he is willing to go to these lengths to steal Whish't Daddy?" he asked incredulously. Both Patrick Barry and the American nodded. Frank scratched his head, letting out a long breath of air. "Okay, then maybe we'll have to do it his way," he said softly. The solicitor asked him what that meant but Frank just shook his head saying he was only thinking aloud. The four men shook hands, agreeing on their plan moving forward. Harry left first and a few moments later the Dubliner slipped through the door. After another ten minutes, Frank and the solicitor made their way down the steps and into the dark streets. They were chatting amiably as they made their way past the cobbler on the corner and neither noticed the little man hiding in the long shadows.

Chapter Twenty-Seven

Somewhere in the West of Ireland - March 1921

The reunion was bittersweet for Frank Walsh. Although his heart leapt with joy upon seeing his son, it also reminded him of his wonderful family, shattered months before by the brutal attack of the Black and Tan's and their terrible captain. He wondered if they would all ever be together again under one roof, healthy and happy as they had been a year before. It had been a difficult decision but he and Fiona agreed it would be best for her to take the girls and go live in London for a while. They could stay with relatives in a flat outside the city while things in Ireland hopefully settled down. The country had gone mad, the violence striking home with a vengeance and talk in the streets and towns and countryside was of a coming civil war that would pit the Home Rule Supporters against those that would settle only for one, united Ireland. And of course, that assumed the British would loosen their fatal grip and leave the country. Frank wanted his wife and his daughters to be safely away from the violence and insanity and he did not think anywhere in the country offered the same security as England at this time. His daughters were scarred by the violence they'd witnessed first hand and Fiona told him Maureen barely spoke in the days following the attack. His wife never mentioned anything regarding Maureen being with child and Frank thought it very possible he'd imagined hearing it during the vicious and sadistic attack. He thought it best to leave the subject alone; certain Fiona would deal with it delicately and in an appropriate manner. Two weeks after his release from prison, he'd seen them off down by the Dublin docks where they boarded a steamship to take them across the Irish Sea. Deidre cried hysterically protesting she did not want to go and Maureen barely looked at her father, her eyes sad and downcast with the hollow look of the defeated. He hugged her tightly, promising things would be alright but she only nodded in reply. Frank thought she'd mumbled the name of Darcy as she walked away. Then they boarded the old ship and soon were gone and he stood on the dock watching the boat move away with the empty feeling of a man whose family has been scattered about like leaves in the autumn wind.

Still, it was great to see Mick. The boy had grown a few inches taller and added a few pounds and the first thought running through Frank's head was whether or not the boy had outgrown the size of most jockeys. A fine peach fuzz covered his upper lip and sat in patches on his rosy cheeks. But the most apparent change in his appearance was the subtle transition from boy to man. He stood differently. He spoke differently, his voice deeper and more serious, his words chosen carefully and offered with discretion. When Da hugged him, kissing him on the head, he could feel Mick pull away slightly, possibly embarrassed in front of the other men. Mick asked about Mammy and the girls and Da told him they'd gone to England which hit Mick very hard.

"When will they be back?" he asked softly. Da only shrugged offering no reply. They left the others so they could speak in private and Mickey led his father towards the stable located a short walk from the men's barracks. He stopped in front of Whish't Daddy's stall and the big, beautiful chestnut beast sauntered over nestling his head in the crook of Mick's neck. Da reached behind his son and ran his hands along the horse's head and face and through the coarse mane of hair running down his neck.

"He looks good, Mick," Da commented as his eyes swept over the shoulders, the rear and along his powerful legs. He bent and ran his hands from Whish't Daddy's haunches down to the hoof, switching from one leg to the next and then raised himself up nodding with a broad smile. "He may be down a few pounds but he looks strong and his legs feel very good, strong and healthy. You've done a fine job with him, Mick. As I knew you would."

Mick returned the smile. "I haven't had much else to do other than listen to these men talk of politics and make their grandiose plans. Grooming and caring for Whishy was a much needed diversion. Although, I do wish I could take him out and let him run with abandon. He's been mostly cooped up and Commander Riordan has asked me to stay close to the camp and keep the horse well hidden. Someone might recognize him and draw attention and that is the last thing they want here."

Da nodded. Frowning slightly, he asked Mick, "Have you seen Darcy?"

The son shook his head up and down. "Yes, he's here. Well, maybe not now, he's most likely on the watch or doing something for the Commander. The men come and go frequently and return at night."

"Did you speak with him?" Da asked.

"Surely, Da, I did. But he seemed a little odd, to be honest. He was very nervous and unsettled. When I told him about the Black and Tans and that they had burned Athy House to the ground he wept like a child. He said he'd heard about if from Riordan but sill it seemed to hit him very hard. He asked about Maureen and the girls and you and Mammy and I told him I didn't know what happened to you all after I left with the horses. That upset him even more, as I guess it should. He told me I'd be best off keeping my distance from the others and he's come by now and then to say hello but he mostly stays away. Like I said, he is often on the watch." Da took in the information carefully but said nothing regarding his brother. He did not know what he would say to Darcy when they met. But he could think of nothing pleasant.

"Do you think we can race him again, Da?" Mick asked, interrupting his father's thoughts. The young man was stroking Whishy's face and looking at him with the admiration of a star struck lover.

"Seems to me son that you're now more man than boy so I will tell you straight away that there is a problem, a question of ownership in the eyes of some important people and until that is resolved we will have a very hard time getting him clearance to run."

Mick looked at his father incredulously. "How could that be? We've had this horse his entire life. I watched as he came into this world. We raised him and trained him and we've raced him numerous times. How could there be a question of ownership now?"

"Ireland is a mad house right now, son. These men here," Da stopped, pointing his chin back towards the barracks, "they want freedom and independence and they will stop at nothing less. The British government is reluctant to let go although I do think there are some who realize they can't hold on much longer. But most of those who rule are trying to keep a firm grip on every last bit that they can. This is about power and the land and in our case, about this horse. He's the finest animal in all of Ireland and there are men who want to take him away from us and they will do whatever they have to do to make that happen." Mick looked at his father with narrowed eyes, considering what he said.

"Lord Montgomery?" he asked. "Is he the one trying to take our horse? He's wanted Whishy since the first time he laid eyes on him. Even I could see that from a distance." His father nodded, again marveling at how the boy had grown so quickly into a young man.

"Montgomery has the money, the influence and the legal system to defeat us. We will never beat him in court. For the longest time son, I thought we could work our way to accommodation with the British. I thought that through industry and by building businesses we could eventually win our freedom and our independence. I thought the British would recognize the tremendous worth of the Irish people and willingly back away and give us what was rightfully ours to own and govern. But I was wrong Mick and as much as I hate to admit it, people like Commander Riordan and your Uncle Darcy were right. The only way to get what is rightfully ours it to take it for our own."

"But how can we do that if Montgomery Castle has all the power? How can we ever keep Whish't Daddy for our own?" Frank had never seen his son so intensely engaged or so desperate on any subject but he knew the horse meant everything in the world to Mick. Placing one hand on Mickey's shoulder he leaned in closely, whispering the words.

"We will beat them at their own game, son," he said looking him directly in the eye. "I have a plan. It will take a bit of time to put it in all in motion. And I will tell you straight it is not without risk. But I see no other way to prevail. But I need your help, son." Mick nodded several times keeping his eyes firmly fixed on his father. "The horse looks very good but we need to make sure he is in fine fiddle indeed. We need him at his best, Mick. I know it's been months since he's raced and he's trained very little. So we need to talk to Commander Riordan and find a place you can work him hard. We both know he is the finest horse in the land. Hopefully we are going to have one last chance to prove it. And if we do than I think he will be ours. Do you think you can get him in shape, Mick? Do you think he's still a champ?"

Mick turned and stroked Whish't Daddy's face with loving care, the sweet smile of a child returning to the young man. "He's a champ alright, Da. Give me three weeks and we'll be ready. We'll run like the wind, Da, we'll run like we never run before."

Frank Walsh moved closer still towards his son and wrapped him in a tight embrace. "You're going to have to Mick, God knows you're going to have to." He hugged the boy again and this time Mick did not pull away.

"These are very serious accusations, Ian," Sir Nevil said gravely as he read the formal charges MacDermott planned to bring against the Under-Secretary, John Harrington. "Treason, spying, providing information detrimental to the forces of the Crown! This is sensational stuff and will demand the man's death if proven true." They sat in the back of a small inn on the outskirts of Galway City. Sir Nevil had business in the town and MacDermott had crossed the country to discuss the matter with his superior. Things had been very tense between the two since the burning of Athy House and MacDermott was looking for a way to get back into his boss's good graces.

"Oh, they will prove true, Sir Nevil, of that I have little doubt," Ian boasted. "At your suggestion, I personally followed Frank Walsh upon his release from Mountjoy. He left with his solicitor and shortly thereafter they met up with an American by the name of Harry Fitzgerald and much to my surprise, no other than Under-Secretary Harrington."

"So what?" Sir Nevil replied impatiently. "We have no proof that Walsh is with the Republicans, we have been over that before. And he is perfectly within his rights to meet with his solicitor and this American chap."

Ian nodded in agreement. "Quite true, Sir Nevil," he said. "But please, allow me to continue. I maintained surveillance on both Harrington and the American. They met up again ten days ago, at the end of February outside of Limerick. And they were joined by one of the known Commanders of an IRA unit that goes by the name of the Twelve Apostles." MacDermott waited for a reaction but Macready only stared at him. "The Apostles are the group of Republicans responsible for the assassinations of the Cairo Gang. This Commander led the attack that killed our brave agents, many in cold blood!" Ian was growing angry just relating the story.

Sir Nevil nodded in understanding. "And if I remember correctly Under-Secretary Harrington had access to the names and addresses of these agents. He was going to have their transit papers prepared, correct?" Ian nodded enthusiastically.

"Exactly, Sir, that is exactly right. Harrington provided that information to the Republican Army and they killed our boys as a result. He is a traitor and a spy and he needs to pay for his crime."

Macready sipped a cup of tea, giving the matter grave thought. If MacDermott was correct than Harrington would swing from a rope in the next few days. But it was a serious accusation needing indisputable verification. He would discuss it with Hamar Greenwood when he returned to Dublin. For now, he wanted to do nothing drastic. "I would like some additional evidence of his espionage, Ian. I think you are most likely correct in your assumptions but one meeting with a suspected IRA Commander may not be enough for conviction. Is there anything more?" he asked.

"Yes, yes Sir," Ian replied quickly. "I had the Commander followed as well and he led us out towards Clare, west of Ennis. We lost him when dusk fell and a heavy rain storm hit but I am quite certain he and his men are hiding out that way somewhere. I am sure if we can capture him and make him talk he will indict Harrington as a coward and a traitor."

Sir Nevil nodded again. "Okay, we should start moving troops out west as soon as possible. The uprising is spreading quickly to these counties and we will need soldiers here soon if we are to stem the tide. Set up a temporary command here in Galway. I have a few visits to make in this region. I will be back in a few days and hopefully you will have more concrete information." Ian understood this to be his dismissal and he left quickly. He would begin writing orders immediately to transfer several units of the Black and Tans to Galway. He'd make sure Butterfield's command was included.

The pub boasted the finest whiskey and most tender chop in all of County Clare. The enthusiastic patrons seemed to agree as the bar area stood two deep and every table and chair was occupied in the dining areas looping around the counter. A thick cloud of smoke wafted up in the thatched ceiling and an old timer in a plaid jacket filled the room with soft melodies from his ancient harp. Michael Cleary shouted greetings to a few men drinking at the bar and patted a few backs while winding his way through tables and chairs arriving at the snug in the rear of the room beside the huge fireplace affording a wee bit of privacy. Taking off his cap, he slid out of his wool jacket and hung both on a nail in the wall before collapsing his big frame into the empty chair across from Frank Walsh. The two men shook hands.

"I am sorry for your troubles," Cleary offered with a shake of his big head. Frank nodded his appreciation. Frank had used O'Malley, the farrier, to help set up the meeting with the trainer from Montgomery Castle. O'Malley had obviously shared the story of the attack on Walsh and his family with the man. "Tea?" Cleary asked, noticing the steaming cup in Frank's hand. "I think I'll be needing something with a bit more bite." He waved the serving girl over and ordered a pint and a swallow of whiskey. Folding his hands he turned his eyes back on Walsh. "Athy House is no more?" he asked.

Frank shrugged. "The cottage, barn and stables are nothing but ash. The horses scattered across the countryside. We recovered three, two of my ponies and Bellweather. Still searching for the rest." Cleary looked at him with a mixture of bewilderment and disappointment. It took a moment to register with Frank but quickly he understood the unspoken question in Cleary's eyes. "Whish't Daddy is fine, if that's what you're wondering. My son took him before the bastards could get their hands on him." Frank thought he saw relief pass across Cleary's comical face.

"Can you rebuild?'

Frank shrugged again. "I am told there is still some question regarding my rights of ownership," he hesitated briefly checking the anger rising in his heart. "That applies to both the land and to my horses." Cleary nodded his understanding and then sighed.

"I see," he said shaking his head repeatedly. The two men looked at each other, their eyes locking in mutual understanding. The girl arrived with Cleary's order and he swallowed the amber whiskey in the blink of an eye. He sipped the ale and then spread his hands. "How can I be of assistance?"

Frank leaned in, lowering his voice. "Your boss is the reason there is any question regarding ownership of my horses and ownership of one horse in particular." Cleary said nothing but nodded slightly. Lord Montgomery had made his wishes very clear. "He wants Whish't Daddy and he will make it impossible for me to race the horse anywhere in Ireland if I refuse to sell."

"Very true, so are you prepared to do so?" Cleary asked. "He will pay handsomely for that big beast."

Frank smiled a sad smile. "Tell me, Michael, if he was your horse would you sell him?"

Now Cleary shrugged. He was surprised to hear Frank Walsh admit to owning the horse outright. It had been rumored over the years that he did but others claimed he was only the trainer working for people in America or Australia. Now that Athy House had been destroyed perhaps it did not matter.

"If I could not race the horse then maybe I would sell him," he said sipping again from the ale. "But if there was any chance at all to race him, I'd go to my grave before I sold that marvelous animal." Frank nodded smiling again. "But what choice do you have?" Cleary asked.

Frank hesitated again, letting his head roam around the cozy pub to make certain no one was listening to their conversation. Satisfied, he nearly whispered. "I want you to take a message to Lord Montgomery for me." The other man's eyes widened. "You tell him I want to set up a stakes race, his horse against mine, War Lord against Whish't Daddy, no other horses in the race." This time it was Cleary's turn to smile.

"What are the stakes?" he asked.

"If War Lord wins, Montgomery Castle keeps Whish't Daddy. If my horse wins, Montgomery uses his influence to have the government recognize the horse and all my land as my own. And I am within my rights to rebuild Athy House and make it the grandest stable in all of the British Isles. He loses nothing. He just allows me what is rightfully mine." Frank sat back relieved he had the idea out in the open.

Michael Cleary frowned, twisting his face awkwardly as if figuring out a difficult puzzle. "He may have nothing to lose but he most likely has nothing to gain. Your horse beat War Lord soundly at the Curragh, an amazing performance, I must say myself." It still bothered him to admit defeat but he could not deny what he had witnessed on that afternoon in September.

Frank nodded in appreciation of the compliment and had expected this objection. "Lord Montgomery can set up the race any way he wants. He can pick the course, the distance, the date and time and if need be we'll run at a weight disadvantage. It should not come down to that. Not with all the trophies you have sitting up in the Castle with War Lord's name on them. But I want to run this race. I need to run this race. So we'll do it however he insists. I only have two conditions. Only the two horses run and my son is allowed to ride Whish't Daddy. Everything else is in Montgomery's control."

Cleary waved to the girl to bring him another pint. He drank it slowly, considering the challenge Frank Walsh had just laid at his feet. He was uncertain if Lord Montgomery would accept the test. He might prefer to use his legal standing to force Walsh to surrender the horse without bothering to race. He had done worse things in the past. But he was a man who liked a good contest and nothing thrilled him more than watching a great match between two outstanding thoroughbreds. And certainly he would get that. Cleary rolled the ale around in his mouth considering the chance of War Lord beating his nemesis. If they could choose the distance, most likely five furloughs, a length War Lord could cover at full speed, and make the track very much to his liking and if need be put three or four pounds more on his opponent,

War Lord could do it, he convinced himself. It would not be easy but if the truth be known, Cleary had been aching for another chance to get even, to demonstrate his horse's superiority ever since the defeat in the St. Leger. He began getting excited at the prospects of an amazing stakes race with only these two marvelous champions. For a moment he thought about the consequences of losing and decided it too depressing, dismissing it all together.

"I will bring your proposal to Lord Montgomery's attention," he said. Frank smiled and stuck out his hand to shake again.

"Thank you, Michael. It means a great deal to me." Frank decided to order a pint for himself and then both men ordered something to eat. Over dinner they chatted about the racing game, the terrible political situation, the terror created by both the Republican gunmen as well as the Black and Tans and the RIC. Walsh told of sending his family to England and Cleary confessed to being happy he had no family to shield from this brutal terror. They finished eating and Cleary stood to leave. They clasped hands once again and as Montgomery Castle's trainer turned to go he hesitated, shaking his head slowly. "I probably shouldn't say anything about this but I think you been through enough, Frank," he looked his contemporary in the eye. "If we can arrange this race, be careful. Lord Montgomery is not to be trusted. I am certain he will have more than one trick to play." He hurried from the pub and disappeared into the night. Frank ordered another cup of tea and sat thinking about the race.

Chapter Twenty- Eight

Galway City - March 1921

The late winter evening was wet and windy with gusts whistling down the narrow, cobblestone streets. John Harrington, dressed in his customary black, blended into the shadows while moving quietly towards the waterfront. Galway City had grown considerably since his last trip out west and he needed to refer to a small, hastily drawn map to find his rendezvous point, an empty warehouse on the water that had once housed crate upon crate of oysters and mussels plucked from the shores of Connemara sixty miles to the west. The building still reeked of fish and salt and seaweed. He found Riordan at the rear of the warehouse looking out of a window onto the blackness of Galway Bay.

"They say another civilization lies at the bottom of that bay, Commander," Harrington said by way of greeting. "A civilization of artisans and goldsmiths and jewelers and craftsman that created the finest goods in all the world, the most beautiful vases and pottery and silverware, exquisite garments lined with golden thread and laced with flawless diamonds, pillows and quilts as soft as a summer breeze and twice as lovely as a sunset, tables and chairs of wood so rare as to be found only at the ends of the earth, chariots of gleaming gold with porcelain wheels made to take flight." He stood next to the big soldier, both looking out upon the dark sea.

"So what happened to this so called civilization?" Riordan asked.

"Legend has it that they angered the gods by creating things more beautiful than the deities created in nature, things more beautiful than a countryside of riotous floral colors, more startling than waves smashing high on the rocky coast of Kerry, more beautiful still than the eyes of a child looking upon a butterfly for the very first time. So the gods punished these artisans and craftsmen and the like, pushing them all, along with their beautiful creations, into Galway Bay and watched in bitter envy as the priceless treasures sunk to the bottom of the sea. Even now, if you look closely when the sun or the moon are shining just right upon the water, you'll see the twinkle of a diamond or the flash of a golden button winking up at you from the depths. Or so it has been told."

Riordan looked at the Dubliner and smiled. "Sounds like the luck of the Irish, doesn't it?" he added with a chuckle. "What do you have for me?"

Harrington took a map from his pocket and spread it out on an abandoned crate. The two men hunched over it and the Under-Secretary pointed to one area and slid his finger along to another. "They're moving considerable forces into these areas from Limerick up to the North across Clare and Galway. They know Cork is lost and most likely Dublin too although they still maintain considerable troops around the capital. They are trying to keep the movement from spreading out West, looking at it as a last resort if you will." Harrington went on to explain to the Commander where the largest caches of weapons would be found, where the RIC barracks would be weakest and where the Black and Tans would augment the Constabulary. Riordan voiced some potential adjustments but Harrington told him he did not make plans, he only supplied information, and money. He placed a parcel of bills and a bag of coins on the crate and Riordan scooped them up quickly.

"There is one other issue," Harrington said while packing away the map. "My understanding is that you have met this Frank Walsh and his son?" Riordan nodded. "There is to be an important race, Walsh's horse and a horse from Montgomery Castle."

"This is of no importance to me," Riordan countered. "I don't give a damn about horse races. We have a war to fight."

Harrington held up his hand. "I understand what you're saying. But this is different. Montgomery wants to steal the horse. The only way Walsh can keep his property is to win the race." The soldier shrugged, unimpressed. "You say this war is about Irish independence, about the rights of all Irishmen," Harrington continued. "What is a more fundamental right than the ability to own your own property? That horse is very well known across our land. If he is allowed to be stolen by the English aristocracy than what have we gained with all this killing? That horse is Ireland's horse. We need to give Walsh every chance to win this race."

The Commander readied himself to leave. "I don't know how we can help other than to keep Walsh and his boy safe, and the horse too. Other than that, I don't know a damn thing about racing."

John Harrington nodded and smiled. "You can help in two ways, Officer Riordan. Find Walsh and his son a place to train the horse adequately and help them get to the race. I think it will be at Montgomery Castle and I know Lord Montgomery will be waiting. Still, Walsh knows his business. Given the opportunity, his horse will prevail." Riordan grudgingly nodded his consent. The two men shook hands and the Commander slipped out the rear door, disappearing into the night.

Harrington looked at Galway Bay and thought about the legendary treasures lying at the bottom. He wished for an Ireland filled with beautiful things once again and an end to all the senseless killing. He left the building from the front entrance and as he stepped into the road he was met suddenly by Ian MacDermott and four Black and Tan soldiers. Two of the Black and Tans grabbed Harrington pinning his arms behind his back. MacDermott stepped up to the Under-Secretary and searched his pockets, pulling out the map and a small notebook. He looked over the crude drawing quickly and then put it inside his own coat.

"You are under arrest Harrington for treason and seditious acts against the crown," he said angrily. "You are responsible for the deaths of fourteen British agents and I intend to see you hanging until dead in payment for your hideous crimes." MacDermott's face was pink with rage but his eyes twinkled with satisfaction on catching his quarry.

Harrington stared at him but said nothing. He knew this would certainly happen one day. He always understood the risks he took on behalf of the battle for a free and independent Ireland. He had no regrets. He took one final glance at Galway Bay as the Black and Tans roughly tossed him into the back of a wagon and rolled down the dark and wet cobblestone streets of Galway City.

The gallows was a crudely constructed thing as hideous as the purpose for which it had been built. It had a small, dark platform made of discarded planks from the waterfront and an arch of grayish timbers to crooked and bent to serve any other use. A thick, brown rope hung from the middle of the arch swaying in the late morning breeze. Slowly a crowd began building in the courtyard off Dock Road where over the past week the make shift court had held the trial of John Harrington. A magistrate traveled from Dublin to Galway, although Hamar Greenwood had argued to move the whole matter to the capital. Sir Nevil Macready interceded directly, forcing the hearing to take place quickly and with as little fanfare as possible. The likelihood of Republican intervention in the process could not be overlooked. A very large and visible presence of RIC, Black and Tans and Auxiliaries moved into and around the city, setting up check points, searching for potential Volunteers, and demonstrating a large and dangerous show of force to dissuade the idea of an IRA attack on the courthouse or the jail. The trial moved quickly, its outcome predetermined. The magistrate heard the testimony of Ian MacDermott and several members of the Black and Tans present at the arrest. He looked over the map of British forces deployed in Western Ireland seized from the Under Secretary. The prosecutor also presented a copy of the list of names and addresses of the British agents that made up the Cairo Gang found in Harrington's office in Dublin Castle. A number of the names of the agents killed in the Bloody Sunday attacks were circled in black ink and the court considered this evidence to be very damning. Patrick Barry, the same solicitor who had represented Frank Walsh, argued on Harrington's behalf but the Magistrate gave him little leeway and quickly found the Dubliner guilty of treason and sedition. He sentenced him to death by hanging and they spared no time setting up the execution.

Most of the crowd came out of curiosity. It was not often a high ranking member of the British Government, even a native Irishman, was to be executed for crimes against the Crown and it would be a sight to remember and talk about for years. Farmers, fishermen and shepherds came in from the outlying countryside and city dwellers left their jobs and homes to witness the historic event. Hawkers set up their tables selling small pies of potato and onions and cups of steaming tea laced with sugar. The morning was warmer than usual for the middle of March with a bright sun shining in a cloudless sky. A light, salty breeze wafted in from the bay. A loud murmur of anticipation rose from the growing crowd, blending voices of righteous indignation for such a horrible crime with the more popular sentiment of English injustice once again served against one of their own. The British soldiers held their weapons high, nervously surveying the potentially hostile mob, hoping to quickly bring the execution to closure.

At the front of the crowd, watching the door of the temporary jail closely, Harry Fitzgerald stood with his straw hat in hand, saddened by the pending death of his friend. He had known John Harrington for more than a decade and found the man to be honest, decent, courageous and kind. He would miss John terribly. He had helped the cause greatly and never wavered from the struggle for Irish independence. The American let his eyes roam around the growing crowd and thought it possible that these people would soon be free and rule themselves and it would be due to the heroic efforts of men like John Harrington. He hoped one day the people of Ireland would recognize his sacrifice.

More to the rear of the mob, and on the fringe almost out by Dock Street, Frank Walsh watched in silence. He had left Mick in a boarding house with a barn on the other side of Galway, leaving his son to feed and groom Whish't Daddy and to tend to the horse while a local veterinarian checked a slight inflammation of his front left leg. It was most likely nothing to be concerned with but they always erred on the side of caution when it came to such things. It also provided Frank with a good reason to leave the boy behind. Mick was growing quickly into manhood but Frank still hoped to shield his son from something as horrible as witnessing a death by hanging. He did not know John Harrington very well and had only met the man the one time after his release from Mountjoy. But the Under-Secretary had been of great assistance these past months. He had helped with Frank's release from prison, with locating Mick in Limerick; he'd helped hide them in the west and helped with their move to Galway City. Frank knew a good man when he met one and John Harrington was a good man. His death would represent one less good man in Ireland and it seemed to Frank the country was in desperate need of good men at this time. He listened to the banter back and forth between the supporters of the British presence in his country and those men hell bent on the fight for freedom, damn all costs. He wondered for a countless number of times if this land would ever know true freedom and if it did would it ever know lasting peace. The screaming and yelling and violent fighting within the crowd suggested otherwise. He scanned the crowd again and then his eyes moved towards the soldiers and troops surrounding the mass of people, guns held at the ready, fearful determination lining their faces. As his eyes moved along the line of soldiers, they suddenly locked in on one man and anger rose inside of him like a fire exploding in a hearth. Near the door to the jail stood the massive and hideous figure of the Black and Tan's Captain, the horrible and hated Butterfield. The man was sneering at the crowd and occasionally swatting at people in the front with his massive hands or poking them with his gun, jabbing at them like they were sacks of hay. Even at a distance, Frank could see the leaky puss sliding down his face and he remembered that horrible goop dripping from the monster's eyes as he raped Maureen with such careless disregard. Frank watched the man carefully, intent not to let him out of his sight.

Hidden behind the crowd, ducked in behind piles of broken crates, barrels and discarded fishing tackle, Darcy Walsh viewed the assembling mass and the surrounding sentries with a mixture of hatred and curiosity. He did not know anyone named Harrington and had never met the man who would be executed. But he had been told the man was a patriot and that he would die for Irish independence and Darcy needed to know nothing more. His hatred of all things British grew deeper and more vengeful. He watched the crowd shoving and pushing each other and listened to the pointless yelling and screaming. Occasionally someone would begin loudly singing one of the rebel ballads and most of the mob joined in stridently, the courtyard filling with the sound of voices lamenting past deaths and defeats and promising glorious victories to come. The scene was taking on the atmosphere of a circus or a carnival and it continued to build until finally, the door of the jail opened and a small parade of people were greeted by a tremendous roar from the crowd followed by deafening silence. Two British soldiers led the group into the courtyard and towards the gallows. They were followed by the magistrate, dressed in flowing robes of black and red with the crest of the British Empire spread across his chest. Next came a large man wearing a black hood with two eyeholes cutout so he could see. He was the executioner and the crowd hissed at his appearance. Two more soldiers stepped out of the jail and between them, manacled at both his hands and feet, John Harrington walked calmly, his head held high and his eyes clear and bright. At the sight of the condemned the crowd grew quiet again, punctuated by the occasional jeering of anger against the authorities or hatred towards the convicted man. The soldiers stopped at the gallows and the magistrate and the executioner walked up the six steps onto the wooden platform. The soldiers escorting Harrington moved towards the stairs but he shook himself free of their grasp, indicating he would climb the steps alone, needing no assistance. When he reached the platform, a priest came forward, moved up the stairs and stood in front of him, sprinkling him with water. He blessed the condemned man and left the platform, disappearing into the mass of people. A silence eerie and complete descended on the courtyard. The magistrate stepped forward and read the charges and the ruling of the court and instructed the executioner to carry out the sentence. The hooded man stepped towards the rope and carefully slipped the noose over John Harrington's head. He took out another black hood and as he began pulling it over Harrington's head the man shook it free, insisting he die uncovered.

"I want them to watch me die with my eyes wide open and a smile on my face," he yelled out in a firm, strong voice which carried across the silent courtyard. "For I see with these eyes the beauty of this grand country and I die smiling in the knowledge that very soon Ireland will be independent and every Irishmen will be free." As these words reverberated across the crowded square, a huge cheer rose from the mob and Darcy felt the hairs on the back of his neck raise up with pride and love and sorrow. He thought of this man's bravery and of the love the people held in their hearts for his courageous act and he was saddened knowing he could never do such a brave thing himself. A moment later the courtyard fell silent again as the executioner pulled the lever opening the trapdoor below the doomed man's feet. With a loud bang the gallows opened and the body dropped quickly. Those standing in the front heard the quick, distinctive sound of the man's neck snapping. In the gentle sunshine of a March morning, John Harrington's dead body twisted in the light breeze coming off Galway Bay. Quickly, shrill voices could be heard keening the mournful sound of a death lamented. Most looked away towards the Bay or stared at the ground with their head's hung low. Slowly the crowd began slipping away. Darcy stayed well hidden in the debris, watching the people move out in sorrow. Then he noticed the familiar face of his brother Frank standing stone still in the crowd. Frank was facing the gallows but watching intently the line of Black and Tans along the wall. He stood that way for a long time until the soldiers began moving out. Keeping a fair distance away, Frank began following them from the courtyard. Darcy looked around carefully, searching for danger from all directions. Seeing none, he slipped from his hiding spot and began discreetly trailing his brother. He knew no reason for his actions other than some odd and powerful premonition that his destiny led that way. The soldiers moved slowly along Dock Street and as they did so the hideous captain who Darcy remembered well, began pointing and shouting directions to his men. The soldiers in the unit moved off in different places taking up their positions. Butterfield continued down the street walking alone. Frank followed the captain carefully, maintaining a safe distance. Darcy reached into his coat pocket and his hands closed around the butt of his revolver. The gun provided little reassurance. He felt his heart pounding relentlessly in his chest. He pulled his hat down over his eyes, hoping to avoid detection while staying close enough to watch his older brother.

Butterfield walked along the Dock Road for ten minutes until he was well clear of the hustle and bustle of the courtyard and the spectacle of John Harrington's hanging. He crossed the street to the bay side of the road and then ducked quickly into a long, narrow building that sat alone between two large, empty lots. It was relatively desolate down on this end of the harbor and when the wind was up it rattled through the old building, muffling most sounds coming from inside. Only a faint breeze blew on this late March morning but he didn't care. He did not know what is was about an execution that raised his insatiable lust to its full and merciless capacity but the sight of Harrington's limp body dropping through the gallows trap door only to be jerked up viciously at the end of the rope and then swing lifelessly in the breeze had created a longing in him that needed to be satisfied. He made his way through the building and down the few massive slate stones that acted as steps leading to a round, small room that looked much like a tiny dungeon. The floors were made of hard packed sand and the walls were of rough stone and damp wooden logs and the place smelled of the sea. In the corner of the small prison, a young girl was tied to the wall by both wrists, her little feet barely able to touch the ground, her tiny smock covered in dirt and mud. A rag had been stuffed in her mouth allowing only a faint moan to escape into the moist air. When she saw Butterfield approaching her eyes opened wide in terror and she tried desperately to cling tightly to the wall. But his big hand tore the smock away from her trembling body and he sliced easily through the ropes tying her to the wall and with a vicious shove pushed her to the ground. Then he pulled down his pants and fell directly upon her.

Frank Walsh hesitated a moment before entering the building. He had no weapon and he knew Butterfield was a terribly dangerous man. Looking about the road, he found a remnant of an old wooden plank lying alongside the building. He picked it up and then slipped in through the doorway, trying desperately to be as quiet as possible. The midday sun came in through the filthy windows allowing him a good view of the two rooms off the hallway and they held nothing but broken furniture and discarded crates. He stopped, listening carefully and quickly picked up the distinctive sound of whimpering coming from the rear of the building. He looked down the narrow hallway but could see little more than the walls and flooring. At the very end it appeared to drop off into an abyss. He crept slowly down the corridor, stepping gingerly, alert to avoid the scraps of paper and chips of wood scattered about the floor. The closer he went, the louder the whimpering became and now he could hear it joined by piggish grunting and moaning. He reached the end of the hallway and looked down into the pit below. He heard the cries of a young person but could see nothing more than Butterfield's huge body lying face down in the dungeon, writhing back and force, groans following grunts of desire escaping from the sordid heap. Frank saw a tiny ankle sticking out from underneath the monster's body and he knew instantly what was happening. A horrible image of his daughter being raped by this grotesque man flashed quickly across his mind, reminding him that memory would stay with him forever. But the sense of uselessness would not. Back in the cottage he had been beaten mercilessly and held in check by armed soldiers. He'd wished every day since that afternoon that he'd been able to save Maureen from that terrible fate. Maybe he could save this poor waif. He took one step down into the pit and raised the wooden club over his shoulder, intent on crashing it down upon Butterfield's head. But the soldier must have sensed something behind him or maybe he heard the shuffle of Frank's feet or the sound of the plank slicing through the air because at the last moment he shifted slightly and turned to look behind him. The shard of wood smashed hard across the Captain's shoulder, splintering into a number of pieces, scattering around his body. Looking at Frank, his one good eye flared in anger and he howled with colossal wrath as he rolled off his weeping victim. Frank noticed in disgust that the girl was no more than a child, barely twelve years old if even that. In a flash, Butterfield was on his feet. He pulled his pants to his waist hiding his manhood and kicked viciously at the young girl causing her to scurry away against the wall. He locked his eyes on Frank and slowly moved his hand to his belt, coming away with his pistol. He shook his massive, ugly head and spit on the ground.

"I should have killed you while I had the chance," he said with disgust.

Frank held his one eyed stare and nodded his head in agreement. "Yes, you should have you fecking bastard. Now it is I who will kill you." With that he launched himself from the first step into the air crashing into Butterfield with all the power of a footballer going for the score. He hit the big Captain solidly sending him sprawling to the hard packed floor of the pit. Butterfield dropped his revolver and it skittered towards the rear of the dungeon. Frank was quickly on top of him, throwing punches filled with all the venom and hatred he had stored up over the past five months. Time and again his fists found Butterfield's block like head and he pounded away repeatedly, at times substituting a sharp poke in the man's good eye or a hard yank on his scrawny hair. The soldier was breathing very rapidly, screaming a rage filled monologue laced with loathsome curses, accompanied by disgusting spittle flying from his mouth. As Frank tired from his relentless assault, Butterfield managed to get a grip on his attacker's throat and began squeezing as hard and as violently as he could muster. Slowly Frank began to slacken and with a final squeeze of the soldier's massive hand he passed out and Butterfield tossed him over like a rag doll. Frank lie still in the dirt for several moments before awakening. He started choking desperately for air. When he managed to look up, Butterfield stood above him like some avenging god, pointing the revolver directly in Frank's face. A few feet away, the young girl screamed but neither man bothered to look her way.

"Okay, peasant," he said softly, still trying to catch his own breath, "now you get what's coming to you. You've had your fun, haven't you? Was it revenge you were after, man? Well, I couldn't say I blame you. You're daughter was a ripe and luscious wench, if I do say myself. I am kind of wishing I had the mother as well." He hesitated a moment, wiping his lips with the back of his arm. Blood ran from his mouth and his nose and he looked at the blood on his sleeve, almost surprised to see it there. "A little blood never hurt anyone, did it," he asked mockingly. "Better than losing your family and your land and your horses and your livelihood I'd guess. Isn't that right, peasant?"

"Go to hell, Butterfield," Frank replied hoarsely.

"Oh, I am going to hell for sure, peasant. Actually I am kind of looking forward to it. At least I'll be with my own kind." He laughed loudly and then looked over at the little girl. "I'll be right with you, darling," he said with a hideous grin. Frank moved towards the girl, hoping to protect her. "Going to be a hero, peasant?" he asked. "Too late for that. I may be going to hell but it won't be as soon as you. Say good-bye." He raised the revolver, pointed it at Frank's head and squeezed the trigger.

Darcy had crept into the building only moments before. He'd slipped into the rear near the dungeon following the sounds of the scuffle and the voices of his brother and the soldier. When he reached the pit, Frank was lying on the ground with Butterfield's gun pointed right at him. The two men were talking. He kept out of site along the wall listening for a few moments, hoping to find the courage to pull out his gun and shoot the horrible soldier dead. He flinched at the mention of Frank's daughter, assuming the man meant his beloved Maureen. Ripe and luscious wench? What could he mean by that? He heard the soldier bate his brother a few moments more and then he saw him raise the pistol and tell Frank to say good-bye. Darcy sprung from his spot along the wall.

No one would ever know why Darcy did not just shoot the man. He had a clear shot and he could hardly miss from such close range. A bullet to the head would have done the job. No one would ever know if it was instinct, cunning, guilt, sorrow or the desire to set straight all the sins of his past, to make good for all the harm he had caused, to in his last moments make right for a lifetime of wrongs. For whatever reason the world would never know, Darcy Walsh threw himself from against the wall, into the pit, landing squarely in front of his brother and when the Captain's gun exploded firing its deadly round, it found the middle of Darcy's chest, touching Frank not at all. And despite the bullet that would end his life entering his complicated heart, Darcy managed to raise his own pistol, firing it repeatedly, squeezing off four shots, each one finding a delicate spot in or around Butterfield's neck, throat and head. Blood squirted heavily from his face and a second hole in his cheek nearly matched the horrible mess that had once been his eye. Both Darcy and Frank Walsh looked on in disbelief as the terrible man crashed to the ground beside them, very obviously dead.

Frank shifted his brother's weight, scrambling around to face Darcy. He was very pale and the light in his eyes was fading rapidly.

"No, Darcy, hold on, wait. I'll send the girl for help."

Darcy, finding the last of his strength, offered his brother a weak smile. "No," he whispered softly. "It's alright. Let me go." Frank shook his head, trying to hold back the tears burning in his eyes. "I'm sorry, Frank, I really am," Darcy said in a fading voice. "Tell her it's… it's…"

His eyes fluttered, closing for the final time and Frank knew with all certainty his youngest brother was dead. He'd never know for sure what Darcy wanted him to tell or to who he wanted it be told to, but somehow he knew it must have been Maureen. The two had always been very close. He looked down sadly on his brother's beautiful face, his heart sick with grief and guilt and loss. When would all the horror cease, he thought? When would all the killing stop? He kissed Darcy tenderly on the cheek, resting his head gently on the ground. Then he moved away sadly, needing to care for the weeping young girl.

Chapter Twenty-Nine

Montgomery Castle, Connemara – End March, 1921

Mick walked the castle grounds for the fifth time and could only marvel at its perfection. Surveying the land and buildings around the racecourse he shook his head in disbelief, amazed that such a beautiful course, complete with benches for spectators, barns, stables and paddocks could be constructed within the confines of Montgomery Castle's property. It was no wonder that the Castle boasted such a fine reputation for its horses and that it was considered the finest of all stables in Ireland and one of the best in the British Empire. To have such a facility at their disposal gave Lord Montgomery and his team a tremendous advantage in breeding, training and racing their thoroughbreds. Mick laughed sadly as he thought of the small, makeshift course down the hill from the cottage in Barreen and longed once again for the comforts of Athy House and the warm embrace of his mother and his sisters. He kicked at the track's grass, finding it firm and unyielding and he knew it had been treated by the workers to achieve a consistency much to War Lord's liking. Whish't Daddy preferred a softer surface but Da had told him the previous evening that the conditions would favor their rival considerably. Negotiations between Montgomery's trainer and Frank Walsh had gone back and forth through a number of correspondences and the conclusions were certainly not an advantage for Mick and Whish't Daddy. They would run a short race, only six furlongs and Mick knew Montgomery Castle wanted no part of a longer race, having witnessed Whishy's great stamina at the Curragh the previous season.

And the race date came far sooner than Mick would have liked. He'd been training his horse for less than three weeks and under less than perfect conditions. Commander Riordan had found a small farm near the border between Clare and Galway and they'd been able to use the tiny facility for most aspects of training. But the course they'd laid out ran through sheep grazing land and it was full of rocky outcrops, scrubby brush and deep hollows where the sheep dug holes to nestle in for warmth. Mick had run Whishy carefully, avoiding any missteps that could injure a leg or cause a fall. And he'd had only four or five days to really push his horse hard, needing time to allow him to recover and rest. Da told him Lord Montgomery knew their horse was being kept in primitive conditions so he pushed hard for the race to happen quickly and Da had little choice but to accept this demand. Mick knew they had a difficult task at hand - a short race on a hard course with a horse that was not in peak physical form. And to boot he'd be carrying three extra pounds more than War Lord. Cleary told them Lord Montgomery insisted on the added weight and would not agree to the race without this stipulation. So Da had agreed.

Mick walked to the starting position on the course. There would be no starting gate. The two horses would line up side by side and then a gun would be fired and they'd take off and run the six furlongs, taking the first turn and racing hard down the back stretch, into the far turn and then down the home stretch which would race past spectators sitting on the wooden benches to the right. The benches reached ten high but Da was unsure of how many spectators would be watching. If Montgomery Castle lost, they would not want many witnesses.

There were three gates off the race course. One led back to the shed row where the barns and stalls were lined up and the horses were held before and after the race. A gate in the middle of the backstretch led to a rocky road used for carting supplies and transporting horses in and out of the castle grounds. Supply sheds lined this road and at the end of these small buildings a larger road running north and south could be accessed. The third gate was at the end of the far turn close by the spectator seating and Da told Mick that the gate led back into the Castle proper, past the hawker's shops and the market and the large buildings where the Lord and his minions lived. This road eventually came to the

Castle's main gate and from there a road ran both east towards Galway City and west out to the Atlantic, a mile and half away. Da told Mick to familiarize himself with the gates and exits in and out of the course and the Castle grounds but he had not told him why. He said to be ready for anything. Mick found no comfort in this cryptic remark. He walked the course one more time, working out in his mind the best spot to give Whishy his way, thinking the far turn might be the best place but knowing he would have to judge once the two horses sprinted from the starting point. He imagined his majestic horse thundering down the home stretch and he suddenly felt confident that despite the conditions and lack of training, Whish't Daddy would prevail. He turned and walked quickly through the first gate leading back to the barns and found his father talking with a man wearing a straw hat who spoke with a strange accent. The man shook Da's hand firmly, patting him on the shoulder as he did. He gave Mick a short wave and then disappeared down the row of barns and stables.

Da took Mick into the stable holding Whishy and the two huddled behind the massive horse. Mick's hand went to Whishy's face and he scratched him gently on his face and neck. The horse licked at Mick's hand. Da put his finger to his mouth, indicating they needed to speak in a whisper.

"We race in an hour," he began. There was something in his voice Mick found disturbing and he listened intently, searching for meaning in every whispered word. "I have your colors in my bag. Your Mom made anther set before she went to England. I want you to wear them with pride, son. I know your Mom would like that." Da started choking up a bit and Mick felt hot tears building at the back of his eyes.

"What's the matter, Da? Is everything alright?" he asked.

Da nodded but his reassurance was not very enthusiastic. "I think it will be fine, Mick. I really do. But you're going to have to be careful, both during the race and afterwards. Montgomery wants this horse badly and he may try anything to get him. That man you saw me with is an old friend. His name is Harry. He warned me that there are many soldiers spreading out around the castle and they may be here to take our horse. There are a fair number of Republicans massing in the countryside as well so the soldiers may be here to deal with them but we don't really know. We can not be sure so you need to be careful. When the race is over, let Whishy cool down a bit and then follow War Lord out of the middle gate on the backstretch. We'll have our wagon waiting back there and load him quickly and be gone. Michael Cleary will be standing by the gate to give us a hand. Do you understand?"

Mick nodded slowly, still unsettled by his father's voice and the sadness in his eyes shrouding his rugged face. "Sure Da, I understand. I seen the gates and I know just where you mean. But I thought we had a deal, Da. If we win the race than Whishy is ours, wasn't that the agreement?"

Da shook his head from side to side. "I am not sure we can trust this agreement. We have no chance but to try. If things work out we'll be on the road back towards Barreen this evening and all this will be a strange memory. But it may not work out that way, son. So you need to do whatever is necessary to get away with our horse. I know you'll figure it out, Mick. You and that horse are an incredible team. Between you both I know you'll do the right thing. I know you'll make me proud." He wrapped his arms around the boy pulling him tightly against his chest. He wondered absently if maybe the son was bigger than the father now but it was a fleeting thought and it left as quickly as it came. Mick was hugging him back very hard and Frank Walsh never wanted to let him go. "I love you, son," he said in a brittle, cracking voice. The boy squeezed him again.

"I love you too, Da. And I won't let you down." They held onto each other for a few long minutes and then Da walked out of the stable without looking back.

Inside the castle Lord Montgomery huddled in his parlor with Nevil Macready, Ian MacDermott and Michael Cleary. The gray light of late morning filtered in from the large window overlooking the east side of the Castle grounds. They could look down upon the race course and see parts of the row of stables where horses were coming and going.

"Take me through this one more time," Lord Montgomery said. "The race goes off in less than an hour and I want to make sure we have everything in place as required." He looked at the trainer and Cleary spoke up.

"We start from the line in front of the shed row and we'll have War Lord on the inside, which will give him the advantage right off the start. The turf is hardest along the rail so he'll like that. Whish't Daddy is carrying three more pounds than our boy so that might slow him down as well. I told Moran to get out quickly but not to burn him out on the backstretch. If he can stay a wee bit ahead of that beast through the far turn I like War Lord's chances down the homestretch. It'll be only the last two furlongs that he needs to go flat out and we been working him that way for the past six weeks. Whish't Daddy hasn't been training much these last months so I don't think he'll have that burst at the end to beat us to the wire." The trainer wandered over to the window and looked down at the track. He pictured the exact spot on the final furlongs where he thought the race would be decided. "We have to have the lead going down the stretch," he added nervously.

Montgomery spread his hands wide. "And if we don't?" he asked. Cleary shrugged in reply. He did not feel he had to tell his boss the obvious.

"We have, my Lord, prepared for all contingencies," Sir Nevil interjected. He nodded to MacDermott and the small Scotsman gladly jumped in.

"Cleary here, has instructed Frank Walsh to have his boy follow War Lord at the end of the race. He'll take his horse through the middle gate, the one I understand is used for supplies," he pointed towards the window in the general direction of the backstretch. "Walsh has his wagon waiting back there to load his horse and get away quickly. I will have over forty men tucked away back there, hiding behind the supply sheds and small buildings so we don't scare the boy off. Once he gets to the wagon we'll surround him and take control of the horse. I have instructed my men to take the animal to your main barn and to lock him away and allow no one in the stable. I told them not to hurt the younger Walsh unless it is necessary but to make sure they have the horse in their possession at all costs." Ian thought of the brutish Butterfield and wondered again why the man had disappeared. He'd not been seen in nearly a week and MacDermott thought it might be a blessing given the task at hand. The operation would rely on speed and cunning, not on brute force and pointless violence. "We also have signs of significant Republican activity in the area so I have another ring of soldiers stationed outside the Castle in case of an attack or any other plan to disrupt the race." He finished with a proud smile, hoping he had impressed Lord Montgomery and Sir Nevil with his comprehensive plan.

Montgomery nodded his approval. "What will you do with Walsh?" he asked.

MacDermott hesitated. "Take him into custody?" he asked looking towards Macready. Sir Nevil shrugged uncomfortably. "He is breaking the law again," the Scot squealed. "He is racing a horse he does not own. We can charge him with horse theft or something along those lines."

Macready shook his head. "Just take him and the boy into custody but charge them with nothing. We will escort them back to Kildare and leave them on the burned out ruins of Athy House." He looked disgustedly at MacDermott, still infuriated by the attack on Walsh's home. Ian chastened, nodded his understanding.

"Hopefully War Lord carries the day," Montgomery declared. He looked at his trainer with a smug grin. "You wanted another shot at this Whish't Daddy and now you have it. Either way by the end of the day the horse will be mine. The question is whether you might still have a job, Cleary. That depends completely on this race."

Michael Cleary turned crimson, embarrassed to be called out in front of the other men. He wished he could answer Montgomery in the way the man deserved but he swallowed his pride, forcing a small grin of his own. "Yes, I do understand, my Lord. I think we'll do just fine." He hesitated a moment and then stepped towards the door. "And as my livelihood is riding on this race, if you don't mind I need to get down to the course and make sure our horse is ready and Moran has his instructions well understood." He bowed slightly towards the others and then hurried from the room.

Mick felt at home back atop Whish't Daddy. The two of them moved slowly along the row of stables, Mick resplendent in the gold and crimson checks of Athy House. The first three rows of spectator benches were nearly filled and most of the patrons whistled or applauded the monstrous horse from Kildare. Mick nodded in appreciation, surprised that the people in the stands would acknowledge any challenger to their majestic War Lord. He searched the course for his Da but did not see him anywhere. He thought this odd. Cleary was speaking quietly with Quiney Moran and both men took a cautious look towards Mick and Whish't Daddy. War Lord looked impressive with his black coat glistening and his muscles rippling as he pranced along towards the starting line. A judge had been selected from a nearby Galway course and he had the task of organizing the start. Stable boys and grooms scattered about hoping to garner the best vantage point to watch the finish. The crowd began cheering and applauding, the noise reverberating throughout the castle property. Lord Montgomery sat high up on the row of benches in a cushioned area near the finish. Nevil Macready sat alongside him, the two men looking tense and stiff as the start neared. Mick looked about but still could not find his father and a dull ache of concern began beating in his chest and stomach. The judge waved the two riders towards the starting line and Mick moved Whishy forward. War Lord was a few paces behind and a familiar voice spoke softly from atop the horse and Mick turned to look. Moran caught his eye and sidled War Lord up close to Whish't Daddy and for a moment Mick thought it might mean trouble.

"Listen to me, young man," Moran said anxiously, "we have but a moment." His eyes swept around carefully, knowing full well they were being watched closely by the crowd. "I know your Da told you to follow me out of the supply gate at the end of the race. Don't, don't follow me at all. Take that monster of yours to the gate at the far turn. You'll be met there and told what to do." Moran began moving his horse closer to the line.

"No wait," Mick said anxiously. "Why should I go that way? Da said the wagon would be waiting by the supply road gate. I really should go that way."

Moran looked Mickey right in the eye. "Do what you want boy," he whispered intently, "but if you ever want to ride that beautiful animal again you'll do what I said, understand?" He waited a moment and Mick nodded, anything but certain of what he should do. "Now, come on," Moran continued. "I mean to kick your arse soundly." He trotted away bringing War Lord to the start. Mick followed, wishing desperately his father was present to tell him what to do. The judge spoke for a moment but Mick heard not a word that was said. His mind was spinning. They had a race to run but he forgot how they'd wanted to run the course. He tried to remember his Da's instructions but his mind came up completely blank. He worried where Da had gone off to and he had no idea what to do when the race was done. He looked about and saw the anxious faces of the crowd and saw their mouths moving but he could not hear a sound. As his eyes took in the growing multitude, he fixed briefly on the face of Lord Montgomery. The man appeared to be smiling at him but in an odd and evil way. His look frightened Mick and he turned away quickly. Suddenly, a gunshot rang out.

The first two furlongs would be something Mick could never recall. He'd not been ready at the start, terribly distracted and preoccupied by the thoughts swirling in his mind. By the time he managed to focus on the race he was staring at War Lord's massive rear end and tasting bits of grass in his mouth as the other horse took the lead. Mick thought it incredible they were only a few lengths behind, once again crediting the brilliance of Whish't Daddy, who had sprinted from the start with little encouragement from his rider. The sounds of the crowd began penetrating his consciousness and he was surprised by the loud noise a small audience could make. The two horses flew down the course into the first turn, War Lord setting a rapid pace and Mick thought Whishy pressing a bit to keep up. As they moved along the backstretch War Lord lengthened his lead, moving almost a full furlong in front. Mick knew he could not leave too great a distance to close or they'd never catch up. He asked his horse for more speed but for the first time in all of their races, it did not come. Whish't Daddy felt sluggish, clumsy and winded. Mick begged the horse for more but they lumbered onward, falling further behind as the far turn approached. Mick felt the sting of wet tears dripping down his face, the thought of losing his beloved

Whishy crushing his hope. He'd never thought they could lose. And it was entirely his fault. He'd not trained the horse properly over the past weeks and he'd let the horse lose too much weight and strength. As they moved through the far turn he thought any chance of victory was lost. Then out of the corner of his eye he spotted Da and saw the tension on his father's face and the heartbreak in his eyes. Everything Da had built over his lifetime would be lost if War Lord prevailed. Athy House had been burned to the ground, his family scattered in the wind, and now his champion horse would be stolen away and Da would have nothing. Mick saw his father wave him on and through the din of the crowd heard him cheering them loudly.

"You can do it, Mick," he yelled. "I know you can."

Mick Walsh laid out over his loving mount and put his lips on Whish't Daddy's ear. His wet tears were falling on the horse's neck and his hands held firmly the reins and the warm, coarse hair on his head.

"Go, Whishy, go. For the love of God, we got to get moving." And there it was! That old familiar feeling of his horse exploding beneath him filled Mick with a sensation of hope, excitement and joy unlike anything in his experience. The people watching that day would say the horse literally flew past his rival. For Mick it counted six or seven massive strides and he knew they'd pull even alongside War Lord. They were out of the far turn and thundering down the home stretch. Unlike at the Curragh, War Lord did not give an inch. Rather like the great racehorse he was, War Lord went full out, giving Moran all he had, striding length for length alongside Whish't Daddy, the two horses mirror images, their legs swallowing huge amounts of grass with every stride, the muscles in their neck, shoulders, hind quarters, legs, every inch of each horse expanding and contracting, their breathing deep and rhythmic, the course flying up behind them in great clumps, the voices of the crowd hitting an incredible crescendo, the pounding sound of the hooves closing in on the finish line filling Mick's ears and mixing with the sound of his own pounding heart.

True champions are born with something unique, a special ingredient that gives them the final push of energy, the last burst of speed, the required amount of strength, something deep in the well of their being that allows them to take that final step, to reach that unreachable limit, to accept all adversary and all challenge and still manage to prevail against all odds. Mick closed his eyes as the finish line approached, sliding himself even further along Whish't Daddy, lying so flat as to be the horse's skin and with the firm knowledge of an intimate partner, felt his horse extend his nose, his neck and his shoulders out across the line, edging his admirable foe by the smallest of margins, but surely and certainly the winner. The crowd was delirious with excitement. Mick wondered what the place would sound like if they raced to a full crowd. As he galloped further along the track, allowing Whishy to cool down, Moran and War Lord moved alongside. The jockey held out his hand and the two men shook with mutual respect.

"Well done, young man," Moran said with an admirable smile. "You two are quite a team." Then he looked around quickly and saw Lord Montgomery moving swiftly down the row of spectators, anger etched across his face and his voice barking towards the judge. "Now you need to get the hell out of here, son. And remember" he said softly, "don't follow me through that gate." With that War Lord pranced down the course, heading out through the middle gate. Mick followed him along the track, looking down the road to where the wagon should be. He hoped to see Da waiting. He was not, but the Black and Tans were. He galloped past the middle gate and moved Whish't Daddy along the course towards the gate at the far turn. As he approached he saw Michael Cleary waving frantically for him to hurry. Mick hurried Whishy along and when they got to the gate, Cleary was holding it open.

"Go through the castle streets as quickly as you can. When you get out of the main gate go west. Go all the way til you can go no further. When you get there you'll know what to do, son. But go now and go quickly and don't matter what happens, don't stop til you get to the water." He smacked Whish't Daddy hard on the rear and the horse reacted, shooting speedily through the gate and maneuvering through the castle streets nimbly and with haste. They passed the shops and stores and residences of Montgomery Castle, dodging pedestrians along the way and as they approached the main gate, Mick spotted two soldiers moving to block the way. He clicked his tongue once and Whish't Daddy understood. The horse bolted hard towards the two

British soldiers sending them diving to the ground for safety and then they were through the main gate and racing away from the castle. As he approached the Galway – Connemara Road, Mick saw a large pack of riders heading towards him from the east. It took only a moment to see the Black and Tan uniforms and he spurred Whishy on as they turned onto the road, sprinting away towards the west.

Mick had no idea how far he had to go or how much stamina his horse had left. He slid the leaden weights from his saddle, dropping them to the ground but it did not seem to help. Whishy had just run flat out for six furlongs and he was obviously not used to the strain. The road was rocky and laced with turns and up and downs and he felt his horse flagging as they got away from the Castle. Looking behind him he could tell the soldiers were closing in on them and he kept asking Whish't Daddy for more but the horse seemed to have nothing left to give. The soldiers were closing fast and Mick could here the pounding of their hooves and the shouts and warnings of the men coming from behind. A shot rang out and he thought he heard a bullet whistle past his ear. He considered pulling up to surrender, not wanting Whishy to be hurt. Then suddenly, as the soldiers were nearly upon him, from behind a small cottage on his left, a pack of men on horses burst out towards him with guns blazing. As Mick flew past he recognized Commander Riordan and he let out a whoop of joy and admiration for the brave Republicans coming to his aide. Remembering Cleary's instructions, he did not stop and kept Whish't Daddy galloping towards the coast. The sound of gunfire remained for a few moments and then fell silent in the distance. The land became flatter with less vegetation and Mick smelt the sea not far away. As Whishy raced over a small bluff Mick saw the majestic ocean spreading out in glorious shades of blue before him. He saw a small fishing village rising up to greet him and he thought for sure he would meet someone in the village that would take him back to Da. He slowed a bit, wanting to give Whishy a break. He felt the sea winds blowing stiffly through his hair and ruffling through Whishy's coat. He thought of Mammy and Maureen and the wee ones and he hoped he would soon be able to help Da rebuild Athy House and that Whish't Daddy would run many more races. He was fairly certain Lord Montgomery would come around and see reason. He'd nearly slowed

Whishy to gentle walk when another bullet whizzed past him grazing his boot. He turned, looking quickly and saw four more Black and Tans bearing down upon them, their guns firing repeatedly, their horses pounding towards him.

Mick took a deep breath and patted Whishy firmly. "Whatever you got left, boy, let's go." And off they went again. Whish't Daddy was laboring hard, rushing headlong towards the little village. They were nearly there when the bullet smashed into Mick's left shoulder, nearly causing him to fall from the horse. Instead he dug into Whishy's mane hard with his right hand, holding tightly to his horse with his legs. But he had no idea where to go. Then he saw a small boy waving frantically towards him and yelling loudly.

"This way, come on, come this way." Mick followed the boy's arm pointing Whishy down a narrow street heading straight towards the water. Bullets were flying over his head and smashing the ground and buildings around him as the horse gave all he had, closing in on the water. Mick panicked momentarily, thinking maybe he was trapped with the soldiers closing from behind and the water offering no escape ahead. Then he saw a long wooden pier. Looking down the pier as Whish't Daddy galloped ahead, Mick spotted a large boat out a ways in the blue-green water. Behind it, trailing from the boat was a big barge. The barge looked closer to the pier but still a short ways off. On the barge stood a man frantically waving a straw hat imploring Mick to hurry. Harry the Horse yelled encouragement as the boy and his horse neared the pier.

"Come on, son," he was screaming as Mick closed on the dock. "Come on, we're moving away. You got to get here now or you'll never make it."

Suddenly Mick understood. Another bullet crashed into the building beside him and Mick knew without turning around the soldiers were pounding down the narrow street closing the gap between them. "This is it Whishy," he said desperately. "I love you boy, let's go." With that, they took off down the narrow, wooden plank, Whish't Daddy's hooves banging hard on the wooden surface, the sound rivaling the gunshots crashing all around them. As they neared the end of the pier, Harry was urging them on, begging them to hurry. Mick looked at the distance between the end of the dock and barge and guessed it to be nearly twenty or even thirty feet. Whishy took the last three strides hard against the pier and then they took off, airborne, suspended over the ocean, time standing still, hoping desperately to reach the far off barge.

Mick's mind wandered back to the early days of training his majestic horse. He thought of the countless afternoons spent racing across the Kildare countryside, Whishy jumping over fallen logs, and small streams and the occasional wider river. The horse seemed to enjoy the challenge of jumping wide obstacles, of trying to go high and far, sometimes splashing his rear legs in the water or banging them on a tree branch but never shying away from the challenge, always exploding with strength and speed and grace. Mick had once asked Da if they should make Whishy a jumper but his father told him no, that the best and grandest champions were thoroughbreds that ran flat out. Mick knew his father was right and he always knew Whishy would be the grandest champion of all. But as Whish't Daddy's legs crashed down hard on the hay lined barge, his rear hooves making it by the thinnest of margins, stumbling a few paces before Harry Fitzgerald helped them come to a stop, Mick wondered if maybe his horse would have been the greatest jumper of all time. He surely just proved it. Harry hurried them both to the safety of a small shed at the front of the barge and in a few moments they were out of range of the gunfire coming from the pier. Mick stepped out from the shed, holding his hand against his injured shoulder, watching in silence as the big ship pulling the barge moved away from the Irish coast. They were bound for America.

Epilogue

Saratoga, New York – 2009

My Grandfather's story captivated my attention and left me aching to know more. It took some searching but I found an old man in Saratoga who spoke the Gaelic tongue. His name was Bernard but he told me to call him Benny, like everyone else. He was eighty-five years old and had left Ireland when he was twelve. He remembered only the stories he'd been told by his dearly departed mother of the Easter Rising, the Republicans and the Bloody Sunday Massacre but he also knew a wee bit of Irish history and for the price of a few pints he was more than happy to read the Gaelic newspapers and letters and translate their meaning. It was an early afternoon during Saratoga's off season so the tavern was nearly empty. We stretched copies of my papers across the bar in a vaguely chronological order. Benny sipped his Guinness slowly, moving along the bar at a leisurely pace, fiddling with his wire rimmed glasses from time to time, and stopping every now and then to look closely at a picture or to reread a particular sentence. He said nothing, managing only the occasional sigh of disappointment or the unexpected murmur of surprise or interest. He took three passes over the letters and articles, consuming an equal number of pints along the way. Satisfied he'd done his homework, he settled back into his bar stool, scratched the white stubble on his ruddy cheeks and looked at me questioningly.

"So?" I asked.

"So what?" he replied.

"What do they say? What are the newspapers and letters about?"

He stood and moved over the papers slowly and selected three different articles, beginning with those. "These are from what was most likely a local paper in Kildare County, the Kildare Word it would loosely translate," he said with the slightest hint of an Irish brogue. "This one is a story about a horse named Whish't Daddy, owned by a small, local stable by the name of Athy House. The horse is apparently new to the racing scene and setting it on its ear with his tremendous performances. In his first season, he wins a bunch of races including one of the biggest races in all of Ireland. Apparently, the horse is ridden by a young boy, a Mick Walsh, whose father is the horse's trainer. The boy never raced before and the writer is very damn well impressed by the performance of this new, young jockey and his new, young horse, racing at the highest level in the country. He goes on to say racing fans are looking forward to the following season and the ongoing rivalry between this horse and another horse by the name of War Lord." He showed me the paper again and I looked closely at the picture of Mick sitting atop of Whish't Daddy. It was the same picture my Grandfather had sitting on the bookshelf in his sitting room, his beautiful eyes smiling back at the camera.

Benny hesitated a moment and then shuffled the papers and took out the one containing the picture of a cottage burning. He shook his head sadly as he handed it to me. "This cottage is part of the stable that owned the horse, Whish't Daddy. The story says the cottage, along with the barns and stables of Athy House were burned to the ground by the British Government and Frank Walsh, the trainer of the famous horse, was arrested for supporting the Republican cause. There is no mention of what happened to the horse or the boy. The newspaper must have been Republican leaning because it states that Frank Walsh had never been connected to the cause in any way but had a brother that was in the IRA. They speculate sadly that Athy House will be no more and their racing days are over."

The next article he handed me had a picture of Whish't Daddy and the word *"Larraidh!"* Benny told me the word meant missing and the story was about the disappearance of the famous horse. He'd last been seen in March of 1921 in a match race at Montgomery Castle against the equally famous War Lord. Opinions varied on which horse had won the race and rumors spread across the country that Whish't Daddy had been killed by people close to Montgomery Castle because he posed too great a threat to their dominance in Irish racing. Others claimed the horse had been let loose to run amongst the wild horses of Connemara and still others said he'd drowned in the Atlantic Ocean trying to escape pursuing British soldiers. Frank Walsh made no comment, saying he'd last seen the horse streaking across the finish line, underscoring that the horse had indeed finished ahead of War Lord. He was continuing the search for both the horse and his son. Montgomery Castle refused comment.

Benny took a breather and washed down another pint. Scooping up the remaining handful of newspaper copies, he sorted them in order and rapidly went through them, explaining what each article meant. The first story, again from the Kildare Word, notified the general public of the landing of soldiers, imported by the British Government to help quell the rebellion. These soldiers had been recruited from men returning from the Great War, men who had seen considerable action on the Continent, hardened men who would resort to violence quickly, men that were to be feared and avoided if at all possible. The writer went on to say these men were being called Black and Tans due to the colors of their make-shift uniforms. My eyes went quickly to the picture featured in the paper of the four soldiers standing side by side and I focused on the circled head of the monstrously large man second to the left. Butterfield, I now knew. It was hard to see his facial disfigurement in the copy of a very old newspaper clipping but it was easy to detect the man's violent, malevolent aura just in the way he faced the camera, staring through his one good eye.

Benny digressed while discussing the next article from a larger paper in Dublin that spoke of the overriding political situation in Ireland at the close of 1920. He orated on the varying positions of Michael Collins, Eamon de Valera, Cathal Brugha and a few others, tending to side with those wanting to fight for one united and free Ireland rather than separating the north and south into separate countries. The article discussed the shifting opinion of the international community as well as the unrest building in other parts of the United Kingdom as a result of the treatment of the Irish people and the negative impact it was having on the British economy as a whole. The piece pointed to the need for a cease fire in the British – IRA hostilities and hoped that the violence sweeping the country would subside in the New Year. Another article from the same Dublin newspaper written towards the end of June, 1922 outlined the ceasefire and truce agreed upon by the British Government and the IRA. This would become known as the unofficial end of the Irish War of Independence. Benny felt the need to expand upon this bit of Irish history enlightening me to the fact that this truce would lead to the Anglo-Irish Treaty drafted the following December, signed by Michael Collins and a few other IRA leaders. However, Benny added, the Treaty would set the stage for the Irish Civil War which would pit the supporters of the Treaty, which included an oath of allegiance to the British Crown, against the anti-Treaty forces appalled by the oath and unable to accept the exclusion of six northern counties from the Irish Free State. The Irish hero of the War of Independence, Michael Collins, would die at the hands of his own countrymen in this horrible civil war.

In a side-bar article, the Dublin paper reported the dismantling of the British governing structure in Dublin, citing a long list of personnel soon to return to London. In a short interview with the second in command of the British forces in Ireland, Ian MacDermott said he was "only too happy to leave this Godforsaken land of cowards and traitors. The Irish people have bitten the hand that feeds them once too often and now we will leave them to their own resources and may God grant them the misery they so well deserve." Benny added that he in turn hoped a bastard like MacDermott was sweating profusely in a hell he also well deserved.

We were done with all the newspaper articles and only the three letters written in Gaelic remained. I pointed towards the pages sitting on the bar and looked at Benny questioningly but he only shook his head. I asked him what that meant.

"I can't tell you what they mean, son," he said with a sad smile. I looked at him with what must have been an alarming look of disappointment and despair. He held his hand up quickly, finished his last gulp of Guinness and stood up. "You need to read the letters yourself, not have someone tell you what they mean. Meet me here tomorrow evening and I will have them translated for you to read." He stuck out his hand and we shook and he moved towards the door. "It's quite an adventure you've been having would be my guess," he said with a wink and a soft chuckle as he left the tavern.

I had a fresh pint waiting for Benny when he arrived at the tavern the following evening. "If you don't mind putting a wee bit of whiskey alongside to keep it company I'd be much obliged," he said, sliding his bent frame into the stool beside mine. I ordered two shots of Paddy's and before clinking our glasses in toast, he smiled impishly, saying, "To Whish't Daddy!" We sipped the amber liquid slowly and he reached into his pocket, removing a sheaf of papers. Separating the copies of the original letters from his translated pages, he passed them over. Then he shifted away, engaging the bartender in conversation, a gesture I'm sure intended to give me privacy, something I would sorely need. The first letter was from Mick's mother, my great-grandmother and it was difficult to read.

My dear son,

I miss you Mickey. More than I would miss the light of a new morning do I miss you. I hope your new life in America is as wonderful and as promising as the many beautiful stories we have heard over the years. I hope you and Whish't Daddy are planning your next race and I know you'll run like the wind and fly across the finish line far ahead of all others. I have returned from London with the wee ones but Maureen has stayed behind. The girls miss you and ask about you all the time and me and your Da tell them you are fine and off on a brilliant journey to a new place where the racing is grand and you'll be champions for the ages. Your Da is trying desperately to manage without you but I know he feels a great loss in his heart. I am not sure he ever really told you how fiercely proud he was of you Mick, but I see it in his eyes now, the loneliness, the emptiness, he carries this burden with him in your absence. All that he is and has been was meant to be passed down to you son and he is all but lost without you. But he is a strong man and over time he will set himself straight and pull things together, God willing. But I am not sure if I ever can. I did not even have a chance to say good-bye to you my dear boy.

On that horrible day when the soldiers came I can't remember seeing you, maybe you'd been down with the horses early. Last I'd seen you that I recall, the night before you were helping Deidre with her numbers and she was laughing beside herself with your silly nonsense. It's a good memory Mick and one I will hold dear to. But I'd much rather have the chance to hug you one more time, to run my fingers through your lovely blond locks and to see that beautiful smile on your handsome face. I wish I could kiss you good night one more time son and to see you rise in the morning with the sleep in your eyes and your hair all tangled and looking to your Mammy for a plate of eggs and wee bit of bread to soak up the grease. But mostly I wish I could look down the hill from the cottage and see you with your Da and with your horses and the two of you working side by side, the two men in this world I love the most, working together doing the thing they love the most in the world, working like partners as much as father and son, loving the thing you do and loving doing it with each other. I do not think there is anything in this world that could make a mother happier than that. Please take good care of yourself my beautiful boy. I will write again soon. I love you.

Mammy

p.s. Do you still have the colors?

The lump in my throat surprised me but I could not help it. Imagining that poor woman, my Great-grandmother, writing to a son she knew she would never see again ached me terribly. Knowing she had left a daughter in England made it worse. And thinking of my Grandfather, alone in America, three thousand miles from his home and his family, reading this sad letter made it that much more difficult. I shuffled the papers and took out the next letter. It had been in a very fragile envelope which I had copied and I looked quickly to see that it had been postmarked in September of 1922 and mailed from Manchester, England. Taking a deep breath I continued my reading.

Hey Mickey!!!!

I am trying to imagine my little brother walking around that great, big country and trying to look like you fit in! I hope you took all the hay out of your hair and washed up a little so you don't smell like a horse! I'm just fooling with you, Mick. You know I miss you lots and I know you'll do just great over there in America. Tell me, are the streets really lined with gold? Well if they are than go outside and scoop up a big pile for your big sister and send it my way. Then I can come and visit you in New York and we can have us a grand reunion. And I got someone to introduce you to Mick! Actually I got two people to introduce you to. When I got over here with Mammy and the girls I met a man and we got married straight away. His name is Tom and he's a chimney sweep but a swell guy and I am sure you would like him. And guess what? We got us a baby! It's a handsome baby boy with the same blue eyes as you got and I think he's going to have a head of curly blond locks like you too. I decided to name him Darcy, after our uncle. Mammy told me about him dying out in Galway and sort of saving our Da's life along the way. I ain't exactly sure what happened but maybe he was some kind of a hero. At least I like to think so. Me and Darcy always was good together and I miss him awful too. It sure is odd being in a strange land with strange people and being so far away from Barreen. And you're a lot further away than me. But neither of us is with Da and Mammy and maybe that's good in some ways but mostly I think it ain't so great. I wonder what you think about it. Manchester is a filthy place and I hope I'm not here too long. I told Tom we got to get out of this place and get to somewhere a lot nicer. Maybe we'll come to America some day or maybe Australia but we got no money for that right now so we'll see. I think you took Whishy with you to America so I hope you're winning a lot of races and getting lots of medals. I don't hear much from Mammy cause I think she was mad at me for staying in England. She don't much like Tom and wasn't even too keen around the baby. So I hope you will write back or I will hear from nobody. I got to go now. The baby's waking up and crying something fierce. This being a mother stuff is really hard work but you don't got to worry about that. Don't forget to send me some of that gold laying around over there little brother. Be good. Say hello to George Washington!

Love,
Maureen

I wasn't very sure if I would have liked my Great-aunt very much. It's hard to tell from just one letter and she had been through an awful lot herself. But I am sure my Grandfather was glad to get her letter and to learn about the baby. He must have been very lonely in America and getting mail from family when he was so far from home must have been like finding a bottle of water while walking across a long, hot desert. Benny and the bartender were engaged in a lengthy conversation regarding fly fishing, a subject I know nothing about so I sorted through my pages and found one more letter I had not read. It was from Mick's Da.

Dear Mick,

Hello son, I hope my letter finds you in good health and making your way in New York. Thank you for your many letters, they are a lifeline for me and your Mammy and we take turns reading them by the fire every night. I am sorry it has taken me so long to write back. It has taken me a while to set things straight but now things are a little better. I am very sorry to hear about Whish't Daddy's leg. A cracked cannon bone has spelled the end for many a good race horse and I think your decision to retire him to stud was a good one. It is a shame in so many ways because there has never been a more wonderful race horse in all the world than Whish't Daddy. You Mick, did a marvelous job training him and I hope you are as proud of what you accomplished as I am. It was a beautiful thing to behold. Changing his name is also a good decision. It will make it much harder for him to be found. Lord Montgomery was fit to be tied when he heard you escaped with Whishy and he swore up and down he would find the horse and bring him back to Montgomery Castle. He had me arrested but they did not keep me very long. Things have changed greatly here in Ireland, some for the better and some for not so good. We are an independent nation now, well most of the country except up North, but now there is terrible fighting within the Republicans and we have a Civil War going on so the killing just continues and I wonder if it will ever end. But anyhow, I got out of jail and went to the courts and now they've ruled I own all the property that makes up Athy House and we rebuilt the cottage and are slowly rebuilding the barns, the stables, the paddocks and the course. They will be much better in many ways but we will be missing our most important assets – you and Whish't Daddy! Michael Cleary works with me now. I made him my partner. Lord Montgomery fired him straight away after the race at the Castle. He blamed him both for losing the race and for letting you get away. They wanted to arrest him too but he used that glib Irish tongue of his to talk his way out of trouble. But he is a good man and a damn fine horse trainer so we are joining forces to rebuild Athy House and to make it the finest stable in all of Ireland. I only wish it was you that was doing the rebuilding with me Mick but in many ways I am glad you are in America and away from the madness of this beautiful country. Harry the Horse was here for a visit and he told me you're doing real well up in that Saratoga place and it sounds grand. Harry will keep you on the straight and narrow and if you keep your nose clean and work hard you'll be the best trainer in all of America. I am glad you received the box with the medals and a few coins to help you along. You deserve them greatly. I am enclosing a number of articles from the papers for you to read. Some are from years back and some are more recent. I thought you'd like to look them over. They will remind you of the early days with that grand horse. I hope someday you find another horse just as grand as Whish't Daddy but that might take some time. So my boy, I will end up by telling you I do miss you so very much. When I am down in the new barn or banging the fences together in one of the paddocks I look up and sometimes I can see you clear as the morning sun. I see you bailing hay or mucking out a stable or piling tack into the wagon. But mostly I see you up on that marvelous horse, sitting in the saddle like you were sitting in an easy chair by the fire. You don't even look like two things, you and Whishy. You look like one, man and horse together as one entity, one perfectly blended coupling, almost as if you are part of him and he is part of you. That's what it looked like when the two of you raced. You could not tell where the horse ended and the rider began because there was no beginning and no end. You and Whishy were one in the same and I never have and never will again see the likes of such a thing. It was poetry in motion as they say. It was everything that is powerful and beautiful, graceful and good in the sport of kings. And I was lucky enough to see it from the very start, up close enough to touch, close enough to see that you and that horse were meant to be, a pairing for the ages. When you have tough times Mick, when things just aren't going well and you can't get a winner down the homestretch despite all your efforts, remember the days of Whish't Daddy. Remember the greatness and the feeling in your heart as you flew to the wire. That will get you through, son. That will take you to the next day. And that's all we can ask for in this world, the chance at another day. Take care son, I love you.

Da

By the way Mick – Teddy is a damn funny name for a horse!!!!

I ordered a shot of Paddy's for Benny and one for myself. With my hand shaking and tears in my eyes, I sipped it slowly and let Frank Walsh's words play over again in my mind. It was pretty obvious to me that he'd not only lost his son but he'd lost his best friend. I doubt they ever saw each other again. I remembered no grand reunion growing up nor did I remember my Grandfather ever going back to Ireland. Some things would remain a mystery. But I hoped not everything. I leaned over to Benny who was sitting silently with one eye on the baseball game playing on the TV. I pointed to the words at the end of the letter.

"Teddy?"

Benny chuckled. "Kind of an odd name for a horse, right? Better name for a bear!" I looked at him questioningly. "You know who that horse was?" he asked. I shook my head from side to side. "That horse mysteriously came out of Europe in the early 1920s. Some say from France but up here in Saratoga we know differently. He was smuggled into America under another name and then changed to Teddy. He never ran a race. They put him right out to stud." I nodded again but didn't really understand. Benny took a pencil from his shirt pocket, took a page from my pile and turning it over to the blank side began to write. When he was done he pushed it in my direction. It took a few minutes to set in but than I understood.

Teddy – Assignation (1930) – Cinquepace (1934) – Imperatrice (1938) – Something Royal (1952) – Secretariat (1970)

"Greatest race horse of all time – Secretariat," Benny said tapping the letter a few times. "Teddy was his Great-great-great Grandfather.

Good bloodlines always prove out," he said with a smile. Benny finished off his whiskey, shook my hand solemnly and walked off with a smile and a quick wave to the barman.

I sat thinking about the whole story and shook my head with astonishment. No wonder he was the greatest race horse of all time, Whish't Daddy was an ancestor to the great Secretariat! I could not help but smiling as I finished off my drink. That must have made my Grandfather very proud, watching Secretariat lap the field down at Belmont on a warm day in 1973. I drove slowly back towards the Saratoga track and my Grandfather's tiny cottage. I had to turn in the key in the morning but there was one more question left unanswered. I opened the door, inhaling deeply of the horse and hay scent and began slowly moving the packed boxes into my car. I peaked in each one but did not find what I was looking for. As I piled the last meager box into the back seat of my Toyota, a feeling of melancholy and disappointment settled over me like a wet blanket. I wandered back into the bungalow for one last look around. The shelves on the small bookshelf were empty, the desk drawers open and bare. Where could they be, I wondered? I peaked into the tiny bedroom, empty except the small cot that had come with the cottage and was to remain behind. I was turning to go when a glimpse of crimson flashed at me from the bed. I walked over slowly, picking up the yellowish pillow with great anticipation and there they were! The crimson and gold color silks of Athy House, frayed and faded, were folded neatly beneath my Grandfather's pillow. I picked them up gently. They were threadbare and fragile to my touch. Whish't Daddy's blinkers looked smaller than I would have thought, their eyeholes slightly torn. The small jacket looked like it would fit a child but the brass buttons still held a dull shine. At the bottom of the small pile I found the saddle cloth and spread it carefully across the bed. It was wide, the crimson and gold checks in an alternating pattern and still with the slightest hint of horse scent rising from the cloth. I stood looking at it in amazement, Whish't Daddy's saddle cloth, hand sewn by my Great-Grandmother three thousand miles away and nearly a century before! It occurred to me suddenly that for nearly the past nine decades, almost ninety years, these precious garments lay beneath Mickey Walsh's head as he slept every night. I stared at them a while longer, and then knowing my Grandfather wouldn't mind, I lifted the silky cloth blanket to dry the tears racing down my cheeks. And when I did I smelled a champion.

THE END

Acknowledgements

This story grew out of a long conversation with Mick Dalton over a number of shots of Paddy's Irish whiskey. He told old tales of raising horses on his farm in Ireland and then longer tales of the IRA going back a few generations. That sparked an idea and the idea grew into this book. Thanks Mick. When I started writing it, I knew horses had four legs and little more and nothing at all about training race horses. A few excellent books helped educate me at least a little. Backyard Race Horse – The Training Manual by Janet Del Castillo and Lois Schwartz was a great primer. Kentucky Derby Dreams – The Making of Thoroughbred Champions by Susan Nusser added considerable detail. Irish Horse Racing – An Illustrated History by John Welcome helped considerably. For excellent color I read the incredible novel SEABISCUIT – An American Legend by Laura Hillenbrand and of course, William Nack's wonderful book Secretariat. Anything incorrect about horses or training is solely my responsibility.

Stormville, NY - December 24, 2015

Printed in the United States
By Bookmasters